JUNK MAGIC

KAREN CHANCE

Karen Chance

Chapter One

There were three doughnuts sitting on Hargroves' desk. Not normal sized ones; I doubted he ate that much in a week. No, these were minis, six little powdered-sugar-coated temptations, one of which had a single bite taken out of it. And doesn't that say everything about the man, I thought evilly. To most people, one of those doughnuts was a bite, but Hargroves could make a single doughnut last him all day.

Sort of like a single lecture.

This one had been going on for what felt like a week, although knowing the boss's tight schedule, was probably more like ten minutes. I'd stopped listening after two because it was always the same thing. My students were wreaking havoc; my students were out of control. I don't know what else he expected.

Thanks to the needs of the current war, the War Mage Corps—the supernatural community's version of the police—had started accepting younger and younger recruits. This last batch didn't contain a person over the age of nineteen. Teenagers. He was giving me magically gifted teens with hormones on overdrive and power to burn and expecting me to churn out spit and polished recruits. Okay, yes, they'd blown up the gym. Again. I was just lucky they hadn't taken the rest of the Corp's new headquarters along with it.

Not that it would be much of a loss, I thought, glancing around the dingy office. Only to have the boss notice. And apparently, number ten thousand and one on the list of things I did to irritate him was allowing my mind to wander during a chewing out.

Although what came out of his mouth next wasn't what I'd expected.

"Which is why I'm promoting you," he said sourly.

I blinked. "Promoting, sir?"

“To train our new task force. They’re to be housed in a separate facility, with rather more security features than this one.” The sour look intensified. “Perhaps you can manage to keep it intact for a week or two.”

I blinked some more, this time in confusion. “But . . . my students—”

“Reassigned to Mage Reynolds.”

“Reynolds?” It took me a second, but then an image of a sandy haired, round faced, jolly tempered mage, fresh off the turnip truck from one of our more rustic offices, came to mind.

Dear God, they’d eat him alive.

“But, sir, we just had a breakthrough—”

“Yes, of the back of the building!”

A comeback leapt to my lips, but I held it back ruthlessly. Not for myself; Hargroves already thought I was stubborn, unpredictable and a bit of an asshole. Which was why he had me teaching.

The supernatural community might be at war, but teaching assignments were thought to be far more worthy of combat pay. And considering what often went on in the classroom, I firmly agreed with that. Magic didn’t like to be leashed, and young, bountiful, reckless magic even less so.

My students needed me.

“Sir, I really think—”

“Let’s go meet your new class, shall we?” Hargroves said, and stood up without letting me finish.

I got up, because he was the boss, but I was frowning when we reached the corridor. And even more so when we left the admin wing and headed across the big open room that served as reception area, training ground and gym, all in one. Part of which was still on fire.

I assumed that was why I was suddenly the focus of half the eyes in the place.

That was better than when I’d first been assigned here, nine months ago, and the stares had been for a different reason. Part fey were not all that strange in the War Mage Corps. Maybe five percent of the whole had some kind of unusual blood in their veins, although it was often so far back as to manifest as nothing more than a faint tinge of blue or green along a cheekbone, or better than average sight in the dark.

Weres, on the other hand, were a lot less thick on the ground.

Of course, we weren't supposed to be on the ground, at least not wearing a war mage uniform. But my father was Guillame de Croissets, from a family with a long history of service to the Corps and many times decorated for his service. He was retired now, but when he'd announced that his daughter Accalia was going to follow in his footsteps, no one had had the gall to tell him no.

Or the courage, probably.

Dad had a temper.

Something he'd passed down to me, along with my dark brown hair and lanky, five-foot-nine build. But my gray eyes were wolf eyes, my mother's eyes, and while they looked human enough, I'd heard that they were hard to meet. Which was probably why a couple of nearby gawkers scurried off when I sent them the glare they deserved, before following Hargroves downstairs.

And started to get nervous.

The Corps' new digs were in a decrepit, thirteen thousand square foot warehouse on an arid bit of desert in the vicinity of Nellis Air Force base. Or, at least, the upper level was. It was mainly taken up by administrative offices, training areas and housing for new recruits, while the newly excavated subterranean sections hid the harder to explain stuff, like the interspecies medical facilities, weapons storage and labs.

And the lock up, which was where it looked like we were headed.

"Uh, sir?" I said, wondering why my new students were already incarcerated. That usually took a few weeks, at least. But Hargroves wasn't listening.

"Open up," he snapped at the guards standing on either side of a large, metal door.

Considering the types of wards draped over it, I didn't know why they were there at all. It could have withstood a nuclear blast, much less an escape attempt. Not that the junkies, scammers and drunks that made up most of its current residents warranted that kind of precaution, but then, it hadn't been made for them.

It had been made for *them*, I thought, after we passed through the door and down a corridor, only to stop in front of a large, well-warded cell.

And, suddenly, I caught a clue.

I also caught Hargroves' eyes, which were looking almost pleased for once. And forgot about my resolution about not pissing off the boss. Because he certainly hadn't made a similar one!

"You have got to be freaking kidding me."

* * *

A couple of very long hours later, I pulled my Harley into my driveway only to find a similar bike already there. The sleek crotch rocket was parked alongside a battered pick up, with a ladder and some paint buckets sitting in the back. I suddenly felt better.

I let myself into the house, which looked less like a war zone than it had for months. A previous issue with another class of students had utterly trashed the place. It wasn't their fault; a mage had used their inexperience to enthrall them and then send them against me, resulting in a fight where I was caught between not wanting to kill my students and not wanting to die at their hands.

The result had been the almost destruction of my brand-new house, something my boyfriend was trying to rectify.

And looking good doing it.

Not that Cyrus ever looked less than edible. But in an old tank riding up to show off sculpted abs, and paint splattered jeans clinging to a better backside than any man deserved, he was stunning. Enough to make me pause in the doorway in admiration.

He heard me, of course. I hadn't inherited my mother's super sharp senses, but Cyrus had the full wolfly package. He'd heard me drive up; hell, he'd probably heard my bike from a dozen blocks away and he'd smelled me before I hit the door. Yet he didn't turn around. He just kept painting my living room wall with the tasteful soft beige I'd picked out, the smooth movement of the roller a counterpoint to the stretch and flex of all those muscles.

I was suddenly very happy that I'd brought dinner.

Dining in was sounding better all the time.

I dropped my keys into a dish and Cyrus finally glanced over his shoulder, the too-long, dark brown hair curling against his neck, because he only remembered to get it cut occasionally. And what looked like two days' worth of scruff on his cheeks, even though I knew he'd shaved that morning. He'd been staying at my place while renovations continued, and I'd found little bits of hair in my sink before I left. It was annoying, like the fact that he appeared to need six towels to take a bath.

A grin broke over the handsome face, and the whiskey-colored eyes lit up at seeing me.

I could deal, I decided.

"Fun day at the office?" he asked.

I took off my jacket and stretched, watching his eyes follow the movement. "No."

"No?" An eyebrow raised as he came down the ladder—with no hands and without looking at it, because Weres have uncanny spatial awareness. "Just no?"

"Just no," I agreed. There were days when I wanted to talk about the job—or bitch, more often. This wasn't one of them.

With tarp-covered holes in the walls, I didn't run the AC much, just a fan over the bed at night. And, even to my human nose, he smelled of paint and sweat and the beer he'd had on a break, the bottle of which was still sitting by the wall. I didn't care.

Hard arms engulfed me, a harder body pressed up against me, and a mouth came down on mine that wasn't just hard, it was hungry. And so was I. I had the tank off and him pushed against the wall in seconds, and was working on the phoenix belt buckle one of his own sort-of-students had given him when he grabbed my wrist.

"Not now."

"Why not now?" He was ready; I could feel it. And, God, so was I! Time to work off some stress.

"We have company."

"What?"

I glanced up to find him looking over my shoulder, where a swivel of my head showed me two lanky teens lounging in the doorway to the dining room, trying not to grin.

They weren't trying very hard.

"Accalia de Croissets, meet Jace and Jayden."

"Brothers?" I guessed.

"Twins," the slightly taller one said. "Fraternal."

Ah. That would explain why, although they favored, they weren't identical. One was milk chocolate, the other dark. One had a buzz cut and the other was growing a very respectable 'fro. One had on baggy jeans that must have been enchanted, because no way were they staying up otherwise, while the other was wearing a track suit worthy of a Russian mobster.

Yet they really were similar. In fact, other than for the piercing in track suit's nose, I'd have been hard pressed to tell them apart by facial features alone. Especially since they both smelled of wolf.

But not of clan.

Normally, having two *vargulfs*—the outcasts of the Were community—in your house would be cause for alarm, assuming you lasted that long. They tended to be desperate, dangerous types with murky pasts, the kind with a lot of power but few restrictions on how they used it, because they literally had nothing left to lose.

But when your boyfriend is one, too, you get a different perspective. Not that it was so clear cut in his case. Because Cyrus was something I wasn't sure the Were world had ever seen before: an outcast by choice.

It had started when his older brother, Sebastian, the leader of the powerful and wealthy Arnou clan, had decided that he wanted to be *bardric*. Humans would translate the term as "king", but that was pretty far off the mark. "First among equals" would be a better version, although it actually meant "war chief", because the only time the clans had ever agreed to submit to one man's rule was when they were threatened with disaster.

And even then, it was touch and go.

Weres didn't play well with others, and resented being bossed around by a wolf outside of their own clan. Like, really resented. Like tear-your-head-off-and-feed-on-your-entrails resented. Yet the war had demanded sacrifices from everyone, and theirs had involved choosing a leader.

It had gone about the way you'd expect.

After weeks of yelling, fighting—sometimes literally—and utter stalemate, Sebastian had come up with an idea. The other clan leaders viewed him as more of a diplomat than a warrior, because he occasionally liked to talk before the head ripping started. In the human world, that would be an asset; in the Were, not so much.

Not that most Weres were quite that temperamental, but any sign of weakness in a leader was anathema. Your Alpha was your life. He could lead you to success or utter destruction, so you damned well wanted him to be the baddest son of a bitch out there.

Which was why, despite the power and prestige of Arnou, Sebastian had been having trouble sealing the deal. But he'd had to seal it, because the next mostly likely candidate was Whirlwind of Rand, the wolf name of the leader of the second most powerful clan. And Rand hated the current human-Were alliance.

If Whirlwind became *bardric,* the Corps would be fighting this war alone, unless you counted the vampires. And nobody counted the damned vampires. They dealt with high level politics and otherworld invasions, which was all well and good and absolutely needed, but what about the little guy on the street? Who protected them?

And they needed protection. The other side knew that the best way to keep the Corps busy was to run us ragged preventing terrorist attacks, and for a while, they'd done a pretty good job. But that was before the Were council started providing support.

Unlike vamps, who tended to stay in their own little enclaves, Weres were a part of their communities. They ran businesses, employed locals, bought homes, and went to farmer's markets. Yes, their kids usually went to special schools, both to teach them clan norms and to keep youthful hormones in check, especially around the full moon. But other than that, and for a few festivals and meetings of the clan throughout the year, their lives weren't markedly different from the guy down the street.

Except that the guy down the street couldn't throw you through a building if you pissed him off.

But the clans kept that kind of thing pretty much in check, and their involvement in the community had been a lifesaver for the Corps. Turns out, super senses were really good for picking up danger signs. Weres could smell magic, and even differentiate between light and dark varieties. Having the clans on board had cut the Corps' workload by an order of magnitude, helping us hunt down dark mage enclaves, protect vulnerable human communities, even stop an attack on HQ.

That last had been an accident. A Were had been in line at headquarters, waiting to get a shaman's license renewed, when he smelled the stench of blood magic. It was emanating off a new arrival so thickly that it had almost knocked him down.

Our enemies had known that getting a bomb past the Corps' fearsome wards would be impossible, so they'd found some old drunk, stuffed him to the gills with life magic, the kind that wards couldn't detect because all magical humans have it, and sent him in.

The magic in his veins was bound to a spell powerful enough to have taken out half the facility and killed who knew how many mages. And it would have, except that the Were jumped him half a second before his body exploded. The vicious attack caused the tainted blood to spirt out everywhere, the magic to disperse, and the Were to be tackled by no fewer than eight war mages for his trouble.

They'd eventually sorted things out, and he'd received an apology and a reward from the Corps. But it showed that, despite every possible precaution, if somebody wants to get to you, they can get to you. Unless, of course, you have paid Were guards stationed all over your lobby, as we now did.

One of them, Hernando, made the world's best tamales. They'd caused the cafeteria's revenues to take a nose dive ever since he started showing up with a cart that he parked outside the front door, 'cause why not double dip? I'd gained at least five pounds, and felt a lot safer, ever since.

But that could all go away if an anti-Corps leader like Whirlwind got into power. Which was why Sebastian and Cyrus had rigged up a plan. Sebastian needed a show of strength to impress the clan leaders, but nothing penny ante would do. So, Cyrus had challenged his brother for leadership of Arnou and then thrown the fight, ensuring that Sebastian looked bad ass enough to win the vote.

As a result, the Weres stayed in the war, a lot of people stayed alive, and Cyrus was made an outcast for life. Or until the war ended and he and Sebastian could admit what had happened and bring him back into the fold. That would entail its own special set of problems, but they were minor compared to a world without family, something that to wolves was literally a fate worse than death.

Which I guess was why Cyrus had made his own.

Two of whom were currently eyeing my bag of tamales.

"You guys want some?" I asked, and had the bag snatched away almost before the words left my lips.

The two ran off, I guess so they wouldn't have to share, and I arched a brow at Cyrus.

"I've been having them do grunt work," he told me. "They need the cash."

"Except now we have no dinner. Guess that means you'll have to take me out."

"I'd planned on it. *Way* out."

I cocked my head. "Do I want to know what that means?"

The grin returned. "Oh, yeah."

Chapter Two

We took both bikes, because my beat-up old truck was not going to make it where we were going, and because the boys were coming along for the ride.

"Jayden and I'll take this one," Jace said, staring in approval at my tripped-out Harley-Davidson Night Rod, with black chrome and blood red accents. Cyrus had a black and silver version, but I guess Jace liked my color scheme better.

So did I, and preferably intact.

"Not a chance," I told him.

"Oh, come on. Then you can ride with Cyrus."

I threw a leg over. "Yeah, but this way, I can *race* Cyrus."

Jace's eyes lit up.

We set out sedately enough, until we left my nice, quiet subdivision behind and hit the open road. Then we floored it. I heard Jace whoop from behind me, while Jayden clung to Cyrus like he was afraid the wind was going to blow him off the back of the bike. Which it just might have, because the open road outside Vegas is *really* open.

And really fun. With long, straight highways that seem to go on forever, surrounded by dusty plains, sweeping hills, and giant azure skies, Nevada has some of the best riding country anywhere. And if you add in the Valley of Fire, with the red hills glowing like embers in the sunset, it turns into pure magic.

My only question was what we were doing out here, especially with the boys. Cyrus and I frequently went camping, but usually for some alone time. Somewhere no one would hear us howl.

I got my answer when we turned off the beaten path and bumped across open country to a busy campsite, where I sent my partner a look. He just took off his helmet and shook out his hair at me; the bastard knows I love that. And then helped poor Jayden off the back of the bike, who was looking about as shaken as a Were can.

"We won! We won!" Jace said, laughing, because we'd rolled to a stop maybe five seconds before they had.

"I don't want to race anymore," Jayden said thickly. And then he threw up.

There was some fussing over him after that, and some teasing from the circle of young men around a campfire, who already had some hot dogs roasting. Jayden went over to sit with them, perking up slightly at the smell of meat, because nothing puts a Were's stomach out of commission for long. Somebody threw a blanket around his shoulders and handed him a stick, and the ride from hell was soon forgotten.

Leaving me looking at the pretty picture of deepening violet twilight, with a rim of reddish orange still clinging to the horizon, and stars blooming overhead. It contrasted nicely with the firelight splashing the excited faces of nine young men, most of them in their late teens, yet looking like kids at their first camp out. Which for all I knew this might be.

"Wanted to get them out of the city," Cyrus murmured, coming up behind me and slipping his arms around my waist. "It's a full moon tonight."

I nodded. Unlike the legends, Weres had full control of when and where they Changed, which was one reason they were so deadly. But the full moon *did* affect them, making them more reckless, less inhibited, and more prone to violence than usual. And that was for people who weren't *vargulfs* with self-control issues.

I could understand why Cyrus wanted his proteges somewhere a little more remote tonight.

And it looked like they planned to stay for a while. There was a ring of tents beyond the firelight, little two-man things that blended into the countryside pretty well. And a beaten-up old Winnebago that definitely did not.

"The new digs?" I guessed. He'd said he was going to up his camping game.

"Better than a tent," he agreed, nibbling my neck. "It has a bed."

"Which we'd get more use out of if you hadn't brought half the city."

"They're sound sleepers."

I doubted that, especially tonight. The moon wasn't up yet, but as soon as it rose, the boys would be off, transformed and chasing unfortunate little creatures all over the wilderness. Leaving the camp basically deserted.

I perked up.

"Dinner first," I told him, because those hot dogs were smelling seriously delicious.

They *were* good, as it turned out, and so was the company. That surprised me a little. The *vargulfs* I'd met in the past had been suspicious, angry, alienated types with little to say. And that was when they were talking at all and not trying to gut me.

But that was sort of understandable when you realized what most of them had been through.

The Were community was governed by a very strict caste system, with the older, richer, more influential families at the top, and everyone else spread down the ladder at different levels. Everybody except the *vargulfs*, that is. They didn't have a clan, and thus had no access to the money, protection, and rights that afforded, including the right to set foot on clan property. More than one *vargulf* had been killed simply for entering the wrong business, without first checking to see who owned it.

The clans said it was necessary to keep their people safe, that *vargulfs* had gotten that way for a reason, and that they were dangerous. And sometimes, that was true. A person could be thrown out of the clans for any number of things, including some pretty bad stuff. Many *vargulfs* were every bit as dangerous as the clans made them sound.

But there were other reasons why someone could end up without clan affiliation. Being born on the wrong side of the blanket, for example, to a father or mother who didn't choose to claim you. Or being born to someone who was already *vargulf* themselves. Or having done something that displeased your clan leaders, even if said something was not worthy of lifelong exile.

And the bad part of it was, there was no way back again. Once you were out, you were out, unless you could convince some other clan to take you. But guess how many of the insular clans wanted to waste resources on someone who hadn't been wanted even by their own families?

Yeah, just about that many.

It was something Cyrus was trying to change.

Born to privilege in Arnou, he'd never thought much about the outcastes of the Were world until he became one himself. At first, he'd thought exile would be easy. He'd even thought that it might be fun, surviving for a while on his wits, free of the responsibilities of being essentially Were royalty, just him against the world.

It hadn't been fun. He'd confessed to me once that killing himself had started to look like a really good option, just a couple of months in. He'd never before realized how much he'd relied on the clan, how much of his strength he drew from it, how much of his identity, until it suddenly wasn't there anymore.

And that was while having something these boys had never known: hope.

Hope that the war would end, and Sebastian could risk telling everyone the truth. Hope that he could avoid getting killed until that happened. Hope that there would come a time when he would wake up from this nightmare, when clan affiliated people wouldn't cross the street to avoid him, and when he could hold his head up again.

Hope that somehow, someday, he could go home.

But what if you didn't have a home, and knew you never would? It wasn't too surprising that a lot of *vargulfs* didn't last long. And those who did were easy pickings for the less respectable elements in Were society, who knew that the outcastes could be exploited without the risk of having a family come down on your neck.

Because these boys no longer had one.

Although you'd never know it tonight. They were laughing, talking and eating—especially eating—like they didn't have a care in the world. It looked like Cyrus had bought out half a grocery store, and he needed every bit of it.

Young men can eat, but young werewolves can eat *everything*, especially on the night of a full moon. I could tell that Cyrus had taken the guys shopping with him, because there was all sorts of junk food scattered around the fire. But there were a few grown up items, too, including potatoes roasting in the embers.

I grabbed one, burning my fingers, and loaded it up with the some of the bacon that one of the guys was frying in a pan, shredded cheese, and chives. Who had thought to bring chives I didn't know, but they went well with everything else. Including the two chili dogs that were slid onto my plate by a short redhead.

"You can't just eat a potato," he said, ducking his head shyly.

Actually, I could, and probably should. Thanks to Hernando's tamales I needed to drop a few pounds before my next fitness evaluation. I suddenly wondered if that was why the Corps' cafeteria was so terrible, to keep us all slim.

It was a theory.

But I guess the moon was affecting me, too, because I wolfed it all down, while the guys joked and laughed and talked. It was obvious that they'd forgotten for a moment who they were and where they fit—or didn't fit—into the world we lived in. Which I guess was why they started debating how it got that way.

"Everyone was a *vargulf* once," one pointed out. He was the stereotypical Were—tall, gray-eyed, and dark-haired—and maybe sixteen or so. I thought his name might be Colin. "I mean, nobody had clans at the beginning, right?"

"Of course, we had clans," one of the others said. He was a dishwater blond with uncharacteristically bright blue eyes. Cyrus had introduced him with the very un-clan-like name of Noah. "We've always had them—"

"We couldn't have," Colin argued. "We were cursed into being, and after the first ones Changed, their families probably threw them out. Just like us."

Things suddenly quieted down, while everyone remembered what that had felt like. Until Jace spoke up. "So, we're like cave men." He glanced around at the night, which out here was calm and wildly beautiful. "I could deal."

"It wasn't that far back," the brunet argued. He looked at Cyrus. "More like four or five thousand years, right?"

Cyrus had been working on beer and bratwurst, and not paying much attention. Except to see how much sauerkraut he could pile on a single dog. It was a lot.

But at that he looked up. "What?"

"The first Weres. They were cursed by the old gods, weren't they?"

"Naw, it's a disease," Noah said. "Everybody knows that—"

"I didn't say it wasn't."

"—just the metaphysical kind. Like the vampires, you know?"

Colin nodded. "That's what I mean. They can be cursed with vampirism, as well as get it through a bite. Just like we can with the Were strain. Right Cyrus?"

Cyrus swallowed spicy cabbage. "That's one theory."

"What, that we're cursed?" Jace said. "I never heard that!"

"You didn't have little werewolf school?" one of the others asked. "That's what we used to call it," he clarified, when Jace just looked at him. "You know, lore and shit."

"I didn't have school," Jace said shortly, and turned back to Cyrus. "Is he right? Were we cursed?"

"I don't know." Cyrus chewed pork. "The ancient Greeks believed that. The legend goes that some guy named Lycaon got in trouble with Zeus—"

"For serving him human meat," one of the boys said eagerly. "I remember that story!"

"—for trying to test his omniscience," Cyrus said, without going into detail. Maybe because he was trying to eat. "But Zeus realized what Lycaon had done, and changed him and his sons into wolves. Which is why the mages call us lycanthropes sometimes—when they're feeling suicidal."

He grinned, showing teeth, and several of the boys bared theirs back.

I noticed that some were also wearing the same type of western shirt that Cyrus had about fifty of in his wardrobe. He could have lent them the clothes, but I didn't think so. The shirts would have been a lot broader across the shoulder, if so. More likely there was a little hero worship going on.

I bit back a smile.

"But the legend doesn't say anything about them turning back," I said. Because I'd studied the lore, too. "So, they weren't Weres, just wolves."

"It's a point," he conceded.

"What do you believe, then?" Colin asked, shifting those gray eyes to me. "Who were the first Weres?"

I shrugged. The real answer was "nobody knows," but I didn't think he'd be satisfied with that. He was looking kind of intense.

"The Norse Volsung saga dates to the thirteenth century," I said instead. "It recorded ancient stories, including one about a father and son who found enchanted wolf pelts that could turn them into wolves for ten days, after which they'd transform back. As far as I know that's the first time anybody wrote about wolves turning back into people."

"I heard dark mages can use our pelts in spells," one of the other boys piped up. "They use magic to strip them off us, then sell them and the power they contain. Maybe that's where the myth started."

"It's not a myth!" Colin said sharply. "We were cursed by the gods, and afterwards the strongest made the clans—"

"I don't know about that," Cyrus demurred. "Even if you believe the legend, it doesn't say anything about—"

"It doesn't have to! That's all that matters—strength. We all know it!"

"There's plenty of things more important than strength," Cyrus said, with a frown. "Decency, kindness, honor—"

"Bullshit!" Colin suddenly stood up. He looked around the circle, and with the firelight splashing his face and leaping in his eyes, he looked more than a little feral. "If we were stronger our clans would have kept us! If we were stronger, we'd have homes! If we were stronger—"

He broke off suddenly and bolted, vanishing into the darkness so fast that it almost looked like he'd disappeared. Cyrus frowned harder and got up. "I'll be back," he told me, and I nodded.

There was silence around the campfire for a moment after he left, except for the soft crackle of the flames and the even softer hiss of the wind. And then Jace spoke up. "Don't mind Colin," he told me. "He had a bad experience."

"A bad experience?"

I regretted the words almost as soon as I'd said them, because one thing you never asked a *vargulf* was how he got that way. But my attention had been on Cyrus and the boy, and my mouth had been on automatic. That was rarely a good thing.

But Jace only shrugged. "Colin's parents were part of a group who split away trying to form their own family, after a disagreement with their clan leaders. But they were attacked a few weeks later by some of their old clan, who didn't want to look weak by letting them go."

"Attacked?" There was surprise in my voice, because that sort of thing wasn't supposed to happen. Yes, clans had a lot of autonomy over their members, but there were rules. A rather large number of them, in fact, as to how acts of vengeance could be carried out.

And sneak attacks weren't among them.

"Didn't they report it?" I asked. "The council—"

"Wasn't in session. There was no *bardric* then, so it would have had to be called to give a ruling. And who was gonna call it? The parents were all dead."

"And the kids?" I asked, wondering if I wanted to know.

"Dragged back to the clan," Jace shrugged. "But not all of them were let back in. The elders made them fight, and only the strongest were restored, while the rest were killed or driven off."

It was said so matter-of-factly that, for a moment, I wasn't sure what I'd heard. "They were made to *fight*?"

He nodded. "Any who were old enough to Change. I think they kept all the littler ones."

"But . . . people can Change as young as nine or ten, some even sooner—"

"And those mostly didn't make it. Colin was one of the few who got away, limping off into the desert after an early round. He'd been given a bad leg wound in the first fight and knew he wouldn't last through a second. But that's also why nobody went after him right away; they thought he wouldn't get far, and they'd round him up once the contest was over. But he got a ride with a norm into town, then ran into Jayden—"

"Wolf eyes in the dark," Jayden said, without looking up from his overloaded plate. "I almost had a heart attack. Thought the clan had come for me for sure."

"He took him back to our camp," Jace added. "We're staying in an abandoned building off Mesquite, so we had plenty of room. He fit in okay."

"'Cept he's angry all the time," Jayden added. "You know he is."

"We're all angry."

"I'm not. Not anymore." He glanced at Cyrus's trailer, and then back at his plate again. "I'm going places."

Jace laughed, and ruffled his brother's 'fro. "Yeah, you're going places, all right."

"Not the hair, man. How many times I hafta tell you?"

The brothers' interaction cut the tension, and in a few minutes, the lighthearted banter was back. Not that everything was forgotten, far from it, but these guys had learned the hard way that you take your fun when you can get it. And they were.

By the time Cyrus came back alone, it almost felt like nothing had ever happened. "Where is he?" I asked, as somebody handed me another beer.

"He's fine. Wanted some time alone."

Yeah, so did I, but not for the same reason as before. I wanted that boy's clan name. Nobody else around the fire seemed to realize that they'd just reported multiple homicides to a war mage, along with a few dozen more minor crimes, if child abuse counts as minor. I didn't intend to point it out since learning that they had a cop in their midst might not go down well, but I damned well intended to act on it.

But I could get the particulars from Cyrus later. If I knew him, he'd already reported everything to his brother. That was partly why Sebastian had agreed to this craziness: Cyrus wanted to use his status as *vargulf* to get information on badly behaving clans. It had been a long time since there had been a *bardric*, and things had gotten sloppy. Sebastian was trying to change that, but he needed information on the inner workings of the clans to do it.

And who better to give it to him than their victims?

I told my inner war mage to relax, lay back, and enjoy the night. I rested my head on Cyrus's leg and looked up at the stars. The fire was throwing ash and burning embers skyward, black and red and yellow. The guys were kicking back beers that they were too young to buy, but that with their metabolisms would never catch up enough to make them drunk. And then somebody pulled out a harmonica.

It crystallized into one of those times that you remember for years. When things, for one brief moment, are so perfect that they don't seem real. The chill of the desert air, the warmth of the fire, the hard muscle of Cyrus's leg under my head, shifting a little because he felt it, too.

And then it got better.

The clouds had been a low cover all day, making things feel a little claustrophobic even in the great outdoors. But they finally parted, sending beams of moonlight down onto the scene, almost like they were putting a spotlight on the camp. We laughed, every one of us, in a spontaneous chorus, because it was just too beautiful. One of the boys even held out a hand, as if trying to catch the rays streaming through his fingers.

And then they were off, transforming at almost the same time, as if choreographed. I felt Cyrus's leg twitch under mine, and knew that he desperately wanted to run alongside them. But that he wouldn't because of me.

"Go," I said. "It'll take me a while to clean up anyway."

"You sure?" It was sober. Because Cyrus knew how much I wanted to run, too, but couldn't. Thanks to a human father and a little thing called Neuri Syndrome, transforming was something I'd never be able to do. But that didn't mean that I'd deprive him.

"I'm sure."

He kissed me quick. "Camper's not locked, but the door sticks."

And then, before I could respond, a huge black and tan wolf was bounding away across the sand.

Chapter Three

I looked around and sighed. Cyrus had forgotten to strip first, and now his clothes were shredded, along with most of the boys'. Weres were hell on wardrobes.

I bundled the empty chip bags, beer bottles, condiments and used napkins into the now rags and let myself into the trailer. I was looking for a trash can—and was pleasantly surprised. Not only did I find one, and with an actual plastic liner no less, but there were other homey touches, too.

It made me smile to see them. Cyrus had an apartment downtown, giving him access to the guys he'd been fleecing at the gaming tables, because nobody cheats at cards like a Were. Their noses are better than a lie detector, sensing the nervous sweat of a mark a mile off.

But while it was a convenient base, the city always made him itch, like a wool coat that was two sizes to small, as he'd put it. He preferred to be out here, under the huge dome of the sky, unfettered and free. And while he could almost certainly have afforded a better bolt hole than this—he was a very successful card cheat—maybe he preferred something that helped him better connect with the boys.

I wondered if he realized that he was well on his way to forming his own little clan. There's no such thing as a solitary Were; the "lone wolf" of legend goes against every instinct they have. And Cyrus's longing for a home was palpable in everything from the chintz curtains at the kitchen window, printed with little Las Vegas signs, to the "who's afraid of the big bad wolf?" fridge magnet supporting a photo.

It was of him and the boys in some kayaks on what looked like the Colorado River. He'd somehow talked them into wearing life vests, and several had zinc covering their noses. It was frankly adorable, and no, I wasn't saying that just because I was stupid about the guy.

Cyrus had started this whole thing with the outcast boys to help them and his brother. But it looked like it was helping him, too. Bad décor and all.

I finished doing the dishes that weren't paper, tossed the rest, stripped and took a quick shower in the tiny plastic cubicle wedged into the hall beside the bedroom. Then I put on the nightie I'd brought in my saddlebags, because I was not afraid of the big bad wolf. Quite the contrary, I thought, grinning.

Full moon sex was the best sex.

And there *was* a bed, a big one that had somehow been shoved into the tiny back room where it took up most of the space. But it was comfy, and my full belly was working against me. I'd no sooner lay down on the soft, rumpled covers that smelled like Cyrus and home and clan than a yawn split my head. Damn it, this was no time to get sleepy! I wanted to stay awake, to finish tidying up, to wait for Cyrus, to—

The door handle jiggled.

"That was fast," I called out. "I'm in the bedroom."

The Winnebago creaked and groaned, but nothing else happened. The damned door must be stuck again. I sighed and got up, grabbing my coat out of the saddle bag because I hadn't thought to bring a robe and it might be one of the boys.

Then I flung open the door.

And found a monster staring back at me.

It wasn't a Were, even a transformed one. I didn't know what it was. And I didn't have time to find out. I had a split-second glimpse of a huge maw of razer-edged teeth, a pair of feverish yellow eyes, and a mass of matted gray fur.

And then it was on me.

The fact that it had to rip open the side of the trailer to get in told me it was big, but I couldn't have said otherwise. Because it moved so fast that it might as well have been a cyclone tearing its way inside. The only saving grace was that I had grabbed that coat.

The long leather overcoats worn by the Corps aren't only meant to hide all the weapons we carry around. They also provide protection, courtesy of the many spells woven into and layered on top of them. Like the ones that kept eight-inch claws out of my chest.

But that's all they did. The repelling charms supposed to send an attacker flying did nothing, the shields I popped out as an instinctive response to danger did nothing, and the force of the attack sent me slamming back into the fake oak paneling above Cyrus's dinette. Where I cut myself on the window glass that shattered behind me.

It fell everywhere, but I ignored it. I was already slinging spells and sending the animated weapons in my coat at whatever was trying to gut me—and trying hard. But I was trying, too, and a war mage about to die is *motivated.*

Which was why the next few seconds devolved into a tornado of magic, flung potions and flying weapons, the latter because a war mage's arsenal can levitate and fight independently.

Not that that made any difference. My weapons were firing, stabbing and blowing holes the size of basketballs in the sides of Cyrus's new digs. But the creature moved like nothing I'd ever seen, so fast that I literally couldn't track it with my eyes, only getting glimpses whenever it paused for a millisecond.

And it didn't do that much.

Even worse, when something of mine *did* connect, it didn't seem to have much effect. The bastard shrugged off bullets and knives like bee stings, barely paused at potions, and didn't seem to mind when half of the roof caved in. And when I rolled off the table, hit the floor, and sent a spell powerful enough to have knocked the damned creature the length of a football field away, the only reaction was the blowback—on me. I went sailing through the door to the hall, like from the recoil of the world's largest gun, while the creature went nowhere.

Except straight at me again.

I caught a glimpse of liquid movement and did the only thing I could think of, namely the opposite of the spell I'd just thrown. Instead of trying to eject him from the camper, I drew it in on top of him. Casting a spell that caused the two sides of the hall to scrunch in on each other like a metal fist, in an attempt to trap the thing.

Which . . . might not have been my best move.

Because it tore free by the simple procedure of ripping the trailer in half. My part must have gotten shoved backwards in the process, because it abruptly went rolling on the two wheels it had left, scattering the fire and knocking me back to my knees. But the distance finally gave me my first good look at what I was fighting.

I almost wished it hadn't.

It had the general shape of a wolf, if wolves were sixteen feet tall. And had strangely elongated limbs, a hunched back, claws like short swords and a maw that looked big enough to swallow me whole. It looked like someone had taken the idea of a werewolf and told some Hollywood effects studio to push it to the limit, and then to push it some more. And to keep on pushing until it broke the brain to look at it, because what was left wasn't the sleek, deadly predator of legend, which was beautiful in its own right.

But something straight out of a nightmare.

It leapt for me again and I forgot my training, at least the part about not screaming and wetting yourself. But I nonetheless managed to throw the worst item in my arsenal: a very nasty little device called a dislocator. It does exactly what the name implies, relocating the parts of your body that it has selected to fuck up to other areas, leaving arms growing out of your sternum or feet quite literally in your mouth.

Or, at least, that's what the illegal street versions do. The Corps' variety isn't so kind. What I threw should have had pieces of the creature springing off its body and adhering to any available surface—the other half of the trailer, the surrounding rocks, each other—until there was nothing left but a scream echoing in the night.

You notice I said *should.*

Because the dislocator landed—I damned well saw it. But the effect wasn't what I'd intended. The creature's body literally leapt apart all right, pieces springing off the trunk and scattering into the air like a fleshy bomb—

For about a second. Then they were flying together again as if they'd been attached by a bunch of rubber bands, ones that had reached their limit and snapped back. Although into what, I didn't know.

All I could see was a storm of fur and bone and sinew, a working mass of body parts wrapped in a fog of blood. It was horrible and fascinating and terrifying, all at the same time. Although not as much so as when it stopped.

And the creature stood there, not in part but all of it, together again as if nothing had ever happened.

And immediately leapt for me again.

But, this time, something leapt for it, too. Out of the shadows came a blur of motion that I didn't identify as Cyrus in wolf form until he landed on the thing's back, ripping, snarling and tearing. And dying, any second now, if I didn't do something!

The momentary paralysis that had left me staring in shock finally broke, and I leapt out of the still moving trailer. I felt dirt and burning embers under my feet, along with some glass shards from the shattered window that I'd picked up when I hit the kitchen floor. I barely noticed. Like I only dimly saw the other wolves gathering around, their eyes shining in the night, reflecting the light from the few scattered logs that were still on fire.

They registered, but they were distant, vague, like the pain in my body where the creature's blow had connected, like the sighing of the wind over the desert, like my heart pounding in my ears.

None of it mattered; only Cyrus.

The darkness brightened, time seemed to slow down, and for a moment, I could see everything: the motes of burning ash in the air, like fireflies drifting across the scene; the beams of moonlight cascading through a gap in the clouds; the surrounding boys, some still in wolf form, others just changed back and crouched low to the ground, disbelief and horror on their faces.

And Cyrus, locked in a battle he couldn't win, but that he would fight nonetheless—to save me.

Then I was up and moving, my coat in one hand, my potion belt in the other. Because I wasn't a damsel in distress; I was a war mage. *I* did the saving.

And I'd better do it soon.

I started running just as Cyrus slashed a gash across the creature's throat, spewing a gout of blood out onto the air. It hadn't even hit the soil when a great claw grabbed him off the misshapen back and threw him what must have been forty feet, into the side of a cliff. I didn't have time to see how he landed or if he was all right. Because the hero-worshipping circle of boys gave a howl, and jumped for the monster who had hurt their mentor.

And were savaged by a hurricane of slashing claws.

"No!" I yelled. "Get back! Get out of there!"

They got back, all except for one. It was Jayden; I could see the nose ring winking at me from the snout of a sleek, dark gray wolf. He was like smoke on the wind, sure footed and lightning fast, and not darting and slashing blindly as the others had been. He emulated Cyrus and went straight for the jugular.

He almost made it.

He was faster than any wolf I'd ever seen—except for the one he was attacking. The giant creature caught him a split second before he completed his leap, snatching him out of the air with those huge jaws. And then snapping them shut, the resulting crunch so loud that it echoed all over the canyon, bouncing off the hills and magnifying in the still, night air.

Along with his brother's horrified scream.

I heard Jace but I didn't see him. I didn't see anything except my target. And Cyrus, leaping out of the dark once more, distracting the beast.

Giving me a chance to strike.

I didn't bother trying to figure out what might work. I threw it all, the whole damned belt, basically everything I had left. While recalling my gun, which had been levitating around the creature's head, pumping lead into a cranium that didn't even seem to notice.

Let's see if you notice this, I thought, and fired.

The potion belt exploded, practically at point blank range, releasing dozens of spells right on target. Cyrus veered away, the liquid muscle under all that sleek fur rippling in the moonlight. Several newly arrived boys, who had also been leaping for the fray, stopped on a dime, their haunches bunching up almost comically around their faces. For a split second, all of us froze, watching and waiting to see if it would be enough.

And then the beast screamed.

It was a horribly human sound, making my skin crawl even as I started moving again. But I didn't hesitate. After seeing it throw off a dislocator in seconds, I knew I didn't have much time. But then, I didn't need it.

Because war mage coats have a number of functions, including one that very few people know about. It isn't seen very often because it isn't needed very often. But in extremis, it can perform one final service for its master.

That one.

I hurled the coat, the final spell I would ever cast over it on my lips, just a whisper in the night. But it was enough. Because I'd had that coat ever since I became a war mage. My father had given it to me when I turned eighteen, just as his father had given it to him, a generation's old family heirloom dating back centuries, to a many times great grandfather who had layered the first foundation spells onto the leather.

I'd added to them as I grew, until it was a tapestry of everything I knew, of all that I'd learned and become. I loved that coat like a friend, like the constant companion it had always been, like my right arm. And like what it was: a repository of my magic and that of the entire de Croisset family, who had served the Corps for eight hundred years with our strength, our honor, and our cunning.

All of which was woven into every fucking piece.

It hit the thrashing body, but unlike the potions, it didn't explode. It didn't hurt the creature at all. Instead, it engulfed him, expanding outward and wrapping him up in what looked like all the leather in the world, a great sheet of it that blocked out the sky.

Until it suddenly contracted.

The monster didn't scream this time, probably because it could no longer open its jaw. It also couldn't see, other than a sea of brown leather, or hear with the muffling folds cutting out any outside noise, or move effectively. It couldn't do anything except thrash about . . .

And slowly suffocate to death.

The thrashing finally stopped, and the coat peeled away from the body. It was no longer a cherished family heirloom, but just a worn old scrap of leather, patched and faded, its magic exhausted. I stared at it in disbelief and grief for a moment, but also in overwhelming gratitude. Dad had always said it might save my life someday. Looked like he'd been right.

But it hadn't saved someone else's.

Cyrus had already Changed back, and had run up to where a wolf had been a few moments before, but where only a boy now lay. I knew it was too late even before I joined him, limping up with a twisted ankle and a bruised ribcage, from where my shields hadn't been strong enough. But the physical pain was easier to bear than what was happening in front of me.

"No! Let me *go*." Jace tore away from the two boys holding him and ran up as well, only to stop in disbelief over the body of his brother. But if he was hoping for a moment to say goodbye, he was disappointed.

The body had been all but bisected by that terrible bite.

Jace went to his knees, his eyes huge and disbelieving. I started to say something, I'm not sure what, but Cyrus stopped me with a look. Well-meaning platitudes weren't going to help, and might easily be resented.

I backed away.

And realized that, while I'd been distracted, the other body had transformed as well. It was still larger than Jayden's, but was now human-sized. It was also vaguely familiar.

Two of the boys rolled it over, revealing limp limbs, a pale face, and a shock of dark brown hair almost the same color as mine. Like the eyes, open and staring and the steel gray of the clans. Colin, I thought dully, recognizing the angry boy from earlier. And, for a moment, it sounded like the hills were whispering the name back to me.

But it was just the boys, belatedly recognizing who we'd been fighting.

And then the hills *were* echoing, but not with words. Unearthly, desolate, ghostly howls erupted in the night, floated over the sand and seemed to merge with the stars. Not just from the throats of the still transformed, but from all of them.

A strange, hybrid pack mourning the loss of not one, but two of their own.

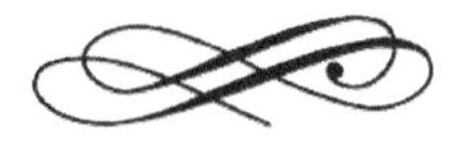

Chapter Four

Yeah. That's it," I said, shoving limp hair out of my eyes.

It was cold this deep in the belly of HQ, where the hot air blowing through the main doors from above never reached. And all I was wearing was the nightie and my now tattered and useless coat. But the monster rotating slowly in front of me was still making me sweat.

Hargroves didn't look any happier, probably because he'd been rousted out of bed—again. If I were him, I'd consider investing in a cot for his office, considering how often that sort of thing happened. But, as always, he was perfectly pulled together, with the purple spotted hanky in his coat pocket jewel bright against the smart gray linen, and the waves of silver-gray hair perfectly combed.

I'd never seen him disheveled, and probably never would. He was old school Corps, brought out of retirement to help with the war, as so many had been. And like most of them, he thought us newbies were slipshod, careless, and less than adequately trained.

I'd often wondered how that last one worked, exactly, since it was their generation who had trained us, but I'd been just smart enough not to ask. And I sure as hell wasn't going to bring it up now. Hargroves' usual mood was set on grim, but tonight he was as sour as I'd ever seen him.

With cause, I thought, looking back at the monster.

It wasn't the one from the desert, although it was hard to tell. The height was the same, the horribly hunched back was the same, as were the elongated arms, which made him literally a knuckle dragger unless he raised those terrible claws for some reason, like slashing out your heart. Mine still hurt where that had almost been done to me, so I found it a little hard to meet the blank stare under that horrible maw.

But I did it anyway.

Old school types weren't the only ones with steel in their spines.

"You're sure?" Hargroves pressed.

"It was memorable."

That won me a glance, probably for the tone more than the words. But he didn't say anything, at least to me. "Jenkins!"

A small man came forward, and by small, I mean maybe four feet tall. He probably had fey blood somewhere in his background, although I wasn't sure as I didn't know him. I'd thought I knew all of the dungeon masters, as the mad scientist types who worked down here were called, but I guessed not.

He was sort of cute, with dimples, thinning, light brown hair and glasses that he shouldn't have needed because there were spells for vision problems. And wards, like the little horned owl tat that my dad had given me when I joined the Corps, along with the coat. At least I still had the owl, I thought, grimacing.

But spells could sometimes fight other spells, and tats took part of your magic. So those glasses told me a lot. Namely that he was more concerned about doing his job than about his appearance. Or about how long he droned on for, I thought, when he started talking.

But unlike Hargroves' lectures, this was one I wanted to hear.

"Are you familiar with cryptozoology, mage?" he asked me. And then went on without a pause for a reply. "It's what norms call the study of legendary creatures whose existence has never been proven: Bigfoot, the Chupacabra, the Lock Ness monster—or the giant bird creature people keep sighting in the desert around Vegas. Big as an Apache helicopter, by all accounts, with a forty-foot wingspan—"

"Cryptids," Hargroves said, cutting to the chase, which won him an annoyed glance from our lecturer.

"Yes, that's the term given them by overly imaginative humans. In fact, most of the supposed sightings are creative mental embroidery by people who have been, shall we say, hitting the bottle a bit too fiercely of late? And who stumbled into the woods and were startled by a bear or what have you—"

"Or a fey," I pointed out, and was talked right over.

"—or, in a very few cases, by a fey or demonic creature temporarily escaped into this world, something that happened more frequently in the past than today, of course—"

"We know all that," Hargroves said impatiently.

He didn't get the verbal steamroller treatment as I had, but he did receive another look, which I could have told Jenkins was a waste of time. That sort of thing slid off Hargroves like water off a duck's back. I'm not sure he even noticed, considering that it was the same expression he wore most of the time.

"You're saying that I fought a myth?" I said, jumping into the brief pause. "Because my ribs think otherwise."

"Not a myth," Jenkins said, pushing up his glasses. "A Relic."

I frowned. "What?"

He nodded. "Long before humans came up with their so-called cryptids, the magical community had its own strange sightings. Only ours were real."

The rotating creature suddenly changed, morphing into dozens of others. Some of which were barely recognizable—a hulking vampire that had to be eight feet tall, with fangs as long as my index fingers; a humanoid fey with glowing yellow eyes, levitating off the ground and throwing energy bolts from his fingertips; a woman with towering white wings—and others that were not even sort of familiar. And some that made my head ache to look at them.

"They come from a time when magic was less tame than it is today," Jenkins twittered on happily, maybe because he hadn't had to fight one, "and more plentiful. And when the creatures it spawned were far more dangerous, as a result. Think of them as the saber-toothed tiger version of a kitty cat—same genus, very different result."

"And we're the kitty," I guessed.

"Exactly so." He looked pleased.

I was less so. "You're telling me I fought a saber-toothed *Were*?"

"Well, the equivalent, yes. Weres used to be far more fearsome than they are now," he added with a straight face, as if a Were child would have had any problem ripping his balls off. "As were other magical creatures, for that matter.

"Then what happened?"

He shrugged. "What happened to the saber-toothed tiger? Evolution, changing conditions—did you know, the Earth used to have much more oxygen in the atmosphere than it does today? Scientists speculate that it might account for why everything grew so large in the past—"

"Jenkins," Hargroves began heavily.

"—Gigantopithecus, for example, was an ape who stood ten feet tall, like a real-life King Kong. There were dragonflies that had wingspans larger than modern day seagulls. And the megalodon shark was sixty feet long! You could have walked, with someone sitting on your shoulders, through its giant maw with room to spare. Not to mention—"

"Fascinating, but—"

"—sloths!" he said, his eyes glowing with enthusiasm. "They were as big as elephants once—"

"Jenkins!" Hargroves snapped.

"Yes?" The small man blinked at him.

"Get to the *point*."

"I was," he sniffed, looking offended, and pushed up his glasses. "The point is, if oxygen levels could affect everything from plants to animals, it shouldn't surprise anyone that fluctuating magic levels can affect us. It was a different era; the world is not static—"

"Then what was that thing doing here?" I interrupted. "We aren't in the stone age!"

"We're not talking about the stone age. That is quite a recent era, evolutionarily speaking—"

He cut off because I grabbed him by the front of his lab coat. "I don't care what era it was! I'm talking about now, tonight. Why are there monsters walking around—"

"Oh, not monsters," Jenkins said, frowning, and not the least bit intimidated. "And not walking around, at least not usually. We have them contained."

"Contained? Contained *where*?"

He blinked at me. "Why, just down the corridor, for one."

"What?"

Hargroves sighed. "He means your new students," he said dryly.

* * *

The room I ended up in a few minutes later was spacious, having been converted from an old holding cell. There had been some concessions made to the fact that its current occupants weren't actually criminals, mainly a screen in front of the toilet for some privacy and a few T.V.s. None of which were currently on because it was the middle of the night.

Things were not particularly quiet, however. The six people meant to be in the bunk beds arrayed around the walls were mostly still up, despite the fact that it was almost two A.M. But I guess when you're stuck in a hole in the earth, however clean and sterile of one, day and night cease to have much meaning.

Two of the guys were playing cards, one girl was brushing another one's hair, and a third girl was on her phone. I doubted she could get bars down here—the Corps' wards were hell on reception—but maybe she was playing a game. The last guy was in bed, with his back to the door and the covers pulled over his head, probably because the light was still on.

He didn't move when I came in, but everyone else did, all conversation stopping abruptly as it had when I'd been here with Hargroves yesterday. He was absent this time, since I doubted that they'd tell me anything otherwise. Of course, that was likely going to be the outcome anyway, because teacher or no, I was the enemy.

I was one of the people who had kept them locked up all their lives.

"Mind if I join you?" I asked, as one of the girls, a petite blonde, glanced at my tattered attire. "Bad night," I added.

She blushed and looked away, but the other young woman, who had been getting her long, red hair brushed, held my gaze defiantly. She'd done the same to Hargroves when we'd visited together, so I wasn't surprised. Anybody who could hold that gimlet-eyed gaze wouldn't have trouble with mine.

Especially now, I thought, stifling a yawn.

"Then why are you here?" Red asked me.

"Sophie," a black girl with a head of Cleopatra braids murmured.

"What? It's just a question. I can't ask questions now?"

"You can ask," I said. "Although you should get used to being rousted out of bed in the middle of the night. It's part of the training."

"Is that what this is? Some surprise training?"

"No." I sat a couple of six packs down on the table, which I guess they hadn't noticed because the tattered folds of my coat had hidden them. But they saw them now, and I saw the card players' eyes light up. "It's a late-night drink and a conversation," I added, taking a bottle for myself, because I could use it.

Red—Sophie, I guessed—didn't do likewise, although the petite blonde that had been doing the hair brushing had no such reserves. "Oh, thank God!" she said. "They don't give us anything down here!"

"Didn't think they allowed drinking at your school, either," I said.

"They don't, but we have ways of getting stuff in. A couple of the guys—"

"Jen." It was merely a monosyllable from Sophie, but the blonde fell silent immediately.

Looked like I'd found the Alpha, I thought, and drank beer.

"What do you want?" Sophie asked again. She had pretty eyes the color of pansy flowers and a scattering of freckles over a slightly snub nose. She was cute, but her expression was as fierce as any Were I'd ever seen.

I ignored her and finished the bottle, because I can be Alpha, too. And because my throat felt like a damned desert. I wanted to go home, I wanted a bath, I wanted to snuggle up to my boyfriend—assuming I could find him. I wanted a lot of things, none of which involved sitting on an uncomfortable plastic chair and sweating some more.

As a result, my voice wasn't as conciliatory as it could have been when I said: "Information."

"Ah. It all becomes clear."

"Maybe to you." I drew out a photo of the so-called Relic that Jenkins had given me. "Ever see anything like this?"

Sophie made no effort to take it. But the card players, who had gathered around to drink beer, were a different story. One of them, a lanky Asian kid with blue-tipped hair, actually picked it up and whistled through his teeth. "That's . . . something."

"Yeah, but what?" The other, a good looking blond with a deep tan, took it from him. He looked like he should be catching waves in Malibu, not sitting in a warded cell. But then, they all did, or at least, they all looked human. That's why they'd been chosen for this little experiment that Hargroves was running on behalf of the Circle.

But looks aside, they weren't that different from the creature on the pic.

Not that different at all.

They weren't as fearsome because they weren't Weres, but they very definitely had abilities left over from a different age. Which was why I hoped they could help me.

And why I flinched slightly when Sophie suddenly grabbed the pic, a fact that didn't elude her. "Relax," she said. "If we don't play nice, they send us back to jail."

"And this is different how?" The third guy asked, climbing down from his bunk to claim a beer. He looked Hispanic, with skin slightly darker than Jace's, but with a strange, iridescent sheen to it when the light hit him just right. I wondered what his ability was.

Guess I should have read their folder.

"That's supposed to change if we prove useful, isn't that right?" Sophie asked, looking at me with a cynical twist to her lips. "They wouldn't just use us and then throw us away again, after the war's over. *Right*?"

On the one hand, I reflected, not bringing Hargroves had definitely been the right move. They hadn't been nearly so open in his august presence. On the other, this was not a marked improvement, especially considering how good I am at diplomacy.

I decided to play a hunch and not try.

"I don't know what they plan to do," I said honestly. "You know the drill as well as I do. Right now, we're in a war and well-trained mages are dropping like flies. They need you, particularly since the other side has no compunction about using everybody they can find with magical ability, regardless of what form it takes. They'll deploy them as cannon fodder, of course, but—"

"And that's different than what the Corps plans to do with us?" Sophie hissed, leaning forward.

Her formerly soft blue eyes flashed gold for an instant. Probably not a good sign. But I'd started this, and I wasn't going to lie to them now. I couldn't, no matter what those higher on the totem pole wanted, not and teach them at the same time. Teaching—especially the war mage version of it—required trust.

If they didn't have any in me, this whole thing was doomed from the start.

"War mages have become cannon fodder ourselves lately," I told her. "For the type of people the Black Circle has been digging up—

"People like us, you mean," the Asian guy said. Unlike Sophie, he didn't sound angry. Just vaguely sad.

It hit me harder than her anger had, because we were supposed to be the good guys. The Corps put their lives on the line, every day, to protect the magical community, and plenty of us died for it. But we didn't protect everyone, did we?

Because magic was like any other physical trait, from hair and eye color to whether or not you liked cilantro: it varied from person to person. Usually, the variance was slight, and mainly boiled down to how much magic your body generated as opposed to the norm. Make too little and you were automatically shut out of a lot of jobs and prestige; make too much, and you usually ended up in the Corps.

Which considering what we went through on a regular basis, sometimes had me wondering who got the rawest deal.

But the point was that magic differed in strength, yes, but also in *content.*

Which was why a bunch of magically gifted young people were drinking my beer, but looking as if it tasted bad. I couldn't blame them. The Circle had decided, centuries ago, that certain types of magical expression were desirable and other kinds . . . weren't.

And life really sucked if your magic was in the latter category.

"Yeah," I agreed. "People like you."

"So, the Circle wants their cast offs to fight the other side's cast offs," Sophie summed up. "And even if we somehow survive, what do you think they're going to do with us? Drape a medal around our necks? They'll put us right back where they found us!"

"They said they wouldn't—" Jen began, her blonde bob swinging around her face.

"And I'm sure the Circle never lies! Like when they told you that you were going to school, that you'd be trained, that you'd learn control!"

"But I have learned control," Jen said, meekly.

"Repression is not control!"

"If you think we're lying to you, why are you here?" I asked curiously. "I understood you had a choice."

"A choice!" Sophie almost spat it. "That's for those of you with normally functioning magic. Did I have a choice when I was taken from my home at the age of six? Did I have a choice when they locked me up in a "school" that's more of a prison? Did I have a choice when they offered me one way, and only one, out of there? Is that what you call a fucking choice?"

I picked up another beer—because hell, I'd bought 'em—and used Were strength to flick the top off. "No," I said, as Sophie's eyes narrowed on my undamaged thumb. "Not really."

"What are you?" she demanded.

"My father is Guillame de Croissets, a decorated, retired war mage."

"And your mother?"

"Laurentia . . . of Lobizon."

Her eyes widened slightly. "You're half Were."

"Just Were," I corrected, because there were no half-Weres. You were either Clan or you weren't, although my case was a little complicated. But I didn't want to go into that now. Or at all. And it looked like Sophie knew something about Weres because she didn't push it.

She blinked and sat back in her chair, belatedly snagging one of the remaining beers. "So that's why you're stuck training us," she said, after a minute. "They thought, if we go rogue and kill you, no great loss."

"Maybe." The thought had crossed my mind.

She thought about that. "Why are you doing this?" she finally asked. "You're not much better in their eyes than we are. We're all just fodder in their war."

"Their war." I reached inside my coat and took out the pic from Cyrus's fridge. It had somehow survived the carnage, and I'd rescued it when I went back for my boots. The Corps currently had the place cordoned off and would for a while, and I thought that he might like to make a copy since it had both Jace and Jayden in it.

I didn't know how many photos Jace had of his brother, but in this one, he was laughing. I looked at it, and wave of pure rage swept over me for whoever had done this. Because somebody had. Relic strains that fearsome might exist in some people's DNA, but they didn't come out without help.

Somebody had turned a boy into a monster, and killed both Jace and Colin, too.

"Their war," I said again, throwing the picture down. "Is our war now."

Sophie slowly pulled the pic over to her, and regarded it silently for a moment. "The man's a Were, too," she said, talking about Cyrus. "He has the look."

"They're all Weres. Unaffiliated—called *vargulfs*—"

"I know what it means."

"Then you know they're outcastes, unwanted by anyone, even more than you. The magical community might not treat you fairly, but you're still housed. You have clothes, food, an education. Yes, I know—what are you supposed to do with it, if you never get out of those schools. Or if you're restricted and watched your whole life even if you do. But that life, the one I just described, the one you're living now? Would seem like paradise to a *vargulf.*

"When the clans throw them out, they have *nothing*. They are literally tossed into the street, in the middle of a world that looks on Weres as dangerous predators, and left to fend for themselves. Most last a few months, maybe a year if they're lucky.

"Many kill themselves immediately because they can't handle the loneliness, the idea of having nobody give a damn about them for the rest of their lives."

Sophie regarded the picture again. "They seem happy," she said, but her voice was less sure than before.

"They were, for a little while. The man in the pic is named Cyrus. He's been trying to help them, to give them a sense of belonging again. It was working—until tonight."

"Tonight?" Her eyes met mine.

"Somebody got to one of them, a guy named Colin, and gave him this." I put a vial on the table. It was empty now, but had contained just enough residue when I took it off Colin's corpse for the lab guys to identify it.

"And what is that?" Sophie asked, wisely not touching it.

I told her.

Chapter Five

For the second time in twenty-four hours, I came home to a house with extra vehicles in the driveway. My old truck was still there, as was Cyrus's bike, which cheered me up. I hadn't known when I'd see him again, because I'd assumed the boys would need him. But nobody drove his baby but him, so he'd clearly made it back.

And so had someone else.

The third vehicle in my drive wasn't one I knew. It was a rental, with the company sticker marring the shiny fender of a brand-new BMW. I frowned at it, but parked over to the side so that I didn't risk scratching the paint. Then I went in—

And almost tripped over a body lying on the floor.

There were a lot of them, I realized, my hand on my newly restocked potion belt. But considering that they were in sleeping bags and gently snoring, I decided that maybe I wasn't about to be attacked again. I slowly unclenched my hand and picked my way across the sprawled forms of Cyrus's boys to the hall and then to the kitchen, where a single light burned.

Two handsome men were sitting at my prep table, having coffee. One of them was Cyrus, with tired lines etched around his mouth and wearing a clean tank top that showed off the powerful lines of his shoulders and chest. I couldn't see his legs, but knew they'd be denim clad, and if he had on footwear, it would probably be boots.

Arnou, his old clan, was based in Jersey, which was why he'd come out to Vegas after the challenge. Some distance had definitely been needed, and I liked to think that my transfer within the Corps also had something to do with it. But he'd embraced the West with enthusiasm, and frequently looked like a cowboy just in from the range.

The contrast with his companion could not have been more striking.

Sebastian Arnou might not have the title, but he still looked like a king, albeit a modern one. A platinum watch gleamed on his wrist, which was probably worth more than my house, especially now. His suit hugged the hard lines of his body like it had been made for them, which it probably had. It was a dark blue power variety that matched his eyes and would have been perfect in a boardroom in New York.

Here in my still somewhat trashed kitchen, it was a bit out of place. But then, so was he. Especially with Cyrus, his outcast and supposedly hated brother, right across the table. If their farce was to work, they *couldn't* be seen together.

My glance went to the kitchen window, which thankfully had curtains drawn over it, and then to the tarp-covered hole in the wall. It was still battened down nice and snug, which was a relief. Although less of one than if I hadn't just passed through a living room full of witnesses!

"Out cold," Cyrus told me, before I could ask. "Gave them redfern."

I relaxed slightly. Redfern was the name for a mix of herbs and magical plants used by Weres to calm the effects of the full moon. In slightly larger doses, it was also a really good sedative.

"Thanks for making coffee," I told him, with a kiss. "Hello, Sebastian."

"Lia." He didn't get up; it wasn't the Were way. But he did the usual hand on heart gesture of a clan member greeting another. I did it back and sat down, and Cyrus slid me over a mug of coffee, fixed just the way I liked it, which was hot as hell and black as sin.

I practically inhaled it.

"We were waiting for you," Sebastian said. "I hoped they wouldn't keep you all night. I had to slip away from my bodyguards, and I can't stay long."

"Any word?" Cyrus asked, more abruptly. Because he doesn't have any more tact than I do.

I didn't take offense, since I'd gotten the easy job tonight. I didn't even want to imagine what it had been like trying to comfort kids—because that's what many of them still were, whatever they thought—who had just seen what they had. I just took out the same vial I'd shown to Sophie.

"Yeah," I said, and put it on the table.

Cyrus picked it up and sniffed it. Normally, I'd have told him not to bother, because I doubted there was much left after the labs finished with it. But it hadn't been washed out, either, and a Were's nose doesn't need much.

"Punch?" Cyrus asked, looking up.

I nodded.

"I assume we're not talking about the Hawaiian variety?" Sebastian said, taking it from his brother. And rearing back after a single whiff, as if his nose might be the better of the two. Or maybe he just wasn't as familiar with Vegas street drugs.

"The fey variety," I said. "It's a derivative of fey wine, a potent narcotic smuggled over the divide from Faerie and then cut way the hell down. The original stuff is said to be able to knock a vamp on his ass."

I hesitated, because this was going to start a shitstorm, but there was nothing for it. "It's what Grayshadow was taking."

Sebastian had no response, other than for a slight tightening of his hand around the white porcelain of his mug, but Cyrus was a different story. "That son of a bitch!"

It was true. Grayshadow had indeed been a son of a bitch. He'd also been Sebastian's right-hand man, who had betrayed him.

Like many Weres, Grayshadow hadn't liked the alliance with the humans. But that had been less important to him that the opportunity it afforded, one that only a truly twisted mind could have come up with. He'd helped to formulate the plan that had made Sebastian *bardric* and Cyrus an outcast, and had then kidnapped Cyrus.

The idea was that Sebastian would be forced to go after his brother himself, since sending the clan to help a *vargulf* would be impossible without admitting what he'd done. And as soon as he made himself vulnerable, Grayshadow intended to kill him and blame the death on his estranged brother. As Sebastian's second, that would have immediately left Grayshadow as clan leader, and possibly *bardric* as well.

It was a good plan, and it might have worked, only I'd found Cyrus before Sebastian had, and caught Grayshadow in the act. He had therefore issued challenge, as it was the only way left to get the position he wanted and avoid punishment. He'd assumed that he would win any fight between him and Sebastian, although not because he was stronger.

But because he was planning to cheat.

He'd been taking punch—a lot of it. Enough to bring out latent magical abilities that, while untrained, were still formidable. Abilities that Sebastian didn't have.

Unfortunately for Grayshadow, I traced him to the arena, and my skills are not untrained. The traitorous second died shortly thereafter, and the problem was solved. But plenty of punch was still out there, and now it looked like somebody was tinkering with the recipe.

"Punch gets you high," Cyrus snarled. "Maybe brings out a few latent abilities—"

"More than a few," I said. "That's why the Corps has a whole division assigned to stop it—or we did. They were mostly pulled off to help with the war, and the stuff has been flooding the streets ever since—"

"Damn it, Lia! It doesn't do what we saw tonight!"

For a moment, I was taken aback, because that wasn't a tone I was used to hearing from him. Then it dawned on me that the boys weren't the only ones who had been traumatized. Stress and pain were written on Cyrus's face as well as exhaustion, and the eyes were haunted in a way that they hadn't been earlier.

I took his hand under the table, and a little of the strain smoothed out. Weres liked touch even more than humans, craved it even, especially after a traumatic event. I suddenly felt it as well, a need for some skin-on-skin contact, preferably full body and in bed. Not sex, not anymore; as tired as I was, I'd probably fall asleep halfway through. I just wanted to hold him.

But we had company so I did the next best thing and answered his question.

"No, it doesn't," I agreed. "This wasn't the usual drug. Someone's refined it, upped the potency, and also played with the formula—"

"Played how?" That was Sebastian.

"It's hard to say, because we just got the sample. And because all fey wine is different, so punch varies greatly, too. It's like chili; everybody has their own recipe, and exactly what goes into it depends on the region it came from, what was blooming the time of year that it was made, the maker," I fluttered my free hand. "A lot of things."

"Then this could be an accident?"

I shook my head. "The guys in the lab don't think so. Street drugs are all about the high; everything done to them is to try and increase that. But this stuff doesn't really get you high. It gets you . . . something else."

"What else?" Cyrus said. "What *was* that thing?"

I debated hedging, because Cyrus did *not* look like he needed that information right now. He looked like he needed a stiff drink and some sleep. But in a real sense, he had formed his own little pack out of those forgotten boys.

And you don't treat a pack leader like a child.

"Colin," I said bluntly. "Just a very different version of him. Colin if he'd been born millennia ago, in a harsher world. Apparently, this new strain of punch does more than bring out a few latent traits. It brings out the latent you, whatever that may be. In humans, that means talents and abilities that have been mostly weeded out of the magical gene pool: telekinetics, necromancers, firestarters, and so on. In Weres—"

I reached into my coat and took out the photo of the creature that Jenkins had given me. I wasn't trying to hurt Cyrus, but Sebastian had to know what he was dealing with. Both of the men just stared at the thing, which . . . yeah.

It was just as bad as I remembered.

"Selective breeding was done in the magical community to eliminate certain traits," I explained. "The junk magic that nobody wanted. Because if someone went dark with some of those gifts, they could wipe out whole communities. But the old abilities weren't entirely eradicated. They still show up sometimes, which is why the Circle runs schools for children with unapproved gifts, where they are supposed to learn to control them safely away from anyone they could harm."

"And if they don't?" Cyrus said, because he knew how the world worked.

"Then they stay there, or in another facility, for life. It isn't a perfect system," I admitted. "But neither would be letting them, and their gifts, fall into the hands of the dark. Only we think that's what somebody is trying to make happen."

"Please explain," Sebastian said, looking concerned. Or as much as he ever did. The smooth forehead was unlined for a reason, despite the butt load of problems he dealt with every day.

I swear the man had ice water in his veins.

It always came as something of a shock, because he and Cyrus looked so much alike. Sebastian had a slightly broader jaw, a narrower mouth, and a more Roman nose. But his hair was the same shade as his brother's, although not as curly, and cut shorter. He looked older, too, despite the lack of lines, maybe because of the air of gravitas he wore like a cloak.

The head of house Arnou did not mess around, and neither did I in answering his question.

"It's awfully convenient right now for the dark to have humans getting high off of punch and then cursing each other into oblivion because they had mage blood and didn't know it. It keeps the Corps busy running around putting out fires, just when we need our manpower the most. It also gives the dark a whole new group to draw soldiers from."

"They're using humans?" Sebastian's voice was sharp, because that was the one universal agreement in the magical world. No matter your politics, or which side you were on, you didn't involve humans in your business. If word got out that magic was real, everybody would be at risk. Humans outnumbered and outbred us by terrifying amounts. Magic or no, we'd be wiped out or destroy each other in the struggle and everybody knew it.

But, clearly, somebody no longer cared.

"That's what the Circle is afraid of," I admitted. "We've had casualties; the dark has, too. And there weren't as many of them to begin with. The fear is that they're recruiting, using punch to sort through the human population and identify those with something unusual in the mix, then cull them out. Train them up, put them under a compulsion, and hey, presto. New soldiers."

"And, if they're really lucky, ones with abilities that you don't have," Sebastian added, because he wasn't slow.

"Didn't have until recently," I admitted. "I've been assigned a new group of students taken from the Circle's schools. They were offered a deal: work for the Corps helping to counter others like them on the other side, and win their freedom. As long as they keep their noses clean, they'll be out, without having to check in with a parole officer for the rest of their lives and without the usual restrictions on travel, jobs, etcetera."

"Sweet deal," Cyrus said, with a look.

Because he didn't believe it any more than Sophie had. The Circle's back was against the wall, more than most people knew. We'd been hemorrhaging mages recently, and calling up retirees was only going to last so long. We needed troops and the Circle was willing to make whatever kind of promises necessary to get them.

But after the war?

"Yeah," I said, and left it at that.

"And this . . . thing?" Sebastian said, one well-manicured finger resting on the edge of the photograph.

It was almost impossible to believe, looking at him, that the two creatures were in any way related. But a saber-tooth tiger and a housecat don't look much alike, either, although they have some of the same instincts. And every one Sebastian had was sounding an alarm right now, judging by the look in his eyes.

"It could just be bad luck," I said, although I heard the doubt in my own voice. "A young Were buys a common street drug. Later, he gets angry, wants to calm down, and thinks "why not? I'm nowhere near civilization anyway. What's the harm?" He takes the drug, only it isn't the normal kind of punch that he's used to, but a souped-up version the dark mages have been using to find themselves extra troops. Only they were giving it to garden variety humans—"

"Which he wasn't," Cyrus said harshly.

"Which he wasn't."

Sebastian's intelligent blue eyes met mine. "And you believe this?"

I shrugged. "It's what the Corps' lab rats think."

"I asked about you."

Yeah, he had.

In for a penny, I thought, and came out with it. "I think it's odd that Colin had just been talking about strength and how important it was. How his clan would have taken him back, if only he'd been stronger. And then he goes and takes something that made him stronger—by a lot. I don't like those kinds of coincidences."

"You think someone gave it to him on purpose," Cyrus said, his voice blank.

"It's possible," I said again. "Someone who wanted to see what would happen, maybe? If you're already experimenting on humans, well, the idea would occur, right? What if we gave our new drug to some other type of creature, and see what might be lurking in their bloodstream? Maybe they could be used as soldiers, too—"

"Not my boys!" Cyrus said, standing up abruptly enough to knock over his chair. "Not my *clan*!"

"They're not your clan," Sebastian said sharply. "Arnou is. It worries me that you seem to be forgetting that."

I didn't know what he meant by that, but maybe they'd had a discussion before I came in. It sort of looked like it. Cyrus scowled, and ran a hand over his face, which was going to have a beard in another few hours.

"I'm not forgetting anything! But Arnou—"

He got up and walked away from the table, although my kitchen was small, so there wasn't far to go. It also wasn't made for pacing. He realized that and turned back around, leaning against the counter with the coffee machine, his arms crossed defensively.

I knew that look, and I guessed Sebastian did, too, because his jaw tightened slightly.

"Arnou is rich and powerful," Cyrus said, before his brother could comment. "These boys aren't. They need protection—"

"As do you." It was flat.

"I can protect myself!"

"Normally, yes. But as a *vargulf*? There are many with grudges against me or our clan who would gladly destroy you to hurt me, as Grayshadow demonstrated."

"He knew the truth about us; others don't. They think we're estranged—"

"Some do. Others suspect something—"

"Suspicion isn't knowing—"

"Which is why we agreed—"

"—and doesn't mean they'd act on it!"

"—which is why you *swore to me*, that if we did this . . . charade . . . made necessary by the thick necked pride of our people, that you would do certain things—"

"That was before—"

"—one of which was to keep a low profile and stay out of sight!"

"I'm not planning on buying a bullhorn," Cyrus snapped. "But you can't expect me to stand by while—"

"That is exactly what I expect."

"—my people are killed!"

"They are not your people!"

And okay, maybe I'd been wrong about the ice water, I thought, staring at Sebastian. And understanding a lot better why he'd been able to herd the cats of the vicious clan council. Only, that's not what they were, was it, I thought, as a shadow grew on the wall behind Sebastian.

It was not shaped like a cat.

I went very still, but Cyrus didn't even seem to notice. "Fine! Then adopt them into Arnou, so they'll have clan protection—"

"And explain it how?" Sebastian looked at his brother as if he thought he might be mad, and I couldn't blame him. To an outsider, what Cyrus had asked might make sense. The boys needed protection; Arnou could afford it. Get them out of the city and away from the new version of the drug until we could run it to earth. Easy, right?

Only no, not easy. Sebastian had already taken flack for adopting me, to keep me safe from my mother's old clan who . . . weren't my biggest fans. But it had been a controversial move, even for a woman with a high-status mother and no baggage. For kids like these . . .

It might be enough for someone to challenge him.

And if Sebastian fell, the alliance fell with him.

"I am supposed to tell the clan," Sebastian hissed, "that they are now responsible to defend, to the death if necessary, a group of outcasts? People disowned by their own families, shunned by those who know them best?"

"They didn't do anything," Cyrus said heatedly. "Not enough to warrant the punishment—"

"I don't care what they did!"

"But you should!" Cyrus's eyes flashed wolf bright in the low light. "You told me that you wanted this title to right the wrongs in our community, to bring order, to defend the helpless! But when you get the chance—"

"We are at *war*," Sebastian roared, his hand slamming down on the tabletop, hard enough to make the coffee mugs dance. "Every day that I keep us in this fight I defend the helpless—as well as the rest of us! But you would have me endanger that for a group of—"

"Careful," Cyrus warned.

And shit. I did not need a knock-down-drag-out in my kitchen. It hadn't yet recovered from the last one.

I bumped the coffee pot off the table, and because it was a cheap replacement for my beloved old one, it shattered in a very satisfying way. Brown liquid went everywhere, including onto Sebastian's nice suit and Cyrus's jeans. The brothers paused to look at me.

"Oops," I said, and grabbed a dishtowel. "Let me help you with that," I said to Sebastian, dabbing at the coffee stains on his trousers and making them even worse.

Oh. I guessed the rag had coffee on it, too. My bad.

"Thank you, Lia," he said heavily. "But I believe I can manage."

"I'm so sorry," I said. "I get clumsy when I'm tired—"

"I find it difficult to believe that Laurentia of Lobizon's daughter could ever be clumsy."

"—and I'm completely whipped tonight."

It was not a subtle hint, and Sebastian—ever the gentleman—didn't need to be nudged twice.

"My apologies," he told me, and stood up. He looked at his brother. "Stay out of this. The clan will look into it; you have my word on that. And you will honor yours and stay out of sight, or I will take steps to see that you do."

Chapter Six

Sebastian left and I finally got that shower. Which turned out to be better than expected when Cyrus joined me halfway through. "You're already clean," I pointed out.

"Not here for the wash," he said, as his arms went around me.

It wasn't sensual, strangely enough, despite the hard hands roaming over my soapy form. Cyrus had every bit of the libido that Weres were famous for, but that wasn't what this was. He wanted touch, the feel of another warm body next to his, the assurance that we'd come through this, that we were both all right, that we were alive.

It always surprised me when he did something like this. He'd seemed perfectly fine in front of Sebastian. Troubled, yes; angry, certainly; but fine, strong, in control. It was only here, with me, in the dark of night and with the boys all soundly sleeping, that he'd let himself be vulnerable.

He didn't cry, although I wouldn't have minded if he had. He had a right to mourn, to grieve, for two he considered to be his own. But he didn't.

He just stood there while I turned and held onto the big body, marveling again that he needed me. That I could calm him with a touch, so light, so whisper soft, that it could have been the water streaming over us both. But it wasn't and he knew it wasn't.

The chest, surprisingly lightly furred considering the thickness of the beard, rose and fell against mine as my fingernails got into the act, scratching up and down his spine. There was tension there, so much that I didn't need to ask if he'd been arguing with Sebastian before I came home. The two brothers had always been close, clinging to each other after their mother died when they were young, but this *vargulf* business had put a strain on their relationship.

I'd gotten the impression that Cyrus had always been the dutiful younger sibling, who had provided constant support to his older brother. But as such, he'd never been given a chance to find out who else he could be. He'd been born into the supporting role, just as Sebastian had been born the heir apparent, with neither of them having any choice about it.

And now that he didn't have to be Cyrus Arnou anymore—now that he couldn't be, by Were law—he'd just been told that he couldn't be anything else, either. Not in Were circles and not outside them. No matter how much those boys needed him.

It must be maddening.

Which was why it was surprising to hear him ask hoarsely: "Are you all right?"

I looked up to see water cascading off Cyrus's face and hair, which didn't mask the concern in those brown eyes. "Me?"

The eyes decided to do a roll. "Yes, you. The one who fought a monster tonight and almost died."

I shook my head. "He wasn't a monster. He was only a boy."

And just like that, the thought that I'd been shying away from all night, the one that had made me fiercely concentrate on work in order to avoid it, reared its ugly head. I immediately deflected again. "How are you, or is that a stupid question?"

Cyrus didn't answer for a long moment. He just turned me around again, I didn't know why. Until those amazingly talented fingers of his went to work . . . on my scalp.

I almost cried it felt so good. And then the rhythmic motion of his hands dropped down to knead the tense muscles in my neck and shoulders, before moving back up to do the same to my temples and head, massaging in the shampoo I'd lathered up with right before he came in. And, damn, it felt amazing!

"You're going to get more than a bath if you keep that up," he whispered, bending over me, his breath in my ear.

"Keep what up?" I breathed, and then realized: my body had turned around to face the wall at his urging, but my hands had stayed behind, still craving that touch. And they'd been touching a lot. "Oh. Sorry."

"Don't apologize." That time, it was a full-on growl.

"Okay," I breathed, trying to keep it together, and not twist around and jump him. This wasn't the time. That wasn't what he needed from me right now.

Of course, I could be wrong, I thought, as a slick, soapy, iron-hard body very deliberately slid against mine.

And then did it again.

"*Unh*," I groaned, from somewhere deep inside. "Don't try to change the subject!"

"And what were you doing?" Teeth scraped across my shoulder, a deliberate tease, as something huge and hot pressed against me.

"I honestly don't remember," I gasped.

"Let's go with that," he said, and pushed inside.

I squirmed, my body trying to adjust around him, and mostly failing because Cyrus was a big boy.

Very big, I thought, as familiar, callused hands slowly slid down my arms, displacing all those bubbles. And moved my own hands up to the wall so I could brace myself. Only I didn't have to, because his hands stayed on mine, huge and warm, like his body as it began to undulate against me.

My teeth caught on my bottom lip, my breath turned hot and heavy in my throat, and my body clenched around him, making him work for it. Which he usually took as validation and a challenge, but not tonight. Tonight, he coaxed my sighs out of me, teased my groans past my lips, gentled me higher and higher and higher until finally, at last—

He backed off.

"What—what are you doing?" I gasped.

"Giving tonight some kind of happy ending."

"I almost had my happy ending!" I said furiously, trying to look over my shoulder.

He chuckled, the bastard. I heard him. "Not yet."

He went back to work.

As it happened, I had three happy endings, the last accompanied by a full body shudder that may have hidden several more. I didn't know. I was too fuzzy brained by then to count, and limp as a wet noodle.

Cyrus wrapped me in towels and carried me to bed, and for once I didn't even feel like complaining about how many he used. My hair was still wet, although no longer soapy; guess we'd kept at it long enough to rinse me off. Not that I cared about that, either.

I cared about this, I thought, rolling on top and kissing him. And taking my time with it, long minutes of soft nibbles and dueling tongues, and warm sighs and beard burn, but I'd deal with it. I'd deal with a lot for this.

I eventually snuggled up next to the warmth of a squeaky-clean boyfriend, who'd had two baths tonight. And who didn't seem all that tired. I grinned sleepily, from under his arm.

"You want to go again?" I asked, as his hand found my thigh.

"I want to you to answer the question."

"What question?"

"Lia."

It took me a moment. He was honestly that good. And then I remembered, and some of the golden glow faded.

"Let's just go to sleep," I offered.

"Mmhm. So you can be off again tomorrow before we can discuss this."

"We don't need to discuss it."

"Don't we?"

The question hung in the air.

More glow faded. But not that much. I'd gotten blackout curtains recently, because the Corps doesn't keep regular hours, and I sleep better in complete darkness. As a result, the only light source was my alarm clock, showing just after five A.M. It would be light outside in less than two hours. I did need to sleep.

But, I realized, I needed something else more.

I fiddled with the sheet that was barely covering us. I could see Cyrus's hand moving underneath it, stroking the still damp skin of my thigh, because he'd missed a spot. I needed another towel, I thought. But that wasn't what came out of my mouth.

"I went to a laundromat the other day."

Cyrus was quiet for a moment. I hadn't told him that that was why I'd been bitching about the towels, because I had to lug them halfway across town to clean up. I very deliberately had not told him that.

"I said I'd get you another washer and dryer," he finally said.

"Yeah."

But that wouldn't change what had happened to the old ones, would it?

Not that anything had happened to them, exactly. As far as I knew, they were perfectly functional, a nice set of shiny new appliances, in white because I hadn't yet decided what color to paint the laundry room when I bought them. I still hadn't; I hadn't been back in there since the incident.

The laundry was just off the kitchen, a narrow little room, but big enough for the necessary equipment, as well as an ironing board that folded down from the wall. I'd been thinking of adding a soaking sink, because potion residue is a bitch to get out, and maybe some additional shelves to hold detergent and such. The house was a new model, never occupied before I moved in, so it lacked the little touches that made a home.

It still did.

Maybe it always would, because I wasn't sure I even wanted to stay here anymore.

I kept telling myself to stop being stupid, that it had been six months, that it was ridiculous to keep trucking the wash all the way across town when I had a perfectly usable laundry right here.

Only it wasn't perfect.

Not anymore.

I could still see Adam's body, so starkly colorful against all that builder's grade white paint. He had been on his feet, but only because a section of the laundry room door had imbedded itself in the wall through his abdomen. I'd replaced the door, and Cyrus had cleaned up the blood, which had splattered the appliances and poured down the body in wide streams to puddle on the floor.

It didn't matter. I could still see it, every time I closed my eyes; still smell it, the sickeningly-sweet scent like pennies on my tongue. Still see the glazed, staring eyes of my enthralled student, the one I'd killed.

"It wasn't your fault," Cyrus said, not for the first time.

But for once, I didn't change the subject—or get angry, or suddenly remember something I had to do. Maybe because it had just happened again, not to a student but to someone about the same age. Adam had been nineteen, the youngest of my former class, and the sweetest, before he tried to kill me.

He hadn't known that's what he was doing. He'd thought he was undergoing something known as the Trials, a test the Corps mandated for all its trainees after the first year or so. Students were told that it would give them a chance to demonstrate the skills they'd acquired by the end of basic training, and to showcase what they could do.

In fact, that was a lie.

It was a test of character.

The specifics of the test differed, because each instructor designed and supervised their own. But they all had two things in common: they were based on an illusion that felt totally real once you were inside it, and they featured a central battle, one that went terribly wrong. Each student saw their teammates die around them, leaving them with the decision to either finish the mission and die, or save themselves and fail. If they chose the latter, no matter how good they were otherwise, they washed out. And if they chose the former, they found out how they faced death by actually doing it.

The test was brutal but necessary. If a dark mage covertly entered the program, he or she wouldn't learn anything new in basic training. But the apprenticeship phase was more advanced, and the Corps did not like the idea of someone using our own magic against us.

Only that was exactly what had happened in my case.

Specifically, an illusion had been laid to convince my students that they were undergoing the Trials right then, and that the only way to pass was to kill me. They hadn't realized that, if you think you're being tested, you're probably not. And that if I died at their hands, I'd really be dead, not just in an illusion.

Or that they would be.

"They gave me a new class of students today," I told Cyrus. "A new group with Relic abilities that could go terribly wrong. And then, that same night, I killed another young man, almost their age—"

"Lia."

"—and now I have to wonder if the Corps is insane, or if I am. I shouldn't be teaching anybody! They should have given me another assignment after Adam, something else, anything else!"

"But they didn't," Cyrus said calmly. "Because you didn't get him killed. A traitor did."

"Then why doesn't it feel that way?"

Cyrus moved from lying slightly below and beside me to the reverse. His body draped over mine, his hands framed my face, and he looked down at me with gleaming eyes. "Because you've got a soft heart under than hard shell, although you hate for people to know it. Because you'd have preferred to die yourself rather than kill one of your students. Because you've been carrying the guilt around for six months for something you didn't do, and it's eating you up inside."

"But I did do it," I told him miserably. "It was my spell; my magic. Just as it was tonight—"

Cyrus's eyes flashed. "You did *not* kill Colin! You saved the rest of us. Look at those boys tomorrow; look at their *faces*. They're here, alive, right now, because you risked yourself to make sure they would be. I thank you for that. They will thank you, too, once the shock wears off—"

"One of them won't."

"Damn it, Lia!" He looked exasperated. "You're a war mage! You must have lost people before—"

"Adults. Trained operatives. Not children."

I sat up, struggling out from under him and hugging my arms around my knees. "And now they're giving me more of them. And not just regular recruits. But vulnerable, marginalized, fucked up kids. I don't want this assignment, Cyrus!"

He lay there and looked at me for a moment. I couldn't see him very well, barely an outline in the dim haze of light spread by my clock. But somehow, I knew he was frowning.

"Then tell them that. Ask for another job. But think about this before you do. None of us had ever seen anything like that Relic, as you call it. None of us, me included, knew how to fight it. Do you think we could have handled it ourselves? Or would there have been a lot more bodies on the ground if you weren't there?"

I started to speak, but he shushed me. "Not finished yet. And maybe think about this, too, while you're at it. I've been wanting to say this for a while, but I've been tiptoeing around, because you never wanted to talk about it and I didn't want to force the issue. But maybe I should have.

"The day Adam died, there was an entire squad of well-armed, well-trained mages here, and only one of you. You didn't have your weapons, you'd just woken up, and you were handicapped by not wanting to kill your own students. And yet you saved all except one.

"How many other instructors would have been able to do that? How many would have even tried, with their own lives on the line? Or taken a bullet and almost died to bring down the bastard who caused it?

"You're better than you know, Lia de Croissets. And the Corps is damned lucky to have you. And tonight, so were we."

I just sat there, suddenly glad for the dark because my face was wet and probably screwed up as well. Not that it mattered when your partner is a Were. I didn't know if Cyrus smelled the tears or heard the slight catch in my throat that I wasn't fast enough to stop. But the next second, his arms were around me and he was whispering nonsense words in my ear like you do for a traumatized child.

It should have been embarrassing; I was a big, bad war mage. I didn't need soothing. Only I guessed I did, because I broke down in his arms, sobbing, for Adam, for Colin, for all the kids fighting this war who shouldn't be. And all the while, Cyrus just held me, murmuring softly, letting me get it all out, even though he'd had just as bad a day as I had.

I was damned lucky to have him, too.

Chapter Seven

My backup coat was being an ass.

I'd hauled it out of the closet after breakfast, which was more like lunch since I'd overslept. Cyrus and the boys had already been up and out, with a brief note telling me that they'd gone looking for whoever had sold punch to Colin. I didn't try to call them back, because it wouldn't have done any good, and it was one of the few things they could do without risking Sebastian's wrath. Plus, they might have more luck than the Corps.

Vegas has a vast network of drainage tunnels underneath it, which have been nicknamed Tartarus by the local down-on-their-luck magical community. They use them as a highway for a sprawling ant-like colony of caverns that contain everything from marketplaces and bars to shantytowns and illicit manufacturing centers. And guess what was being manufactured?

The Corps knew that most of the punch flooding the streets came from Tartarus, but with the war taking up the majority of our resources, we didn't have the people to patrol it effectively. This was unfortunately not a secret. Production had really been ramping up lately, with a lot of new players getting into the game.

I wished the guys luck, but they had their work cut out for them.

Sort of like me with this coat.

I scowled down at the shiny new leather, which didn't have so much as a scratch on it. The only time it had been worn was in the class where I'd learned to enchant it, and where I'd used it as a test subject, not wanting to risk my family heirloom. That had been years ago, and ever since, it had occupied a dark corner of my closet, where I had learned the hard way to keep it well away from the other clothes. I'd found more than one garment shredded or burnt, because my learner coat had a temper.

As it was currently demonstrating.

I reached for it, and had my hand slapped away by a sleeve for my trouble. I tried again, and had my hand enveloped in a leather "fist" that wouldn't let go. Until I zapped it with a spell, only to have it zap me back.

Son of a bitch!

"Oh, this I gotta see."

I looked up to find Caleb, a fellow war mage, lounging in the doorway. He was big, black and imposing, a solid mass of 'tude eyeing up my pathetic excuse for a coat. His own coat, on the other hand, was looking good, well-oiled and supple, with a hem that wafted a little too energetically around his calves, but overall . . .

"Don't even," he told me flatly.

I put on my best be-a-pal face, and may have even fluttered an eyelash or two. I was desperate, okay? "I'm desperate," I told him. "I need a coat."

"What happened to your old one?"

"Involucrum."

Caleb winced. "Shit."

"Yeah." I blinked rapidly, cursing myself for being sentimental, but the loss cut like a bitch. I didn't even know how I was going to tell dad. Or what I was supposed to do for a replacement, after reaching out for my badly behaving item and getting the crap shocked out of me for my trouble.

"Damn it! Did you see that?"

I received no sympathy from Caleb. "Some of us weren't lucky enough to get handed an heirloom," he said heavily, crossing his arms. "I've gone through three coats so far in my career, and this one is still new. I'm breaking it in—like you're going to have to do."

"If it doesn't break me first. Or fry my damned arm off!"

"You have to show it who's boss."

Yeah, only I was pretty sure it already knew that, and didn't think it was me.

It was my backup for a reason: I'd never liked it. They'd told us in spellbinding class that it was a fallacy that magical objects developed personalities. That we humans just liked anthropomorphizing things.

That was a load of crap.

This thing hated me.

"Have to show it soon," Caleb added meaningfully.

"Why?"

"You got company."

I grabbed a regular old jacket, useless magically but good, thick leather, the kind I used when riding to keep the road and my flesh from meeting too energetically, and followed Caleb into the living room.

"Well, shit."

"Nice to see you, too," Sophie said dryly.

They were all there, my whole new class, which frankly gave me hives. And not just because they were supposed to be back at HQ and safely locked up. But because of what had happened the last time I had students here.

I looked at Caleb, who shrugged. "Just the delivery guy."

"They said they needed the cell," Sophie informed me. "Something about a nest of dark mages they dug up, hiding out in the desert somewhere."

"Hey, is that your bike in front?" That was the Hispanic guy, his brown hair sticking up everywhere.

"Uh, yeah," I said. "Look—"

"You got anything to eat?" That was Malibu, with his blond locks equally disheveled and his plain blue T-shirt wrinkled. He also hadn't shaved, although his beard wasn't too noticeable as it was blond, too.

"Yeah, I'm starved." That was the Asian guy. "We didn't get breakfast."

"Because somebody gave us all of five minutes to get ready," Sophie said, looking pointedly at Caleb.

I could have told her to save herself some time. Caleb didn't have a shame reflex that I'd ever noticed. Which he demonstrated by corralling the brunet and the blond, who'd been heading off in the direction of the kitchen, despite not knowing where it was.

"It's okay," I told him. I looked at the guys. "You know how to cook?"

They blinked at me as if I'd asked them if they spoke Navajo.

"None of us do. Brought up in a prison, remember?" That, of course, was Sophie.

“Don’t look at me,” Caleb said, which was fair. He was the king of take out.

I sighed, and wondered if a bunch of hungry Weres had left anything to cook. “Intros first, then I’ll feed you,” I said.

“Blue hair over there is Aki,” Sophie told me. “The male model is Chris.” Malibu waved and pushed the Hispanic guy forward. “Dimas,” Sophie dutifully added. “Didn’t you get papers on us?”

“Left them somewhere.”

She rolled her eyes. I was cementing myself as a slipshod operator. “That’s Jen,” she said, nodding at the shy blonde with the 1920s bob and the love for beer. “And Kimmie,” she added, talking about the chick with the braids, who unlike everybody else, was looking surprisingly good, with a full face of makeup and a fashionable blue jumpsuit. “Kimmie doesn’t sleep,” Sophie added, as if reading my mind, which maybe she was for all I knew.

“At all?” I asked Kimmie, who shrugged.

“Only if I expend too much magic and have to recover. Otherwise, I don’t need it.”

“Must be nice,” I said enviously.

“Not really. You run out of Netflix shows after a while.”

“Food?” Aki said, looking worried that I’d forgotten.

“This way.” I led them down the hall and into the kitchen.

It was a snug fit with eight of us, especially since Caleb counted for at least one and a half. But there was food left, although a big dent had been made in the grocery haul that I’d lugged in just a few days ago. I wondered if Cyrus was planning for his guys to stay here for another night.

And then I wondered something else.

“Uh, Caleb? Where is everybody staying?”

He gave me a look I didn’t like. “Think of it as a boarding school—”

“Caleb!”

“We’re out of room, Lia. The Corps is bursting at the seams—”

“Hargroves said there was a special facility—”

“Yeah, it’s under construction—”

“He didn’t mention that!”

“Probably slipped his mind.” We exchanged looks. Nothing slipped the old man’s mind. The bastard.

“Then another room at HQ,” I said desperately.

"Take it up with him—"

"Yeah, like getting on his calendar isn't a three-week ordeal!"

"You seem to manage okay. Weren't you cozied up in his office just yesterday?"

"To get chewed out!"

Caleb shrugged. "Maybe screw something else up?"

I glared. "I thought they were prioritizing the dangerous criminals for cells and letting the rest go with fines—"

"They are. We're still overrun." He put on his serious face. "You know the deal. The war has become a free for all for every lowlife from here to the border—and beyond. We need every bed—"

"So do I! I can't house six more people. This is a three-bedroom house!"

"Some can sleep in the living room—"

"I have *vargulfs* in the living room!"

Caleb paused. "Do I want to know why that is?"

"No." I slammed down my biggest frying pan and dumped half a pound of bacon into it. Then did some mental math and dumped the rest into another one.

"We can bunk up in two rooms," Sophie said. Her eyes had been shifting back and forth like at a tennis match as me and Caleb argued it out. "Guys in one, girls in another, if you have enough beds."

"That's the problem; I don't. Half the rooms aren't even furnished."

"Get us sleeping bags and we're good on the floor," Aki said. "Or . . . or just a blanket—"

He looked panicked. In fact, now that I noticed, they were all looking panicked. Including Kimmie, who was backing toward the door to the yard. "I'm not going back there," she said, her voice trembling slightly. "Do you understand me? I'm not."

"None of us are," Sophie said. "Come on, Kim. Put the knife down."

Which was about the time I noticed that one of my kitchen knives was missing from the rack.

It was now in her hand, and she was almost to the door. That shouldn't have been a problem since the only thing beyond my back yard was desert; there were no neighbors to freak out that way. But when she tried the door and it stuck, thanks to a bent hinge from the last disaster, she panicked.

"I won't be locked up again! I won't be locked up again!"

Her eyes were wild, and when Chris tried to get the knife back, she slashed at him. It didn't connect, but that was more because of cat-like reflexes on his part than anything else. Or maybe Were-like was more accurate, although I'd seen Weres who moved slower.

That was fortunate, since I suddenly found out what Kimmie's talent was. A moment ago, there had been one knife, shining under the kitchen fluorescents. Now there was a solid dozen, glinting in the air in front of her.

Multiplier, I thought.

Shit.

And then they were coming this way.

They hit the shield I'd thrown up, but because it had been split second, there were gaps and one got through. And one immediately became another dozen, which required putting up another shield. And then more and more, piling them on top of each other to try to plug the holes, while Sophie yelled and Jen fled and Chris tried to grab one of the knives, God knew why. Forcing me to have to send a spell to knock him back toward the laundry room.

My heart tightened at the sight of him splayed against the door, but the fight was over the next second. Somebody had left the kitchen unnoticed by everyone, slipped around the side of the house, thrown open the stubborn back door and enveloped Kimmie in a hug from behind. And when Caleb hugs you, you stay hugged.

The knives abruptly dropped to the ground, and then she was sobbing against the big chest, saying "I'm sorry, I'm sorry, I'm so sorry," over and over again.

I looked at him and he looked at me, above her head. "Yeah. I'm gonna take some PTO."

Of course, I couldn't allow Caleb to do that, not when they were my students. So, while I turned over the bacon, which had started to smoke, and the kids picked up a whole laundry basket full of kitchen knives, and Sophie held Kimmie and tried to calm her, I got on the phone to HQ. It didn't go well.

Hargroves wasn't there, but then, the boss didn't handle scheduling anyway. And the guy who did was a dick. His name—I kid you not—was Alistair Fitzgibbon, and he looked exactly the way that sounds: thin, haughty, British, and as pale as a vampire.

"Just for a few weeks," I said, balancing the phone under my chin while I tended to the bacon.

"Not for a few days. Are you aware that we're at *war*, Mage de Croissets?"

"You know, I'd heard something about it."

"We need every man—"

"And woman?" I said, just to be difficult. Because the Corps tends to forget about us. But this time, it didn't even phase him.

"—and anything else I can get! You try doing a schedule with half your operatives on medical leave and the other half—"

"I understand—"

"—who probably should be! This place looks like a convalescent home—"

"—but—"

"—with people staggering about—did you know, my own assistant is on crutches? Not because of the war, you understand; the boy falls over his own two feet if you don't watch him, and took a stumble off the curb. The *curb*. Who breaks an ankle on a three-inch drop?"

"However, I *really* think—"

"Donovan, that's who. Which means I have to fetch and carry everything myself. Assistant," the tone was acerbic. "I should be credited with assisting him. He can't even make coffee, not if you expect him to carry it, too—"

Caleb took my phone. "Fitzgibbon, it's Carter. I'm taking a week's PTO," he said, and hung up.

"I can't let you do that," I said, dumping up the half-charred bacon.

"You can't afford not to." He held up one of the strips. "You said you could cook?"

"I like them that way," Aki piped up.

"You like them any way," Sophie said dryly.

"So, if anybody else doesn't want theirs—"

"Here," I handed Aki the platter. "Dining room's through there."

I started some eggs.

"I can set the table," Jen offered, reemerging from the living room.

I showed her where the dishes were, put some oil in a pan, and dumped in the potatoes. "Can I help?" Caleb asked.

"You can start some toast. And don't think we're not going to discuss this."

"Discuss what? You need help; I'm here to help." He looked around. "Although a toaster would be nice."

"Toaster oven—it does four slices at once," I said pointing it out.

"And this works how?"

"I'll show you," Sophie said, getting up. That amazing head of red hair was in a ponytail today, and bouncy with curls that I guessed she hadn't had time to brush out.

"I thought you didn't know how to cook?" I said.

"Toast is not cooking." And, okay, couldn't argue with her there.

Breakfast was finally completed, somehow. I even found some sausage to add to the bacon, which had mostly been eaten by the time everything else made it to the table. I discovered that the kids really liked orange juice, and went through a gallon of it along with what remained of a gallon of milk. I bumped up my visit to the grocery store to today.

After they ate, I started everybody on clean-up detail and dragged Caleb into the living room. He had that look, the crossed arms, crossed legs, leaning against the wall look of a man waiting for me to catch up. I hated that look.

"You were just put back on active duty," I said, keeping my voice low, why I didn't know. The talking, jeering, laughing, and occasional crash of another piece of my crockery biting the dust covered any convo we might have. But I didn't feel like broadcasting Caleb's problems to the world.

"Yes. And this is active."

"Caleb, you were *blind* for months—"

"And now I'm not."

Yeah, which was why he wore a magical tat by each eye. I didn't know how bad his vision was, but it probably wasn't good. He shouldn't even be back yet, but as Fitzgibbon had said, that was true of a sizeable chunk of the Corps right now.

"You know," Caleb said, when I just stood there, wondering what would work, "I'm starting to feel unwanted."

"It's not that—"

"Okay, then what is it?"

"You *need* your time off. You need to heal."

"I'm certified competent to return to duty—"

I rolled my eyes so hard I thought I saw the inside of my skull.

"—and besides, what are you planning to do today? Go grocery shopping?"

I didn't answer.

Caleb's eyes narrowed, and his stance widened. I'd seen that before, too. It was his interrogation posture, the one that, all on its own, made perps nervous.

It wasn't making me feel all that great, either.

"You want to tell me what's going on?"

No, I didn't say, because Caleb wasn't the type to be put off. And because I did kind of need him. I just needed him to understand what he was getting into.

A few minutes later, we were sitting on the couch, which had been shoved up against the far wall and covered with a tarp so that nobody dribbled paint on it. Caleb was holding the picture of the Were-creature and scowling. I sat there watching my ceiling fan go round and round, wondering when was the last time was that I'd dusted it.

Never. Never was a good contender. I was a failure as a housekeeper and not much better as a cook. I sometimes wondered what Cyrus saw in me.

And then I remembered last night. Okay, there was that. Although it might be the last intimate moment for a while with a house full of Weres and a bunch of magically gifted young people with who knew what kind of abilities.

Because I *had* glanced over their paperwork, and magnifier hadn't been on it.

I wondered what else they were hiding.

"This is bullshit," Caleb said, pulling my attention back to him.

"Okay."

"No, not okay!" He turned angry eyes on me. "We're having enough trouble fighting normal enemies, if you can call the fey normal. What the hell are we supposed to do with *this*?"

"I don't know. I mean, I took it down, but—"

"Your entire family line took it down, Lia. That coat was a goddamned marvel, oldest I've seen in service. And you had to burn it just to stay alive. What are the rest of us supposed to do?"

"I don't know," I said again. "But that's why you need to think long and hard before you sign on. I'm going after these things—"

"Lia!"

"I have to. Cyrus isn't going to let this go. It's not in him, Caleb. And I can't let him do this alone."

"So, you'll stick your head in the noose, right alongside him?"

"If necessary. I'm kind of hoping it doesn't come to that. But you could help me out if you want—"

"By doing *what*?" Caleb was still staring at the photo, which . . . yeah. It did kind of draw the eye.

I gently took it back. And looked up to see a bunch of new responsibilities in the doorway, still splashed with water from the sink. Multitasking was not my forte, but maybe, for once, it didn't have to be.

"Grocery shopping?" I asked hopefully.

Chapter Eight

An hour later, the kids were off destroying a grocery store with Caleb, leaving me free to visit the compound of a certain Were clan. Colin's former family home was well out into the desert, past miles of dusty roads and pale blue skies, in the middle of a natural fortress of low-slung hills. It was also down what I called an anti-road, the kind that seemed to have more rocks and potholes than drivable surface. But eventually, I made it.

Only to discover that the compound had a lot in common with the road.

Someone had been burning trash, and the smell lingered on the air, along with the smoke. It had drifted across a dozen trailers, an old wooden house that looked like it was busy trying to return to the earth, and a bunch of long, thin, white plastic tarps. The latter had been made into tents by shoving poles up the centers every six feet or so and anchoring them down along the sides with a bunch of old tires and bricks.

Otherwise, there wasn't much to see. Vegas soil dusted everything, and a few scraggly bushes clung to life here and there. The bushes were desert flora, brown and low slung, the kind that sprang up on their own. There wasn't a piece of deliberately planted grass or a tree in sight.

But there was green. Something was growing under those tarps, visible in glimpses when the wind caused the edges to flap. But I couldn't see what it was from here. And a couple of the biggest, meanest dogs I'd ever encountered had been chained outside, with their hackles rising.

Until I got close enough that they could smell me, that was, and the change was immediate. One whined and tried to lick my hand in a show of submission, and the other hunkered down and tentatively wagged a tail. I can't transform, but the smell of Clan is unmistakable.

And dogs do not challenge wolves.

But other wolves do.

"It looks like a war mage, but it smells like Clan. So, which is it?"

I looked up from petting the good boys to see a skinny, sandy blond in a wife beater and dirty jeans, leaning against the side of a metal Quonset hut. It looked like old military surplus, and appeared to be in use as a tool shed. There was a wheelbarrow just behind the guy, a couple of dusty sacks of fertilizer, and a coiled hose that didn't seem to be attached to anything.

I couldn't see any further, because he was in the way, and while he didn't have hackles to rise, the aura around him was the same: suspicious, unhappy, belligerent.

Funny; that exactly matched my mood, but I forced a smile anyway.

"Both. Lia de Croissets. And you are?"

My question was ignored. "Ah. Heard about you." He looked me over. "Yeah, you look like Clan. What you doing with all those humans?"

"My job."

"There's more to life than work," he said, moving closer.

A wave of wolf musk, mixed with the sour tang of sweat and the reek of clothes that hadn't been laundered in a week, hit my nose. It was enough to make my eyes water, but my smile didn't falter. Being polite—AKA respectful—was practically a prerequisite to getting anything out of the clans.

"Yeah, but I'm single minded. I also like to know who I'm talking to. Mr. . . . ?"

"You can call me whatever you like, darlin'."

I was starting to have to work to keep the smile on my face. "I'd like to call you by your name."

He sighed. Apparently, I was not responding to his charms as well as he'd have liked. "Cloud-Leaper."

"And who gave you this name?" I asked, unconsciously falling into clan-speak.

But it was a lucky accident, as it pulled the first hint of a smile out of him. "My gran. As a boy, I used to run up the bluffs and jump off. Thought that, if I could only get high enough, I could touch the sky. Then I transformed and found I could leap higher than anybody. It was an easy choice."

"Sounds like it."

"And what do they call you, then?"

I didn't answer, because I didn't have a clan name. That was given after the first time you transformed, which I could not do.

"And your human name?"

"Don't use it. Don't need it. We stopped being human a long time ago, only some of us forgot." He looked at me pointedly.

I didn't take the bait. I also didn't keep trying for a name that he didn't want to give. The clan rolls would have his wolf name recorded, and I could get it that way.

"Mind if I take a look around?" I asked instead, and started toward the Quonset—only to find a well-muscled arm in my way.

Sometimes being polite wasn't enough.

"Long as you got a warrant," I was told. "Otherwise, you got no business here, *mage*."

I smiled wider. One of the dogs, the more submissive of the two, slunk off as far as its chain would allow, hiding around the side of the nearest, makeshift tent. The other whined and gnawed unhappily at its chain.

"That's the thing about war," I said. "Rights often get suspended. Like the one to refuse a search when there's reason to believe that there's contraband on the property."

It was, of course, pure bluff. I was here to get an errand out of the way so that I could concentrate on helping Cyrus. To be precise, I was here because Colin's family were shit and I wanted to get a look at the other kids. They might be in danger, and an eyewitness account from me could help Sebastian force their removal pending an investigation.

I had not suspected that the crappy clan had anything to do with the current drug problem, as I'd assumed that Colin had gotten his on the streets.

Had assumed until right now, I thought, as the skinny blond shivered all over. It caused me to instinctively stumble back because I knew what that meant. And thereby barely avoided the maw of huge teeth that tore through the air a second later, right where I'd been standing.

I threw a shield up, leaving me looking at a crazed, light tan wolf twice as big as me that was pawing and lunging and snarling, trying to bite through my protection. He didn't succeed—war mage shields are no joke—but he did make a hell of a ruckus. Enough to call in backup in the form of two more transformed Weres, who bounded out of the wooden house, one of them large enough to get his withers caught in the doorframe—

For about a second, until he tore through the wood, blowing out the sides as if a tank had just rolled through.

Even worse, an old pickup was headed our way down the road, stirring up a dust cloud behind it. It had what looked like a dozen guys on it, sticking out of the cab and hanging onto the back. And while I didn't know that they were Weres at this point, it seemed a safe bet.

It was the only thing that was safe.

I had not expected a problem, at least not of this magnitude. Less because of the Corps, whose authority many clans did not respect, than because of Sebastian. He was *bardric*, with the authority of the council behind him, and I was an adopted member of his clan. To attack me, especially without provocation, was to attack him and the whole of Clan Arnou.

Yet I'd been attacked anyway. Which meant that not only did these guys have something major to hide, but that they intended to kill me and hide the body. At this point, they had no other choice.

The truck screeched into the melee, which was already bad enough with three huge Weres hammering on my shields. And I was treated to a rare sight: a nearly simultaneous transformation of what had to be eight or ten more Weres. I couldn't count them accurately because it looked like a waterfall of fur flying off the truck and straight at me, but it didn't matter. No shields were going to last long under a barrage like that.

Defense: limited. Offense: doubtful. Retreat?

Retreat, I decided, but did not start edging toward my ride.

The Weres seemed to have overlooked it for the moment, and I needed that to continue. Otherwise, they'd destroy my bike and leave me stranded. And at that point, it really would be game over.

I sent up a distress spell, burning bright against the pale blue haze of the sky, just in case there was anybody within range, and then prepared a distraction. I needed the Weres off me and looking elsewhere long enough to make a break for it. Then we'd see who was faster: Harley Davidson's finest or a panicked Were pack.

But I had to get there first.

I'd loaded up the jacket before I left, but I'd have to drop shields to use much of it. So, a spell it was, then. And if you want to get someone's attention, threaten their livelihood.

Or, you know, outright destroy it.

A second later, the first tent went up in a fireball big enough to have taken out the house. But I couldn't see inside the house; there could be children in there. The tent, on the other hand, was empty except for a lot of very suspicious looking plants.

Which were now going up in flames.

Even better, the wind had picked up, blowing sparks onto the other tents and causing half of the Weres to suddenly veer off. They changed back into now-naked humans, mostly men but a few women as well, and started scrambling, trying to get hoses attached and water flowing. But half wasn't enough. I sent another fireball to engulf the truck, which must have had a nearly full tank, because it went up with a satisfying *whoosh.*

And then my phone rang.

I put it on speaker, hoping for back up, and instead got Caleb in the dairy aisle.

"I am not buying a dozen kinds of milk!" his harassed voice informed me—or informed someone.

"Caleb?"

"Almond, coconut, low-fat, one-percent, two-percent—"

"Caleb!"

"—whole, organic, lactose-free—"

Several more Weres had broken away to go for the truck, giving me the best odds that I was likely to get. I started edging toward the bike, blowing things up in the opposite direction in the process, trying to keep everyone's attention focused elsewhere. Another tent went up, along with a windmill, the burning arms of which sent spirals of black smoke flooding into the air.

And, finally, I spotted what looked like salvation: a big, freestanding gas or possibly propane tank.

"—it just goes on and on. Who the hell needs this many kinds of—"

The tank got the biggest fireball I had magic left for, and—oh, yeah. That worked, I thought, as a mushroom cloud of flame went skyward. The Weres stopped beating on me long enough to stare, and I dropped my shields, shoved one out of the way with a magical assist, and ran.

They were right behind me, but no shields meant no restrictions. That meant snare charms grabbing onto necks and dragging them off course; it meant bear traps—or in this case, wolf traps—latching onto paws and biting down, crushing bones and then slamming into the ground, refusing to budge; it meant potion bombs and lasso spells and levitating guns blasting full out, because I wasn't playing, either. It meant demonstrating that the odds weren't as uneven as you might think, as an unleashed war mage was a platoon, all on her own.

I heard howls and human screams, curses and yells for help. I felt the sun beating down on me, the blast of heat from the fires rolling over me, the hot breath of an apex predator on my neck. I sent a spell behind me, heard a yelp and a thud, but didn't turn around to see what had happened.

"Lia? Lia, what the hell?" Caleb was yelling, but I barely heard him. Because my I was almost there, my bike was just ahead, I could practically feel the chrome under my hands—

Then something leapt for me, from impossibly far away, slamming my body down to the ground and my head onto a rock.

And then there was only blackness.

* * *

The jangly sounds of Vegas at night rolled over me, along with smears of neon decorated with strangely distorted faces. People were everywhere, but looking as if they were reflections in a fun house mirror. They crowded in from all sides, getting close—too close. And then they were suddenly distant, what had to be a block away or more.

It left me rearing back when they lunged at me, and stumbling drunkenly in shock when they suddenly disappeared. I found a wall, a crumbly bit of brick, and held on, because the street was doing it now, too. One moment it fell out from under me, leaving me plunging down a deep, dark hole; the next it was so close that it felt like my knees should be up around my ears.

Up-down, up-down, to the point that I could barely stand, and it didn't help when some of the fun house people gathered around me in a semi-circle. The gyrations made it appear as if they had ridiculously elongated necks, like human giraffes, which was weird enough. But it also allowed them to poke their strange, distorted faces into mine.

Even worse, which of them had the giraffe necks changed from moment to moment. Leaving me surrounded by monstrous creatures who alternately lunged at me and retreated, back and forth, back and forth, back and forth, until I wanted to scream. And then I did scream, when one of them spoke.

"Are you all right?"

The words were benign, but the sound wasn't. Oh, God, it so wasn't. It was unbearably loud, as if the man was shouting in my face with a bullhorn.

I tried retreating, but I was already backed up against a building. I couldn't go anywhere. And they were all crowding in now, suffocatingly close, these weird people with their loud voices and their grabby hands and their springy giraffe necks—

"She's not all right," a woman bellowed. And, suddenly, there she was, with a tiny face, but huge sparkly red lips, and brilliantly white teeth the size and shape of a donkey's, and an enormously long tongue that snaked out when she spoke again. "Grab her—"

"Auggghhh!" I lashed out, not with anything lethal, because they hadn't hurt me yet, and training held. But it was a shockwave spell, forceful enough to push them back. And with the bizarre world I'd fallen into, they looked like they literally flew away.

I didn't waste any time. I ran. Although that caused its own set of problems.

One minute, my feet felt like they were melting into the pavement, making every step a sucking nightmare. The next, it was as if I'd affixed clouds to my soles, causing me to levitate off the concrete. And while it's not easy to run through melting tar, it's even harder on air.

Not surprisingly, I wasn't making great time, something complicated by the approach of two more distorted figures in police uniforms.

That would have been fine; I wasn't hurting anyone, after all. Only they didn't seem to think so. I kept trying to get away, sucking footsteps and all, and they kept following and harassing me. Until I finally had enough and stuck them to a wall with a web spell.

I staggered off down an alley, which was a mistake because it led straight into Fremont Street, and the neon extravaganza arching overhead. Viva Vision, as it was called, was usually a tacky, but colorful, addition to the old-time Vegas ambiance. Arching across the home of penny slots and mile long beers, it was a world away from the upscale glitz of the Strip.

But tonight . . . tonight it was hell.

Music boomed from multiple stages, loud enough to deafen me. People crowded in from all asides, jostling me. And neon pink fireworks exploded overhead, dazzlingly bright.

I stared up at them, completely overwhelmed. I knew they were just a light show projected onto a LED covered canopy, but they looked amazingly real. And just like with the giraffe necks, they were telescoping down at me, until it felt like being caught in a war-time barrage. Or as if I'd flown up into the middle of an actual firework display.

Maybe I had. Colorful bursts detonated everywhere, including under my feet, making it impossible to run or even walk. Not that I probably would have been able to anyway, as I couldn't feel my feet anymore. I didn't know where to go or what to do, and I couldn't see anything, except brighter and brighter explosions, bursting in front of my vision, blinding me. While their *boom-boom-boom* reverberated deafeningly in my head.

I fell, what felt like miles, face planting into the middle of the street screaming and flailing as the sensory overload intensified. Hideous things dove at me, colors shouted at me and the ground convulsed underneath me. All while I tried to concentrate long enough to fling the spells to make it stop, to make it all stop!

But instead, somebody else did.

A spell whispered around me, soft and silent, but powerful enough to have made my hackles rise on another occasion. Not tonight. Tonight, I grabbed hold of it like a child with a favorite teddy bear, dragged it closer, tried to bury myself in it. Because where the spell went, darkness and silence followed.

I felt strong arms lifting me, whose I couldn't tell, because the spell was making everything hazy. It was as if a black blanket had been thrown over my head, but with a thin weave, allowing me to get glimpses through the fabric. I closed my eyes; I didn't want glimpses.

And then the spell tightened, and I was gone.

Chapter Nine

I knew where I was before I opened my eyes. "Crap."

"She's awake," a familiar voice said.

I hauled myself the rest of the way back to consciousness and saw the Corps' leading physician, Arturo Sedgewick, bending over me. The rotund little doctor was scowling, which was par for the course since the war had flooded his clinic with patients. Sedgewick was more into research than healing, which was just as well considering his bedside manner.

Typically, he shoved me back down when I tried to sit up. "Stay there. Or I'll have you strapped to the bed."

I would have had something to say about that, but the room was spinning hard enough to make me dizzy. And his nose, already fairly pointy, kept growing and stabbing out at me at random intervals. It made me want to duck and dodge, like sword fighting Pinocchio. I refrained and closed my eyes again.

Only to hear Hargroves clear his throat on the other side of me.

Great.

"Is she lucid?" he demanded.

"As much as she'll be for a while," Sedgewick said dourly. "She's lucky to be alive. That dose would have killed anyone else. Were physiology truly is amazing."

I sat up abruptly at that, despite the threat, because Sedgewick was known for being a little too interested in Were physiology. He'd gotten into trouble not too long ago for doing a forbidden autopsy on a dead Were, and I didn't want to be next. Although it felt like I might be, any minute now.

Oh, God.

"What did I just say?" Sedgewick demanded, gesturing at some hovering orderlies.

But to my surprise, Hargroves waved them off again. "Are you going to be sick?" he asked me, stepping back a pace to preserve the mirror-like shine on his oxfords.

"Probably."

He passed over a trash can. I guess the clinic was out of the usual kidney-shaped basins they used for such things. Like they must have been out of water and napkins, because nobody offered me any of those, either.

They had found a hospital gown to stick me in, one of those ridiculous paper-thin things with no back that was like trying to wear a tissue. I gathered the equally thin blanket that had been draped over me more securely around myself, so that I didn't flash the boss. Assuming I hadn't already done that.

Sedgewick stood there, eyeing me hopefully, probably anticipating autopsy number two. But when I just sat on the edge of the exam table, clutching my trash can and stubbornly continuing to breathe, he sighed and padded off. I seriously thought about using the can, but literally felt too bad to be sick.

"What the hell?" I croaked.

"That is what I would like to know." Hargroves' little pebble eyes varied between blue and gray depending on what he was wearing. They were gray today, because he had on a snazzy charcoal pin stripe with an emerald silk pocket square folded so perfectly that its little blue dots lined up in regimental rows along the creases. I wondered if magic had been involved. I decided that I didn't care.

The pebble eyes abruptly became pebblier and shot out at me like rocky asteroids.

I yelped and flinched back, and he said a bad word that contrasted with his genteel suit.

"Sorry," I said, which was ignored.

"You were found wandering about downtown in a state," he informed me sharply. "You attacked several groups of people, made a spectacle of yourself on one of the busiest streets in Las Vegas, and for a finale, grabbed onto the spell Mage McGibbon was using to calm you so tightly that you pulled him into your fevered state. He had to be carried back here on a stretcher alongside you."

Yeah. Some of that was coming back. "Is McGibbon okay?"

"Other than for screaming at the bedside light to stay away from him?" Hargroves asked dryly. "Yes, he'll recover—in time. What I want to know is why you have enough punch in your system to kill a platoon."

I blinked at him slowly, because I had to remember how. "Is that what's wrong with me?"

"You didn't know?"

I paused before answering, because breakfast was debating whether or not to make a reappearance. It finally decided in the negative, and I answered thickly. "No."

"Then tell me what you do know."

"It'll be in the report—"

"Yes, and we both know how assiduous you are at filing those. Give me the shorthand version now."

I swallowed bile and tried to drag my fractured thoughts together enough for a summary.

"Checked out a grow farm off 95 that I didn't know was a grow farm. Owners objected and attacked. I lost and blacked out, and the next thing I knew, I was inside a fun house mirror and the sidewalk was eating my shoes."

Hargroves gave me the look that deserved, but honestly, it was the best I could do. I needed time for the room to stop spinning and for my stomach to settle down from imminent disruption to seriously perturbed. I needed a bed and a shower, probably in reverse order as it felt like half the sand in the Mojave had been imbedded into my flesh. I needed a break.

What I got instead was a silence spell clicking into place around us.

Great.

We were in the bowels of the Circle's HQ, which meant that the best wards available were already protecting us from prying ears. And the only people down here were fellow members of the Corps anyway. But apparently that wasn't good enough for Hargroves, which made me clutch my makeshift bucket even tighter.

This was really going to suck.

"You weren't merely given a dose of the so-called punch," Hargroves informed me. "You received the same adulterated drug we found in the Were's system last night—a great deal of it."

I looked at him blankly for a moment, not sure that I'd heard right. "What?"

"The drug that turned the Were into that . . . thing, that throwback," he said impatiently. "Sedgewick isolated it from your blood."

I stared at him some more, trying to compute that. "I had the same dose as Colin?"

"No, you had five times as much, enough that it should have killed you. Or, more likely considering the limited effects that drugs have on your kind, it should have turned you into a monster dumped into the middle of the city. Yet it does not appear to have had any effect at all, aside from making you punch drunk."

I would have pointed out the inadvertent pun, but I was too busy freaking out. "They planted me there like a bomb."

Hargroves' head inclined a fraction of an inch, like a tutor finally getting through to a particularly dense student. "Indeed. Why merely kill you when they could use you instead? Yet drug dealers would have no interest in killing civilians, some of whom might be their customers, or in inviting the attention of the Corps. We have our answer as to whether or not this drug is being weaponized by our enemies. It is."

I swallowed thickly, and thought about that. And about what a creature like the one Colin had become could have done if it had magic at its disposal. I thought hard.

"But their plan didn't work," Hargroves repeated. "Despite the dosage, you did not Change. I would like to know why."

I didn't say anything.

"I would like to know *now*, Lia."

The use of my first name shocked me enough that I met his eyes, and there were no weird sensory calisthenics happening this time. Just the usual intense, brooks-no-bullshit-here energy that I could have really done without. Because either way I answered, I was about to be completely screwed.

If I lied and he found out, or if I chose not to tell him, I'd be out of the Corps on my ass, probably immediately. He wouldn't normally have that kind of authority—there'd have to be hearings and meetings of the disciplinary council and reams of paperwork. Getting rid of a war mage wasn't easy, or I'd have been fired years ago.

But during a time of war?

A lot of rules got bent, and frankly I had made way more enemies than friends. A woman war mage was viewed by the old boys' club as suspect enough. But a Were woman?

They'd been jonesing to get rid of me for ages, and this was the perfect opportunity. So, I had a decision to make, and Hargroves, damn him, had come down here to force me into it when I was woozy and barely functional. He was a bastard, but he was a smart bastard, you had to give him that.

"Of course, I could have answered the question myself," he pointed out, as I continued to just sit there. "Or had Arturo do it for me. The blood sample he took from you could have been sent 'round to the Corps' best labs. But I suspected that that might cause you some . . . complications."

I met his eyes again, this time in surprise. Had he done me a favor? And if so, why? We weren't exactly close. He treated me the same way he did any of the younger generation of mages, as if he smelled something bad when I entered a room. But, come to think of it, he didn't treat me any worse, which I guessed was something.

Or maybe in a time of war, any competent mage was worth preserving.

At least, I had to hope so, because I was about to risk a lot more than a job.

I put up a hand and the silence shield became opaque, darkening to the point that there weren't even any shadows moving beyond it anymore. Hargroves glanced up and then back at me, and his lips tightened a fraction more. Another minute and he wouldn't have any left.

"This can't get out," I told him.

"I surmised that."

He waited.

I paused, trying to force out the words, but old training died hard. Especially a lifetime's worth of it, first learned at my mother's knee. "Never say it, Accalia," she'd whispered, while stroking my hair. "Never let that word pass your lips."

But, of course, it had. I'd had to tell Cyrus, since getting involved with me was arguably more dangerous than being a *vargulf.* Sebastian knew, too, having guessed the truth before I said anything.

It was the main reason he'd allowed me into Arnou, to protect me from Lobizon, my mother's clan, who were determined to turn me. Or to do worse if they ever found out why they couldn't. No one else knew the truth besides my father, and I liked it that way.

But Hargroves was right: a blood test would turn it up—if the doctors knew what to look for. And he would make sure that they did. The old man would get his answer, one way or the other; better that it came from me.

Yet I still barely got the word out.

"Neuri." I cleared my throat, since that had been a rasp. "I was born with Neuri Syndrome."

Hargroves didn't so much as blink, which shouldn't have surprised me. The immediate, savage reaction I would have gotten from almost any Were wouldn't make sense coming from a human, most of whom wouldn't even recognize the term. As was clearly the case here.

"It's named after an ancient Russian tribe who were rumored to be able to Change into wolves," I explained. "Although I'm not sure why since Changing is the one thing carriers of Neuri can never do."

Hargroves frowned. "I was under the impression that you cannot change because you chose not to be infected. That you are what they call a rogue wolf."

I shook my head and once again had the words stick in my throat. This wasn't the sort of thing that was discussed with outsiders. It felt wrong, almost obscene. I made myself continue anyway.

"I was Wolf Born—"

"Meaning?"

"Most Weres are bitten by their parents after they reach the age of five or six, the earliest that a child can usually hope to withstand the infection. Before that, it is often fatal. But some acquire the Were strain in the womb, which is considered a sign of strength—assuming the child survives."

"Then you should have been born able to Change."

I didn't answer. I started to, but the pain hit all at once, not blindingly hot and burning, like an open wound, but cold, hollow, and filled with desperate longing. I shook it off angrily, my lips unconsciously forming themselves into a snarl. And it must have been a good one, because Hargroves' right hand twitched.

But he caught whatever spell he'd planned to use before it materialized, and I took the chance to get myself under control. And then to explain before I pissed him off any more than I already had. "Normally, yes. But Neuri intervened. The syndrome occurs occasionally when the mother is Were but the father is not, which is why female Weres rarely marry outside the clans. Basically, it's a milder version of lycanthropy, one that acts like a vaccine, preventing the carrier from getting the full-blown disease."

"I see."

I doubted that. Doubted he could have any idea what it had been like, growing up with sweat soaked sheets for days around the time of the full moon; tossing and turning with the call of the wild surging through my veins; hearing the howls of the pack loud in my ears, pulling on me like a physical tug. And then a yank and finally a heave as I grew older and the call intensified, leaving me gripping my bed in fear and longing and self-hatred, wanting to run with them, to feel the ground being eaten up under our paws, to see moonlight gleaming off heavily muscled flanks that moved like lightning, to . . .

To experience things that I would never know.

"Neuri is seen as a major threat by the clans," I said hoarsely, after a moment. "It could decimate a clan's strength if allowed to run wild, not to mention alienating it from everyone else. The higher clans usually intermarry among themselves, for prestige or alliances, but nobody is going to marry into a clan that might have Neuri. They might even attack it instead. For that reason, along with prejudice and tradition, babies born with the syndrome are commonly killed at birth."

"Killed?" Hargroves frowned some more. "I assume you mean in the distant past."

I didn't answer. Mentally, I was back at my mother's bedside, the sickly smell of a hospital ward strong in my nose, antiseptic overlaid by a profusion of flowers, neither of which covered the stench of approaching death. I could still hear the beeping of machines I didn't know the names of echoing in my head, along with her labored breathing.

"Mother hid my condition," I finally said, my voice expressionless. "Leading Were clans have a hierarchy, like old European nobility, and there weren't many ahead of her in clan rank who could have challenged her decision to refuse to let me be turned. And those who could have done so refrained out of respect or friendship. But then the clan chieftain died and his successor decided to push the issue. Laurentia of Lobizon's only daughter could not be lost to them. The farce had gone on long enough."

"And yet, you were not turned."

I shook my head. "Mother managed to avoid the summons to appear before the elders, and thereby risk a new ruling, by pleading illness. It wasn't a lie. She was diagnosed with pancreatic cancer when I was twenty-three.

"She held on for almost two years, because twenty-five is the age of majority among the clans, when I would be considered fully adult and able to choose for myself. She went through a great deal of pain to shield me, including a number of pointless surgeries and treatments that were never going to work, but might buy a little extra time.

"She missed my birthday by less than a week."

"My sympathies," Hargroves said, and actually sounded like he meant it.

Maybe he did.

We were all well acquainted with grief these days.

"The clan couldn't do anything as long as she lived," I continued. "But two days after she died, I was attacked by eight clan members determined to bring her only child into the fold before time ran out, whether I liked it or not. They forgot: I was Guillame de Croissets' daughter, too, and a war mage in my own right. Not to mention that, while Father is retired, he's far from helpless."

"An understatement," Hargroves murmured.

I didn't respond. I didn't want to break down in front of the boss. But the pain was just as bright, just as strong, just as enraging as it had been that night, fueling my response. And father's, too. Grief takes many forms, and ours had been written in blood.

"In the end, there were six dead Weres, two fires, five million dollars in property damage and headlines in all the Newark papers. The Circle covered it up as a gang war, but I received a black mark on my record for letting the fight become public as well as a transfer out here."

"So that was why." Hargroves looked like he'd wondered. "And your old clan?"

"They would have killed me in retribution once the furor died down, but under Arnou's protection, they didn't dare. But it's safe to say that I remain . . . unpopular."

"Yet they still do not know of your affliction."

"No. And it needs to stay that way," I said grimly, and he inclined his head half an inch, his version of a nod.

A commotion started up outside of our bubble before I could say any more and Hargroves dropped the shield. I looked up to see Caleb filling the doorway, looking belligerent, with his coat whipping about as if in a high wind. Maybe because he had a crowd of my new students behind him, and babysitting did not appear to have gone well.

Either that or I looked worse than I thought, because he was glowering at the boss in a way that was unwise if he wanted a promotion anytime soon.

He tossed me something and Hargroves caught it—fortunately. I would have sat there while it bonked me on the head, judging from the fact that my hand didn't lift until the boss was already examining it. I pretended to be pushing back a strand of hair before anybody noticed.

"Your phone?" Hargroves asked, looking at Caleb.

"No, hers." Caleb transferred the glare to me. "You scared the hell out of me! I called to ask about milk and it sounded like I dialed into a goddamned a war zone! Then you cut out and I had to listen to a couple of assholes deciding whether or not to kill you. They hadn't made up their minds when somebody noticed the phone and that happened."

"That" was putting a boot through it, by the look of things.

"I found it in the dirt," he continued, before I could respond. "After we finally got there—"

"We?"

"Well, what did you expect me to do with them?" he hiked a savage thumb over his shoulder.

"I expect you to get them out of here," Hargroves said, unamused. "They do not have clearance for this. They do not have clearance for anything!"

Sophie looked like she had something to say about that, but several of the others dragged her out before she could.

"Your distress signal was noticed by a patrol returning from Reno," Caleb added. "Along with a farm in the process of burning down and a bunch of highly illegal fey plants, most of which were crispy fried by the time we arrived—"

"And the people?" I interrupted.

"The patrol didn't find any people. Just tire tracks."

I shook my head. "There were trailers there, a half dozen or so, and a bunch of Weres on a truck—"

I cut off, but too late. The magic word had been uttered, and damn it! Hargroves had been smart to talk to me when I was woozy as hell.

"Weres?" he said, very deliberately.

"Yeah. Did I not mention that the punch growers were Weres?"

He just looked at me.

"I got a name off of one: Cloud-Leaper. I can ask about it, find out what human name he goes by and if he has property registered anywhere else."

Hargroves looked at me some more. His eyes said that he understood exactly how much this revelation complicated things. But I expected a measured response, since he was always measured.

I didn't get it.

"I hate this shit," he said, causing me to blink, because the American phrase sounded weird coming from an uptight Englishman.

"Um," I said.

"I hate that I don't have the people to properly patrol this territory. I hate that an operative almost died due to that. I hate that two very concerning issues, both having to do with Weres, have decided to crop up right before the Conclave—"

And, damn. I'd forgotten that the agreement between the Circle and the Were Council had only been for a year, and had to be renewed annually. The clan leaders were meeting in Vegas less than a week from now, and yeah.

The timing could have been better.

"—and I especially hate that I don't have anyone else to trust with this, anyone who knows the clans well enough to pick up on what is going on, anyone—"

"Who isn't your resident troublemaker."

He didn't bother to deny it.

"But I don't," he seethed. "So, this is your job—your only job—until we get that damned Conclave out of the way! It has to go off without a hitch, do you understand?"

"I—yes, but—"

"I don't want any buts. You can use Carter on this."

"But I'm on vacation," Caleb said, and immediately looked like he wished he hadn't when the boss rounded on him.

"Rescinded!" Hargroves snapped, and strode out of the room.

Caleb looked at me.

"Well, at least you're getting paid now," I said, and saw him scowl.

Chapter Ten

"I was already getting paid," Caleb growled. I had slung on some spare clothes that a medic brought me from my locker, since mine had gotten the scissor treatment after I was brought in, and we'd started climbing the steps back to the lobby. "That's what PTO means: paid time off."

"Well, now you'll have it for later," I pointed out.

"Like any of us is ever getting a vacation again!"

I frowned. "You were already insisting on helping out. I don't know why you'd rather do it for free—"

"Free means I don't have to write anything down. Free means off the clock and therefore off the record—"

"What do you think might need to be kept off the record?"

"How would I know? With you I never—"

He cut off when a siren started up, but not the kind that indicated a fire. That one was loud, blaring, and intended to get the attention of anyone in the building. This one was different.

This was meant for war mages only, being silent and almost impossible to detect for anyone without a Circle tattoo somewhere on their body. It was designed to alert the Corps to the fact that we had a breach without letting potential bad guys know that we'd been warned. And it did its job well.

My skin tightened painfully, as if I'd just received a massive sunburn all over my body, and the hair on the back of my neck stood up. And then felt like it was trying to pull out of my skin when the alarm intensified, all but pulling us up the stairs and causing Caleb to curse. I don't know why; he shaved off most of his hair anyway.

"Hey, what is that?" Sophie demanded, looking around as if she could feel it, too.

But she didn't get an answer. I was too busy hitting the wall after being shoved behind Caleb as he tore past.

"Stay there!" he threw back over his shoulder, probably because I was still wobbly and had no business being in a fight right now. Or maybe he wanted me to protect the kids; I didn't know. And I didn't have time to find out. Another alarm hit, hard on the heels of the first, but this one . . .

Was new.

Or new to me, since I had only a fraction of my mother's abilities, with senses heightened barely above those of a normal human. I couldn't usually hear things a mile off, or name every spice in a dish, or see almost as well at night as in the daytime. But I could suddenly see something, and with perfect clarity: a flash of dark eyes flickering wildly across my vision, like those of a hunted animal.

The image was as clear as if I was staring right at it, and was quickly joined by a smell. It was strong, almost overpowering, and not the usual mustiness of the stairway. I breathed in the stench of stark panic, heard pounding blood and rapid breaths, and felt skin prickling fear and indecision, along with the impression of a wild fluttering in my throat that made it all but impossible to swallow. It was terror given tangible form, but it wasn't mine.

My heart rate was more or less normal; my breathing unbothered. But someone was coming out of their skin—literally. And I experienced it right alongside them.

For the first time in my life, I knew the agonizing crack of reforming bones, the waterfall of a thick, magical pelt spreading over my body, the incredibly strange sensation of a new face pushing its way out of mine. The sensations were so overwhelming that, for a second, I just stood there, gasping and trying to grab a snout I didn't have. Because the changes weren't happening to me.

"What is it? What's wrong?" Sophie was shaking me, and one of the boys—I didn't see who—was whistling between his teeth.

"Told you—mages be cray, yo."

And then I was moving, as another blast of distress flooded down the stairs, almost strong enough to knock me over. My new students pounded after me, all those feet making the stairwell echo loudly in my ears, even though most of them were wearing sneakers. Something about that, about them running headlong into danger, pulled me out of the fog and I rounded on them.

"No. Stay."

"What the fuck?" someone said loudly.

It was Chris, the usual laid back surfer dude, but he wasn't sounding so relaxed right now. Maybe because the voice that had come out of my throat hadn't sounded like mine. Low, guttural, and menacing as hell, it should have shocked me, too.

Instead, I was grateful for it, as the whole class stopped on a dime. I turned back around and raced ahead, and when Aki tried to follow—I could hear the peculiar sound of his sneakers, all worn down on one side for some reason, giving a little lisp to his walk—Sophie threw an arm over his chest. I could distinctly make out the soft sound of her touch impacting the buttons on the front of his shirt.

And then I was through the door to the lobby and out.

A blast of sound and sensation hit me, making the quiet stairwell feel like an oasis. But I wasn't tempted to go back, because the door had been blunting more than just the five senses. A tornado of terror battered me as soon as I stepped out, like a physical blow.

I somehow stayed on my feet, even while the emotions of a panicked wolf hit me on all sides. Every instinct I had wanted to find, to help, to *protect*, but training held. And caused me to take a second to size up the situation first.

It wasn't good.

In front of me was a ring of leather coated war mages standing like rocks in the middle of a crashing surf, motionless against the blurred panic going on behind them. The only motion was in their coats, fluttering around their legs as if caught in a strong wind, and the occasional twitch of a hand hovering over a weapon's belt. Or the weapons themselves in the case of one mage who had already deployed his arsenal, leaving them circling his head like a deadly cloud.

In front of the mages was a ring of wolves, facing inward and already transformed, with bunched muscles in their haunches and torn clothing littering the ground around them in a confetti of colors. Their bodies were tensed and ready, their hackles were raised, and snarls and growls were emerging from behind bared teeth. They looked like they were about to pounce.

Outside the circle, the high rafters of the old warehouse were ringing with the distressed sounds of normal people who had showed up to renew weapons' licenses, to report a disturbance, or to apply for a permit, only to find themselves caught in a situation. I saw flashes of wide eyes and dropped jaws, probably because many had never seen a transformed Were before. Some were rushing to get away before they saw even more, while others had stopped to gawk, with one lady letting a slew of paperwork slide out of her hands unnoticed, which scattered everywhere.

But all of that was a haze at the edges of my vision, vague and indistinct, almost irrelevant. My eyes noticed it because they'd been trained to notice everything, and to size up a situation quickly in order to determine the best course of action. Only, this time, I wasn't coolly assessing anything.

This time, I was furious.

And then two Weres sprang for the small wolf at the center of the circle, who was apparently the cause of all this, and what could only be called a roar echoed through the room. It was loud enough to drown out the panicked background noise and the ambient music the Corps had recently started playing in the lobby for some reason. The roar didn't sound like a wolf's howl; it didn't sound like anything I'd ever heard. Which should have been a surprise since it was coming from me.

It wasn't. And neither was the sight of two large wolves changing course mid-attack, their haunches bunching up around their faces as they veered off to the side. Or half a dozen more war mages' weapons springing into the air as if on strings. Or the several hundred heads that suddenly jerked in my direction, some stopping and craning their necks to see past the deadly circle.

Nothing mattered except the boy, because he was a boy, a desperate, hurting, still defiant cub, crouched low to the floor but howling his fear into the air, along with his defiance.

At least, he had been a moment ago. But he'd paused at the roar, too, and turned his head as I started toward him, pushing a war mage whose face I didn't bother to register out of the way in the process. "Lia—" someone said, sounding shocked, and was ignored.

I could smell the cub's fear as I approached, a tsunami of sensation. And below that, a deep, dark ocean of agony that didn't know where to go or how to cope. He'd been in pain before, but never like this. For the first time in his life, he was alone.

And was slowly realizing that he always would be, because it was Jace, who had lost his brother barely two days ago.

"No," I rumbled, and again, barely recognized my voice. "Not alone."

Someone was shouting a warning, someone else was calling my name—Caleb—who was also yelling at our fellow mages to "Put the goddamned guns down; she's got this!"

I didn't know if I had this. I didn't even know what this was. Except that I was drawn by that horrible pain, that terrible loneliness, and by the strange feeling of possession sweeping over me. A war mage took a small step forward and I growled at him. I saw his eyes fly open in surprise, and although I was currently unarmed, he stepped back.

I turned my attention back to the cub, who was almost nose to the floor now, in a position of respect and submission just short of rolling onto his belly. But he couldn't do that, couldn't risk it, not now. His eyes flickered from me to the encroaching circle, but he wasn't looking at the mages.

And for good reason.

"*Vargulf*," a fully transformed wolf snarled, the voice like an industrial sized file scraped across stone. It was harsh enough to cause a man, fleeing just behind him, to let out a little scream.

It didn't faze me. Weres can talk while transformed, although few do as it isn't often necessary. The scents coming off the clan, the small changes of expression, the odd telepathy that close family members shared, was usually sufficient.

Like the kind I was suddenly getting from the cub.

Some of the images I recognized: the paint splattered figure of a young man, at a faucet outside of my house, carefully washing off a bunch of brushes; the circle of happy faces around a campfire, jumping with leaping flames; the full moon, flooding over sand, turning a spreading circle of blood black and terrible. . .

But others were new to me: a terrifying race through the night on all fours, blood pounding in his veins, his brother at his side, and the howling of a pursuing pack in his ears; a dilapidated room with dirty windows, but with their meager possessions arranged carefully on cinderblock and plywood shelves; his brother, laughing for the first time in months, with hope in his eyes and the neon lights of Vegas behind him—

"It's *vargulf*!" the same wolf growled, his pelt red and ruffled and angry. "Get away. We'll deal with this!"

It was what they were paid for, I realized. Because these weren't a random clan who had wondered in here. They weren't even from the same clan, with no less than four distinct family signatures hitting my nose. And when I concentrated on their wolf forms, I could see a hazy figure of the men and women they'd been a moment ago crouched in the middle of each.

That wasn't normal, any more than the rest of whatever was happening to me. But it did allow me to recognize them as the Weres who'd been contracted by the Corps to sniff out dark magic attacks. And now they thought they were protecting us from something else. Because a vargulf wasn't a traumatized child to them; he was a serious threat.

One they were about to eliminate.

"Touch him and die," I said, my own voice so rough now as to sound almost transformed.

It shouldn't have, because the rest of me hadn't changed. And for some reason I found that surprising, looking down at my human body and barely recognizing it. Spindly arms instead of heavily muscled ones; pale, hairless skin instead of a shiny pelt; a face that felt curiously flat and unremarkable, rather than sleek and purpose built for a predator, with an elegant snout of knife-like fangs.

It threw me, but not as much as the voice. Low, guttural and fierce, it was the audible equivalent of a dead-eyed sheriff waiting for the other guy to go for his gun. And it wasn't a bluff. I meant every word, and the Were knew it. I saw his hackles rise, his teeth flash as they snapped in the air, his eyes narrow.

I'd just challenged him for the boy's life, and Weres do not back down from a challenge.

"You would fight for that *thing*?"

Something leaped in me, a vicious, primal joy, a resounding 'yes' springing to my lips so fast that I had to bite them to keep it back. Something in me wanted to fight; something was glad to fight. Something wanted to take on all of them, right here, right now, and savage them for daring to touch what was ours.

The rest of me thought I might be going mad.

"I don't have to," I said, my human mind battling down whatever the hell was going on. "I am ordering you to stand down and go back to your stations. This boy is no threat."

"He's an outcaste! He's here to cause trouble!"

"No." I glanced at the cub, who was staring up at me with a mix of confusion and wonder in his eyes. "He's here for his brother."

I didn't have to ask if I'd guessed right. In the crouched wolf form in front of me I could see the huddled figure of Jace, the remaining twin. The body of his brother, Jayden, was still downstairs, in the morgue along with Colin's corpse. I hadn't seen it, but I knew it had been brought here by the Corpsmen who had swarmed the bloody camp after I called them.

And I doubted that Sedgewick had let a nice, juicy corpse get away from him.

A new flood of rage swamped me—no wonder he'd been so uninterested in me; he already had a body waiting for dissection. Assuming that he'd waited. And the curtain of red that fell over my vision at that thought was thick enough to make it difficult to see.

It would have been followed quickly by shame—that I hadn't even thought to ask about Jayden, that I'd left him in Sedgewick's filthy hands—but wolves don't feel shame. And I was in wolf mind now, almost fully, for the first time in my life. And while I didn't understand it, I understood one thing perfectly.

Someone had to bleed.

* * *

"Lia!"

A voice was talking from somewhere nearby; a familiar voice; a friend.

"Lia, come on. Let him go, okay? We can talk this out."

I didn't understand the words. They didn't make sense. Let who go?

Then I realized: there was a body underneath mine, with a pulse beating heavily in a thick neck—a human neck. My teeth were buried in flesh, and something was dripping down my chin. Rich and meaty, it tasted like pennies.

"Lia, can you hear me?"

I looked up and saw a big, dark figure crouching not too far off. Caleb, my mind finally informed me. Friend.

"You know me," he said, echoing my thoughts. And crouching down, getting in my line of sight. "We're friends. Fought side by side."

Yes. Friend. War friend.

I smiled and somebody screamed.

Caleb ignored it.

"Yes, we're old friends," he said, as if reinforcing it. "And as your friend, I can ask a favor. Can't I?"

I blinked slowly at him.

"Can I . . . have that?"

I looked down, where his eyes were focused. A man was underneath me. There was blood on his neck.

"He's not going to challenge you anymore," Caleb said, slowly and carefully. "You won, alright? He's submissive."

I growled, unable to answer as my teeth were still buried in the man's flesh. I could rip it out, I thought, almost idly. I could feel the gush of warm blood, see it pour over the floor, saturate the old carpet tiles. They needed changing anyway—

"Lia!" I looked back up. "He challenged you and he jumped for the boy. He was wrong. He fucked up and found out. Just . . . just let me have him now, okay?"

Caleb's hand reached out and I growled, deep in my throat. My prey. Mine.

"Hit her with a stun spell," someone said.

"We've hit her with five!" someone else snapped.

"Then try something else!"

"We've tried everything nonlethal and she shrugs it off. What do you suggest we do? Kill her?"

"She's going to kill him if we don't!"

"Shouldn't have challenged," a rougher voice said, a wolf voice.

"No, he shouldn't have," someone else said. Another new voice, but this one . . . this one, I knew.

It rang like bells in my ears, sweet and joyous. I made a happy little sound, and a new figure replaced Caleb. Mate.

"He shouldn't have," Cyrus repeated, smiling at me.

I smiled back, although that was not a thing that wolves did. But I was betwixt and between now, my mind caught between two identitics, and unsure which was me. I was still unsure when Cyrus reached out a hand and did what Caleb had been denied.

He touched my prey.

"He was a fool," Cyrus said, speaking to the others but keeping those whiskey-colored eyes on mine. "Lia is Arnou. She outranks him in clan order, something of which he was well aware. When she gave a command, he should have listened."

"She's honorary," a man's voice said, melting halfway through the comment from wolf speak to human. "She hasn't been bitten, doesn't Change. He thought she had no right—"

"Don't talk to him!" Someone else said. "He's *vargulf*, too! You dishonor yourself!"

"I'd do a lot more than that to get my brother back safely."

The speaker came into view a moment later. Fiftyish, hair half gray, half still a vivid red. Lined, weather-beaten face under a short beard. Strange expression as he regarded me.

But he made obeisance, getting low, almost to the ground since he had to be lower than me and I was currently crouched over my prey. His brother, I realized. My brain almost broke as conflicting commands raced through my synapses:

Get off him.

No! Ours!

Let him go!

Wild yips and growls and aborted howls flooded my brain, ones I felt all the way to my bones. Like the reply. *No!*

"Lia," Cyrus's voice came again. "He made a mistake. His brother begs forgiveness, and for the Were's life. He asks that you show pity."

My eyes flicked to the brother, now face down on the floor in front of me. Close enough to grab his brother's arm, to jerk my prize away. Yet he did not.

He just waited, as he should, for my decision.

"Your choice, of course," Cyrus said, sounding diffident. "But as for me . . ." Our eyes met, and he shrugged. "I'd let him go. He isn't worth the trouble his death would cause, and Sebastian—"

My ears pricked at the clan chieftain's name. Cyrus bent low, to whisper in my ear. Not that it mattered; right now, I could have heard him from across the room.

"He would probably prefer not to have any more trouble."

Listen to him! My human half screeched.

The wolf mine was calmer. Blood lust still surged, and outrage, and joy, a strange mix of emotions that the other me didn't understand. But slowly, my teeth released the man's jugular, and the flesh around it. Slowly, I pulled back and sat up, the room swaying a bit around me.

I licked my lips, tasting warm copper; somebody cursed; and the man's brother silently pulled him away.

The strange haze I had been experiencing broke a second later, and I snapped fully back into my human mind. One which saw Jace, still in wolf form, crouched low behind Cyrus; saw a ring of naked humans, many still on all fours, watching me intently; and behind them, the usually bustling lobby filled with war mages, what must have been hundreds of them, all standing silently, all looking at me with sober, accusing eyes.

Chapter Eleven

"What the hell was *that*?" It was one of my new students, following us out of the door to HQ and into the blazing sun of the parking lot. It was so bright out that I covered my eyes, and so hot that I was surprised the asphalt wasn't melting. It was like walking into an oven set on high.

"Damn, it's hot," Aki said, gasping a little.

"Screw the heat!" Chris said. "I want to know what just happened in—"

"Stuff it," Sophie said tersely, and to my surprise, he did.

Yeah, I thought again.

Alpha.

No one else said anything, including me. I didn't know how much they'd seen, and right then, I didn't care. My stomach was roiling and I felt like throwing up. The taste of blood was strong in my mouth, human blood, and I didn't have anything to wash it away. I stopped by Hernando's cart, but he wasn't there. He was back in the lobby, huddled with the others, talking . . .

About God knew what.

Cyrus reached behind the cart and stuffed a bill into the simple shoebox where Hernando kept his cash, because nobody in their right mind steals from a Were. And then snared me a soda out of an ice chest, something orange with a Mexican name on the side. It was lukewarm, with the Vegas heat making a mockery of anything that wasn't a deep freeze, but it was welcome.

I took a drink, swished it around my mouth and spat it out. I didn't look at what splattered on the concrete. I very carefully didn't look.

"You alright?" Cyrus asked, his voice low.

I didn't answer. Thought I might throw up. I would have liked to blame the overly sweet soda, but it would have been a lie.

I could remember everything now, as I hadn't been able to before: the wolf jumping for Jace; the terror in the cub's eyes; the small body nonetheless squaring up, because Weres don't die huddled in a ball on the floor, not even children; a roar that shook the rafters, erupting from my throat but not sounding remotely human or even remotely Were; and the attacking wolf falling out of his arc and back into human form, sprawling awkwardly on the floor; and then—

And then I was on him.

I remembered my very human teeth sinking into his flesh, proving that we are predators, too. Remembered him struggling underneath me, unable to rise despite the fact that I wasn't using magic to hold him down. Remembered when my teeth snapped shut around his jugular, and we both knew it was over.

I might have killed him, I thought blankly. Followed immediately by knowledge that that was a lie, just my human brain trying desperately to soften the truth. The truth was that I would have killed him, if Cyrus hadn't intervened. I might have shared the kill with Caleb, but I wouldn't have forgone it for him.

I knew I wouldn't have.

My body started to shake, and Cyrus repositioned himself between me and the others. "Take them onto the house, would you?" he asked Caleb casually.

"And what are you going to do?" Caleb demanded, his voice containing a thousand questions he didn't vocalize.

"Get dinner. We'll bring enough for everyone."

Caleb looked like he doubted that, but didn't call him on it. I'd have to satisfy his curiosity eventually, along with that of a lot of other people. In fact, I didn't know why I wasn't being arrested right now. And I guessed Jen felt the same, because she tentatively touched my arm, the sunlight gleaming on her blond bob.

"You're not in trouble, right?" she asked. "I mean, they're not going to charge you with anything, are they? You were defending him—"

"No, it's fine," I said, even though I wasn't sure that it was.

And I guess my unease came through in my voice, because her frown grew. "But we could tell them, even though they all saw—"

"It's fine," Cyrus said, more forcefully.

"How can you be so sure?" Sophie demanded. She'd taken down her ponytail, and her red hair was a staticky flame around her face. "We all know what the Corps is like. We've dealt with them enough."

"Because this isn't Corps business. A challenge was issued; a challenge was accepted; and one wolf lost. Even if Lia had chosen to end him, the Corps couldn't bring charges. There is a treaty. And no Were court would convict her."

"The Corps doesn't have to convict her to kick her out. And then where will we be? I doubt there's a lot of other trainers willing to take us on!"

"This isn't just about us," Jen said, frowning at her friend. "Lia could have been—"

"It's about us if we get sent back. This is our chance, our one chance, and we only just—" she broke off, probably because the other students had started to look a little wide-eyed. But Caleb intervened before anything blew up—possibly literally.

"If Hargroves intended to make a big deal out of this, he'd have already done it," he said in his brooks-no-discussion voice. "He was watching the whole thing."

"Hargroves?" Aki asked.

"The big boss. The old guy in the snazzy suit."

"The one who came to see us with Lia," Sophie added, looking more subdued. She glanced at Kimmie, but the other girl was keeping it together today. In fact, if anything, she appeared more belligerent than scared.

"The Corps needs us, and we need Lia," Kimmie said flatly. "And nobody died—"

"Kind of a close thing," Aki murmured.

"—so they're not going to do shit."

Aki looked less than reassured, but he didn't say anything else. I didn't either, but mostly because I was focused on a different problem. "Hargroves was there?" I asked Caleb.

"You didn't see him?"

"She was kind of busy," Chris commented, eyeing me. It looked like there was at least one student who wasn't sure he wanted to be trained by a crazed war mage who went for other people's throats in a conflict.

Couldn't exactly blame him there.

"He, uh, arrived about halfway through," Caleb acknowledged.

"Halfway through?" I asked.

"About the time you went for the jugular."

I felt my stomach clench, and a little more bile join the burning sensation in my throat. And I guess I wasn't subtle, because Caleb decided to change the subject. "Come on," he told the class. "We have stuff to do."

Aki looked like he was going to object, and maybe Jen, too, who was still regarding me with concern. But people don't generally argue with Caleb. The only thing that happened was the small group following him across the parking lot through the shimmering desert heat, although a few of them looked back at me over their shoulders.

"How's he getting them back?" I croaked, watching them leave.

"No idea," Cyrus said, and then his arms went around my waist from behind, and his face buried itself in my neck. "Thank you."

It was barely a whisper, but it was enough to stop the tremors that had started spreading outward from my core. The feel of his body against mine, of his strong arms around me, of the steady beat of his heart helped, too. He was warm and solid and there in a way that I really needed right then. But the comment didn't make sense.

"For what?"

"For protecting Jace. I put him in danger; you got him out."

I turned in his arms, careless of any watchers from inside the building. "I'm feeling a little off right now," I said shakily. "So . . . what?"

I didn't get an answer, unless you counted a tackle from a half-naked boy. Cyrus had loaned Jace his leather jacket, which he'd wrapped around his waist, making him look vaguely like a Scotsman in a leather kilt. He felt like one, too, when he grabbed me, the thin boy arms having the grip of a man twice his size.

"Thank you," he whispered, his body trembling, too. "Thank you. I thought—I don't know what I thought."

You thought you were about to be torn to shreds, I didn't say, because there was no need. And because he was currently squeezing all the breath out of me. He finally let go and turned to Cyrus.

"But Jayden—"

"I took care of it." Cyrus's voice had a wolf growl in the back of his throat. "He'll be returned to us tonight—unmolested."

Jace buried his face in Cyrus's shirt, then suddenly collapsed, sobbing, onto the hot pavement. Because it was all too much and he was just a boy. I stood awkwardly by as Cyrus did everything right—crouched down, hugged him, rubbed his back, and told him that it would be okay, when we all knew it never would.

For Jace, there would always be a hole in his heart, no matter how long he lived. I'd dealt with that since my mother died, the realization that there are some wounds that don't heal. You learn to live with them, to not think about them every single day, to function again because life goes on. But healing?

Yeah, that was a lie.

But it was a lie that Jace needed right then, and gradually, the tears slowed down. I realized that Cyrus must have come here to demand the body back, and had probably brought Jace in case a family member's signature was required. I didn't know how things had gone so terribly wrong, but with a lobby full of Weres, it wasn't hard to guess.

"This was my fault," Jace said, almost as if he'd heard my thoughts. "We signed the papers, then Cyrus went outside—"

"Through the back, to the impound yard," Cyrus added. "They wanted to know if I could get a scent off a bike that had been left at the grow farm—"

"A bike?" I asked.

"—and I did. It was yours. I think the clan who attacked you tried to destroy it. They . . . did a good job."

I decided not to ask.

"I was supposed to sit in the office and wait for him," Jace added. "But I thought I smelled you and you were . . . upset. I was worried and went to look and . . . they grabbed me."

"That wasn't your fault," I told him firmly. "None of this was."

"They saw him come in with me, but waited until he was alone to pounce," Cyrus said, his voice roughening again. "Cowards. If you'd ripped that bastard's throat out, it would have been—"

He stopped himself, but not because there was a child present. Jace had probably seen more violence in his short life than most war mages, and was already nodding along. Instead, the pause was because of the loud contraption that had just rattled up behind us, announcing its presence with a pop and a belch.

"What—" I coughed, waving a hand in front of my face in search of clean air I didn't find, because the beast's exhaust was polluting it all.

"Needs an oil change," Caleb yelled, to be heard over the engine. He was in the driver's seat, although of what, I wasn't sure. It was old and rusted and looked like something that would embarrass a junk yard. "Old surveillance van," he shouted cheerfully. "I commandeered it for a school bus. What d'you think?"

I was fortunately too busy coughing up my lungs to answer.

"Wanna ride?" he asked Jace, who looked from me to Cyrus.

"Go on, *canagan*," Cyrus told him. "Lia and I will be along in a while."

Jace nodded and climbed on board, as quickly as if a clan leader had just given him an order. It made me frown, but I didn't comment since the three of us weren't fitting onto Cyrus's bike. I watched Caleb rattle away in what was definitely a road hazard and probably illegal, rolling coal all the way to the main street. And then I turned my thoughts to the food Cyrus had promised.

"Tamales?" I said doubtfully, wondering if Hernando would even sell them to us, a *vargulf* and whatever the hell I was these days. But Cyrus shook his head.

"Better. Come on."

* * *

Cyrus's cramped apartment was even more cramped than I remembered, since it now had two large chest freezers shoved against a wall of the living room.

"Redecorating?" I asked, as he dumped the bike's saddlebags onto a beat up, two-seater sofa.

"Something like that," he said, and hugged me.

I didn't know if it was part of his wolf nature, or just a facet of the man, but he had a wonderful stillness about him. I felt it slowly seep into my bones as we stood there. The room helped, too, being dim except for a little light leaking through crappy plastic blinds, and was colder than usual even for Vegas air conditioning.

Weres ran hot and loved the AC. It left the room an oasis of tranquility that served as an added balm on my frazzled nerves. It seemed to be doing Cyrus some good, too, because after a moment he rested his chin on my head and sighed deeply, beathing in my scent.

"You need anything?"

Just this, I thought, and hugged him tighter.

He smelled wonderful. He usually did, although he rarely wore cologne. Most clan wolves didn't, as it was considered rude and somewhat suspicious to mask their scent. It made other Weres think that they had something to hide. That didn't matter anymore, but I could still only detect suntan lotion, soap, a light coating of sweat from the ride over—

And the breakfast burrito he'd had, hours ago, the peppers a spicy bite in my nose; and the exhaust from his bike, still clinging in microscopic particles to his clothing; and the smell of the cigar another rider had been holding, the smoke from which had drifted over to us when we paused side by side at a traffic light . . .

"Lia?"

"It's okay."

I buried my face in his shirt and shoved everything away, concentrating only on the trace of wolf musk underneath it all. He smelled like home; he smelled like clan. But today, it was stronger, sweeter . . . *more.* It reminded me of Jace's terror, back at HQ, being less a scent than an emotion given form. As if I could breathe in Cyrus's love, support, and concern with every breath.

It was intoxicating.

He must have agreed, because he held me for a long time, his arms tight. "I know you hate when I ask this," he finally murmured.

"Don't."

"I just want to know that you're all right."

"I'm fine."

"You sure? That would have rattled anybody. There's no shame in admitting—"

I released him and stepped back.

He sighed and rubbed the back of his neck with one hand while regarding me from under his bangs. They were too long and fell in his eyes, making him look boyishly handsome. He appeared harder, older, and fiercer whenever he got tired of messing with the thick mane nature had given him and did a buzz cut, which lasted all of a week at the rate that Weres' hair grew.

But he hadn't done that in a while, and the dark strands in front of the concerned brown eyes made me want to brush them back, to smooth away the lines on his forehead and to tell him that I was good. That I just had to wait for the drug to finish working its way through my system and everything would be fine. But I didn't.

I didn't trust my voice not to crack.

I didn't know what was wrong with me. One moment I was gripping Cyrus's shirt, feeling his love for me like a tangible thing. The next, I was pushing him away, all but gasping in confusion and pain. My emotions were all over the place and I couldn't seem to rein them in or even parse exactly what they were.

It left me feeling off balance and vulnerable, not to mention furious with myself. I was a war mage; I dealt with next level shit all the time. I should be better at this!

But the things I shrugged off didn't matter, whereas that scene today had hit every button I had.

"Lia?" I looked up to find that Cyrus's look of concern had grown. I realized that I was hugging my arms around myself hard enough to bruise. I wanted to hug him instead, but I was afraid that if I did, I wouldn't be able to let go. And I didn't want any questions I couldn't answer, or for him to worry about me even more.

Cyrus worried a lot. It came with dating a war mage, especially a prickly one with enough baggage for ten people. I sometimes wondered if he was a secret masochist.

"You know," he said, after a pause. "When young Weres first change, their clan takes them into the wilderness. Sometimes for a week, sometimes two. It's usually phrased as a camping trip—"

"I know what they do."

"—and it is, I suppose. But it's mostly to let them run and sniff and play to their heart's content, until the built-up energy from all those days since the bite, when they couldn't yet turn, when they felt like they were coming out of their skins all the time, is finally expended. I wonder . . . how much energy would twenty-seven years cause?"

"I didn't Change!" I made my fingers release my arms. They did so slowly, awkwardly, as if they were made out of wood instead of flesh. Only to be immediately captured in Cyrus's grip.

"But something happened today. We both know that. I don't pretend to know what it was, but we need to—"

"I'd like a shower."

It was abrupt, enough to be rude, but I needed to get out of there. I needed to get out now. And Cyrus seemed to realize that, dropping my hands with that same concerned look on his face. But he didn't say anything else.

I turned and went into the bedroom.

Chapter Twelve

Cyrus's place was the stereotypical bachelor pad. The building dated to the seventies, and as far as I could tell, so did the decor. There was brown shag carpeting on the floor, breaking down with every step because it was so old, and sending clouds of tiny filaments into the air. There was "wood" paneling on one wall that had never seen a tree, and some geometric wallpaper on another, peeling a little along the seams, in gold and beige. There were even what might be original, avocado-colored appliances in the kitchen, paired with an accent wall in eye-searing orange.

Add a few beanbag chairs and a lava lamp, and the place would be totally groovy.

It was also tiny, which along with helping me with my remodel, explained why Cyrus slept over a lot these days. There was a welcome mat sized foyer, a tiny galley kitchen, and a living room/dining room combo so small that I had no idea how it was supposed to serve both purposes. Which was likely why he ate on the sofa while watching T.V.

The bedroom wasn't much bigger, being mainly a walkway around the queen-sized bed that he'd had to get, because nothing larger would have fit. Fortunately, he didn't have a lot of belongings to take up space, since he hadn't taken much with him from Arnou. Having to run for your life in the middle of the night before your old clan guts you will do that to a person.

He also hadn't acquired much since moving to Vegas, unless you counted a framed poster of the Rat Pack and a lamp designed to look like a woman's fishnet-covered leg. He'd found both at an old junk shop outside of town and thought they went with the retro vibe of the place. It was an "if you can't beat 'em, join 'em" sort of thing, I guessed.

But there were some differences from the last time I was here. Like the neat rolls of sleeping bags stacked against the wall opposite the bed, what looked like a dozen or so. And the clothes bulging out of the room's lone, sliding door closet, which had once closed easily. And the change in scent . . .

I stopped with my hand on the dresser and just breathed for a moment. My eyes had closed without me telling them to, and since it was approximately noon, the usual nighttime noise of the surrounding streets was far into the future. My senses should have been registering pretty much nothing.

But tell them that.

There was a tangle of unfamiliar scents snarling the room, which I finally recognized as belonging to some of the lost boys Cyrus had befriended. I doubted he was housing them all here—there simply wasn't room. But he was definitely feeding them, and providing a safe place for their belongings.

I couldn't be sure of the number because some were mere traces, barely a whisper in my nostrils, their scents old and decayed. But others were fresh, vibrant and vivid, as if they'd been here very recently, painting the darkness in leaping wolf shadows behind my eyelids. One of the latter was Jace, his quick, mercurial nature mimicked by his scent. It was elusive, like being caught in a scattering of leaves blown by the wind, teasing me from all sides. And then gone again, just as quickly. And immediately behind it—

Jayden.

The boy's scent was so tangible that I actually reached out a hand to touch it. But like quicksilver, it slipped through my fingers, as fast as he'd been on that terrible night. Yet so vivid that I could almost see him, bright as a flame in the darkness.

I wondered, could Cyrus see him, too? He must be able to; he'd had these gifts far longer than me. But if so, how could he stand it?

Even worse, how hard would it be, when the scent began to fade in another day or two, slipping away like a second death? When even the last trace of the boy he knew was gone? It felt vaguely like the place was being haunted now, but I thought that the echoing stillness, the absence of any sensory memory at all, might be worse.

We have to keep Jace out of here, I thought blankly. We have to—

A head lifted abruptly from my neck, almost in a jerk, but it wasn't mine. At least, it wasn't normally mine. But I could see it as I had the boys, without the need for eyes. It was sleek and dark, like a shadow on a wall, and not in a human shape.

And, suddenly, I could see something else, too.

A woman was coming down the hall outside, her scent painting a trail in the air behind her. It was yellow; I had no idea why, but I could see it streaming out like a pale scarf caught in the wind.

She'd taken the stairs because the elevator was acting up again. She was panting, her heavy breaths and heavier footfalls coming closer, and she was carrying something. I could hear it crinkle in her arms.

Groceries? Shopping? I didn't know, but she was laden down and distracted. It made her vulnerable. Prey.

Now she was struggling to open a door down the hall with keys that jangled on my nerves, loud and clanging, despite the fact that I shouldn't have been able to hear them at all. Like her low cursing when she missed the keyhole—soft muscles, and now bad reflexes. *Prey,* something said louder, my nose twitching.

A scent cloud surrounded her, painting me a picture as clear as sight: the salty tang of her sweat under a dash of cheap perfume; the smack of her hairspray, too much for a young woman, but perfect for someone older who was trying to preserve an expensive hairstyle in the Vegas heat; a hint of lavender body powder covering a trace of Ben Gay.

The sounds confirmed the scents, with the soft *swish, swish, swish* of hosiery rubbing together on her legs when she moved, which no young woman would bother with in this temperature. The clip clop of sensible shoes. Her breath, still labored after some minutes—all of it said older, out of shape, or injured. PREY.

"Lia?"

The voice jolted me back into myself somewhat, and I opened eyes that I couldn't remember closing. And saw a man standing in the doorway. The bedroom was darker than the living room, as the wall of the next building blocked most of the light through the lone window. Some sunlight muscled its way in anyway, but was confined to dim, dust filled stripes across the darkness, which didn't help with visibility. It left the man barely a shape against the gloom, and for a moment, I didn't know him.

My hackles rose, ruffling the hair at the base of my neck. I made no sound, but I could feel him tense nonetheless, as if some of the air had been sucked out of the room. "Lia?" he said again, more carefully this time, and it confused me. I knew that voice.

I knew that scent, too, flooding the air abruptly as my senses refocused closer in. I drew it into my lungs, reveling in the strong, masculine heat of it, and the knowledge that it brought. *Home, pack, mate.*

Yes, I knew him. I felt the tension leave my body, and I slumped slightly against the dresser. And then turned and scrabbled at it, because part of me knew that I was acting weird. "I, uh, was looking for some clothes. I thought I left some here."

"You did." Cyrus's voice was almost wary. "We moved things around somewhat. A few of the boys were rousted out of their digs and had to bunk with me for a while, and there's not much room."

He approached, his footsteps silent on the soft carpeting, even to my ears. But I didn't need extra senses right now. He was being careful, telegraphing his movements, keeping them slow and elegant and easy.

I didn't know why, but it reassured me.

"I put them in here." He opened a drawer of the dresser and I retrieved a pair of jeans, an old t-shirt, and some underwear. And then just stood there, torn between taking a shower and going to rip an old woman's throat out.

Cyrus didn't say anything, and thanks to the low light, I couldn't see much of his face. But he didn't move, and I'd have to get past him to make it out the door. I wondered if that was deliberate, if he was aware of how on the brink I was.

Or if he was just waiting for a response, because that was how normal people acted when someone helped them out, Lia!

"Thanks," I whispered.

"Sure."

The expression, what I could see of it, was casual, the stance loose limbed and relaxed. We might have been talking about the weather—or about the clothes I'd left here after a recent trip to Zion National Park. He'd laundered them for me; I could smell the detergent, the supposedly unscented kind that Weres preferred, because anything else was overpowering.

I might have imagined that eerie tenseness a moment ago, when I thought he was blocking my path.

"I'll be right outside the door if you need anything," he told me steadily.

Or maybe not.

I went into the bathroom.

The door closed behind me and I sank against it, hearing it creak under my weight and not caring. For a moment, I just stayed there, breathing deeply and trembling, trying to separate the sticky strands of that other mind from my own. It wasn't easy.

Possibly because there were people—*prey*—all over the building. Vegas was not a city of early risers, and most were sleeping—*vulnerable, off guard*—snoring through last night's binge and today's hangover. I could hear the creak of a mattress down the hall, as an overweight body repositioned itself—*too out of shape to run, an easy take down*—and someone else yawning, having just gotten up—*disoriented, oblivious*. I heard a child coming up the stairs, singing the jingle from some cartoon, blissfully unaware—

Stop it!

I froze there, panting and afraid—of myself, which was so weird that it broke my brain to even think it. But my stomach rumbled, reminding me that I hadn't eaten today. And something hungered.

I needed to go back to HQ, I thought shakily. I shouldn't be out here now, running around the city with a monster clawing in my veins. Cyrus should have left me there—

For what? So that Sedgewick could rip me open, as he was probably doing to Colin right now? So he could figure out what made us tick, when he would never understand that, any more than norms understood his magic?

We were magical creatures, too, mystical, strange, wonderful and terrible, and never had I felt that more. But I was something else, as well. I was Lia de Croissets, a war mage daughter of a war mage father, the scion of a distinguished line going back hundreds of years, and I was *better than this*. I didn't stalk people in their apartments or attack children in stairwells, like a monster out of a fairy tale. I didn't care what I'd ingested, I was in control.

But I stayed there for a while longer anyway, having slid down to my haunches, the tile cool under my butt. And waited, to see which side would win. It was a tense few minutes, with my senses feeling like Sedgewick's nose had briefly looked, back in the infirmary.

One would spear out into the world, becoming hugely sensitive for a moment before shrinking back down to let another have a go. Like when the tile wall opposite suddenly rushed at me, going ninety miles an hour, and causing me to flinch back and rattle the door, because I thought it was going to hit me in the face. And I hadn't recovered from that before sight gave way to sound and I could hear *everything*, for what had to be a mile around.

"Lia?"

The single word sounded like it had been spoken through a bullhorn, deafeningly loud and echoing. Cyrus, damn him! He was back in the bedroom and he couldn't see me like this! Something in me panicked at the thought, knew this wasn't normal, not even for the wolf I wasn't.

So, what did that make me?

Crazy, I thought, but couldn't say, any more than I could answer my boyfriend. I couldn't even think with a dozen car horns suddenly blaring in my ears. And that wasn't all.

A couple was arguing, their words loud and cutting, before a vase hit a wall, shattering in a tinkling of tiny fragments; another was making love, the woman soft and groaning, but getting steadily louder and louder; slots were ringing as some gamblers hit them early; people were talking; ice was dropping from an ice maker in a crash like a glacier cleaving; a police helicopter was flying overhead, the *chop, chop, chop* of its blades like hammer blows against my senses; some children were crying, others were laughing, and the boy on the stairs was singing his little song at what sounded like operatic levels. And I couldn't do anything but lay on the floor and writhe while it all cascaded over me.

And then cut out, just as fast as it had come, leaving my ears ringing and my mouth gaping open in shock.

"Lia? I'm making coffee. You want some?"

No, I thought, slowly getting back to my hands and knees, a snarl on my lips. I don't want any damned coffee and you know I don't. I want to be left alone!

"Lia?"

"No, thanks, I'm good!" The words came out surprisingly normally, even cheerful. But Cyrus hesitated, probably because they'd also come from somewhere near the floor, and normal people with lilts in their voices don't crawl around the bathroom tile!

But it was too late to do anything about it now, so I just held my breath, hoping he couldn't hear that, too, and would just go away. Go away and let me deal with this. Go away before you feel like you have to take measures that somebody isn't going to like. That somebody might just fight you over, and I don't want to fight you!

Please, *please* go away.

And, after a moment, he did. I could hear the previously silent footsteps on the carpeted floor getting fainter and fainter, along with the worried breaths he was taking—because he hadn't bought that, hadn't bought any of that. But he was back in the kitchen, rustling around making coffee, because he had to cover his story.

We were going to pretend that everything was normal, that I wasn't clawing at the walls and that he wasn't playing the part of my jailer. But he was. The kitchen was just on the other side of the wall from the bathroom, because they shared water lines, and he'd grab me before I got halfway across the living room. And he'd hear if I tried the window—

Damn it! I wasn't going to try the window! I wasn't trying anything! I was going to get a bath, before my lover decided that I really was mad!

And before I decided that I agreed with him.

I stood up, jerked off my shirt and bra, and tossed them on top of the commode, because there weren't a lot of options. The bathroom was as tiny and dated as the rest of this place, with Pepto Bismol pink tile and coordinating accessories, and a mirror that must have been original, because a quarter of the silver film had worn off. But there was plenty left to show me back my face, and while it was pale and my pupils looked like twice their usual size, there was no other difference.

At least, none that I could see.

But I could feel it, like I could feel the blood running through my body. Not just in my heartbeat or the pulse in my throat, but everywhere, every inch of veins or capillaries, all the way down to my fingertips. They pulsed oddly, like I'd just run a marathon, even though I hadn't done anything but to cling to Cyrus as we tore through town. My toes, too, throbbed in my boots, hard enough that it felt like they might tear through the leather.

I took my footwear off and felt somewhat better, then stripped down the rest of the way and—

And stopped abruptly, at what I saw when I peeled off my jeans.

My legs were bruised and battered up, but I'd had road rash that was worse after forgetting to wear my leathers. There was nothing that looked serious—except for a gauze pad the size of my hand on the outside of my left thigh. I frowned at it.

I hadn't noticed it at HQ, because I hadn't been in the head space to notice much of anything, but now I wondered how I'd missed it. Or how I'd gotten my jeans on over the thing, because it was held on by a metric ton of medical tape. I unwound it, taking much of the gauze along for the ride except for the bits soaked with blood and clinging to my flesh.

But eventually, they came off, too, and—

And then I stood there, staring at an ugly, raised wound in a very familiar shape.

I let my fingers trace the raised flesh as another shock radiated through my system. And tried to tell myself that I was wrong, that it was just a coincidence, that it wasn't what it looked like. But there was just no doubt about it. It was a bite, and not one made by a human mouth, but by something much bigger and more savage.

A Were bite.

Someone had bitten me.

Chapter Thirteen

Blood stained the fabric of the bandage, colored brown now with oxidation, but still fresh enough that I could smell it. It was recently spilled and yet the bite looked weeks, maybe months old. But it hadn't been there yesterday. And neither had the rips in my jeans right over top of it.

I guessed it shouldn't have surprised me. The Weres at the grow farm had wanted me to Change. And my rogue status—the name for clan-born who chose not to turn—was common knowledge. So, they bit me to ensure that I'd become the monster they'd wanted me to be.

But Neuri had saved me. For the first time in my life, I felt a swell of genuine gratitude for my life-long affliction. Followed quickly by a wash of sadness and longing so hard that it almost threw me to my knees.

"Lia? Sure about that coffee? It's almost ready."

I jerked and looked over my shoulder at the closed door. Cyrus was back again, and probably wondering why he wasn't hearing any water yet. Or if I'd gone completely crazy and was shivering in a corner, wild-eyed and slavering.

Which, frankly, wasn't that far from the truth.

"No, I—I'm fine. I'm starting the shower now."

I was true to my word, reaching up and turning on the water, and running it as hot as I could stand it. But I didn't get in. I just stayed where I was, staring at my wound, the one I'd evaded my whole life. And wishing . . .

What? That it had worked? Because in that case, I'd be dead now.

The Corps might have had to assign a couple dozen mages to take me down, if I'd turned into a creature like Colin. But if that's what it took, then that's what they'd have done. Overwhelming me with sheer numbers, and with enough magic to exhaust whatever reserve I had of my own. And Sedgewick, damn him, would probably have been there, pad in hand, taking notes on which spells worked the best and how long I lasted.

I should be on my knees, thanking every god I could think of that I'd been born the way I had!

But I wasn't on my knees, and I wasn't thankful. I was mourning, yet again, stupidly, uselessly, desperately, for something that I could never have. I thought I'd buried this, dealt with it, moved the hell on years ago.

Because that was the smart move. That was the only smart move. The other way . . . lay madness.

And yet, here I was, slumped against the wall and on the edge of sobs, feeling inadequate, incomplete, broken all over again. Mother had always said that I wasn't any of those, that I was exactly who I was meant to be. I'd known that she was lying, but I'd never guessed, not once, not until today, just how much.

I let my head come to rest on the slick tile by the shower. It didn't help, but at least I couldn't see the mirror anymore. And the flat human face I'd always secretly despised.

I couldn't see much of anything, with the heat from the shower having combined with the too-cold air conditioning to form enough steam to fill a Turkish bath.

It boiled around the tiny space, so thickly that it was hard to make out my hand in front of my face. That was a problem, because my eyes couldn't help my very confused brain to sort things out anymore. I was no longer sure what I would see if I looked down. A damp, bruised up, very human body or . . . something else.

I got into the shower to distract myself in the hard-hitting spray, because the one advantage Cyrus's place had was decent water pressure. But it didn't help, either. If anything, the steam was even worse in here, whiting out everything.

I lathered up, trying to wash the crazy off along with the sweat, blood and dirt of the past two days. But it felt weird; my hands were clumsy and the wrong shape, and my body was strangely unfamiliar under my touch. But, if I closed my eyes, I could almost see that other form, that other me.

Could see my hand gripping the bar of soap hard enough to have it squeeze up through my fingers, while slipping from human pale to the elongated, fur-covered paw of a predator. Weres, even normal ones, didn't really look like wolves, and not just because of the too intelligent eyes. They were far bigger, stronger and faster, but there was also a human elegance there, a sleekness not found in their animal counterparts, a strange, savage beauty.

My mother had had that. I had a flash of memory of her coming home from a run, the early morning mist wetting her fur. I'd only been a child, and she had been a huge, tawny wolf with brown in her mane and gold in her eyes. She'd curled around me, her tail tickling my nose, protective of her lone, disadvantaged cub. The one who couldn't Change.

I'd wondered then what I would have looked like, had I had her gift. Had we been able to run together, hunt together, do all the things that Were mothers normally did with their offspring, and which we'd never been able to share. I *could* see it now, that elusive, other me: I had brown fur maybe, or possibly black; I wasn't sure. But I could glimpse enough to know that I would have been duskier than her, sleeky dark and dangerous, a proper daughter for a brilliant, courageous mother. The kind she deserved—

Goddamnit!

I pried the mangled soap off my fingers, stripping them down with quick, savage motions, and got out of the bath. I fumbled into my clothes without even bothering to dry off, too busy pushing my thoughts back, pushing them down. I didn't want to know what I was missing. I didn't want to see! Just stop thinking, I told myself fiercely. Just stop everything!

I bent over and ran a comb through my mane of soggy hair, jerking out clumps along with the tangles, uncaring that it hurt. I wanted it to hurt, wanted it to bleed, wanted to have something, anything, to distract me. It sort of worked.

Until I pulled the boots back on. The heavy, steel toed things that I wore in my capacity as a war mage weren't designed to fit wolf paws, especially not the elongated feet of a Were. But I shoved them in anyway, because I didn't have those, no matter what my very confused brain currently thought.

The clunky footwear didn't go well with my "See Red Rock Canyon" T-shirt, which had started out as crimson as its namesake, but was now a washed out pink and a little girlie for the boots. And neither complimented my pale, freaked-out expression. But right then, I didn't care.

I didn't care about anything.

I went back into the living room in a temper.

"It's times like these I wish I had a car," Cyrus said as I came through the door.

The mundane phrase stopped me, catching me off guard. As did the fact that he wasn't waiting to pounce on me. He had one of the freezers open and was bent over it, looking for something.

"What?" I said. "Why?"

"For the food."

"What food?" I looked around, but the only comestible in sight was the coffee, sitting in a carafe on the counter. It didn't smell good. The familiar odor, usually so welcome, made my nose wrinkle in distaste.

But Cyrus didn't seem to notice.

"For the wake." He'd looked up from the freezer he'd been pawing through with an elongated package in his hands, wrapped in white butcher's paper. "We're going feed the boys first; it's still too close to a full moon to leave them hungry, and I don't want anyone doing anything stupid. Then we're going to see Jayden off according to Were custom, out in the desert. Sound like a plan?"

I just stood there. I had no problem with the plan. Jayden was *vargulf*, meaning that there were no cemeteries open to him, unless we buried him alongside humans. And I thought he'd prefer the wide-open spaces, the huge bowl of the sky, and the beauty of the desert to that. I was just a little surprised.

"That's really why you came back here? To get dinner?"

He nodded and patted the top of one of the freezers. "Bought these a month ago. With a bunch of young, growing mouths to feed, I have to take advantage of whatever sales I can find. Got a deal on pork the other week and loaded up."

He started digging a mountain of what looked like ribs out of the nearest chest and piling them on top of the other freezer like Jenga sticks. I watched him build a mountain of meat and continued to feel off balance. Because I hadn't thought that we were really here for food.

"Okay," I said and walked over to help, but I guess my tone must have given me away, because he shot me a glance.

"You thought I was taking you off for an interrogation."

I'd actually thought he was taking me away from other people in case I went nuts again. And after the last half hour or so, I wasn't sure that that hadn't been a plan. But interrogate sounded better.

"The thought had crossed my mind."

He went back to rooting around in the freezer. "Nope."

"Nope?"

"Nope. But this will take a while—as long as you need for it to. And you know where everything is. You want a nap, a snack," he gestured around, a bag of frozen peas in hand. "*Mi casa es tu casa.*"

I just stood there some more, frowning. "I don't want a nap."

"Okay." The peas were tossed aside and more pork hit the other freezer top.

"You're seriously not going to ask me anything?" I said.

He shot me a glance. "I know you, Lia."

"Meaning?"

"Meaning no way are you going to want to talk about this so soon. I might get something out of you eventually, when you've processed it, or I might not. But today?" He paused to examine something in a frost covered wrapper. "Not a chance."

I frowned harder. "You don't know that."

"Oh. So, you do want to talk?" He tossed the mystery item back into the cold and leaned against the freezer, waiting politely.

My frown tipped into a scowl, because no, I didn't. But I hated that he could read me so easily. "We do need to discuss one thing," I said, because it was true. And I might as well get it over with while I was already uncomfortable as hell, rather than ruin another day.

"Okay." He crossed his arms.

On a human, that would have been a closed off, defensive stance, but Were body language was different. In the Were world, even a fraction of a second could make the difference in a fight, like the time it took to uncross arms or legs before Changing. Tangling yourself up was therefore the Were equivalent of a house cat slowly blinking. It said I trust you; I know you; I'm willing to be vulnerable around you.

It made me feel even worse than I already did, but this needed to be said.

"You called Jace *canagan.*"

"So?" The big shoulders shrugged. "It's a term of endearment meaning 'little wolf'. You know that."

"It's a term of endearment in the *clans*. Jace is *vargulf*—"

"Says the woman who just went to the mat for him."

The posture hadn't changed, but the face was suddenly a lot more closed off.

I persisted anyway, because he needed to hear this. "Just because I don't want to see him ripped to pieces doesn't mean I don't know where he ranks—or doesn't rank—in clan order—"

"If you merely wanted to protect him, you could have done it with a spell," Cyrus pointed out, the dark eyes steady on mine. "You didn't."

"My magic was acting up. I wasn't thinking—"

"Oh, you were thinking. Just not with the human mind."

"You weren't even there!" I wasn't sure when Cyrus had joined the party at HQ, but it sure as hell hadn't been before the challenge was decided. Or else the red wolf would have had someone else's fangs in his throat.

"No, just missed it," he agreed.

"Then how can you—"

"I saw you," he said, and then moved so fast that his hands were cupping my face before I could twitch. "I don't claim to understand what happened back there, but I saw you—Accalia of Arnou, Laurentia of Lobizon's daughter. For the first time, I saw the wolf."

I stared up at him for a moment, until the room went swimmy and I couldn't see his face anymore. "I don't have a wolf. You know that—"

"I thought I knew that, just as you did. Thought you'd been denied that part of yourself. But it seems we were both wrong."

In a moment, I was going to cry, and I didn't want to cry. So, I wrenched away. "I don't want to talk about this."

He sighed. "No. Didn't think so."

"I want to talk about Jace!" I rounded on him. "I know you think you're helping him—"

"I am helping him."

"—but have you thought about where this goes? Sebastian already said no—he's not going to adopt those boys into Arnou. And if you think you can change his mind—"

"I don't. I know my brother."

"Then where does this lead, Cyrus?" I spread my arms. "You're going back to Arnou someday, and they can't follow you. And they're not likely to be welcomed by any other clan. If you get them used to this—"

"To what? Having full bellies and sleeping protected?"

"—to *belonging*, to being part of something again."

The idea of Cyrus making a little *vargulf* clan had seemed cute at one point. It didn't anymore. Not after what I'd seen, not after how vulnerable those boys were, how willing to die for a clan they didn't even have!

They were already clinging to him, craving the same thing I was, so I knew how badly it hurt. Because they might be able to Change, but that was only half of the equation for Weres. The other half was clan, and all the words that went with it—home, love, belonging, acceptance—all the things that he was dangling in front of their noses, but which they could never have.

He might think he was helping them; I knew differently.

"What happens when that's no longer true?" I demanded. "When the rug gets pulled out from under them again?"

"That isn't going to happen."

"How?" I stared at him. "How does that not happen? They're outcastes—

"Stop calling them that!"

The change was immediate and mercurial, as it often was with Weres. One second, Cyrus was calm and relaxed, as loose limbed as a cowboy leaning on a bar. The next, his eyes were flashing with a light that had nothing to do with the sun striping the room. And the small bones of his face, usually as still as anyone else's, were moving under the skin.

He caught it; his control was far too good to change when he didn't want to. But the fact that he'd had to stop himself, that he'd had to exert that much control, told me everything I needed to know. And then he confirmed it.

"I can't, Lia."

"Can't what?" I asked carefully.

"Abandon them. If Arnou won't take them, I'll make my own clan. But those boys need protection. You saw what almost happened today, and for no more reason than Jace existing—"

I stared at him in disbelief. "Yes, it did. And the same thing will happen to you if you keep this up. Cyrus, you can't—"

I stopped, because a muscle in his jawbone had just come out, the one that said that his wolf wasn't the only stubborn one. And because I didn't know how to get through to him. He'd spent so many years in Arnou, as a virtual prince of the Were world, that he didn't know how to be anything else.

It simply hadn't occurred to him that he couldn't merely waltz into the Circle's HQ with a dozen Were guards on duty, dragging another *vargulf* along. Or that he couldn't do anything else, either, that even partially intersected the Were community. That he was a leper, an outcast, a pariah, who damned sure couldn't make his own clan!

That needed the consent of the entire Were council, a body he would literally be torn to pieces before he ever reached. Not that it mattered; they wouldn't speak to him anyway. No one in power would except for his brother, who couldn't admit it. He knew that; he'd been raised knowing that. And yet, even after all this time, he still didn't understand.

I was beginning to wonder if he ever would.

"Next time you need something from the Circle, call me," I finally said, because he already knew what I'd been thinking. It was all over his face, but his voice was light when he answered.

"I tried. For some reason, you weren't answering your phone."

I suddenly remembered the shattered thing that Caleb had tossed at me. I hoped he'd taken out the sim card first. "The growers did the same thing to it as to my bike."

He winced. "Ouch. Okay, help me load all this up, and we'll swing by and get you another one before we eat."

Chapter Fourteen

We did not swing by and get another phone. I had an old one at the house that would do in a pinch, and no intention of lugging a crap ton of frozen pork through the Apple store. It was crazy enough to be speeding through Vegas with it sticking out of saddlebags and threatening to fall from the grocery sacks I was clutching in my lap.

I didn't care. I was too busy doing my impression of a dog hanging its head out of a car window—something I totally understood suddenly. Because there was a whole new world I'd never imagined, just waiting to be discovered.

It started out with the usual city smells, just ramped up to the point that it felt like they were slapping me in the face: baking asphalt and exhaust; hot grease billowing out of the open door of a fast-food restaurant; a spilled soda in a gutter, its sickly-sweet aroma sizzling in the heat; and garbage, sweat, and cigarettes—the latter all from the same car, which seriously needed cleaning out. But it got weird fast, because the car . . . *wasn't there*. It had passed by minutes ago, with a ghostly outline flickering in front of my eyes that we rode straight through.

The same was true of half of the people I saw. Some were in the present, reeking of suntan lotion and pool chemicals, their skin glistening under the still punishing heat of the afternoon sun. But others were like the smelly car: hazy, ghostly figures from the past that formed a crowd so thick that it looked like a festival had descended onto the city.

Most of the scent-people were dim, with the traces that formed them being hours or even days old. But others were almost as rich and vibrant as the flesh and blood counterparts they walked alongside or darted through the middle of. I blinked furiously as we zipped past, unsure at times who was real and who was a scent memory.

And wondered how the hell Weres kept them all straight!

"You okay?" Cyrus asked, probably because I was sniffing up a storm right by his ear.

"Uh huh." It was as much as I could manage with the entire last week or two of Vegas street traffic all fighting for my attention. Something that went from amazing to overwhelming real freaking fast.

"Hold on, we're almost there."

I nodded, too overwhelmed to speak, and he put on a burst of speed, cut through the lower level of a parking garage, and headed into calmer side streets.

My arms were half frozen by the time we finally arrived back home, my thighs were burning from clenching the seat, and my shirt was drenched with sweat. I was never so glad to see my driveway in my life—right up until I noticed the smoke billowing out of my back yard. A lot of it.

"Shit," I said, trying to disentangle myself from the packages of pig.

That was easier said than done, and before I managed it, Caleb showed up. "You read my mind," he said, eyeing the haul. "But I have a grocery order coming with hamburgers, sausages, chicken . . ."

"It won't go to waste," Cyrus assured him, swinging off the bike and grabbing one of the sacks.

I'd have given him the rest, too, but didn't get a chance. I was mugged by a starving mob of teens a moment later, who denuded the bike and then streamed around the house, their spoils held high above their heads like a triumphant army. Leaving me looking pointedly at Caleb.

"What's going on in the backyard?"

"Relax, we're having a barbeque—"

"I don't have a barbeque."

"—and what back yard? It's a patch of desert."

"It's a xeriscape," I told him, climbing off the bike.

"You good?" Cyrus asked, regarding me narrowly.

"Yep."

The suspicious expression didn't change, probably because I was lying. I wondered if he could smell it, like I could smell his unease. It radiated off him in waves, as hot as the sun off the pavement, as confusing as my own emotions that kept tripping over themselves. His concern was welcome, but not—I didn't need a babysitter! Annoying but not—how nice to have somebody in my life who gave a damn. Worrying—because if Cyrus was concerned, should I be, too?

Probably, but I was too busy getting distracted by a thousand different things, most of which were completely irrelevant to anything at all. But my brain was unused to this amount of sensory input, and had no way to sort it all out. And now that we were no longer moving, it felt like the neighborhood was folding in on me, an origami structure of pale blue, stucco and desert brown, trying to force all its varied sights and scents down my throat, all at once.

I could tell that Caleb had had corned beef for lunch—with Thai chilies and spicy horseradish mayo—making my nose twitch; that someone inside the house was making lemonade, probably with the soon-to-be-too-old lemons I'd bought for the purpose a week ago; that the guy with the Goldendoodle down the road had let his dog shit on my lawn again and not bothered to clean it up; and that someone else badly needed an oil change, the burning smell searing a fiery line though my senses, causing me to gasp and my eyes to water—

Until Cyrus abruptly bent over, arms full of pork, and kissed me. And for some reason, that simple touch brought me back to myself, like a dash of cold water in the face. He took his time, not caring any more than I did about the melting ice dampening our shirts, because they were already wet anyway. And then even more so when he grabbed me around the back, one armed, and dragged me into him, his mouth plundering mine, deepening the kiss until I forgot about everything else, until I forgot my own name.

"Better?" he asked me, after a moment, his breath in my face, mingling with my own.

"Better." And this time, I meant it.

Cyrus nodded and headed through the front door, bearing what was left of our haul, and I stood there, staring after him like a lovesick teenager and not caring.

Caleb cleared his throat.

"Still in the honeymoon phase, huh?"

"Guess so." Only I thought that term was bullshit. The stumbling, fumbling, constantly pissing someone off by not knowing their triggers phase was more like it. Cyrus and I had never had the honeymoon, both being too damaged to flow easily into a relationship of any kind. Even the I-just-want-to-hold-someone thing that we'd started out as. The sex had been great from the beginning, but the rest . . .

Was much better now.

I followed Caleb around the side of the house, after the kids, while he took the opportunity to insult my still newish house.

"This is not a xeriscape," he informed me.

"You live in a condo," I pointed out, a sprawling, uber chic, masculine steel and glass thing overlooking the Strip. His downstairs neighbor was a Saudi sheik's younger son who was 'discovering himself'; the gal above him, when she was in town, was a fairly well-known film star. Caleb did not do a lot of grubbing in the dirt.

"That doesn't mean I don't know how," he informed me, when I pointed this out. "And xeriscapes have stuff in them "Cacti, fountains, attractive piles of rocks—"

"Is that the official name? Attractive piles of rocks?"

"—none of which did I find back there."

"I have a cactus," I said defensively.

"That sad thing in a pot on the back stoop? You do know you have to water them occasionally, right?"

"I water it!"

I was pretty sure.

"When? Last summer?"

"You know, houses don't come together all at once. I'm still in the process of—" I began, and then stopped dead as my back yard came into view.

It was normally a boring bit of dirt with a small tree next to the neighbor's fence on the far side. There was nothing else back there except for a tool shed which I had yet to stock with tools because it had acquired spiders. And a nice view of the desert from the rear and left of the house.

It was kind of minimalist, but I liked it. It was at the back corner of the subdivision, meaning that, unless somebody developed the land behind me, I could enjoy the feeling of living in wide open spaces but with all the advantages of the city. Eventually, I planned a few stone pathways, maybe some more cacti, possibly a fountain . . . and to fill in the large scars that had just been carved into my dirt.

"What did you *do*?" I demanded, turning on Caleb.

"No need to thank me," he said, clapping my back.

"I wasn't planning on it!"

"We'll spread the dirt back out when we're done. It'll look the same—"

"It will not!"

"—or maybe better. And in the meantime, we have somewhere to cook!" He yelled the latter over his shoulder, having jogged off to tend to the nearest smoking trench.

There were two of them, each about six feet long, carved slap into the middle of my xeriscape. There was a new mountain of dirt, from the trenches I assumed, toward the back of the lot, and coals burning merrily at the bottoms of the pits. There were also grates piled haphazardly on top, which worried me.

I did not own any grates.

And now neither did anyone else in the neighborhood, I assumed, because said grates looked like they'd been sourced from all over. There were a handful of different shapes that belonged on barbeques, several that appeared to have been ripped off of firepits, and one that resembled the gate of a decorative iron fence that a neighbor had recently put up. I glanced around apprehensively.

The last thing I needed was a posse coming to retrieve their stolen stuff. But all I saw was dust, waves of heat coming off the blacktop, and a lone, whirlybird lawn sprinkler wobbling its way around and around Mrs. Kovacs's flower bed. She was gonna get a ticket for that; it wasn't anywhere near seven P.M.

Maybe I could trade her misdemeanors, I thought, eyeing her missing gate as Sophie emerged from the back door of the house.

She'd changed from the khakis and blue eyelet top she'd been wearing earlier into a more climate appropriate set of white shorts and a knitted green and white tank. Her red hair was up in a messy bun and her fair skin was flushed. The latter might have been because of the heat, or the fact that she was carrying a gigantic pot.

It was my biggest one, the kind used for stews and mass quantities of soup, and looked like it weighed a ton. But she made it to the grill, putting it down with a thump before anyone could help.

Chris and Jen, who had been spreading out charcoal in the other trench, wandered over to see what was going on. Aki likewise showed up to peer into the pot, and looked disappointed that it contained only water.

"Cyrus said we gotta boil the ribs before they hit the barbeque," Sophie panted at me. "Or they'll take forever to cook."

"They'll take forever to boil, too, if that's all you got," a man said.

I didn't remember his name, but he was one of the guys who'd been with us in the desert the other day. He had the typical overgrown Were haircut, in his case a shock of blue-black that was falling into his eyes, and half covering the jagged scar on one olive-colored cheek. It takes a lot to mark a Were so deep that his natural healing abilities couldn't compensate, but that wound must have laid his face open to the bone.

An expensive healer might have been able to smooth it out some, but I didn't think that was in this guy's budget. He was wearing a wife beater and a pair of old jeans, the kind that were clean enough but discolored at the knees and hem as if he hadn't always had a way to wash them. The lack of ready access to a shower might explain the cloud of cheap cologne that wreathed him like a halo, and caused my new, overeager senses to almost gag.

That was weird for a Were, especially one who smelled clean enough underneath it, but I guessed old habits die hard. He was also older than the rest, maybe mid-twenties, and raw bone thin. But he sounded like he knew something about food.

"Used to work in a kitchen," he added, accepting my scrutiny without comment, and I nodded.

"No problem," Caleb told Sophie. "We can bring out some more."

"We're going to need a lot," she said doubtfully. "And this is the only big one I could find. Where do you keep the rest?"

"The rest?" I asked, because she was looking at me.

"Of your pots."

"Why would I need multiple stew pots?"

"You mean this is the only one you have?" Caleb asked, sounding surprised for some reason.

"Who has more than one stew pot?"

"I do—"

"You never even cook."

"No, but they come in those sets from the store, right?" I looked at him blankly. "You know, the kind with five or six different sized pots and matching lids?"

"Okay? But what does that have to do with—"

"But I only use the frying pans, to cook a couple eggs in the morning or a grilled cheese once in a while, and eventually, they get scratched. Then I have to buy another set, and the big ones just accumulate—"

"Another set . . . of what?" I asked, confused.

"Of pots."

"You buy another set of pots every time your frying pan gets scratched?"

"Of course."

I looked at him some more.

"You can't use a scratched pan, Lia," he said condescendingly. "The nonstick coating can flake off into your food."

Before I could even try to respond to that, I heard a commotion coming from the direction of the house. I looked up to see Sophie, who must have left while we were talking, leading Kimmie this way by the hand. Or dragging her might be more accurate.

Kimmie had also changed from the jeans and button up shirt she'd been wearing into a cute pair of cut off overalls. They were embroidered with different sizes of daisies and matched her yellow t-shirt and the couple of daisy pins in her braids. She was bright, sunny and cheerful, except for her expression.

"Just eight or ten," Sophie was saying. "Like that one."

She pointed to the pot of water, now sitting on what had once been somebody's firepit grille, and just managing to avoid falling into the hole.

"In a line down the grates," she added, when Kimmie just stood there.

"I can't—"

"Sure you can. It's easy. They're just pots—"

But Kimmie wasn't finding it easy. Her head was shaking and she was backing away. "No, I can't. They said not to—"

"They aren't here," Sophie said patiently. "And we signed up for this, right? To start using our abilities? We have to begin somewhere."

"Not with her," Chris said, scowling. "She's the weak link; you know that."

"Shut up!" Sophie said. "She's fine."

But Kimmie did not look fine. She was backing up, and appeared to agree with Chris. "No, I'll screw it up. I screw everything up—"

"You don't," Sophie said, encouraging her. "That's them talking, the teachers and so-called therapists—"

"I can't, all right? I can't!"

"—acting like we were about to go off like a bomb ever since we were children. But they're not here. Nobody's here—"

"Hey," I said, because Kimmie clearly didn't care who was here. Kimmie was starting to panic again, with the whites showing all around her eyes and her head shaking furiously.

"No! I'm a good girl. I'm a good girl!"

"It's okay," Sophie said, finally realizing that easing Kimmie out of her phobia wasn't going well. "It's no big deal, Kim—"

But Kimmie was no longer listening. "I'm good, I'm good, I'm good, *I'm good*—"

And crap, I thought, because the pitch on that last phrase was practically a scream. I readied a knock out spell, and glanced around to see if there were any knives out here. There was one, along with a pair of firepit tongs, both of which were disappeared by the scarred Were before I could so much as flinch.

Guess he'd heard about what happened yesterday.

And what was about to happen today, because the mismatched grilles had started to tremble, all along the two lines. I didn't understand why until Jen gave a cry and stumbled back, and I saw the burning coals underneath them begin to rise, making the trenches glow like gashes staring straight into hell. And then spill over the top to scorch the sand, like lava flowing up from the earth.

Chris wasted no time jumping acrobatically out of the way, covering as much territory in one go as a transformed Were. And then Aki grabbed Jen and disappeared, only to reappear with her over by the house. I started to call for everyone else to do likewise, since burning coals were beginning to fall off their mountains and bounce across the landscape.

But, just as fast as it had started, it was over. And I found out what Sophie's special talent was, and why she was the glue that held this crazy group together. But it had nothing to do with magic.

"It's okay, it's okay," she murmured, enveloping a shaking Kimmie in a tight hug. "This is my fault, all my fault. I shouldn't have pushed you—"

"I'm a good girl! I'm a good girl!" It was still a scream, but wheezy now, as if she'd started to hyperventilate.

"Yes, you are." Sophie's arms tightened, and her eyes closed. "Yes, you are."

Chapter Fifteen

I stayed outside for a while, despite it being approximately the temperature of hell, to help cook some veggies for a pasta salad that someone was making. I didn't think that the Were with the scar, whose name was Danny, needed the help, as he seemed pretty handy around a grill. But I wanted to give Sophie some time to get Kimmie to bed.

Apparently, duplication was tiring, not to mention remembered trauma.

"Sooooo, what's the deal with them?" Danny asked, nodding after the girls.

I flipped over some zucchini, to give it those nice diamond shaped grill marks. And wondered how to explain mage politics to a guy who probably knew nothing about them. It was almost as hard as explaining the Were world to an outsider, and I'd never had much luck with that.

"They're the human equivalent of *vargulfs*," I finally said, and saw his eyebrows rise.

"Didn't think humans had those."

"Every society has outcasts," I said, before I thought. But he only nodded thoughtfully.

"Suppose so. But I heard they lock them up, not throw them out. And try to reintegrate them?"

"Sometimes." I decided not to mention the success rate on that.

"Then they do better by them than the council does by us."

"Sebastian is working on that," I said, looking up from basting some squash.

Only to meet cynical dark eyes that suddenly looked a lot older than his years. "Yeah. Good luck to him."

"It's hard to undo hundreds of years of mistakes," I pointed out. Because Sebastian really was trying. But he had about a thousand other things competing for his time, and the council was completely intransigent on the subject of *vargulfs*.

"Mistakes?" A dark eyebrow raised. "Unusual word choice for a clan wolf."

"Yeah, well, I never was my clan's favorite daughter."

"So I heard. Guess they don't like the company you're keeping."

"Naw. I was on the outs way before that."

He laughed suddenly, and it changed his whole face. "You're not what I expected."

"And what did you expect?"

He flipped over some onions. "Dunno. But Lobizon and Arnou? That's high tier stuff. Not the kind of woman I'd expect to be slumming with a bunch of *vargulfs*."

"There's nothing wrong with *vargulfs*—"

"Tell that to King Sebastian."

"I have!" It was a little sharper than normal, because Sebastian wasn't a king and Danny knew it.

"Then tell him again, because nothing is happening. Except that a bunch of Weres feel empowered to attack a kid in the middle of the Corps' HQ, and nobody did anything about it . . . except for you."

I frowned. "Sebastian can't fight every battle at the same time. Not and win. He's prioritizing the war right now because he has to, but afterward—"

"Afterward may be too late. A shake up like this is the best time to transform a society, when some catastrophe has already cracked its foundations and people are open to change. But the social lines will solidify again soon enough; that's just how people are. And who knows when we'll have another chance."

I frowned some more, because that had sounded a little too practiced to be the first time he'd made that speech. I wondered what the guys were talking about among themselves, when Cyrus wasn't around to hear. And then I wondered if they didn't have a point.

Because this war had to mean something. Too many people had died for everything to just go back to the status quo. Especially when the status quo sucked.

But to my surprise, Danny didn't push it any further. He seemed pretty Zen overall, which was what I needed right then. Politics could wait until I wasn't as high as a kite.

We slowly baked together under the hot sun, while slathering olive oil onto more zucchini, squash, red peppers and onions. They started to be seriously fragrant, and I realized that I hadn't eaten since . . . I wasn't sure. I stole a zucchini slice.

"Needs salt," I told him.

He passed the salt.

"They doing a mayo-based sauce or what?" I asked, after a minute of chewing.

"Balsamic vinaigrette, with a little mustard and a little mayo mixed in." He gave me a small dish from the folding table where he'd parked his utensils, and where he'd been concocting a sauce. I dunked the remaining zucchini in it and—

"Bitchin'."

He grinned. "My old restaurant used to make it that way."

"You must have started young." He didn't look much over early twenties now.

"Twelve," he confirmed. "It was family owned. And I was rolling silverware and refilling condiments even before then."

I didn't say anything, because talking about the past with a *vargulf* could be iffy. He shot me a look, as if he knew what I was thinking. "It's okay," he said. "You can ask."

"It's your story. You tell me what you want, if you want."

The raised eyebrows were back. "Most people would wanna know who they had in their house."

"And Cyrus doesn't know you?"

I got the cynical look again. "His standards might be different from yours."

I ate another piece of zucchini. "Okay."

"My parents owned a restaurant. It was profitable. One of the clan leaders decided he wanted it, and offered them a price. They turned him down.

"They wanted to leave it to me. That's why they were training me, so I'd know how to run it. I was never much in school, but I could cook. They figured it was my legacy.

"But the next thing we knew, my father was brought up on charges. They said he raped this girl. I knew it was bullshit; my old man worked twelve hours days and practically worshipped my mother. Plus, he was a straight arrow, as much as they come. He didn't have it in him.

"But they said it anyway."

"What happened?" I asked, pretty sure I already knew.

"Her family challenged. Dad was old—I was a miracle baby—but they paired him with her brother. Young and fit and ready to tear my old man's throat out. So, I took the challenge instead."

He touched his cheek. His wavy dark hair was just past his shoulders, but not up in a ponytail or manbun, or any other concession to the heat. I guessed he preferred it loose to cover his scar.

"I lost. Knew more about cooking than fighting. I'd have gotten myself killed, but the girl's family intervened at the last minute. Said they'd take exile."

"Yeah. Because a death would have to be reported to the council," I said dryly.

I suspected that was why Colin's clan had kicked everyone out who they wanted to get rid of, and then murdered them. Because nobody cared what happened to *vargulfs*. Or, apparently, how anyone got that way.

That kind of thing was what Sebastian was trying to change, and why Cyrus had been willing to choose exile to get his brother into power. This wasn't only about the war; it was about restoring some kind of order to the Were community. The war had just provided a pretext.

Danny nodded slowly, with the same calm, steady motions he seemed to use for everything. A red pepper had sufficiently charred, developing a blackened crust all over, and he expertly started scraping off the burned bits with the side of his tongs. They fell away into the fire, revealing the sweet, red flesh beneath.

"Yeah. So, just like that, we were out. And once you're out, the clan bank can call in any debts you owe. Like our mortgage. Dad had no choice but to sell the restaurant or lose it—to the same Were who'd initially wanted it, at half the price."

I didn't ask what had happened to his parents afterward. I was pretty sure I knew that, too. A shock like that at their age, and knowing that their son was now condemned along with them? It wasn't hard to guess.

And I supposed I was right, because he didn't elaborate. "After everything, I came out here. Hoping for a new start, but it's the same story everywhere. You're in or you're out, and when you're out, nobody wants to know you. Nobody cares. Until Cyrus came along, and . . ." he shook his head, looking up at the house. "I don't know how he does it. But it's like he makes you believe again, you know?"

I glanced back at the house, where my boyfriend was presumably organizing the chaos. "Yeah," I said. "I know."

* * *

I finally went inside, carrying the platter of grilled veggies and feeling half grilled myself, and barely managed to fit through the door. I found Aki dicing more peppers and onions at the kitchen table, Jen and Cyrus adding hot sauce to something they were concocting on the stove, and a bunch of Weres—like, entirely too many Weres—helping Chris to bring in the grocery order that had just arrived. And laughing over the sheer amount of food, because Caleb was nothing if not generous.

He didn't like it to get out, but his family came from wealth. Like wealth-wealth, the kind with multiple houses and private planes and servants to do the cooking. Which probably explained why he had no idea how to buy pots.

I danced backward when the Weres started tossing a cantaloupe around like a basketball, and looked for a safe place to put down my platter. But I didn't see one. Every surface was covered in dishes in the middle of prep; the fridge, when I finally elbowed someone aside and got it open, was stuffed full to running over; and I couldn't even ask anyone to take the thing from me, because a radio was blaring as loud as a club.

Aki yelled something and I tried to pass him the dish, only to find him attempting to give me one. We shrugged at each other, a guy with dreads passed in between us and popped a cookie in my mouth, and another guy muscled in with a ladder, I guessed to fix the flickering overhead light. And I decided that my help was not needed here.

I passed off the tray to the first Were I could find with empty hands, and made my escape into the hall.

And found it to be an oasis of calm compared to the kitchen. It wasn't exactly quiet, with the sound of the radio still loud enough to shake the floorboards, but it was empty. And dim, because I had a bulb out here, too.

I took a moment to get my breath back, and to eat my cookie. It was peanut butter—not a favorite—but my stomach didn't care. My stomach demanded more after the first bite as it simply hadn't with the zucchini.

And then roared at me to hurry up, in a way that had me staring down in concern.

I finished the whole thing, despite the fact that it was almost as big as my hand, then licked my fingers clean as I made my way into the living room.

Only to discover that it had been transformed, too—into a dorm.

"Hey."

Someone greeted me, but I didn't see who since my nice living room, with the bay window and the tasteful paint job, was now a shanty town of draped blankets, sleeping bags, and cots. There were also a few inflatable mattresses scattered about, along with more blankets, pillows, and personal items, denoting people's individual spaces, which they'd already carved out. And they'd carved out a lot.

It looked like a dozen or so were camping in just this one room, which made me worried about the rest of the house. Although nobody was in residence except for the young blond Were from the camping trip. Noah, I thought, dredging up the name after finding him reclining on a sleeping bag and playing with a beat-up Switch.

He raised a hand when I peered over the blanket delineating his turf, and I raised one back.

"She's in the bathroom," he said, before I could ask.

"Kimmie?"

"Both of them. Her and the redhead."

"Thanks."

He sniffed. "You smell like peanut butter."

"There's cookies in the kitchen."

"Really?" he thought about it. Then made the decision that I would have. "Not worth it."

"Good call."

"The bath in the bedroom, not the hall," he clarified, as I started to backtrack. "The rest of us are using the hall one."

I nodded and made my way toward the master, stopping to glance in the guestroom on the way. It and the room next door, which I intended for an office if I ever got around to buying furniture, should have been empty. But instead, they were filled with more sleeping bags and air mattresses, with the office also having a mound of backpacks piled high against one wall.

I had no idea why.

I had a handful of students, and most of the Weres had homes.

So why was I suddenly running a Motel 6?

"They'll be gone in a few days," Cyrus said, coming up behind me. I hadn't said anything as I made my way through the kitchen, but of course he'd smelled me. "But Jace needs them right now, and I didn't have room—"

"It's okay. Where is he?"

Cyrus rolled his eyes. "Where the food is, where else?"

That explained why Cyrus was wearing one of my aprons and carrying around a sauce-covered wooden spoon. He'd positioned himself where he knew the boy would be, just in case. It made me love him a little more, which I hadn't thought was possible.

"Didn't see him in the kitchen," I said, although I could have easily missed him.

"He's doing laundry with a couple of the guys. It seemed to help him to have something to do . . ." Cyrus trailed off, probably because I'd stiffened.

It was a stupid reaction and I knew it. The laundry wasn't haunted except in my messed-up head. For everyone else, it was just a place to wash clothes and they'd needed one.

What was he supposed to say?

But it bothered me, like having all these people here bothered me. It shouldn't have. I'd grown up with all kinds of people, some related, some not, roaming in and out of the house all the time, and triple or quadruple that during a time of mourning. I'd been almost buried under Weres after my mother's passing, bringing more casseroles than dad and I could ever hope to eat, touching my face and hands and arms, and telling me how sorry they all were. Right up until the clan's brutes arrived to forcibly Change me, when they'd suddenly disappeared.

The memory of that betrayal, and betrayal it had been, whether they agreed with the clan leaders or not, still hurt. I'd been vulnerable and grief-stricken, and they were my mother's friends and family—*my* friends and family. They should have protected me. But they'd vanished into the mist instead, leaving dad and I to fight for our lives alone.

Maybe that explained why all this was making me antsy. Maybe I didn't trust Cyrus's new "clan." Or maybe it was my failure the last time I had students in the house that was troubling me.

I wondered if the washer still had dried blood in the crevasses. I wondered if we'd gotten it all, or if traces would still be discernable to a Were's nose. I wondered if they were able to smell him, the boy I'd killed.

I didn't know. I just knew that I was about to come out of my skin suddenly, and that I wanted them gone. I wanted them all gone!

"I'm sorry," Cyrus said, sensing something from me. "Some of the guys had started a load before I noticed—"

"It's okay," I told him, and turned toward the bedroom again, but he pulled me back.

"We shouldn't have come back here," he said, his voice rough. "I should have kept you at my place."

"The funeral is tonight. They need you—"

"You need me. But I thought . . . maybe it would help you, too, to be around people."

"I'm around people all the time."

"No, you work all the time. You don't go anywhere, Lia. You come over to my place or we come here, but otherwise—"

"We went to Zion a month ago."

"Because I practically kidnapped you. I thought it would do you good."

"It did. It was fun."

He took my face between his hands, and they were so big that they cradled my whole head in warmth. Like looking up into brown eyes that were suddenly heartbreakingly sad. "I wish I knew how to take the pain away. Knew what to say to make it better."

"You don't have to say anything. This," I covered one of his hands with my own. "This is good."

"I can have them hit up a laundromat," he whispered, his forehead coming down to rest against mine. "I didn't before because the clothes were already wet—"

"And because you didn't know how to tell them that you livc with a crazy woman?"

He enveloped me in a hug then, holding my head against his chest. "You're not crazy, and I don't know too many women who wouldn't be on my ass right now, for dropping a couple dozen houseguests on her unannounced."

"It's clan custom," I said looking up. "Did you really think I'd say no?"

"No, but I'd planned to clear it with you first. But nobody at the damned Corps called me until this morning, and then all they said was that you needed a ride. I thought you'd left your bike somewhere, not that—"

"I was drugged off my ass?"

He nodded. "That's why I took Jace, to kill two birds with one stone. I didn't realize there was a problem until I saw the condition of your bike, right before all hell broke loose."

I winced. "Sorry."

"It's not your fault. Those bastards should have called me as soon as you were brought in. I'm supposed to be on the contact list for emergencies—"

"You are on the list. In fact, you are the list."

"Then why the hell—"

"Sedgewick. Maybe Hargroves, too. They didn't know what they were dealing with, and didn't want anybody causing trouble until they figured it out."

I stopped there, because I'm not a fool.

But Cyrus's jaw clenched anyway. I felt it against my head. "And what, exactly, would I be causing trouble about, if they were just trying to help you?"

Damn. Sometimes I really wished I had a dumber boyfriend. "Cyrus—"

He pulled away so that he could see my eyes. "What was the plan, Lia, if you'd turned into something like Colin? What were they prepared to do?"

"I liked it better when you were tiptoeing around my feelings back at the apartment," I told him honestly.

"Answer the question."

Yeah, only I didn't want to do that, because the atmosphere in here was already getting hard to breathe. Cyrus was shedding power, trying to avoid a Change, but he was losing because he'd already figured out the answer and his beast didn't like it. No, scratch that, his beast was furious, I thought, as the broken light bulb came back on and then abruptly shattered, raining down shards of glass everywhere.

And shit.

Chapter Sixteen

"They don't get to decide that," Cyrus growled, his voice so full of wolf speak that I could barely understand him. "They don't get to decide *anything* to do with you!"

I put a hand on his arm, a light touch because his beast would not appreciate restraint right now. He accepted it, although the muscles under my palm were bunched and tense. But not Changing.

Not yet.

"You saw what Colin could do, and that was without magic," I said softly, trying to diffuse things. "They couldn't risk the equivalent of a nuclear bomb going off downtown—"

"And did they think about what they risked from Arnou if something happened to you? What they risked from *me*?"

I gazed up at him. The hall was dark, but his face was fierce. He hadn't Changed, yet I could see the wolf, and I didn't need extra senses to do it.

But right then, I had them, and my beast liked what she saw. Liked the lean lines of his face, both that of the human and of the hulking predator who hovered just out of reach. Liked the bared teeth, the very non-human expression that called to her, that showed his ferocity. Liked his anger.

Liked it so much that she slid against him, not the man but the wolf, twining her body around his and calling him out, drawing him forth. For a moment, I could almost see the two of them, the dark, red eyed female, sleek and savage, and the massive, black and tan Alpha male. They were circling each other, taking the other's scent, curious but cautious.

Because they'd never met, had they?

The idea floored me for a moment. Cyrus and I had been lovers, off and on, for years now, starting out in Jersey shortly after he broke with Arnou, and continuing on for most of my time in Vegas. Our wolves should have met long ago, only they couldn't have, could they?

Not until now, when whatever I'd taken had brought mine closer to the surface.

And they were taking full advantage.

He was larger than her, by a good deal. Cyrus's family were big men and they made big wolves, dwarfing the punier clans. Such things shouldn't matter when choosing a leader, but Weres were no less superficial than humans, and Sebastian's stature had definitely helped his chances.

As Cyrus's was doing now.

But my wolf was holding her own, undisturbed by his size. Maybe because whatever she lacked in bulk she made up for in speed, easily evading his attempts to get closer. But then circling around and coming back, almost as if she was teasing him.

She was dark lightning, and he was quickly confused. And then intrigued, unsure why he couldn't catch her. I had the impression that she was laughing at him, or maybe with him, because his befuddlement quickly changed into something else.

He liked this one.

And apparently, she liked him back, too, because the next moment, I felt the two heavily muscled bodies come into contact once more, this time pushing against each other, testing the other out. Their claws were sheathed, but that could change in an instant and they both knew it. Yet they apparently thought the reward was worth the risk.

She liked how big he was, how solid. Liked that she wasn't sure she could take him. Wanted to try.

For his part, he seemed fascinated by her scent, butting his head against her, dragging it along her fur. She snarled a warning when he got too close to her neck, and he bared his teeth in return. Yet he backed off, unwilling to allow this to descend into a fight.

He liked her. He wanted her. He tried to mount her, but she growled and slipped out from under. She wasn't having it, yet she looked at him over her shoulder, a come-hither look that could have been playful or a trap.

Or possibly both.

I wasn't even sure, and he was just as confused, with the great face displaying an almost human-like puzzlement as he stared after her. Not that it lasted for long. Because Cyrus in either guise was a take-charge type of guy, in the habit of going straight after what he wanted.

And he wanted her.

He bounded after her, in whatever metaphysical plane they were occupying, and she evaded again—but halfheartedly this time. More as if she was putting up a show than genuinely trying to avoid him. But then, she didn't have to.

"Lia—" Cyrus said, half strangled. And then stopped, as if he didn't know what he was asking.

I did, but I couldn't give him what he wanted, couldn't release her, couldn't manifest my alter ego and set us both free. Couldn't do anything but shiver and shake against him, feeling his beast's frustration as if it were my own. It wanted, it hungered, it *liked* this one, the darkly dangerous predator at its side. And that was rare among Weres, who often found that their beasts were not compatible even though the humans were.

It led to all kinds of trouble, including married couples breaking up because their beasts couldn't get along. Or resulted in strange, blended families when the original couple wasn't willing to part, and had to invite their beast's preferred partners to join them, something that rarely worked out. It was why some clans required both prospective pairs to be compatible before a marriage was allowed, as there was often at least some disconnect that needed to be resolved.

But not here.

And it was tragic, because our alter egos didn't understand. They weren't human and didn't think as humans do. They saw, they approved, they wanted . . .

And discovered that they couldn't have.

I heard Cyrus's wolf howl in my mind, a cry of pain-filled yearning. She was the one he'd waited for, hungered for, ached for; why wouldn't she come to him? Why wouldn't she Change?

And she didn't understand any more than he did. Syndromes meant nothing to her, just human words for the cage she had never been able to escape. But she tried suddenly, as she hadn't in years, throwing herself against the bars, battering them with her anger, her loneliness, her pain. Gouging them with claws she'd never used, because they weren't real, any more than she was.

Just a phantom . . .

"She's real enough," Cyrus whispered against my hair, but it didn't help, wasn't true.

Neuri was an evil, wicked thing, destroying my other half before she was even born, but leaving her spirit to haunt me. And now she would haunt him as well, with the knowledge of what we could have had. A perfectly matched pair, so rare, so prized, and so not to be.

"You deserve better," I told him shakily, because it was true. Better than a fucked-up war mage with PTSD who didn't even know who—or what—she was.

A finger tilted up my face. "There is no one better," he said savagely. "There never has been. There never will be."

I searched the strange, whiskey-colored eyes. In sunlight, they were simply brown, with a bit of variation near the pupil with a brighter color that was almost, but not quite, gold. But here in the darkened hallway, where they made their own light as his power rose, they were burnt umber and deep copper, blending into an almost sherry-red, and appeared completely sincere.

Hell, they probably were sincere; he probably believed that this could work, as I once had. But it couldn't. This was worse than when another Were's wolf didn't like you—far worse.

Because ours did, and now they knew it and so did we. And, suddenly, that half of a life didn't feel like enough anymore. Not even close.

How could I say I loved him and condemn him to this? Our beasts were part of us in a way I hadn't understood before, because how could I? I couldn't share it.

But he could, and with another like him—

"There is no other!" Cyrus's eyes flashed because I must have whispered that aloud. "There never will be!"

"So, you'll live like this? A half life—"

"It's not half!"

"It is! I just never realized before. How much you gave up to be with me. How much you lost—"

"I lost *nothing*." I suddenly found myself backed into the wall, a furious Were in my face. He still hadn't Changed, that iron control holding, but it was by a thread. I could feel his power circling me, a staticky cloud of it, but I wasn't afraid.

Like my wolf, I reveled in it, drew it closer, wrapped it around me like a cloak and saw his eyes flare, neon bright for a second. He loved my courage, had told me that once, although this wasn't that. I didn't need courage with him. I was safer like this, with him standing as a bulwark between me and the world than I ever could be anywhere else.

I loved it here, but I didn't deserve it.

And, for once, we had to face that.

But Cyrus beat me to the punch. "Your mother chose to be with your father," he said harshly. "A human war mage who never accepted the bite; never Changed. Do you think she felt that she lost out? Do you think she resented him?"

"No, but—"

"Then am I so much weaker than she was? So much less willing to sacrifice—"

"You shouldn't have to sacrifice! That's the point—"

"Is it?" His head tilted. "But she did, didn't she? A high-ranking member of one of the chief clans, yet her position was destroyed by her marriage, and her status in the clan eroded. She could have gotten it all back by repudiating him, by saying she'd made a mistake, by turning her back . . . yet she didn't. I wonder why that was?"

I had a sudden flash of the two of them, with mom sitting on dad's lap like they were newlyweds although they'd been married close to two decades at that point. They'd been pouring over an app they'd found that added dog ears and a snout to any photo. And scrolling through their phones' memories, putting the new "accessories" on everything and giggling like children.

"She loved him," I whispered, because she had. And he'd loved her, to the day she died. Hell, to this day. He'd never dated again, although it had been years.

I wasn't sure he ever would.

"Strange how that works," Cyrus said, as if that changed anything. But our situations weren't the same and he knew it.

Dad hadn't Changed because it would have cost him his career, there being rules about deliberately taking on a transformation and thereby splitting your loyalties. Not to mention that the Were strain can often override anything else, potentially costing him his magic. And because it wouldn't have helped.

Mother was a noble of the great house of Lobizon, one of the twelve clans who had first founded the ruling council. She was expected to make an illustrious marriage, maybe even to birth a new clan leader, not to lower herself to couple with a nobody. Even had father accepted the bite, her status would have been in the gutter anyway, as a newly turned Were from none of the old bloodlines wasn't viewed as much better than a human.

They hadn't seen the point.

But Cyrus and I weren't facing that choice. I couldn't take the bite and join him, not at any price; the truth of that throbbed on my thigh even now. And there was another consideration as well.

"It's not just about what you'll miss," I said. "It's about what you risk. Had things gone differently today, had something happened and you went berserk at HQ—"

"Then there would be a lot of dead war mages on the ground."

The flat assurance in his tone frightened me as nothing else had.

I felt my nails dig into his arms. "No, there wouldn't be! You don't understand the power of the Corps, Cyrus—"

"Or you the power of Arnou. You grew up in Lobizon, but you were never treated as part of it. You think more like a war mage—even when you shouldn't."

"And you more like a wolf!" I wanted to shake him, to make him understand. The Corpsmen might look puny to Weres, some of whom when transformed were three times their size. But they weren't. And the thought of what might have happened today sent a shard of pure ice down my spine. I gripped his arms harder, made him hear me. "Sebastian is a diplomat; he's not going to risk the alliance for me, nor should he! And you're only one man—"

"He's not, though," someone said, and I looked up to find Noah standing there, backed up by several more Weres from the camping trip whose names I couldn't recall. "He has us now. And so do you."

Damn! I'd forgotten that I was currently surrounded by creatures with way better hearing than average. And that I needed to watch my mouth.

But it was too late now, and the three of them must have heard enough, because they were looking pretty worked up.

"You saved us the other night," one of the other Weres added, a guy with skin so dark that it blended into the dim light of the hallway. He'd solved the problem of quick growing Were hair with dreads wrapped at intervals with different colored thread, which reached past his shoulder blades. "You put your life on the line, yet you think we wouldn't come after you? That we wouldn't tear that place up?"

"We ought to do it anyway," the third Were said. He was a tall redhead named Jason, with a prominent Adam's apple, a skinny, lanky build, and hair in a Carrot Top-like snarl. He should have looked more than a little goofy, but his voice was halfway to wolf speak and there was nothing funny about it.

"After what happened to Jace," Noah agreed. "I mean, what more can they do to us?"

"They can kill you," I said, gripping his arm before I thought. It wasn't a great idea to touch a wolf you barely knew, but he didn't react.

"They can try." The bright blue eyes were steady on mine. "Let's see how well that goes for them."

The other two were nodding along, and I felt something rising in me, threatening to stop my throat. Fear, but not for myself. For a moment, I couldn't even speak.

Luckily, Cyrus could.

"No." He didn't raise his voice or offer any explanations, but he didn't have to. An Alpha's word was law.

But I wanted to make sure they understood, that they *got this*. "Nothing happened, so there's nothing to avenge. And the Corps is a lot more formidable than you're giving them credit for, not to mention that there are all kinds of wards throughout that facility that make it into a death trap. And there are Weres on duty now—"

"Yeah, Jace told us." The growl was evident in the black Were's voice now, too.

"—from at least four different clans! So, assault the Corps, and you're assaulting them—

"You assaulted them," Noah pointed out. "Or one anyway."

It looked like Jace had spilled everything. And why not? I'd been too out of it to ask him not to and Cyrus had been too focused on me. It was safe to assume that everyone knew everything, at this point.

“I challenged,” I corrected. “And won a fair fight—”

“Then maybe we’ll challenge,” the black Were said, glancing at Cyrus, who didn’t say anything. But he didn’t have to. The atmosphere, already oppressive, thickened to the point that I felt like I was about to choke on it.

And I guess the boys did, too, because they almost visibly shrank as their Alpha did the Were equivalent of banging their heads together.

“Lee’s just talking,” Noah said quickly. “You know how he is.”

“Talk about something else,” Cyrus growled. “This discussion is over, you understand?”

The boys nodded and he left after giving my shoulder a squeeze. Because talking privately in this house wasn’t possible right now. They started after him, but I pulled them back.

It kind of surprised me that it worked.

They’d just been publicly slapped by the man they considered their clan leader and probably wanted to go off and lick their wounds. But at a call from me, they paused. I decided not to question my luck, and drove home the point while I had the chance.

“You can’t challenge,” I told them. “You’re *vargulf*—”

“You think we don’t know that?” Lee said bitterly.

“Based on what I just heard? Yeah, I think you don’t. Those wolves who watched my fight did nothing but stand there because clan law says they have to. Challenge was issued; challenge was accepted. Nobody interferes with that.

“But clan law doesn’t apply to you. If you had challenged, they wouldn’t have merely watched. They’d have torn you to pieces—”

“They'd have tried!” Lee’s eyes flashed yellow in the darkness, brightly enough to shed a golden glow over his dark skin.

“They'd have succeeded!” I snapped, wondering what I had to do to get through to them.

“We know that,” Noah interjected, shooting Lee a warning look.

“Yet you’re still talking like it would be a fair fight. *It wouldn’t be*. Clan law—”

“Yeah, only maybe we’re tired of clan law.” Lee said. “What has it ever done for us? What is it ever going to do, but keep us down? It doesn’t protect us? Okay, then it doesn’t protect them, either.”

“Meaning?” I asked carefully.

"Meaning, if you hadn't been there, if they'd torn Jace apart, a young guy just trying to get his brother's body back? Yeah, then all bets are off. Those fuckers should be *glad* you were there. You protected them as much as Jace, maybe more. But if they want a fight? We'll give them a fight!"

I stared at him, nonplussed for a second, and Noah cursed. "That's great. Bring that up here—"

"He's got a point; you know he does—"

"Who has?" I asked, confused.

"Guy in Tartarus, another *vargulf*," Noah said tersely. "Always shouting a bunch of nonsense—"

"It's not nonsense!" Jason chimed in, and then started to look a little uncomfortable as Noah stared him down. "Not all of it."

"What guy?" I asked again.

"Name's Lyall," Noah said. "Don't know where he stays, but he shows up at the market under Decatur pretty regularly." He paused, and then came out with it. "He's getting attention. Getting a following. People want some payback and think the war might be the right time—"

"Shut up!" Lee told him. "What are you doing? She's a war mage!"

"She's also Lupa and she asked. What was I supposed to do? Lie?"

I just stood there for a moment as the boys argued, caught completely off guard. Lupa was the official term for the Alpha female of a clan, either the Alpha's mate or a female leader in her own right. Lupa was not what I was, because this was not a clan and I did not have responsibility for these boys.

But according to clan custom, if I didn't challenge it now then I accepted it, and became den mother to a bunch of *vargulfs*.

Cyrus, what the *hell*?

"I'm not Lupa," I told them clearly. "I'm sorry; I don't know what Cyrus told you—"

"Nothing. He didn't have to," Noah said, regarding me strangely.

"Then I don't know where you got the idea—"

"From you."

I frowned. "From me? I never said—"

"You didn't have to," Jason broke in. "You and Cyrus are a thing, and you fought for us. You damned near died for us. And then again for Jace. If that doesn't make you Lupa, what does?"

I just looked at him for a moment, caught flat footed yet again. But we were interrupted before I could figure out a reply. Sophie poked her head out of the door to my bedroom, looking cross.

"Hey, can you guys keep it down? I just got Kimmie off to sleep."

I started to ask why she'd put her in my bed, instead of one of the many others available, but frankly, I had bigger problems right now.

"Yeah," I said. "We'll just be another few—" I turned back around but didn't finish the sentence. Because just that fast, the boys were gone.

Chapter Seventeen

I vacuumed up glass from the shattered lightbulb and tried to do it quietly. Then I rescued my sim card from Caleb, who'd just returned from a pot run—of the metal kind—and called in a query for everything that the Corps had on some guy named Lyall from Decatur. I also phoned the clan archive, asking about Cloud-Leaper, because they weren't going to give the Corps a damned thing.

Both queries would take a while, the Corps' because they were overworked and the clans because they didn't like me. And I could probably double that after this morning. But I'd get answers eventually or I'd get nasty, and in the meantime, I needed a break.

Even by war mage standards, it had been a shitty week. So, instead of checking on Kimmie, who was asleep anyway, I decided to take a few hours off. Maybe have a late lunch and hope that it dissipated some of the effects of the drug.

Of course, that would have been easier if Caleb had gotten out of the way. But when I reentered the kitchen, I found him parked by the stove with the air of a man who had no intention of moving until somebody fed him. Something that would have worked better if he wasn't dealing with an Alpha Were.

"That's your secret?" he asked Cyrus, looking at the four large cans of baked beans on the kitchen counter. "Opening cans?"

"No, the secret is the onions, peppers, homemade barbeque sauce and bacon that you dress them up with," Cyrus said mildly.

I doubted that he was any happier than I was after our abortive talk, but he gave no sign of it. A clan's Alpha was required to be stoic, calm and controlled at all times, because the clan took their cues from him. A worked-up Alpha was a sign for the rest of the family to go into battle mode, and that was the last thing we needed here.

But he wasn't in the mood to put up with any shit.

"Pork," Dimas added, suddenly appearing out of nowhere and making me jump. He had a habit of disappearing for long stretches, then showing up looking like he'd been there the whole time. And then I noticed: the hand he had on the countertop was no longer medium brown, but off white with gray veins, the exact color of the quartz.

Taking a break, I reminded myself, and didn't ask.

"Bacon is pork," Cyrus pointed out.

"Yeah, but to do it right, you need pork shoulder. Like making carnitas, you know? Only you shred it into the beans."

"See, that's what I'm talking about," Caleb said. "Let's do that."

Cyrus didn't bother to reply, just gestured at the apron he was wearing, which proclaimed "No Bitchin' in the Kitchen."

Caleb frowned. "I'm not bitching, and it's well known that I'll eat anything, but the boys—"

"See, he's thinking of the children," I told Cyrus, who rolled his eyes.

"—might prefer the pulled pork. Maybe with some mac and cheese on the side—"

"We have plenty of sides," Cyrus informed him.

"We also have plenty of mouths. I thought you wanted to feed them up?"

Cyrus quirked an eyebrow at him, while layering bacon slices onto the already dressed-up beans. "Are you offering to make said mac and cheese?"

"I don't cook."

"Oh, that's a shame. It means you don't get a vote."

"But I *eat*—"

"Yes, you eat baked beans."

Caleb looked at me. "You know, your man is—" he began, right before I popped a forkful of beans into his mouth. They were having to be done in batches, because my oven couldn't handle that many dishes at once, and these had just come out. So they were hot and saucy and had now-crispy bacon on top, having shed all its fatty goodness into the beans.

Caleb didn't complain about the steam they were sending up. For once, Caleb didn't complain about anything. He swallowed the forkful, then grabbed the utensil away from me and went back for more.

I smacked his hand. "Not a chance."

"How long until dinner?" he whined, which looked ridiculous coming from a guy who could take Mike Tyson in a fair fight. But I wisely didn't say so.

"Go ask Danny."

The restaurant owner's son had taken on the role of pit king, fishing the tenderized ribs out of the boiling liquid when they were ready and setting them to charring on the grill. He seemed to be doing a bang-up job, judging by the smells drifting this way. And, honestly, I couldn't blame Caleb; my own mouth had started to salivate.

"I just did. He said another hour, which is ridiculous. It's after three now!"

"You won't starve," I promised, wrapping foil over the beans to keep them warm.

"Tell my stomach that," he grumbled.

"Everything would go faster if there were fewer people in here," Cyrus said pointedly, which was true. My kitchen remained packed.

"Who can we lose?" I asked, because everyone seemed to have a task except for Caleb, who was already on his way out of the door to "assist" Danny.

An ice-cold beer found its way into my hand.

"Seriously?" I looked at Cyrus. "I was helping!"

"Help outside," he suggested, and gave me a little push.

I would have argued, but the backyard couldn't be any hotter than the kitchen, where the bubbling pots, constantly running oven and press of bodies had become oppressive. The air conditioner was simply not designed to compete. By contrast, a small breeze slithered in through the door when Caleb opened it, beckoning enticingly.

I decided that Cyrus had this, and ventured forth.

A few minutes later, I was sitting under the lone piece of greenery in my back yard—unless you counted the cactus—drinking my beer. A rainbow of colored pots now littered the purloined grills, bubbling merrily away; a few racks of ribs from the early cooking with my stew pot were now kissing the flame for the first time; and a couple more tables had been dragged out of the house to provide surfaces for the platters of finished meat.

Things appeared to be handled out here, too.

"Didn't think they had trees in Vegas," Sophie said, coming over to join me. She had a beer in hand which was sweating almost as much as I was, and which I guessed I should say something about. But I'd brought them alcohol back at HQ when I wanted to grill them, so it seemed hypocritical. And with the Corps deeming them old enough to fight, it also felt stupid to tell them that they couldn't have a beer on a hot day.

I took another swig of my own drink and repressed a sigh.

This mentoring thing was a bitch.

Sophie was taking in the leafy canopy above us. "I expected a barren desert," she added. "But I see these everywhere."

"Sweet acacia," I told her. "It's why I bought the house. It has little yellow puffballs in spring. Messy, but pretty."

Sophie looked as if she was trying to visualize the puffballs. After a while she gave up, sat down and watched Danny instead. He was posing with a spatula for Jen, who was wandering around, taking pictures with her phone. Of him, of the food, of everyone, as far as I could tell.

She doesn't want to forget this, I thought, and felt something uncomfortable under my breastbone.

"Danny better hurry," Sophie said, as Cyrus's boys began edging closer to the burning pits. "Or we're gonna have a riot soon. And I'm not sure I won't help."

"He said an hour, but that was maybe fifteen minutes ago."

"Really?" she brightened. "God, I could eat a whole rack by myself!"

"Grab it early."

"Why?" She balanced her bottle between her crossed legs and scraped sweaty red hair off her neck. "There's plenty."

"You've never seen Weres eat."

She shook her head. "We had a Were at school for a while. He was always hungry."

I raised an eyebrow. "In school? His clan allowed that?"

"Mage mother. Corps used it to claim him, and I don't think his clan liked his talent much anyway. Firestarter."

"Ah." It explained why she knew something about Weres.

"He used to slip out at night to get more food. I mean, they fed us enough, but he was a bottomless pit. I gave him my dessert most days and he'd eat it in one bite. We started giving him orders after a while, for beer, candy, whatever. He never took any money—"

He never paid, I thought cynically.

"—and it was pretty cool, until they transferred him."

"Transferred?"

"To another facility. For Intransigents. That's what they call us when—"

"I know."

It was the term for kids that the Corps had given up on, the ones who were never getting out. They held them at the schools for a while, after they started to get out of hand, but as soon as a bed opened up elsewhere, they disappeared. It made the regular facilities look better, since the students who remained were better behaved.

And kept up the façade of the system being about schools instead of prisons.

Sophie nodded, and took a moment to tie her hair up into a bouncy ponytail. Then she licked her lips and glanced at me. Here we go, I thought.

"Listen, about Kimmie," she began.

"It's okay."

"Is it? I kind of got the idea that maybe this," she gestured around vaguely, I guessed at the piles of charcoal from the earlier incident, "was more than you bargained for."

"No, it's fairly standard."

"Standard?" Her voice acquired an edge. "What about it is standard?"

I closed my eyes. I was hot, hungry and feeling really odd. I'd had hell of a day, and I had a funeral to go to tonight for another kid I hadn't managed to save. I just wanted to finish my beer in peace.

But that obviously wasn't happening until I cleared some things up.

"Let's cut to the chase," I said. "You're worried that I'm getting freaked out. That I plan to tell Hargroves that he saddled me with a group of powerful, but highly unstable kids who've been through a lifetime of trauma and might go off at any moment—"

She bristled. "That's not what we are! That's not what any—"

"That's exactly what you are. Some of you, maybe all of you, but it's not the point. And don't interrupt."

She blinked at me.

"But I'm not going to do that, okay? And, yeah, considering that my last class set the gym on fire and the one before that tried to kill me, this doesn't feel all that different. Magic is chaos, but you'll learn to leash yours."

It was an indication of how upset she was underneath the calm exterior that she didn't even ask about the attempted murder.

"And if we don't?" she said instead, her hands gripping the beer bottle almost hard enough to snap it. "We can do a little more than set something on fire."

"I hope so. The other side certainly can. And you'll have to hold your own against them soon enough, right alongside the rest of us."

She blinked some more, as if she'd expected me to lie. But she rallied quickly, because this kid didn't have a spine problem. "Or die trying?" she challenged.

"Or die trying. That is, if you decide to stay."

"We don't have a choice!"

"You do. It's just not one you like. But there are worse things—"

"There's nothing worse than going back! Nothing!" she got up abruptly, as if intending to walk away, then sat back down just as fast. And abruptly leaned in, invading my space in a way that would have disturbed a human.

Fortunately, Weres have a different standard and I recognized the pain on her face. This wasn't an attack. I doubted she even realized what she was doing.

"You don't know what it's like there," she told me. "No, they don't kill us. They don't even hurt us. But it's . . . it's a living death. You can't use your magic, even when it builds up inside you like a volcano about to go off. You have to swallow it, repress it, try your best to eliminate it no matter how much it hurts, or risk being put in the danger group. The group that doesn't go anywhere, not even on those carefully guarded "field trips" they take the rest of us on. So they can say we have a normal life.

"Normal!" she laughed, and it was bitter. She sat back and gestured around, more wildly than before. "*This* is normal! Did you know, Caleb didn't lock the back of the van this morning? We could have jumped out if we wanted. Or later, he asked Dimas to go with him to get the damned pots. They went alone, just the two of them. Dimas could have overpowered him at any time; Caleb turned his back on him for at least five minutes, searching for cookware under the sink!"

"Is he really unaware that they sell frying pans separately?" I asked, trying to lighten the atmosphere, and it was the wrong move.

Because she was suddenly back in my face, and this time, her eyes were solid gold. It was like looking at a tiger, a deceptively sweet tiger with freckles over her nose and cheeks still slightly chubby from baby fat. But who could nonetheless rip your throat out.

I would have flinched—anyone would—if I hadn't grown up with creatures who could transform in an instant and do the same thing, to the point of touching my nose as they menaced me. Those last few years in Lobizon had seen a lot of that, and I'd gotten very good at staring into the eyes of a predator. But it took everything I had to sit tight, to look back unflinchingly, to appear like we were having a normal conversation.

And not to ask why Sophie was so sure that Dimas could kill a senior war mage with impunity.

Then she sat back again, and it was almost as big of a transformation as the Change. Her eyes were suddenly back to blue, and her face was tragic as she looked out onto the mundane scene in my back yard. It was literally just a barbeque, and a pretty shit one so far. But her gaze was filled with wonder.

"We never had anything like this," she whispered. "No one watches us here. No one threatens us. Most of the people aren't even wearing weapons."

Most of the people *are* weapons, I didn't say, because I'd already screwed up once. I just let her talk. It seemed to be helping.

"We went to the beach one time," she said, after a minute. "I'd never been. My parents were always going to take me, but then the Corps came. . . I was so excited. So scared but so thrilled to be getting out for once, to see the waves, to splash in the water, to sit in the sun and eat a terrible hot dog. To be normal, just for a day . . .

"And they ruined it. There were so many war mages, just so many. I was only ten, and the rest of my class weren't much older, but they sent an army to guard us. They kept their hands on their weapons most of the time, and followed every move we made with suspicion. I finally asked one, 'why don't you just kill us?' Because it was obvious to me, even then, that they hated and feared us.

"Do you know what he said?" she asked, turning to me. "Do you know what he told a ten-year-old girl?"

I shook my head.

"You haven't done anything . . .yet."

I winced, but didn't reply. I wasn't sure what to say. I'd have liked to wring that man's neck, but honestly, the same sentiment might have come from half the Corps.

Those special schools took manpower to guard and were expensive to operate. Plus, they perpetuated the problem in a lot of people's eyes. Some of the kids grew up, got out, and had kids of their own, sending that so-called junk magic into the next generation.

Of course, when pressed as to what the alternative was, that same group tended to get cagey. Nobody liked to remember when people like Sophie were just quietly disposed of, with the argument that it was good for the magical community. Or later, in a slightly more enlightened age, when they were sterilized, to ensure that their problems died with them.

No, nobody liked to remember that.

But you could see it in their eyes sometimes.

I bet Sophie had seen it a lot.

"Some are crazy," she admitted, still staring outward. "I don't dispute that. I hear them sometimes at night, screaming themselves hoarse in the basement, in warded cells they never leave. Until they take them away, and nobody ever sees them again. I used to wonder: did they start out that way? Or did they start out like me, but weren't able to learn enough control?

"And will we end up like that? Me or Kimmie or Dimas . . ."

She shook her head after a moment, and glanced at me. "But staying is a risk, too, right? We're cannon fodder, just like you. We're all supposed to die on cue, and maybe take a few of the other side with us."

"Maybe," I agreed steadily.

She frowned, looking genuinely puzzled. "You just say things, don't you?"

"You levelled with me. I thought you wanted the same. Or would you prefer a lie?"

"No."

And, for the first time since I met her, Sophie seemed to be listening. Not with hackles raised, defensive before I even opened my mouth, but genuinely, sincerely. I decided to honor that.

"They did this before, in the Middle Ages," I told her. "During the Vampire Wars. Gave people willing to risk their lives a pass from the murder squads who used to hunt them. Gave them a way out.

"But freedom came at a price, and a lot of those who volunteered never came back. This is war, and you're too young to fight it. But so are the rest of the students I've been getting lately. You're seventeen, right?"

She nodded. "Well, in a month."

I tried and probably failed to keep the anger off my face. "That means you're only a year or two younger than them. Too young—far too young. Still a child, but fighting an adult's war. We're eating our own, but if we don't . . ."

I stopped myself, because honesty or not, there were some things she didn't need to hear. Some things I wished I didn't know. It was an ugly fight, and getting uglier as the war dragged on and both sides became more desperate.

"There's no good solution," I finally said. "But you don't have to do this. You can go back to the schools you came from, buckle down, bite your lip when you want to answer back, and do what you must to get out of there. And maybe, by then, this will all be over."

"Or it'll be worse," she said steadily.

"Or it will be worse," I agreed. But maybe that wasn't her problem. Why fight for a world who hated and repressed you? For a moment, I was afraid she'd ask, because I didn't have a good answer.

Or any at all.

But she didn't. "And if we stay?"

"I will train you, and try my best to protect you. But there are no guarantees."

She sat quietly for a moment, her eyes somber, then got back to her feet. “There never are. But for once at least there’s no bullshit about it.”

She walked off.

Chapter Eighteen

I watched Sophie walk away, and felt shitty. She was in a bad situation, but it was a brutal world. I wouldn't have helped anything by lying to her; I knew that.

So why did I feel like crap?

Maybe I *should* tell Hargroves that this wasn't going to work. And get my new students shipped back home, or what passed for it, whether they liked it or not. They might hate me, but I was used to people hating me; I was a cop, after all.

And it would be better than burying another kid.

But I doubted that the Corps would see it that way.

They needed help and were determined to get it. But the older "graduates" they'd let out of the school system tended to have a chip on their shoulder for some reason and wanted nothing more to do with them. And they weren't trusted anyway, since they often made their way into the arms of the dark, who at least didn't lock them up or keep them on a leash for the rest of their lives.

We might be the good guys, but honestly, it was sometimes hard to tell.

So, no, the kids wouldn't go home. They'd be assigned to another trainer instead, one who didn't screw up as often as me. And who wouldn't understand them, because he hadn't been on the outside looking in his whole life, and didn't know what it felt like.

Or maybe I was being an arrogant asshole, and just assuming I could handle them better than anyone else. I sighed and leaned back against the tree, holding the still cold bottle against my overheated cheek, hoping for some relief. It wasn't much use, having already reached the tepid stage. Cold out here had a definite shelf life.

And arrogant asshole sounded about right.

Only Hargroves must have thought that I could do something, or he wouldn't have entrusted them to me. Or maybe he'd just thought it fitting: sending his problem children to the most problematic member of his staff. I wondered what he thought now?

I sighed again and watched Cyrus and Caleb muscle out of the back door. I guessed Caleb had gotten tired of threatening Danny, who hadn't seemed too bothered by it, and had decided to do something useful. He had a thick roll of white fabric over his shoulder, while his companion was carrying a washtub full of ice studded with bottles.

Cyrus was, of course, mugged before he'd gotten six yards, leaving him with an empty tub and an exasperated look on his face.

Looked like dinner was still going to be a while.

I leaned my head back against the tree trunk, and closed my eyes, hoping for a moment of peace to get my thoughts in order. But that wasn't what I received. Without visual stimulation to distract me, other senses came online.

A lot of them.

It suddenly felt like I was the tree, sending little roots shooting out everywhere. Only these roots were turbo charged and set on fast forward. Little ghostly roots . . .

I should rein them in; I knew that. After the craziness at Cyrus's apartment, the plan had been to ignore all the strangeness until it faded out, and blended back into my normal experience. That was the smart move and I had committed to it.

But the thought caused a pang under my breastbone, a persistent, aching sense of loss. My new world was slipping away before I'd ever even explored it, and I wasn't likely to get another chance. War mages do not experiment with weird, magical drugs if they want to remain war mages. This was my only opportunity to discover my mother's world, to see it as she had, to understand.

And after today, I kind of thought I'd earned it.

Just for a moment, then, I let myself drift.

There was no immediate difference, except that the chaos in my thoughts slowed down, and a languid heat took over. Not the sticky, burning, oh-God-it's-so-*hot* of summer in Vegas, but a floating, comfortable feeling, more soothing warmth than fire. My wolf liked it here, liked the sun on her body and the wind in her hair. Liked all the people scurrying around, some of whom were now bringing out plates, cups and platters to decorate the tarps.

I couldn't see them, but I could trace their actions by the smell of the food they carried: potato salad, its sweet pickle bright and tangy on the breeze; the pasta dish I'd helped to cook, its spicy, vinegar smell unmistakable; Cyrus's fatty, bacon-y beans; buttery garlic bread, with the charr from the grill marks coming distinctly to my nose; a fresh salad, its cool, green notes singing through all the rest; and corn on the cob, grilled over an open fire and smeared with cotija cheese and Mexican spices.

And even without the smells, I would have followed the action from the sounds: the *clink, clink* of dinnerware; the scuff of shoes over sand, with Aki's oddly worn sneakers distinct among the rest; the "oh, shit, sorry" of a near collision between Jen, her slightly breathy voice rising in surprise, and the lower tones of Danny, bringing over a platter of ribs; while the *whack, whack, whack* of the back door constantly hitting the side of the house pounded out a steady beat.

That last should have upset me—I'd just had the damned thing painted—but it faded into the languor drenching my limbs in honeyed warmth. Fittingly, a bee was droning around the branches overhead, looking for a late bloom. I could hear its soft buzz, even trace the movement of its miniscule wings, like I could discern the *shush, shush, shush* of the tree's small leaves, moving in a breeze so faint that I shouldn't have been able to feel it.

But I could, and it carried word of everything going on in the neighborhood. And suddenly, my senses expanded again. I heard a chainsaw gnawing through the tops of some bushes in the distance; Mr. Patel muttering at the end of the block as he struggled with a car that wouldn't start; and a couple of kids down the road defying the heat to bounce a basketball against a driveway.

The driveway was cracked. I could tell whenever the ball encountered the edge and bounced off to the side. Probably the Wallers; they'd needed to get theirs sealed for a while.

Yeah, it was definitely them. I could hear the Rodriguez's little yappy dog going nuts next door, because it was a vicious creature who hated all known forms of life. Or maybe it was just hungry, as Mrs. Rodriquez was cooking something that smelled wonderful. I could discern it in flashes through the haze of barbeque smoke, something with chili and lime and coriander. And then somebody cracked open a bottle of tequila, and the pungent, spicy smell cut like a knife through the haze, making me whine slightly.

"Lia?"

The word drifted over the scene, but wasn't important. I was beginning to understand why dogs stared blankly out of windows for hours, seemingly well entertained. Because they were, I thought, almost laughing as the world around me exploded outward.

I didn't know how far a dog's senses extended, but mine felt like they went on for days. Literally. It was like they could time travel, with the sounds coming to my ears all being in the present, but the smells . . .

Went back for *weeks*.

The newer ones were thick, like the boys' shadows I'd seen darting around Cyrus's apartment. As if I could reach out and touch them if I tried. Others were more like smoke, torn apart and shredded by the passage of time, some a little, some a lot, but often still recognizable. And the ones that repeated, over and over, gouged colorful scent trails in the landscape.

I didn't know why they were colorful, but they were, creating a topographical map of the neighborhood, only with people instead of mountains. Like the old woman whose name I didn't know who lived several streets over. I'd never paid her any attention; probably never even seen her, but I could see her now. She was vividly depicted in my mental landscape, with her trips with her walker to the mailbox every day carving a dark blue scent scar into the world.

I suddenly knew other people's habits, too, including ones that they'd probably prefer I didn't. Like Mrs. Lake's visits to the hunky new neighbor's house, where the pink color that my mind had assigned her and his dark blue merged into a shade of purple that I doubted her husband would like. Or the stoner down the street, who had bright green ganja leaves painted on the side of his van but whose house was suffused by a sickly yellow, as he'd recently moved on to heroin. Or the hoarder three streets over, with the stench of human decay emanating from his living room; how long had it been since anyone saw him?

I could see him; he was white and gray in my mental landscape, the color of ashes, and staring sightlessly at a T.V. It was still on; I could hear the tinny sounds from here, but not make out the show.

And wouldn't have been able to concentrate on it if I could, not with that smell in my nostrils.

It reminded me of beef jerky: dried out and concentrated. He had a window open and must have died in the spring, when the weather was still cool. The air had desiccated him over the intervening months, sucking all the water from his flesh until it left behind something almost mummified, except with no wrappings.

And that, and the open window, had allowed little visitors to pay their respects.

"Lia!" Somebody was shaking me now, but I barely noticed, being too busy recoiling from the insect-covered cadaver. I could hear the little *scritch-scritch* sounds they made; and almost feel their tiny legs moving over my own skin.

I backed away, not able to deal with the immediacy of it. And burst back out of the house of death to find the rest of the neighborhood vibrant and alive, with rainbow hues zipping about everywhere. My senses careened right along with them, out of control for a moment until I managed to steady them again.

Only that didn't work so well since they were all flowing together, as if into one uber sense stronger than any of the original five on their own.

I didn't understand it, and no Weres had ever described anything like this to me. But maybe they hadn't understood how, or hadn't wanted me to know all that I was missing. And I had been missing a lot, so much that it felt like I'd been blind all my life and was suddenly able to see.

It was overwhelming and intense and strange and wonderful, and I didn't know how to process it. All I knew was that the colorful scent trails were *everywhere*, crisscrossing the landscape like a subway map, some as dark as the Marianas Trench in front of the old lady's house, others barely a sheen on the day. But all of them were trying to tell me their stories.

And they were so easy to read!

I discovered that I could pick one out and follow it like a trail without moving an inch. The one I chose was gold, as vivid as Sophie's eyes, and followed a young boy on a bike, his tires threatening to melt into the hot asphalt. I hopped from there to the bright orange spilling out of a family's car; there were groceries in the trunk, including a bag of oranges that smelled so sweet that I could taste them, their flavor bursting on my tongue. And then I jumped to two little girls in a kiddie pool, splashing in the water, their delighted laughter causing their light-yellow color to flash brighter and brighter, like sunlight.

One of them was healthy; the other wore a bandage where the ports for the chemotherapy she was taking had scarred her tender flesh. She was sick, but she was happy. Her friend had come to visit—her scent was faint on the house, instead of well rooted like the sick girl's—and they had had baloney sandwiches for lunch. It was a good day—

A dog ran by, cutting across their yard. He and I hopped a fence, chased a squirrel down a sidewalk, and dodged out in front of a car, the exhaust strong in our noses. The driver of a car had been in an argument with her boyfriend. I could smell his scent on her, like I could taste the blood pooling under the skin of her cheek where he'd hit her, and the salt of the tears in her eyes. They were as distinct as the Cheetos on the floor mat, which one of her kids had spilled when she was bundling them into the car.

Then she was gone, in a panicked swerve around a group of children getting off a school bus. The dog spun on a dime and ducked through them, too, only that proved to be a mistake. Because there were so many, all with different scent stories, all hurrying off in different directions, that it broke my brain a little.

A dead goldfish resided in a leaking thermos, having been stolen by a boy who didn't understand that it wouldn't make it back alive on tap water from the school's water fountain and the remains of his apple juice; a girl had started her period and it must have been her first one, because she was panicking, her heart going a mile a minute as she raced to get home before anybody noticed; another girl had thrown up her lunch, and it was probably deliberate, since she'd brought mouthwash to try to hide it; a third girl greeted the dog, laughing as he jumped up to lick her face, and rewarded him with a piece of chicken she'd kept out of her lunch . . .

And then it sped up, all the information flooding at me, as if a dam had burst. I suddenly knew that the bus driver chewed tobacco despite the ulcer that had already formed in his mouth; that a back tire on the bus was worn and about to blow out; that one of the older guys had half a blunt in his pocket, which had been shared around by at least three of the other students earlier because their scents were still on it; that a girl had just had a perm, the sharp, chemical scent pervasive in the air around her; that a boy had been wearing the same clothes for three days, a probable sign of neglect; that somebody had a cavity forming in a tooth; that somebody else was chewing spearmint gum; that several more kids were throwing a football around behind the bus, the sunlight on the rubber allowing me to trace its arc across the sky—

I mewled in confusion, as understanding hit of why dogs spun about when engulfed in a crowd, unable to decide what to sniff first. But I wasn't a canine and couldn't manage it, or even sort out which senses I was supposed to be using to try. Sight, smell, and taste had no discernable difference anymore, and the strangeness of it was threatening to overwhelm me.

"I think she's sick," someone said, the words enough to jolt me out of the other-mind I'd slid into. They were harsh, angular, foreign. For a moment, I didn't even understand the meaning. Just looked at them, floating in the air in front of me, like jagged, transparent shapes distorting my mental landscape. "I don't know what's wrong; she was all right a minute ago. But when I came back—"

"She's not sick," someone else said.

"How do you know?"

"I've seen this before. She just needs to eat."

And then the confusion snapped and my eyes flew open, to see Sophie looking stressed and holding a couple of beers, and Cyrus—

Holding something else.

Oh, I thought, staring at it like an acolyte seeing the face of God. I grabbed it. And didn't register anything else for a while, the piled high plate in front of me completely absorbing my attention.

There were a few beans on there, dribbled around like a sauce, but nothing green, nothing bread-y, nothing extraneous. Just a mountain of ribs studded by a couple of hamburger patties and a fat sausage unlike any that I'd had in the house. God bless Caleb, I thought fervently.

And then I didn't think again for a while.

I came out of the food haze an unknown amount of time later, dimly aware that I had sauce on everything, that my jeans didn't fit right, and that I was happy. Deliriously so. I pushed the empty plate away, spilling a few stripped bones onto the ground, and another ice-cold beer appeared in front of my nose as if by magic.

"No, you're nothing like a newly turned Were," Cyrus said, with a thread of laughter in his voice.

I downed the beer, sat back, repressed a belch, and regarded him hazily. It seemed to take a moment to remember how to speak, with an idea in my head but nothing coming out of my sauce-stained mouth. "What?" I finally croaked, and it sounded like wolf speak.

Cyrus just grinned and leaned over and kissed me. He had barbeque sauce on his lips, and I grabbed the back of his head and licked it away. There was more laughter at that, and then spontaneous clapping, and I glanced up to see that we had an audience of essentially everybody.

"What happened?" I asked, feeling like I was surfacing from a dream.

"We need to get you to the desert."

"Why? Is it time?"

"It is for you," Cyrus said dryly. "Come on."

Chapter Nineteen

We headed for a place in the desert so far outside of Vegas that I doubted any tourists would ever find it. Which was just as well since my dignity was shot to hell. Cyrus had avoided having me stick my head out of the window the whole way there by taking me on the back of his bike, but I'd been sniffing up a storm anyway. And was continually amazed at the new world I discovered.

Even the dust was fascinating.

Instead of the dry annoyance I was used to, clogging my throat and coating any exposed skin whenever I rode, it was a revelation. It carried motes of a campfire in the distance, or maybe a wildfire burning some of the local mesquite. It brought traces of cinnabar, sulphur and salt from desert deposits likely miles away, yet peppering the breeze like spice. But most of all, it introduced a multitude of growing things.

The latter surprised me the most, and not just because the Mojave wasn't exactly green and lush. But because scent, sound, and sight were getting jumbled up in my head, and becoming impossible to separate. Resulting in a multisensory experience that had me staring around in awe.

There was the constant background hum from the creosote bushes that grew everywhere: earthy yet refreshing, with the smell of soil after rain. They smeared the horizon like the sea, calm and green, except where tiny, yellow flowers danced in the breeze like sunlight on waves. And like the ocean, many of them had been there for time out of mind, being among the longest-lived desert dwellers.

They were interspersed with Dorr's sage, fresh and bright, like cool mint on my tongue. Its bushes studded the landscape with a deep blue violet, the branches hanging so heavy with summer flowers that they mimicked pools of water in places. And like water, they murmured softly as we passed, like tiny waves licking the shore.

But the softer elements ended there. Because prickly pear was next, its sharp, fruity scent bursting on my tongue, like underripe strawberry mixed with bubblegum, and in my vision, with fireworks of yellow, hot pink and mauve, the colors of its flowers. Its sound was just as aggressive as its scent, with high, almost bird-like trills, as if a scattering of pissed-off parrots had descended onto the desert sand.

Those were the loudest notes, either so close or so numerous as to threaten to drown out everything else. But interspersed among them were other sensations, adding variations on a theme. And making the already rich landscape even more complex.

The rose-like odor of Palmer's penstemon was ever present, which I'd been considering for my yard because it was so hardy and so sweet. It sounded like a glissando of bells but flashed on the horizon like colored lightning. Pink and white and pale violet, it shocked me with its power, sending frissons over my skin even from this distance.

It was joined by the elusive vanilla scent of Ponderosa pine, which smelled so soft but sounded like thunder in the mountains. The massive trees were too far away to be seen, but I could feel them stretching arms high into the sky, providing nests for all types of scurrying and flying things. While their roots reached deep, deep, so very deep, communing with stone and earth and water, as if they alone stitched the world together.

And, finally, came the overripe cantaloupe reek of a Joshua tree, flowering late on the top of some hill and born aloft by the breeze. It was merely an echo, high and soaring, as if from miles away. But it was as aggressive as an opera singer, making the distance immaterial in its determination to be heard.

There were other notes, as well, like every bit of animal scat for miles that found its way to my nose. But instead of being disgusted, I breathed it in, filling in the gaps between the flora. Until I could almost see the animals, too.

My eyes caught flickering images of a mule deer, twitching its overlarge ears as we zipped by; of a desert tortoise with the rock-like protrusions on its shell helping it to blend into the landscape; of a

Gila monster peeking out of its den; and of a whole flock of roadrunners flitting through the sand and across the sky, to the point that it was almost filled with them.

Or maybe that was merely one bird who moved around a lot; I didn't know anymore. It was getting to be too much, this new way of seeing, and once again felt more like an assault on the senses than a broadening of them. Halfway to our destination, I grabbed the back of Cyrus's shirt and buried my face in it, allowing the familiar musk to suffuse the air around me. I badly needed something to ground me and he did the trick.

After a while, I could smell only him.

That changed when we arrived at our destination, and everyone piled out of Caleb's makeshift school bus, which despite its appearance had somehow kept up. The old truck that I no longer used much, but kept around for when I needed to haul things, had come, too. Danny had stuffed the Weres into the backseat and truck bed, somehow fitting in the overflow from the van, and as soon as it stopped, they spilled out like water.

Seeing them move so fluidly reminded me of those at the grow farm doing the same, in a long line of different colored fur. And, for an instant, the landscape around me wavered, and was replaced by another rocky backdrop, this one in the midst of a savage assault. I could hear the crack of breaking bone, taste the fear in my mouth, see the blood, sweat and bile flying, along with what looked like a severed limb—

And then I was back, panting slightly and very confused. Because that wasn't right. Was it?

My attacks yesterday had been mainly defensive, or aimed at objects when they weren't. They'd hit the house, the lines of illegal plants, and the fuel tank—even the windmill, churning circles of black smoke into the air. I remembered all of that clearly. But they hadn't torn through flesh like a tornado; I knew they hadn't!

Yet, suddenly, all I could smell was blood.

"You doing okay?"

That was Danny; I recognized him by scent even before he spoke, the scent of cologne heavy in the air around him. Which was just as well, since I discovered that I was bent over, hands on my knees, staring at dirt. I straightened back up to meet worried, dark eyes.

"Yeah. Just a little dizzy."

"Not surprised. Cyrus drives like a bat out of hell. You want a drink or something?" He hoisted an ice chest. "I brought water, soda, sports drinks . . . "

"I'm good."

"Well, let me know if you change your mind." He moved off as Cyrus came back over from greeting everyone.

"I'm fine," I said, before he could ask me, too. "Just a . . . bit overwhelmed."

"It takes people like that," he said, rubbing my back. "Some worse than others. You want to sit in the truck?"

I shook my head. "No. Go do . . . whatever you need to do."

He hesitated for a moment, concern on his face, because my big, buff, boyfriend was turning into a mother hen. But he took me at my word and jogged over to where some Corpsmen were standing by one of HQ's white medical vans, which had just pulled in behind us. I guessed he must have asked them to meet us here, as we had no good way to transport a body.

I would have gone over to say hi as well, but tonight, I didn't trust myself. The stench of the two men's magic was strong in my nose, cutting through even the bloody haze that the rest of my senses were still toying with. It made my lip curl into a half snarl, which was ridiculous.

I had magic. Was I going to growl at myself next? I decided that that was perfectly possible today, took Cyrus's advice and went and sat in the truck.

The door snicked shut behind me, and I closed my eyes, trying to block it all out. But as before, it didn't work. I could sense *everything*, from Jace's suddenly rapid heartbeat, pounding from the center of a protective circle of Weres, to the metallic *clang-clang* of the van being opened and a stretcher being rolled out of the back. From the cry of a bird I couldn't identify, its metallic *chip, chip, chip* farewelling the day, to the voices of a group of Weres I didn't know, but who must be *vargulfs*. Because they greeted Cyrus calmly as he walked up to them and started chatting about something . . .

Wood. They'd brought the wood for the funeral pyre. The men hoped they'd found enough, but weren't sure as it wasn't exactly easy to source in early June.

I watched them pull it from the back of a pickup even older than mine. They were quick and efficient, taking no time to empty the bed, but it upset me, nonetheless. That wasn't the way this was supposed to go.

The clan ought to gather the wood themselves, scouring their territory for it, with each person bringing back a piece. But that was a tradition from when the majority of Weres lived in heavily wooded areas, where fuel was easy to come by. And where you'd spend hours looking for just the right branch, one that spoke to you.

I'd missed out on that with my old clan's bullies on my heels. I'd visited my mother's grave after the ceremony, but I'd had to pass on the funeral itself, never getting to lay my piece on the pyre. I'd been in hiding, unable to properly send her off. Her only daughter, the one who was supposed to lay the first branch, yet it had been denied to me . . .

I felt an anger rising, a fury undimmed by the passage of years. And now the same thing was going to happen here, because what were Cyrus's boys supposed to find? Saguaro? Yucca?

Yet they were doing it, I realized. Jayden's clan, or the closest thing he had, circled around him. And then transformed, shedding their clothes along with their skins and running with silent wolf paws into the twilight, causing the mages to stop and stare.

And then to scramble back into their van when they saw me looking at them, boring holes through them with my gaze. This wasn't for them. They needed to leave. They needed to leave *now*.

They did, in a squeal of tires that I barely noticed, like I barely saw my eyes in the mirror, glowing red with the setting sun. Because I was getting down from the truck, I was searching around the ground, I was looking for something; I wasn't even sure what. Couldn't think.

Until Cyrus put something in my hand. "Here," he whispered. "Take this one."

My fingers closed over something woody, and I looked down to find myself holding a slender branch. It had long, skinny leaves and big, beautiful pink blooms. They looked almost like orchids, or maybe angel trumpets, with a cup-like body, yellow stamens and mottled pink petals.

They didn't look remotely like something that should bloom in the desert.

But I guessed I was wrong, because they smelled of earth and sky and wild, growing things. These hadn't been cultivated in a hot house, intended to decorate a huge vase in some casino. They were a desert flower, with a faint, but noticeably sweet scent.

"Desert willow," Cyrus confirmed. "The guys who brought the wood got here a little early, and found a clutch of them blooming by a dried-up creek bed. They gathered what they could without hurting the plants."

"They're beautiful," I growled, the wolf in my voice. "But I should find my own."

"I think that, under the circumstances, Jayden would understand." I looked up at him, and my eyes flooded with tears. "Come on," he told me gruffly. "It's almost time."

The Weres who'd brought the wood were like Danny, being several years older than the guys Cyrus had called to surround Jace all day. They'd stopped for fried chicken on the way here; I could smell it. And they must have eaten a lot, because they were calm, with their movements sure and unhurried as they finished building the pyre.

I didn't have to ask why they'd waited. They hadn't wanted the mages here, any more than I had. Hadn't wanted them to see.

It made me worried, because my students had come, too. I didn't turn around, but I didn't need to. I could pick them out by their scents, which formed an uneasy cloud around them and the bus, which they were still standing beside.

They weren't sure that they were welcomed, either.

I should have thought of that. I'd been too busy thinking about me to wonder how they would manage. They weren't even used to normal human things, like going to a grocery store or having a barbeque. How the hell were they going to react to this?

And that was assuming that the Weres would stand for having a bunch of humans at an event that in no way concerned them. They were coming back now, in twos and threes, bearing their offerings to the pyre in their mouths. Nobody had Changed back; it took too much energy, and they would only have to Change again, after the pyre had burned down to ashes.

They were going to run tonight, run as a group, run until they couldn't run anymore. And then sleep together in a big pile, soft and warm and there for their brother, who had lost so much. My students couldn't do that and wouldn't be welcomed if they could. Even another clan wouldn't be.

This night was for family.

I turned to Cyrus, about to tell him that I'd take my group back. That they could ride in the truck with me and he and the boys could meet us later. But before I could, something amazing happened.

Jace hadn't run with the others, nor had he transformed. That was against tradition; he should have been leading them. But I wasn't sure he knew that.

I wasn't sure what he knew, this boy without a clan, only what he did. He walked over to the group by the bus and took Kimmie's hand. I hadn't noticed until that moment that she'd come, too, as she had been so quiet and so far in the background that she blended into the shadows. But I saw her now, her dark eyes uncertain as Jace gave her a floral laden branch, as Cyrus had done for me.

But after a brief hesitation, she took it and followed him. And one by one, the others did the same: Jen, her short, blond bob painted red in the sunset, her blue eyes liquid; Sophie, her fiery hair like a flame, and gold glinting deep in her pupils; Aki, his blue hair purple as it fought with the sun, and his usual boisterous personality dimmed. And finally, the last two boys, with Dimas barely a glimmer on the night, his changeable skin reflecting the desert like a mirror.

For once, even Chris didn't have anything to say.

But Cyrus did, after the body had been positioned atop the pyre, and the flowers and branches laid. He delivered the eulogy as the day surrendered to night and the stars bloomed overhead. It was strong and hopeful, and more than words. It was like the smell of the desert in my nose, like the whisper of the wind over sand, like the strong bond of connection I could feel flowing through me and every person there.

I didn't know if the others could sense it, too, but they felt like parts of my own body. Their breath caught in my lungs, their blood pounded in my veins, their sorrow flowed down my cheeks, mingling with my own. I could almost see a ribbon of energy streaming through each of us, binding us, knotting us together. I didn't know all their names, but I knew *them*, in a primal way I had never felt before.

It was like the senses I'd experienced on the road, all mingling together into one. We felt like a single entity for a moment, with our breath in sync as well as our hearts. It was beautiful.

And so were the flames, lit by Jace at each corner of the pyre as Cyrus's voice faded away, and that quickly leapt toward the stars overhead. But not high enough. Not even with the magic fuel smelling faintly of juniper that the pyre had been doused with.

I started forward, to help it along with a spell, hoping that that would be allowed. But then stopped halfway. Because someone else was there before me.

I hadn't even expected her to come, much less to participate. But there she was, kneeling by the pyre, her eyes closed, the flames splashing her body. Kimmie, so afraid of her power but so determined to help, with the two warring strains purely visible on her face.

And then whited out as the fire suddenly sprang off the pyre like a wild thing, billowing higher and higher and higher as if reaching for the stars with hands of pure, white light.

Kimmie was pulled back by the others, some mage, some wolf, her eyes shining with the flames she had multiplied out of all reason. I felt the heat, but not much of it, as she'd multiplied the wood, too. The pyre, so short and inadequate a moment ago, now towered over the surrounding desert, maybe a couple of stories high, with flames leaping up hundreds of more feet into the air.

The light spangled all below it, like a star come down to Earth, turning night back into the brightest of days. For a moment, we all caught our breath in wonder, amazed at the pyre's power and strange, otherworldly beauty. And then the whole thing went up, in a whoosh that deafened me and sent us stumbling back, as the entire edifice was consumed in an instant, transformed into a single, great spire of light . . .

And then was it was gone, like a snuffed-out candle, leaving only a haze of ash swirling into the heavens that seemed to go on forever.

Chapter Twenty

My phone rang halfway back to Vegas. I was returning with those of us who couldn't transform, leaving those who could to other pursuits. For once, I'd watched the boys run away across the desert with no envy in my heart. I guessed it was too full for such things tonight.

And then it felt like it stopped in my chest, when I heard Sebastian on the other end of the line.

I didn't know why I reacted so strongly. I knew he was in town, and would be until the Conclave was over. But there was something in his voice that let me know that this was serious.

"I've been trying to reach you all night," he began, without the usual pleasantries. Considering that Sebastian was a diplomat, that wasn't good.

"I was out of range," I said. "Cyrus is—"

"I wasn't asking about him. Where are you now?"

"On my way back to Vegas. I should be there in—"

"Can you meet me at the Wolf's Head instead?"

"Uh . . . I guess?"

"Good. How long?"

"I don't . . . maybe an hour?"

"Make it less."

The call ended with me staring at my phone and wondering what the hell.

"Problem?" Caleb asked. He was riding shotgun, having entrusted his bus to the boys, since it was larger. They'd be back in town tomorrow, with Danny driving and Cyrus riding the bike. Leaving us with only one form of transportation tonight and me with a dilemma.

"No. Just a quick diversion."

"It better be quick. We got clean up to do."

"Hey, take your time," Aki said from the back seat.

"I'm not doing any more dishes." That was Chris, sounding belligerent from the truck bed.

"I left a lot of it soaking," Caleb informed them. "It won't be that bad."

"Says the man who doesn't know how to cook."

"But I do know how to do a gag spell."

The peanut gallery got noticeably quieter after that.

I'd have preferred that they didn't, as the jabber was a distraction from my thoughts, which were grim. And became grimmer when we turned into the dirt road that led to the Council Grounds, also known as the Wolf's Head, a large, rock cut stadium inside a natural formation of cliffs. It should have been dark tonight, with the monthly meeting of clan leaders more than a week in the past, but no.

"What is *that*?" Caleb asked, sitting forward at the sight of a haze of light spilling out of the top of the cliffs, turning them a dull red and frankly somewhat ominous.

That wasn't helped by the huge torches burning in front of the entrance, shedding yellow puddles that reminded me of eyes. That was by design, as the formation had been chosen as much for its appearance as its size. Pointy shards of rock jutted upward toward the star field like wolf's ears, and the entrance was through a narrow passage along what, if you squinted, looked like the snout of a crouching beast.

The image was heightened tonight by the vehicles scattered out front, on the hard packed dirt that served as a parking lot. They reminded me of pieces of meat, shredded by those powerful jaws. And wasn't that just a wonderful thought to have?

"Lia?" Caleb said, when I didn't answer. "I asked what that is."

Trouble, I didn't say, because my brain didn't know that yet. But my gut did, and was clenching as we rolled to a stop. I left some space between the truck and the rest of the vehicles, and parked off to one side before turning to Caleb.

"Wolf's Head. It's where the clans meet," I explained. "If I'm not back in a few minutes, take the truck and go home. I'll get a ride with Sebastian after."

"After what?" he asked, his eyes on the glowing rocks as though having some of the same thoughts as me. "And you've had a hell of a day. Can't this wait?"

"No. You don't ignore a summons." And that was exactly what that call had been, although I had no idea why. Probably had something to do with this morning, though.

Great.

"You're just trying to get out of clean up," Aki said, forcing a laugh and attempting to lighten the atmosphere.

It didn't work.

"We'll go in with you," Sophie said, eyeing the two burly guards standing on either side of the entrance.

They were big guys in suits with gun bulges under their arms that they didn't need, because they were Weres. They looked like they could handle themselves, but were far less impressive than the usual council guards, who were nowhere to be seen. I frowned, my eyes scanning the area as if I thought they might have wondered off somewhere.

The job of guarding the Wolf's Head rotated between the local clans and was considered an honor. The last time I'd been here, the two wolves at the entrance had been a matched set of giants, with seven feet tall frames draped in four hundred pounds of muscle—and that was in human form. Both had been minimally dressed—in loin cloths and ceremonial necklaces—in case they needed to transform quickly. And should have looked like professional wrestlers on Halloween, or cosplayers doing a burly version of ancient Egyptian guards.

They hadn't. Torchlight had gleamed on the precious metal in the necklaces and the oil on all those muscles, or maybe that had been sweat. But they'd stood out, as hard as the rock face behind them, and just as intimidating.

Yet tonight, there were just a couple of overdressed guys who looked about as tense and unhappy as I felt. It made my spine itch, and didn't seem to be doing Sophie any good, either. Because her voice roughened. "We'll all go."

"No!" I turned in my seat to look at her, squashed in between Aki, Jen and Kimmie in the back seat. Kimmie was snoring in a corner, wiped out by her display back at the funeral site. But the others were bright eyed and curious about another new thing they got to experience tonight.

Only they weren't; they definitely weren't.

"None of you is going in, you understand?" I said.

"Why not?" Dimas asked, poking his head through the sliding rear window. He and Chris were sharing the truck bed, since nobody else was fitting onto the back seat. But with the windows open now that the desert had cooled, they could hear us, too.

"Yeah, why not?" Sophie agreed, looking past me. "I've never been inside a Clan structure before—"

"And you're not going in this time, either!" I snapped, anxiety making my voice harsher than I'd planned.

"Why?" she repeated, bristling. "We're suddenly not good enough?"

"That's not what I'm saying—"

"Then what are you saying? I thought tonight was all about inclusion—"

"It was, it is—"

"Well, it doesn't sound like it. It sounds like we could go to the funeral, because it was out in the desert where nobody could see us. But as soon as there's other people around, we get hidden away."

"I'm not hiding you!"

"Then why can't we come with—" she broke off, probably because of the massive, transformed Were who'd just jumped onto the hood of my truck.

He wasn't one of the guards, who had remained by the entrance. He'd probably been lurking in the shadows around the cars, although how he had I didn't know since he was approximately the size of a car himself. And heavy enough to dent my hood, while the three-inch claws on the end of his paws damaged the paint.

I didn't mind that so much; the old clunker already had an impressive collection of scratches and dents, and the blistered paint job was mostly a thing of the past. I did mind the disrespect, however, especially when I recognized the beast's markings. I managed not to throw the truck into reverse and watch the bastard hit the dirt, but it was a close thing.

I slammed out of the door instead, getting in his face, which was easy, since he was busy getting in mine.

There were some squeaks from inside the cab, despite the fact that the girls had already seen plenty of transformed Weres tonight. But Ulmer was a different story. Ulmer was freaking huge.

He'd have paled in comparison to the monster that Colin had become, had they been standing side by side. But they weren't. And with the added boost of looking down on me from the hood, he was a mountain of black and gray fur.

But not a sleek and silky one. Instead, Ulmer's coat was a mess of old battle scars that caused the fur to stick up in tufts, giving him a shaggy, unkempt appearance. It matched the deep tear that bisected his face, the mostly missing right ear, and the absent left canine that caused his muzzle to be slightly lopsided.

He was a mess, but he was a deadly mess, which was why the clan elders had appointed him as Sebastian's bodyguard, after three assassination attempts recently. Sebastian had been less than pleased about that, as I doubted Ulmer was great company. But to give the shaggy bastard his due, there'd been no more near misses since he'd come on board.

Maybe it was the stench, I thought, as a blast of fetid breath hit me. It was almost bad enough to cause me to step back a pace, but I caught myself in time. And stared defiantly up into narrowed, golden eyes.

Right before the end of that bisected nose smeared wetly across mine, leaving a trail of mucous that slimed its way across my cheek.

"What the fuck?" I demanded, and did step back then, the gross factor overriding any attempt to look cool.

Sebastian's bodyguard grinned, showing some broken, yellow teeth, but plenty of whole ones, too.

"About to ask you the same," he said, with the wolf speak so thick in his voice that I doubted anyone inside the truck understood a word.

But they understood something, because the next second, Sophie tried opening the back door, only to have Caleb reach over and slam it shut again without a word. "What the—"

And then I guessed he made good on that gag spell, because she said nothing more.

I kept looking up into the huge face of what was supposed to be an ally, and wondering why I was being treated like a threat. I decided to ask, because I'm the kind of person who asks. "Is this the way you treat clan, Death Stalker?"

I used his Were name since he was transformed, and as a sign of respect. But good manners had no effect, except for a slight lip curl. It seemed that we weren't doing pleasantries tonight.

And then he confirmed it.

"It's the way I treat trespassers, No Name."

"I *have* a name. And I suggest you use it."

"Human name. Weak name for a weak link."

My hand flexed, itching to show him exactly how weak I was, but I pushed my magic back down. It would hurt him, but it wouldn't teach him a damned thing. Weres like him had nothing but contempt for human displays of strength, including magical ones. I could beat him— probably—but I couldn't force him to respect me, or to have any patience for Sebastian's willingness to add a Were to the clan who couldn't even transform.

And then I decided to hell with it, and used a spell to shove him off my truck.

It was not a punch, not quite, but he came off the dirt like a tornado—snarling, maw agape, and eyes narrowed down to slits. I just stood there, trying to look unaffected, and I must have managed it. Because the glistening yellow fangs stopped a hair's breadth from my throat.

"You dare use magic here, little bitch?"

"Bitch? But I don't transform, remember?"

"Don't, or can't?" the words were a rumble, from deep inside his chest. "I hear it's the latter."

"Of course, it is," I said, getting impatient. "I didn't take the bite—"

"We could change that," he said, pushing at me, his breath forming a noxious cloud around us. It smelled like blood, as if he'd been eating some unfortunate creature before I arrived. It smelled like death. "We could test a theory."

"What theory?" I asked, but didn't get a reply. Because Caleb was suddenly behind me, weapons holstered but coat flapping open in a nonexistent wind, showing off exactly how many he had.

"*I* have a theory," he said. "Want to hear it?"

I got a hand on his chest, leaving me stuck between a rock and a very hard place. And wishing that I'd told Sebastian two hours, and dropped everyone off at home first! I should have known this was a bad idea.

"Sebastian called me," I told Ulmer shortly. "Your boss wants a word—"

"With you. Not outsiders."

"—and he said now, so I was in a hurry. But they're not coming in—"

"They die if they try!" the snarl was back in his voice and more pronounced than ever.

"And we find out if I can strip the hide off a wolf with one spell, instead of the usual three," Caleb murmured, his hand on his belt.

"You're not helping!" I said, shooting him a look. "Listen, just take everyone home, okay? I'll be back in a few—"

"We're not going anywhere."

"Damned right!" Sophie said, sticking her head out of the window. I guessed the gag had been wishful thinking on my part. "Is he threatening you? What's he saying? It sounded like a threat!"

I would have put a hand on my forehead, which was developing a stress headache, but I needed both of them to keep two Alphas—and maybe three if you counted Sophie—from going for each other's throats.

"Give me a moment," I told Ulmer, and dragged Caleb back to the truck. I looked at the kids, who were staring at me with varied expressions.

Sophie, of course, was ready to throw down, despite not knowing what she was dealing with. We were going to have to work on that. Chris was glaring at me, as if wondering why the hell I'd brought them here, which . . . yeah. Dimas, predictably, had faded into what I'd started to think of as his liquid state, meaning that he rippled like water, reflecting the images around him. And the remaining kids were subdued and silent, with wide eyes except for Kimmie, who had somehow remained asleep.

I handed Caleb the keys to the truck. "I'll be fine. Clan is clan. He's not going to hurt me."

I ignored the growl from behind, which I swear I could feel in my bones.

"He just likes to put on a show—"

"Like you did this morning?" Ulmer grated.

I ignored that, too.

"—and after I deal with whatever this is, I'll catch a ride back."

"You'll catch a ride with us," Caleb said stubbornly.

"Caleb—"

"We'll stay in the truck," he said. "But I'm not leaving you here alone."

"Yeah. Look at him," Jen piped up, surprising me.

Until I glanced behind, and saw Ulmer bearing his fangs, with thick lines of mucous, spit and God knew what dropping down to wet the desert sand. He looked like a slavering beast out of a nightmare, the kind that would have had Red Riding Hood shitting herself and running for home, grandma be damned. I sighed and turned back around.

"Outsiders aren't allowed in Wolf's Head—on pain of death—when the clan council is in session," I told them. "It isn't right now, or it isn't supposed to be, but it still wouldn't be good if you went in there. Like really wouldn't."

Sophie, of course, started to say something, but I skewered her with a look. "But it won't come down on you if something goes wrong, it'll come down on me. I'm the only clan member here and I brought you. That means I'm responsible for you. You screw up and I'll have to answer for it."

And it looked like I was going to be answering for enough as it was.

"Do you get it?" I asked her, to be sure.

She looked mulish, but Jen shot her a look. And then proved that she wasn't as beta as I'd thought. "We get it. We'll stay here, waiting for you."

"I don't see why," Sophie said stubbornly. "If the damned council or whatever isn't meeting right now, then why does it matter—"

"For God's sake, Soph, it's like sacred ground or something. You remember Uluru?"

"What?"

"That big red rock in the Australian outback?"

Sophie looked understandably confused. "What about it?"

"You know that show we watched, where all those tourists were climbing all over it? The tour companies had hammered rope ladders into it, to make it easier for them, even though the Aborigines consider it sacred and had asked them not to touch it. You remember what you said?"

Sophie looked uncomfortable. "It's not the same—"

"It's exactly the same. It's their stuff. They say who goes in and who doesn't, and if they don't want us there, then we stay here. *Right* here."

Sophie glared at her, and then at me.

"A human with a brain. Will wonders never cease?" Ulmer growled from behind me.

I continued ignoring him, because that seemed to be working.

"If they hurt you, and we're out here and don't even know—" Sophie said stubbornly.

"The only way I get hurt tonight is if you come in after me," I told her. "They can't touch me without Sebastian's approval, and don't have any reason to anyway. Unless you give them one by trespassing on council ground. Then all the clans that use this place will be demanding recompense—from me. You get it?"

She glared some more, because Sophie was not a young woman who liked being told what to do. But she didn't appear to like the idea of getting me into trouble, either, because she finally sat back against the seat. "Fine. But if you don't come out—in one piece—there will be hell to pay."

Chapter Twenty-One

Little one is feisty," Ulmer growled, as we approached the entrance. "Should have been a Were. Unlike some."

"I can be feisty," I said, wondering what his problem was tonight.

Not that he was ever warm and cuddly, but provoking me wasn't his usual style. He typically sent me a lip curl whenever we met and then ignored me, as if I was beneath his notice. Which as a rogue, I probably was.

So, the fact that he was being this open in his dislike meant that I was already in trouble.

And then he confirmed it.

"You can be stupid," he growled. "Not the same thing!"

He'd held his comment until we'd passed through the entrance and left it behind, entering the twists and turns of a maze of high, narrow stone passages that branched through this place like a warren. Some were artificially straight, having been cut into the rock, while others had the dips and ripples of natural formations, carved by the wind and rain over millennia. All were dark, being only occasionally lit up by a smoking torch.

Very occasionally, since Weres see a lot better at night than I do.

That left the passageways dim, and even worse, any sound soon hit walls or dead ends and bounced back, causing a strange echoing void that few voices managed to escape. Cry for help in here and even a Were was unlikely to hear you. That thought didn't help the itch at the bottom of my spine, which was getting higher and making my legs jittery, probably because they wanted to run back out of here.

Instead, I looked up at some strips of buff-colored cloth that had been stretched over the passage to provide protection from the sun. They were dark orange tonight, reflecting the light off the stones, and hadn't been changed in a while, which had left them pretty ragged. As a result, the effect was less modern sail shades and more laundry left out on a line. They were flapping in a slight breeze, enhancing the effect of somebody's long johns, but through the gaps the stars peered down.

I decided to stop being a pussy and came to a halt, wanting to know what I was getting into. Ulmer stopped with me, as if delighted to elaborate. Only maybe delighted wasn't quite the right word.

"Alright, what is the problem?" I asked.

"You! You are the problem!"

"For what? Not being able to Change?"

"For being part of the ruling clan, but acting like a fool over a damned *vargulf,* and in public! How do you think that makes Sebastian look? Did you stop to think, for one second, what would have happened if you'd killed Gonzago?"

"Gonzago?"

This simple question seemed to enrage him even more. He snarled, the sound echoing ominously up and down the corridor. "This! This is what I mean, you stupid girl! You didn't even know that you took down the head of the Brightwater clan. He couldn't back down once you challenged—he's a *clan leader*. He had to fight, and you damned near killed him in the process! What do you think would have happened if he'd died, hm? What do you fucking think?"

I started to answer, then paused, because there were none that he'd like or even understand. To a clan wolf, especially one whose honor was now tied to that of the leader of the Were world, the sooner a *vargulf* died the better. A dead outcaste caused no problems, and that was all Jace was anymore: not a person, much less a boy in need of protection. Just a source of trouble and potential embarrassment.

It made risking myself for him looked like the height of folly, and arguing the point would get me nowhere.

So, of course, I did it anyway.

"May as well let Jace die, and decrease the surplus population, is that it?"

The words surprised me as much as they seemed to Ulmer, maybe because they came out in wolf speak, a smooth, silky growl, instead of my human voice. Or maybe because there had been no conscious thought behind them. At least not my conscious thought.

Shit.

Ulmer had transformed back to his human state, or as close to it as he ever got, while we talked. That left him naked, but it was honestly hard to tell, with a shaggy head of gray/black hair that almost reached the small of his back, a massive beard, and enough wiry gray body hair to count as a pelt. His human eyes were brown, but occasionally flashed the gold of his alter ego. And the scar across his face was the same, only deeper, almost bisecting his nose and lifting his lip in a perpetual snarl.

He was just as fierce in this guise as the other, although at the moment, he looked more puzzled than anything else.

"What? Who the hell is Jace?"

"This! This is what I mean, old man."

I heard myself paraphrase his own insulting words back at him and tried to stop, but something didn't want to stop. Something wanted to provoke him, and was doing a damned good job, judging by the expression in the suddenly narrowed eyes. But that only seemed to make me louder.

"You didn't even know you were talking about a child, one who had just lost his brother, who had *seen him die*. He was traumatized and helpless, and couldn't back down once a much larger wolf challenged him, because was a *child*. What do you think would have happened if he'd died? That I wouldn't have savaged all of them? That I would have left a wolf alive who had happily watched a cub be torn apart and done nothing? What do you fucking *think*?"

I had backed him into a wall, not realizing it until my fist punched the stone beside his head and I watched the massive block crack halfway up the cliff face. Pieces of it rained down onto the burly man, who was looking at me with another expression, but it wasn't anger this time. More like someone who suddenly realizes he's alone with a psycho.

"You're mad," he said.

"Furious," I snarled, and strode off in the direction of the stadium.

I was practically blind with anger, so much so that I was surprised I didn't face plant into another wall. I could almost feel the beast pacing inside, wanting to come out, but trapped and fuming. She wanted to go back and teach Ulmer a lesson. She wanted to see him bleed. She fought me every step that I took away from the arrogant bastard, who would have never dared to speak to our mother that way, but who treated us like dirt beneath his feet. And our cub even worse, as trash, as *nothing*.

So, yeah, I was lucky that the main entrance was shorter than the tunnels in the fortress surrounding it. Or maybe it was Ulmer who was lucky; I didn't know anymore. But while the other passages had been designed to trap and confuse an enemy long enough for him to become lunch, this one was abbreviated, a deceptively friendly, come-on-in-and-sit-a-while invitation that anyone with any sense refused.

But I didn't have much sense, as I was proving in spades tonight. And before I knew it, I was spilling out into a large, brightly lit space. So bright, that I had to put a hand up to give my eyes time to adjust, and even before they did, I knew what I'd see, as a thousand terrible scents hit my nose, all at once, like a belt to the face.

"What the fuck?" It was my own voice that spoke the words this time, and my own thoughts behind them, but I was too shocked to be relieved.

"My question exactly," Sebastian said, striding over.

My eyes adjusted enough to see him some out of the blur, not in his usual suit, but in a black linen caftan that flapped around his ankles, with black embroidery edging the low-cut neckline and sandals in the same color. He looked like a desert sheik, lean, dark and strangely elegant, although a fashion statement this wasn't. It was the sort of thing a *bardric's* entourage took along in case he burst out of his other clothes, because the leader's dignity wouldn't support letting it all hang out like Ulmer.

That meant that something had startled Sebastian enough to force a change, which would normally have shocked me as he was nothing if not controlled. But I didn't have to ask why tonight. I didn't have to ask anything.

Because the stadium in front of me . . .

Was full of corpses.

Or, to be more precise, it was full of pieces of corpses. Arms, legs, heads, and the occasional torso littered the sand, and what looked like an ocean's worth of blood had splashed the long rows of rock cut benches that surrounded the big open space. They were a mottled red-brown anyway, so the slaughter didn't show up as much there, but that wasn't true of the sand beneath our feet, which had been brought in to cover the more sophisticated carnage that sometimes happened here.

This was the official place of challenge, where evildoers were made to pay for their crimes, and things often became bloody. But not like this. I'd never seen anything like this.

Except briefly, in a vision out in the desert, I realized. Had that been when this happened? Because it had to have been recent. The blood was still liquid in spots, although it was no longer warm . . .

"Recognize them?" Sebastian said, his voice rough, as he crouched across from me.

I realized that I'd sunk to one knee beside the nearest body. It had a large stain seeping out from underneath, which the cop part of my brain had already started to assess. That was made difficult by the fact that much of the blood had seeped away into the sand, but the wound the victim was lying face down on must have been severe, because there was still plenty pooled around.

I might have been wrong about the timing, I thought. With the fact that much of the blood had already formed a gel like consistency, some had started to coagulate into dark clots, and a black, cracked rim had begun eating at the edges of the puddles . . . my best guess was that this had occurred earlier than my vision. Possibly as long as six to eight hours ago, although the lack of humidity might have fudged that somewhat—

"Lia!"

I looked up to find Sebastian staring at me. He didn't look angry; more concerned, with a line in between the dark blue eyes that were so different and yet so like his brother's. They examined my face for a moment as though they barely knew it, and I stared back, seeing two different creatures merging in and out of one another.

The sun bronzed figure in black was crouched in the dirt, but the shadow of his alter ego loomed over him. It was a tawny giant with fire lit eyes, or maybe those were some of the many torches that had been scattered around and were now shining through the illusion, or whatever this was. I still wasn't sure and didn't care, just stared up at him in awe, caught in surprise as always by the beauty of our other form.

And then I noticed—he wasn't alone.

I didn't mean just the people who had gathered in groups at a couple of the lesser entrances, who were being rousted out by some of Sebastian's squad. Wolf's Head was currently occupied by several smaller clans whose territories had been impacted by the war and who had nowhere else to go. So, instead of the passageways beyond the stadium branching off into classrooms, recreational centers, communal kitchens and meeting halls, they now boasted what looked like the beginnings of a small town.

Or so I'd been told. I didn't make a lot of council sessions. But the people trying to peer in looked normal enough, despite the wolf shadows I could see behind them.

But others didn't.

Sebastian was trying to talk to me, but I was busy watching shadows flitting around the arena the way the tourists had in Vegas, or the phantom boys in Cyrus's apartment. Scent people were everywhere, and gathered most strongly in the areas around the bodies. Or what was left of them.

Some of the clouds were smeared, blurred by people passing through in the hours since, but others were strong and bright, with the lack of wind inside the huge walls keeping them intact. So much so that I could see dim recreations of the battle in places: a wolf on his belly, fighting desperately to get away, his fingernails carving long trenches in the sand as he was dragged off. Another had been thrown against a wall, the blood splatter around where he hit still visible on the stone although the body itself was gone. And several teeth had been knocked out of someone in human form by a savage blow, causing them to go flying.

But most of the dead were Changed, which made sense as they'd been fighting for their lives, with blood splattered fur everywhere. There was everything from tawny to russet and from brown to black, with plenty of beautifully mottled coats in between. And while they were ripped up and stained from the battle, they were still there.

So, hunters hadn't done this. The dark mages who stalked Weres for their skins would never have left a fortune to rot on the desert sand. Nor would any have been bold enough to come here on a hunt to begin with.

I turned my attention back to the teeth.

I'd found them by smell. Someone's shoe had almost buried them in sand, when its owner staggered back from a blow to the gut. The attack had brought up his dinner—tacos and cola, by the smell of things—and splattered it all over another wolf that had been running by, trying desperately to get away from someone.

I could see the panicked wolf, but not his pursuer. I only knew that he was there because of the scent void around him, just nothingness beyond a splatter of puke, some of which had hit him, too. I could trace it as he moved along, even through the sickly-sweet odor of death that permeated this place. But he and the other attackers were simply . . . missing.

"Are you alright?" Sebastian demanded, a hand on my shoulder.

"Can't see them," I said, staring around. It was as if the dead had been attacked by ghosts.

"See who?"

"The people who did this. They're . . ." I sketched an absent body with my hands, showing where it had been standing beside a decapitated head, which I assumed had not been levitating in mid-air. But whatever had been holding it wasn't registering.

"Must have used scent suits," Ulmer said, coming up. He'd found a pair of jeans somewhere, but his feet were still bare, and now stained pink from where he'd splashed unconcernedly through a puddle. So much for the crime scene, I thought, my human mind cringing.

Not that it mattered; the Corps would never be allowed in here. I was the closest to an investigator this scene was ever going to get, which probably explained why Sebastian had called me. But all I had here was half a story.

And then what Ulmer had said registered.

"They used what?" I said, looking up.

"You cover yourself head to toe in a hazmat type thing, or whatever you can rig. Garbage bags and duct tape will work if you use enough of 'em. Then smear on some noxious potion, maybe two or three. And Bob's your uncle, no one can follow you back to your house and rip your guts out."

"Some of the criminal elements preying on the Were community have been using them for a while," Sebastian added. "To keep their identities secret. I'm surprised you didn't know."

"The Corps doesn't deal with Were issues all that much."

And that went double when it was Were on Were violence, which this definitely had been. These bodies had been savaged, literally shredded at times, not gunned down. There was also no potions' residue splattered about, or decaying spells shriveling up in a corner, as would have been the case after a magical attack. This was butchery, done with claws and teeth and overwhelming strength.

Weres did this.

And I was pretty sure I knew what kind.

"No, they expect us to police our own," Sebastian said, looking aggrieved, despite the fact that that was by the clan council's own request. But said request had been made before his time, and was obviously not one he agreed with.

"As opposed to?" Ulmer growled. "We don't need mages interfering."

"Clearly we do! Or we need our own investigative force, as I've been trying to tell the council. If this was the work of hunters—"

"Not hunters," Ulmer and I said simultaneously, causing Sebastian to blink.

"Then what was it?"

I just shook my head. I was pretty sure I knew, but it wasn't something I wanted to discuss out in the open. But I still had a question.

"I don't smell any potions."

Sebastian grimaced. "No, whatever the attackers used seems to work a little differently. Instead of masking a person's scent with unpleasant odors, it . . . removes it. Like cutting a piece out of the natural world. It is something we haven't encountered before."

"There's a lot of that going around."

The blue eyes narrowed. "So I hear. But right now, I'm more interested in why the clan who attacked you yesterday have been butchered, and dumped into the middle of our sacred ground."

Chapter Twenty-Two

What?" I stared at Sebastian, but didn't get an answer. Instead, he simply strode away, with the air of someone used to being followed.

So, I did, and Ulmer followed me, the two of us picking a path through the forest of the dead. The Were remains were bad, being torn up and fly strewn now that darkness had fallen and the scavengers of the desert had come out to feed. But the human ones were worse.

Their skins had been discolored by the heat that they'd probably lain in for hours, although not like a sunburn. They were the hue of charred roast beef, with no healing possible anymore. Just meat on the grill.

I swallowed and tried to find somewhere else for my eyes to rest, but unless I looked straight up, there wasn't anything. Corpses were everywhere. And in such a savaged condition that I couldn't even count them all.

And then Sebastian was shoving a new one in my face, or the head anyway.

It was human, or a Were who had shifted back after death, which sometimes happens. But it was hard to tell much more than that. It had a melting quality, as if the skin was dripping off the bones. It looked like a Halloween mask with no head inside it, probably because the skull had been pulverized by the vicious blow it had taken to one side.

Said blow had splattered blood all over the face, further obscuring the features, but Sebastian seemed to think it proved something.

"Cloud Leaper, of the Windward clan. You put in a request for information about him earlier today. I would like to know why."

I stared into the glazed eyes of the Were I'd spoken to briefly at the grow farm, before he changed and attacked me. And still had trouble recognizing him. But the signs were all there, now that I knew to look for them.

He still had the same sandy blond hair, which Sebastian was currently holding him up by, the same thin face and stubbly beard, and the same slightly gray teeth that said he hadn't visited a dentist in a while. But while the face was largely untouched, the body was missing. Only a few inches of spine dangled out of the severed neck, along with some ropy muscle that indicated that this head hadn't been severed so much as ripped off.

I swallowed some more.

"The heads were all pulverized like this, we don't know why," Sebastian added. "But there isn't an intact one in the bunch."

And no, there wasn't. The bleeding mountain behind him, which appeared to be where all the heads had been brought for identification, would have been gory enough, but someone had turned the skulls into mush. But not as if they had been trying to obscure the features. Cloud Leapers' face was bloody, but intact, as were many of the others.

They appeared to have been pulverized at random, in a rage-fueled frenzy.

"This is him, isn't it?" Sebastian asked impatiently, when I took my time assessing things. Usually so good at appearing human, he turned the grisly body part he was holding toward him and scowled at it. And then used a sandaled toe to search around the pile at his feet, disturbing some flies.

They rose up in a thin black cloud, with some taking off from the opened, dead eyes of the victims, where they'd been feasting. And I swallowed my lunch back down for what had to be the fifth time. "It's him," I said, my voice thick.

"Good. And?" His remained calm, but that probably wouldn't last long if I didn't get my shit together.

I gave myself a mental slap.

"*Bokors*."

"I beg your pardon?"

"It's another word for necromancers. The Corps has mages who can sometimes peer inside a dead brain and retrieve information. It's often inconclusive, especially after any time has passed. But it looks like whoever did this didn't want to take chances."

The blue eyes narrowed. "Someone didn't want these people talking, even after death."

"No." And they wouldn't be. Whatever brain matter they'd had, had been turned into sludge. I looked away. "How did you know he attacked me?"

"You told the archivist. Don't you remember?"

It was smooth, without so much as a minute hesitation. It was also a lie. I'd been shell shocked all day, but not giving people more information than they needed had been ingrained into my psyche through years of training and natural reserve. I hadn't just decided to spill my guts to a librarian I didn't even know.

Which meant that Sebastian had a spy at HQ who'd sussed out the truth, probably after my little display this morning.

Great.

This was why it was hard having a foot in both camps. I ought to tell Hargroves that he had somebody on the take, or somebody with loose lips, or somebody sleeping with one of the Were guards who didn't understand the meaning of discretion. But if I did, and the suborner of war mages was found, he'd just be replaced by another. And it would damage the tentative alliance that we needed so badly.

So, it wouldn't go into my report. And neither would this, but for a different reason. Sebastian was *bardric*, which meant that the buck stopped with him—on everything, but especially when it came to keeping his people safe. And having a whole tribe butchered, and then left to rot in the middle of the Wolf's Head, the local symbol of his power?

Somebody was making a statement, and if he didn't figure out who and go medieval on their ass, it wasn't going to look good. Especially not with Conclave bringing the leaders of the Were world here to witness his failure. The Corps couldn't be involved in this; it had to be his fight.

I looked up, and saw the weight of it on his shoulders.

He knew.

"I need to talk to you privately," I said, and got a jerky nod in return.

"This way."

* * *

But of course, it wasn't that easy. Weres banded together in times of trouble, and the ones here wanted reassurance. They wanted to be close to their *bardric*, to see him rant and rave, to hear him promise death and destruction to their enemies.

And they wanted it now.

Sebastian was mobbed as soon as we reached the nearest corridor, where his people had been holding back the crowd. I guessed the plan had been to find a room somewhere and talk, but that was clearly not happening right away. And even Ulmer's furious cursing and shoving couldn't do anything about it.

But despite the bodyguard's concern, I didn't think these people had assassination in mind. They looked freaked out, with their children clasped close and their eyes wide and fearful. And Sebastian noticed.

He stopped to reassure them, standing in the middle of the milling throng, letting them close, letting them touch him, like he hadn't almost been killed three times in the last few months. Because whatever else you could say about the man, he wasn't a coward. Of course, he wasn't stupid, either. He also had Ulmer and a dozen of his men watching the crowd, ready to leap on a problem at a second's notice.

He didn't need me.

I took the opportunity to slip away and try to locate the guards who were supposed to have been at the entrance. It wasn't hard. They were laid out in a nearby rock-cut room, on sheets that had been spread on the floor, while several women tried to make them presentable.

Since they were in pieces, that wasn't going well.

"Sunseeker. They're going to want blood," one of the women said, when I asked their clan affiliation.

Since Sunseeker was among the larger and wealthier local clans, she was probably right. I was surprised that they weren't here already, raising hell. But we likely didn't have long.

"Did anyone see what happened?" I asked. Because that attack couldn't have been quiet.

But to my surprise, she shook her head. She was probably still on the right side of forty, if only just, with caramel colored skin and hair that remained long and ebony dark. She was wearing a simple outfit of jeans and a lighter denim shirt with the sleeves rolled up, but climbing her inner arm was a gorgeous tattoo of a single feather in oranges and reds, and in her right ear was an elaborate beaded earring that didn't look like you could buy it in a shop.

Red Mountain, I thought, an all Native American clan of mostly Shoshone and Paiute people, and one of the groups currently in residence. Only this woman was looking like she wished she wasn't. They had relocated to try to avoid the war, but it had followed them here.

"No," she told me, dusting dried blood off her hands. "We were asked to avoid the arena. Guess the local clans didn't want us hanging out our washing in their sacred space." She made a face. "Sacred, when it's just used for killing."

"Your clan doesn't handle things that way?" I asked, because the carefully arranged challenges in the arena were nothing like the slaughter outside.

Dark eyes flashed in my direction. "No, we have this crazy habit of talking things out, rather than gutting each other."

"You know that doesn't always work, Sienna," the other woman said. She was still kneeling by one of the bodies, I had no idea why. Nothing was going to make that collection of clawed remains look human again.

"Which is why there are fines and jails, not to mention jury trials with actual evidence," her counterpart said. "Anything else is barbarism, plain and simple. We should be past that by now!"

"It's tradition—"

Sienna had some colorful ideas for what tradition could do to itself, which she expressed at length.

"Sebastian wants what you do, but it isn't so easy," I said, when she finally wound down. "For trials, you need judges, an extensive court system, investigators to gather evidence—and tribal leaders willing to accept rulings on their internal affairs. And so far, they've been resistant—"

"Of course, they've been resistant, the hidebound old bastards! The well-run clans don't think they need supervision, and the sloppy, corrupt, or power mad ones don't want it showing them up. But what they want doesn't matter; we need change! If this hasn't shown that, I don't know what would!"

"I hear you," I repeated, because Cyrus and I had talked about this many times. "But establishing so many courts would also require raising clan dues, and it's like pulling teeth to get them to pay up as it is. Arbitrating disputes between different clans can be done by the Clan Council, who volunteer their time. But anything more extensive—"

"So, if it's hard, it isn't worth doing?" she demanded.

"I didn't say that—"

"Not to mention that just the idea of decent oversight might prevent things like this! The very idea that we could be attacked here, at Wolf's Head itself!" She looked outraged. "This must be investigated!"

"It will be—"

"By you?" She looked me up and down with sharp dark eyes. "Accalia de Croissets, I take it? Heard you'd been adopted by Arnou. Didn't quite believe it though.

"Didn't think Sebastian would be that smart."

"Smart?"

She shot me a look on the way to the opening that passed for a door. "That not the usual response you get?"

"Not so much." That won me a bark of a laugh, but no explanation as she grabbed a barefoot young girl who was running past and said a couple sentences in a language I didn't know. But I recognized a name, at least. "Jack?"

"My son." The girl took off into the milling crowd, and Sienna turned back to me, fast enough to cause her long hair to swing.

She had a strange energy about her, lightning fast and with abrupt, staccato movements that reminded me of something, but I couldn't place it. Not a wolf, though. But it matched the rapid-fire delivery that left me scrambling to keep up.

"He's the one who raised the alarm," she added. "I assume you want to talk to him?"

I nodded.

She looked past me at the butchered remains on the floor, and shook her head in what looked like a mix of sorrow and disgust. "Tell me you're here on behalf of the Corps. Tell me we're about to be overrun by investigators who know what they're doing. That you're going to get to the bottom of this."

"I'm . . . here on behalf of Sebastian."

Keen dark eyes met mine. "Of course, you are. That's why he adopted you. To keep stuff like this quiet until he could figure out how to spin it. It's all politics with that one—"

I opened my mouth, but she shut me down.

"I understand the reasons. I know politics better than most; I've been dealing with them all my life. But that kind of attitude won't fly this time. The war isn't nice and neat with a PC answer for everything. It's messy and dangerous, and if we're going to survive, we're going to have to ruffle a few feathers. Get a little messy ourselves. Or wait to get butchered like those poor bastards out there!"

"Meaning?" I asked, because I wasn't sure where she was going with this.

"Meaning, call in the Corps, if you haven't already! We need help with this—no matter what Sebastian thinks."

"I'm sure he has plans for how to deal with the investigation," I said uneasily, because that was what I wanted, too, and had since I first saw this place. But I'd just finishing thinking about how difficult involving anyone else was likely to be. "However—"

"However what? They should already be here!"

"—the Corps might not be the best choice. For one, it doesn't know how to investigate Were crimes—"

"And we do?"

"The clans police themselves, Sienna," the other woman said. "You know that—"

"Yes, seems to be working well!"

"—and they're overworked right now," I continued grimly, "without the manpower to take on the oversight of a new, large, and mostly unknown group. Not to mention that no tribe would submit themselves to Circle justice—"

"Then they need to start! Or we need to come up with an equivalent system. I've spent my whole life witnessing Were violence being called justice, and I'm sick of it. Seen too many bastards get away with brutal crimes because they were stronger—as if strength was ever a guarantee of wisdom! Seen too many small clans be bullied by larger ones, while the council does nothing. But you—you could change that."

"Change it . . . how?" I asked, feeling cornered. Not least because she'd just physically backed me into one. "You're talking about overturning thousands of years of—"

I stopped before I said the dreaded T word and pissed her off again, but it didn't help.

"The humans slaughtered each other for thousands of years, too. That was their tradition, but they found a better way. Why can't we?"

"Perhaps we can, but—"

"Good, I'm glad we agree. So, I take it that you are investigating this?"

"Trying to," I said, my head spinning.

"And the Corps?"

"I just explained—"

"Why they can't do it. But you're Corps, aren't you? You could put together a crew made up of Weres, train them in the Corps' investigative techniques, and—"

"Wait. What—"

"—Sebastian could use them on things like this. It's what we've needed for a while—"

"That isn't what I'm doing—"

"Well, why not?"

"I—the Corps would never allow it, for one, and I already have a job—"

"Yes, and from what I hear, it has designated you to deal with Were matters for at least the last year or so. You're the one who found Sebastian's daughter when she went missing, and cleared up that mess with Grayshadow, although nobody ever really understood what happened there. But you were obviously involved—"

"At Sebastian's request! I can't just go around—"

"Why not?" The woman was wearing a bunch of silver and turquoise bracelets that clinked together when she put her hands on her hips. I stared back at her, unused to feeling quite this dominated. She was maybe five foot two, giving me six inches on her, but somehow managed to convey the idea that she was looking down on me.

"Who are you?" I asked.

"Sienna Thunderbird, Lupa of the Red Mountain Clan."

Okay, that explained a few things.

"Well, Ms. Thunderbird, I don't have the authority to simply make up my own department. It doesn't work like that—"

"Then who does have the authority? Because somebody needs to deal with this before the perps become emboldened to do even worse."

"I'm sure that Sebastian—"

"Wonderful! It's settled then. I'll let my people know they can rely on you."

I was about to make the response that bit of steamrolling deserved when a young man ducked into the room. He looked about twelve in the face, with still-chubby cheeks and innocent brown eyes, but he was already too tall for the six-foot door. He was dressed in a football jersey and jeans, but had a waist length braid running down his back.

She pushed him at me.

"Here you go. Your first witness. Jake, tell Mage de Croissets all you know. She's the head of our new investigative squad."

And then she left, leaving me staring after her with my mouth slightly ajar.

"That's the typical reaction," the other woman said dryly, getting up. "Laura Bright Feather," she said, holding out a hand. "Sienna's cousin."

I took it and found her grip to be strong, as all Were's were. But other than that, she didn't exactly scream otherworldly predator. She was what is often referred to as fluffy, a motherly sort of woman with a short, modern haircut that suited her pleasantly round face. She was dressed similarly to her boisterous counterpart, except for an embroidered floral blouse instead of an Oxford shirt, and without all the jewelry.

She did have an elaborate earring, though, and saw me notice it.

She touched it briefly. "Our people believe that you can't get into the afterworld without a piercing."

"What happens when you Change?" I asked, because Weres didn't often wear jewelry. Sienna must be very confident in her control, because bracelets could cut into the flesh of suddenly larger limbs, and necklaces, especially strong ones, could choke you. I supposed that earrings would make the switch easily enough, but you still didn't see many people wearing them.

But I guessed spiritual matters won out over convenience.

"We look fabulous," Laura confirmed, and I laughed.

She patted my shoulder. "Don't let Sienna worry you. She's just frustrated. She's been the voice of reason for many years, but nobody listens. I think she's decided, if you can't beat 'em, join 'em."

Great.

"She'll try to railroad you, but just stand your ground. She'll respect you more—"

"And bully me less?"

Laura shrugged. "There's always a first time," she said optimistically, and left.

I watched her go, wondering how much trouble the stubborn Lupa was likely to make. I decided to let Hargroves or Sebastian explain things to her, depending on who she cornered next, and turned my attention to the young man. And discovered that he wasn't looking at me.

Chapter Twenty-Three

I watched the boy's Adam's apple bob up and down as he looked at what was left of a clan's best defenders. Laura must have doubled over the sheets when I wasn't looking, hiding the worst of the damage, but it didn't help much. A ripped-up body under a sheet, as it turned out, looked a lot like a ripped-up body under a sheet.

I suddenly remembered that I was dealing with a kid, even if he was taller than me. And probably a traumatized one at that. Weres might be exposed to more violence than most humans, but what I'd seen today wasn't normal, even for us.

"We can go somewhere else," I offered.

But the boy was made of the same stern stuff as his mother, and shook his head. "It's okay. Saw worse out there."

He jerked his head in the direction of the arena, and I used the opportunity to maneuver us around so that he was facing the door to the outside. "Yes, I heard that you discovered the . . . situation."

"Situation." He choked out a laugh. "Yeah, I guess so."

"Can you tell me what happened?"

I'd made my voice softer, and that and the fact that he was no longer staring at corpses seemed to help. I also decided that I might have underestimated his age. I revised my guess upward to maybe fifteen, taking into account the acne on the otherwise smooth cheeks and the hint of peach fuzz on the upper lip. He also had lashes as long as a girl's and would probably turn heads in a few years.

"Got a drone for my birthday," he told me tersely. "Wanted to try it out. We're not supposed to go into the arena, but a lot of us do anyway. The back tunnels get . . . claustrophobic . . . after a while."

"You're not allowed to go outside?"

He shrugged. "Sure. As long as we take a couple of adults with us, who usually don't want to stay for long. And it has to be in daylight and in sight of the lookout stations up top. And we have to have a good reason."

I thought that having a bunch of kids cooped up in an unfamiliar place dealing with a move, a war, and what was likely a bunch of antsy adults ought to be reason enough. But then, I wasn't a parent. I'd probably be overprotective in their position, too.

Of course, they might have loosened up the restrictions after a while, had everything gone according to plan. But probably not now. And Jake seemed to be thinking along the same lines, because he suddenly scowled.

"Everybody's so focused on the war, on keeping us safe. Yet it got in anyway. Looks like nowhere is safe anymore."

"We'll look after you," I promised.

Which . . . may not have been my best move. Angry dark eyes met mine, and then the floodgates opened. The formerly quiet, scared teen started talking and couldn't seem to stop.

"You can't! The hunters came for us at Red Mountain, and I—we barely got away! Then they followed us here and—"

"Those weren't hunters out there."

"Then what *were* they? Why would anyone *do* that?" he gestured wildly in the direction of the carnage. "*How* did they do that? And who were those people? I never even saw any of them before and now they're dead. Did you see—"

"Yes—"

"—what somebody did to them? They were torn *up*. But nobody seems to know why, and nobody will tell us anything! We're just supposed to go back to our rooms and wait until the adults figure it out, but we *can't*. How can we go back there? How can we stay here at all? But if we don't, where do we go? The war is everywhere—"

"And so are your protectors," I said, griping his arm.

But he just looked at me, shaken and miserable. He needed comforting, like the frightened kid he still was. But his mother had been busy trying to deal with the fallout and I was a lousy substitute.

Not for the first time, I wished that I had Cyrus's easy way with people. Even when he was being stern, they gravitated toward him. And damn, didn't I wish he was here right now!

But he wasn't, and this boy needed something.

Or someone.

"Is your dad around?" I asked, and immediately wished I hadn't.

"No." Jake jerked out of my grip. "He's dead. Five years now."

"I'm sorry."

He looked away, hiding tears. "It was natural. Heart attack."

Which made it exactly no better at all.

"Mom took over after he died. And she's done a good job." His gaze came back to me, and it was fierce. "But she can't fight the whole world, and neither can I—and now we're stuck here, in a freaking massacre. I was in *school*; I'd just joined the softball team—"

"You went to a human school?" I asked, surprised.

He gave me a jerky nod, caught mid-sentence. "All the kids do, at least in our clan. Mom said we have to live in this world, so we might as well start early. It's worked out okay, except a couple of the guys accused me of having a period—" He stopped abruptly, and flushed. "Sorry. It's just, I get a little snippy around that time of month, and they noticed—"

"It's okay," I told him. "You know, I went to a regular school, too."

He blinked at that. "Really?"

"Lettered in track and softball."

His eyes lit up. "You played?"

"All four years. I was the star hitter in my last."

That actually won me a small smile. "I can hit, but coach said I have a better arm. He was thinking of making me a backup pitcher . . ." The brief joy in his face faded, when he remembered that that wasn't going to happen now.

"What grade are you in?" I asked.

"Tenth. Or I was. We're homeschooled now."

"Then you can still try out next year."

He abruptly looked away again. I didn't blame him. To someone of his age, leaving his school and friends behind had probably felt like losing the whole world.

He dashed an angry hand across his eyes after a moment. "You really think this'll be over next year?"

"Maybe. It has to end sometime, right? But in the meantime, Sebastian is strong and smart. He isn't going to just ignore this, or sweep it under the rug."

"That's what Mom's afraid of. She said that's what politicians do."

"Not Sebastian. He'll fight for you. And so will I."

He looked at me in surprise, as if he'd expected a different response. "That's . . . you're nice to say that." He looked me over and then realized what he was doing and blushed again. "You're . . . they said you're that Were war mage. Lia something?"

"De Croissets."

"And you're really a rogue?"

"Yeah."

"Why?"

I shrugged. "You already said it. I wanted to be a war mage and they don't take Weres. Not even a Were with magic."

"Well, they should!" The copper-colored cheeks flushed again, this time with anger. "We'd be better for a lot of things than the damned mages—" he stopped, maybe realizing that he was talking to someone in that category. "Uh, I didn't mean—"

"It's okay. Some of them are damned mages." I smiled at him, and got another smile in return, a bigger one this time. "So, you went to the arena to test out your gift. And got a surprise."

"Yeah."

"When was this?"

"A couple hours ago. I . . ." he paused, but he didn't lie to me. He obviously wanted to, but his mom had raised him right. "I freaked out," he admitted. "Just turned around and ran back to my room, and didn't tell anybody for, like, fifteen minutes; I don't know why. But then ma came in to tell me that dinner was almost ready and . . ."

"It's okay," I said, because the Adam's apple had gone back to work.

"I lost my lunch," he admitted. "She was worried until she found out why, then ran off to raise the alarm. I know I should have already done it, but—"

"That was enough to rattle anyone. What happened after your mother alerted the clans?"

"It got crazy. Like completely batshit. People were running and yelling—I think half of them thought we were being attacked—and the rest headed for the arena to see for themselves. Ma made everyone get out of there, something about not disturbing the crime scene, only some of them already had. But she cleared them out and called the *bardric*, and he showed up a little while later. I don't remember exactly when."

Probably not long. If anything would make Sebastian burn rubber out of Vegas, this would be it. Only something didn't add up.

"Those bodies had been there longer than a couple of hours," I said. "Maybe a lot longer. Didn't anybody notice? See anything, hear anything?"

"It's hard to hear thorough the tunnels," he said, repeating what I already knew. "They twist and turn and sound fades out. And nobody is supposed to go into the arena itself. But I thought a few minutes wouldn't hurt, just to make sure the drone worked okay—"

"I get it." Or, rather, I got his point, but not how a massacre had happened and nobody noticed. Especially in a facility populated by beings with super senses. "You didn't smell anything, either?"

"Smell?"

"From back there," I gestured into the labyrinth where I guessed the makeshift town had been set up. "Nobody noticed the blood, the viscera, the—" spilled shit, I didn't say, because battlefields are ugly in so many ways, and I didn't want to remind him.

But all he did was blink at me. "Who could smell anything from all the way back there?"

I didn't answer, but my senses suddenly woke up to do it for me. I could feel those little tree roots shooting outward, crawling around the space, mapping it without the need for eyes. Informing me of what each small dwelling had been cooking for dinner, including one whose pot of rabbit stew had been spilt on the floor in the confusion.

Its scent mingled with the dust on the floor and some rat droppings somebody hadn't found under a sink. The sink had a leak, which was dampening the drywall and loosening the wallpaper glue on the other side of the wall, in the same room where somebody was hiding a bottle of booze under his bed. He'd spilled some around the shape of the bottle; I could see it in my mind's eye, a blank patch in the middle of the field of sharpness. Like I could see the open bottle of glue on a desk in the house next door, where a kid had been assembling a model airplane on a desk—

I blinked, and things snapped back to normal.

But it suddenly occurred to me that maybe my new senses weren't Were standard, after all.

* * *

"Mage Jenkins," I told the Corps' operator a few minutes later. I'd taken a moment to make a call, after sending Jake off with a task to keep him busy. He was a smart kid; I was pretty sure he knew what I was doing, but he hadn't argued.

Maybe he wanted something to occupy his mind, too.

As a result, he was currently assembling the other kids into the community kitchen/cafeteria that was used for tribal get togethers, and seeing to it that they all got fed. One of the first things I'd learned in this job was that, no matter how upsetting the situation, always offer food and drink. People find it difficult to panic and eat at the same time, and witnessing death usually makes them want to do something life affirming, so they typically don't argue.

The result: they feel better, and you get a calmer, more rational bunch to deal with.

In this case, it also had the bonus of getting the kids out from underfoot, along with some of the adults who'd gone to help. And I needed the space. Because I was about to do something that would not improve with witnesses.

Assuming that anybody ever answered the damned phone, that was. I had to listen to a terrible light jazz rendition of "Poker Face" three and a half times before Jenkins, AKA the Mole Rat, AKA the four-foot-tall, glasses-wearing, cryptid enthusiast I'd met with Hargroves what felt like a lifetime ago, finally came on the line. And was just as charming as the Corps' functionaries tend to be.

"What?"

"Jenkins?"

"Isn't that who you asked for?" he demanded.

"Yes, I need—"

"Which took me by surprise, since I've left you half a dozen messages today and you've responded to exactly none of them. But my shift ends in ten minutes, so of course you finally decide to—"

"What messages?"

"The ones on your answering machine? I called your house three times, then tried your cell. Do you ever bother to check—"

"I was away for part of the afternoon, and out of range for the rest—"

"Typical! What if there'd been an emergency? What if—"

"You mean, there wasn't an emergency?"

"What? No—"

"Then why did you call me six times?"

"Because I heard through the grapevine that you ingested the same dose as that boy Colin, yet you didn't turn—"

Great.

Fucking great.

"—and naturally, I want you to come in so that we can test your blood—"

"Sedgewick already has my blood."

"Yes, but he isn't sharing!" The outrage was palpable. "I've tried reasoning with him, but you know how he is—"

Unfortunately.

"—and he won't spare a drop. Even said he didn't have it anymore, that the director made him throw it out! As if I'd be stupid enough to believe that—"

"Then just use whatever they drained out of Colin," I said irritably, because I knew they had. "Sedgewick probably did the autopsy by now—"

"That won't help. The boy *turned*. Or Changed, or whatever the proper word is. You didn't. So, I need your blood. It might allow us to develop an antidote to this new street drug that seems to be making its way around. Something we could put in a dart or—"

"I don't think a dart is going to help," I said dryly.

"Well, it couldn't hurt, mage! And nobody else seems to be working on this, maybe because they couldn't find you, either. You do realize we are in the midst of a war? If you are going to be gallivanting about the countryside, the least you could do—"

"How would you like to see a Relic attack up close?" I said, before he went on another tirade. "A fresh one?"

There was sudden silence on the other end of the phone.

"It happened this afternoon, possibly as little as six or seven hours ago," I added. "The Relics themselves are gone, but they probably left all kinds of interesting—"

"Where?" It was clipped, but I had his attention, at least.

"You have to come now, and alone. And you have to wait at the entrance and call for me to come get you. And this is off the books—like off-off, you understand?"

"I understand that I need an address."

"And I need your word that I'm not going to get burned for this. And that you understood and will obey what I just told you. No one knows about this or gets anything you find unless I give the okay. I need that made very clear."

"That's not procedure, as you know perfectly well—"

"Hargroves gave me jurisdiction on these matters. This is my investigation, and I'm offering you a spot on my team. But I can rescind it if—"

"All right, all right!"

"Also, don't tell anyone you're from the Corps when you get here and don't wear your uniform—"

"I never wear a uniform." He sounded vaguely offended. And I had a sudden, vivid recollection of a pair of fuzzy pink slippers peeking out from under his trousers and lab coat.

"Just wear something that won't immediately make people think about the Corps," I said. "You're a friend doing me a favor, that's all, and bring your forensic kit—"

"Are you going to talk me to death or tell me where this is?"

"I need—"

"Oh, for the love of God! Yes! Off-off. Wait at the door. Look normal. Bring my kit. Now where the hell is it?"

I told him. The line immediately went dead, leaving me holding the phone and hoping I wasn't going to regret this. Technically, Hargroves *had* given me carte blanche with this investigation until Conclave, so I wasn't technically breaking the rules. But I didn't think he'd envisioned anything like this.

The treaty made it clear: Were business was Were business and the Corps was to stay the hell out. If Weres attacked humans or interfered in Circle affairs, then it was a different story. But as long as they stayed in their lane, we had to as well.

There were no exceptions.

So, if the clans found out that I had deliberately involved the Circle, or if Hargroves discovered that I was risking the treaty . . .

Yeah. Goodbye job, pension, and possibly freedom. So why the hell had I done it?

Because Sienna had a point. Because we needed answers and neither group was likely to get them alone. And because, for once, my background might actually serve as a bridge instead of a wall, allowing for some cross-species cooperation to nail whoever did this to the goddamned wall.

At least, that's what I told myself.

And then Sebastian came to find me, and I was out of time.

Chapter Twenty-Four

"Unacceptable!" I'd rarely seen Sebastian angry, but I was seeing it now. Which was a bad sign considering that we hadn't even gotten to Jenkins yet.

But this was impressive enough, with the *bardric's* power rattling things on the desk in the groundskeeper's office, which he'd commandeered for our talk. I'd put a silence spell on the room as soon as we walked in, before spilling my guts about the events of the last few days. Not that it was helping much.

Because "speaking privately" had a different meaning when you were with a bunch of Weres.

I glanced behind us, to where various locals were trying to peer through the frosted glass panel in the door, to the point of pressing their faces against it. The guards positioned outside kept dragging them off, but others just took their place. And I didn't see that changing.

They wanted Sebastian to come back outside. They liked the feeling of safety he gave them. They did not like the closed door.

And then one of them simply opened it and came inside.

The rest almost fell in after Ulmer, but his bulk blocked them and he calmly shoved them back out again. There were some squawks of protest, but nobody tried getting past him. Or if they did, they couldn't budge the bulge.

Except for one tiny boy, who breeched the sanctum simply by crawling through the big man's legs. That might have tripped up a human, especially one of Ulmer's size and age, but he wasn't one. And he made a light-footed, almost balletic movement out of the way.

The little brown-haired interloper, on the other hand, who was all of maybe a year old, stopped abruptly upon seeing Sebastian.

And froze in place, as if he'd not quite gotten this far in his clever plan. And now that he had, it was too much and his face scrunched up, and he began looking around for mama.

"And who is this?" Sebastian picked him up, with the ease of a man who had a teenaged daughter at home and knew the drill.

The incipient crying jag cut off before it began, once the tyke realized that he wasn't in trouble. His thumb found his mouth, and he sucked on it happily, gazing at Sebastian with big gray eyes. But someone else was less reassured.

"*Bardric*," a man's voice squeaked in a way that a wolf's just shouldn't, no matter what form he was in. And then he went down to one knee, while literally quaking in his boots. Possibly because the last *bardric*, elected a century ago during a war among the clans, had been a real bastard.

And because, as a war time leader, Sebastian wasn't hedged by many rules. He could kill with impunity and never give a reason. And, unless the victim was someone from a prominent clan, nobody would probably even ask for one.

Although why the man thought that applied here, I had no idea. But maybe seeing a field full of corpses had shaken him. Sebastian seemed to think so, because he did nothing but jiggle the boy on his hip.

"This one is yours, I take it?"

The man, who hadn't met Sebastian's eyes yet, nodded. He had brown hair like his son, and the stereotypical Were build: stocky, muscular, and a decent height, maybe six feet when he wasn't kneeling in terror. But he seemed unusually timid for a species who normally ran the other way.

"He's a fine boy," Sebastian added. "Strong and inquisitive. He'll make an impressive wolf one day."

"Yes, *bardric*. He—his grandfather was Vilkas of Graymoor, better known as—"

"Sword Breaker. Yes, I've heard the stories."

The man finally looked up, and Sebastian handed him his son. "He fought alongside my father in the wars," he added. "Clan Graymoor were good friends to Arnou, and still are."

"Yes, sir!" the man, so afraid a moment ago, was now hugging his son and staring at Sebastian with wide eyes. "Yes, always!"

Sebastian's own eyes softened, and he bent forward, lowering his voice. "I was wondering, could you help me keep everyone out of the arena? Sienna's people have been doing it for hours and need a break, but I don't have many people here and it's a grisly sight." He ruffled the boy's hair. "Especially for ones so young."

"Of course! I—I'll get my whole clan on it. All of us!"

The crowd behind him murmured assent, and someone started organizing things even before Sebastian smiled the man out and closed the door. Suddenly, instead of a frightened mob, he had a group of loyal soldiers doing his bidding. And, like them, I wasn't quite sure how he'd managed it.

But the smile didn't last, and the blue eyes that met mine a second later were no longer luminous or kind.

I sighed and redid the silence spell as Sebastian stared me down.

Ulmer intervened before his boss resumed the tongue lashing the kid had interrupted. Which suited me, since it had felt a lot more like literally being flayed than a verbal attack had any right to. But Ulmer missed the undercurrents in his quest to find himself a perch that could bear his weight.

"Sorry, I was checking with the cavalry," he informed us, after scraping a steel framed arm chair across the tile.

"What cavalry?" I asked, because the fight had been over for hours.

"Our remaining force from Vegas. Called them in before you arrived and they just got here. They're hooking up with some of Sienna's people who know the area."

"To do what?"

"What do you think? To find whoever did this, of course."

"And if you do find them?" I asked, feeling my blood pressure spike. "What then? Because you can't take them—"

"Like hell we can't. You'd be surprised—"

I grabbed his arm, which wasn't easy because it was thicker around than most people's thighs. Many Weres were more heavily muscled than the average person even in human form, and Ulmer was no exception. Which would do exactly fuck all if he caught up with a bunch of drugged up Relics!

"No, you'll be surprised—for about a second," I told him. "Your people can't take them—"

"What the hell are you talking about? And get your hand off me—"

"Call them off!"

"I'll do no such thing! And how are you this strong?"

"Do as she says," Sebastian said.

"What?" Ulmer looked up at his *bardric* in confusion. "Why? We have half the council on the way here—"

"The *council*?"

"—so you're going to want some answers—"

Sebastian's jaw tightened. "Just do it."

Ulmer did it, because that voice had brooked no argument, going to the door and speaking briefly to someone outside. Then he came back, arranged his bulk in the steel reinforced chair, and scowled. "What the hell?"

"What is the council's ETA?" Sebastian asked, as I redid the silence spell for the third damn time.

"An hour or so. I just got off the phone with our informant on Moon Shadow's staff."

Sebastian's jaw tightened some more, to the point that I was afraid it might shatter.

"You knew some of them were already in town," Ulmer pointed out.

"In town, yes. But we don't need them here!"

"Maybe not, but they're coming. Gotta figure out what to say."

Sebastian snarled something in wolf speak that even I didn't understand.

But I guess Ulmer did, because he rolled his eyes. "Yeah. Probably not that."

"The council is coming here?" I asked, which was a mistake. Because it brought Sebastian's blue lasers back to me.

"Allow me to explain something," he hissed. "You may be a war mage, but you are *Arnou*! My adopted sister that I brought into the clan at a good deal of political expense. I expected better than this of you. I deserve better!"

"You do," I agreed, because it was true. I didn't know what strings Sebastian had pulled to get me out of the mess with Lobizon, but the cost had probably been high.

"Then why do I find out only now that one of my clans is making the drug that turns us into monsters?"

The groundskeeper's personal effects cascaded off the wall, including a smiling portrait of the man and who I assumed were his two sons. The glass shattered when the frame hit the floor, but I didn't think Sebastian noticed. The people outside the door suddenly sprang away, however, because silence spells don't block Were power.

Especially not that much power.

Ulmer sighed and sat back in his chair. "Did I miss something?"

I quickly filled him in while Sebastian paced, his sandals making slapping sounds on the tile floor, which wasn't doing my nerves any good. And neither did Ulmer's expression when I finished. I was suddenly grateful for the beard, because the part of his face that I could see . . .

"You didn't think it necessary to tell us about this?" he asked. "To make a report before you took the day off with your *vargulf* boyfriend?"

I felt a reply spring to my lips, but bit it back because he was right. The thing was, I had made a report, but to Hargroves, not Sebastian. I technically had two bosses now, but I'd forgotten that in my confusion and one had been left out of the loop. And it had cost him.

It had cost a lot of people.

"I wasn't thinking clearly," I said, and managed not to wince at how lame that sounded.

"Yet you had the foresight to call in a query on Cloud Leaper."

"I knew the Corps wouldn't find anything—"

"No, but we might have!" Sebastian said, whirling on me. "Now the only lead we had is dead, along with his entire clan! And you knew what they were doing—all day—yet told us *nothing*."

I just sat there, trying not to squirm, because he was right. I'd fucked up. And my mistake might have gotten a lot of people killed.

Not that I knew for a fact that Arnou would have found Cloud Leaper and the rest before karma caught up with them, but I didn't know that it wouldn't have, either. As the leading clan, it had a lot of resources to draw from, and the loyalty of the other clans. I might have prevented this, if I'd been thinking more like a wolf than a mage.

"I'm sorry," I finally whispered, and heard him scoff, an angry expulsion of air.

"Yes, that's helpful!"

"She did tell you about the drug," Ulmer said, to my surprise. I guessed they must have discussed it after the late-night meeting of the brothers in my kitchen.

"But not that a clan was making it! We could have interrogated them, found out who they were supplying!" Sebastian's hand hit the desk and I heard an ominous crack.

"That would be the dark mages who put them up to it," I said evenly. Staying quiet would be more prudent right now, but I'd already done that and look where it had gotten us. "A small clan with meager resources would be exactly the type that the dark would approach—"

"To do what?"

"To interrupt the war, at least that's what the Corps thinks. To keep us so busy running after drugged-up Weres that we can't focus our attention elsewhere—"

"Yes, because everything is about the Corps," Ulmer cut in grimly. "They view the world with blinkers on; I thought you had more sense!"

I looked at him in confusion. Not because of the sentiment, which was common among Weres, but because he was acting more like Sebastian's advisor than his bodyguard. Or in some position of authority, at least, because he shouldn't have been in here otherwise.

He should be outside, guarding the damned door.

"I've recently appointed Ulmer as my Third," Sebastian said, before I could ask.

"Quite a promotion," I said, eyeing the big man.

He eyed me right back, a half-amused twist to his lips. Because the last person to hold that office had tried to kill Sebastian and usurp his position, and he knew I was thinking about it. But his response was mild, maybe because he already had enough problems.

"I'll earn it, seems like. If a pissant bunch of bastards like Windward dared to drug a member of Arnou, then they had a backer, and a powerful one."

Sebastian scowled at both of us. "Whoever they were working with saw their lack of judgement as a liability, and removed them. And did it here, to use their deaths to make me look weak. And with the council on the way, they're doing a damned good job!"

Ulmer leaned over, rested his giant arms on his equally large thighs, and sighed. Because yeah. This was bad.

And his next words confirmed it. "There's sure to be a challenge now."

"As if it wasn't sure before!"

"You're being challenged?" I asked Sebastian, because that was the first I'd heard of it.

He ran a hand through his dark hair, which was just as much of a tell as cracking the desk had been. He didn't do that sort of thing. He couldn't afford to.

If a clan leader was the rock for his or her people, then a *bardric* was the whole damned beach. He was the shoreline that the waves of fortune broke against, but who never faltered, never even looked like he noticed. Only here, among family, he could afford to let a little of the inner turmoil show.

I supposed that I should have been honored that he trusted me that much, especially after my recent failure. I wasn't. Instead, a little of his anxiety passed over, and I felt my own body tense uncomfortably.

This is why people like heroes, I thought, remembering the identical shining eyes of the father and son. They wanted to believe, wanted someone who could make this crazy world make sense, and let them feel safe. It was the same way people looked at war mages, when they weren't busy cussing us out.

But then, that's why they cussed us out, because they knew we'd handle it, knew we'd take all their negative emotions, their fear, their panic, and make it all right again. We were the bulwark that the magical community depended on and we never broke, either. It was only from the inside that you began to realize just how fragile that protection really was.

Sebastian looked at me, and our eyes met.

"Not yet. But there are rumors that Whirlwind is tired of the human alliance, tired of the war, and tired of Arnou being considered the leading clan. He may challenge at the start of Conclave. All he needed was cause."

"And now he has it," Ulmer said heavily.

"But Whirlwind is my father's age," I said, frowning. "Maybe even a few years older. Not on his deathbed, but in a contest with you? He'd be lucky to last five minutes!"

"It's not that simple," Ulmer told me.

"It is exactly that simple! If he's challenging for *bardric*, he can't appoint a champion. He has to fight himself—"

"Or assassinate me first, before the Conclave begins," Sebastian said evenly.

I stared at him, then glanced at Ulmer. And suddenly understood why the clan had thought they needed him. Random disgruntled types were one thing, although anyone can get lucky.

But someone with the resources of Clan Rand?

I felt a shiver go down my spine.

"But he hasn't had much luck," Ulmer said, "and Conclave is almost here. So maybe he upped the ante."

"How?" Sebastian demanded. "They've already tried a car bomb, an ambush, and half a dozen snipers—"

"Half a dozen?" I broke in. "I thought there'd been three attempts, and what car bomb?"

Sebastian sighed. "Panicking the clan would serve no purpose, and some attempts are normal, even expected. But the constant barrage that I've received lately—"

"Then you need help! You need—"

"Who?" the blue eyes were impatient. "My brother?"

"Yes!"

"You know that's impossible—"

"If he thought your life was threatened, he'd find a way—"

"Which is exactly the point!" Sebastian said, proving that blue eyes could burn. "If anything could make Cyrus risk returning to Arnou, this would be it. And getting himself killed by his own clan won't help me!"

"Then maybe it's time to admit what happened—"

"And risk a challenge from a dozen leaders, instead of just one? May I remind you why we had to do this in the first place? And that assumes the Conclave wouldn't view that farce we pulled as reason enough to remove me, all on its own! I need Cyrus, but right now—"

"You can't have him, and that is well known," Ulmer said thoughtfully. "So, let's break this down. Somebody starts turning monsters loose on the Were community, right before the big meeting, then slaughters a bunch of us at our most sacred spot. Yeah, we know it's because Windward, the stupid fucks, botched things and drew the attention of a war mage who they then foolishly left alive. But to everyone else—"

"I look like a weakling, and unfit to lead," Sebastian said grimly.

Ulmer inclined his head.

"And if you're assassinated before you deal with this, it will utterly destroy Arnou's reputation. And with your brother now a *vargulf* and ineligible to replace you, that leaves the field clear for Whirlwind to step in and save the day. Rescue us all from the terrible monsters and claim the throne that he thinks should always have been his—"

"Wait," I cut in. "Are you implying that Whirlwind is behind the drugs? That he'd actually turn his own people into—"

I broke off, ashamed at how shocked I felt.

Ulmer gave me a pitying look. "If it put his fat ass on the big seat, I don't think there's too many things that old schemer wouldn't do. And he's drugging up *vargulfs* and killing off clans that have always been a problem anyway. Probably looks on it as a public service—"

"This is speculation," Sebastian said. "You have no proof."

"It's a working theory, and I'm not making a case before the council. But you tell me someone else with the resources and the chutzpah to even think—"

He broke off, because something sliced through my silence spell. Not a sound, which would have been preferable, but a feeling. Panic, a full-on flood of it, as if every wolf here was suddenly screaming for help.

And was just as suddenly silenced.

Chapter Twenty-Five

The groundskeeper's office was just down a corridor from the arena, so it shouldn't have taken long to get back there. But I put on the brakes before we'd gone five yards, because something was wrong. Something was very wrong.

The people Sebastian had sent to guard the gates were standing around in the hallway, looking lost, with vague expressions on their faces. One was staring at the wall with a bemused look, as if he'd never seen it before, and they all had the vibe of having just walked into a room and forgotten why they were there. Or having just been spelled.

I flung a spell of my own to drag Sebastian back from the gate, which he'd nearly reached. Because, even in human form, he was faster than me. But I was determined and the net spell held, despite him transforming almost immediately.

"What are you doing?" he demanded, with his now huge body fighting it every inch of the way. "Let me go!"

I did not let him go. I grabbed Ulmer's arm instead. "Is there another way out?"

He scowled at one of the bemused Weres. "You know damned well there's not. That's the whole point of this place—"

"Then make one, and get Sebastian out of here. Scale the walls if you have to. I'll slow them down."

"Them? Who the devil is—"

"What's going on?" Sebastian raged. "What do you think you're—"

"Dark mages. And saving your life. Go!"

"I'm not leaving my people!"

"It's you they want! This was a trap. Killing Windward was done to draw you here—"

And that seemed to light a fire under Ulmer at least, who said something profane and changed with a snarl, putting himself between his *bardric* and the end of the alleyway. Sebastian snarled back, and I thought the two were going to have at it right there, even though they barely fit in between the walls. But I didn't have time to worry about it.

I grabbed my phone, which, of course, was dead. If I'd tried to call out earlier, I would have realized that something was wrong, but I hadn't. I'd been chatting in the office while the trap was sprung, just as I'd been lying under a tree in my backyard when it was set up.

I'd been on the back foot all day, just a little too loopy, a little too slow. And now, I was about to pay for it. I sent up a distress flare, even knowing how useless it was, because who would see it out here?

And that was the last thought I had that wasn't in the *oh, fuck* category, because the enemy were coming. And even though I couldn't see them yet, because of the way the corridor twisted, there were a lot. My shield almost buckled at the first volley that came ricocheting down the hall, and just that fast, we were out of time.

"*Go*!" I yelled at Ulmer, who was trying to corral his *bardric*, and started running ahead, reaching for a gun I didn't have because I didn't have anything. For the first time in years, I'd left the house unarmed, not thinking to grab even my crappy, second-best coat.

I'm going to die, I thought, and threw everything I had into my shield, gathering strength and pushing it out in front of me in a wall of magical power, while Sebastian's entourage poured into the hall from a rock cut doorway I'd just passed. The thick stone must have shielded them from the effects of the disorientation spell, but they nonetheless seemed pretty oblivious. A few of them were still holding coffee mugs or saucers with small slices of cake.

I grabbed one of them by the lapels of a very nice suit, just as the gate gave way. And was immediately replaced by the shield I'd reinforced to the thickness of a bank vault's door and sent barreling down the corridor. It slammed into place, knocking several mages off their feet on the other side, and I shook my captive.

"Guns?"

"What?" He was a handsome young man with the traditional Were coloring, plus an added flush of confusion on his cheeks.

"Do you have *guns? Weapons? Anything?*"

"We do." A small, grandmotherly-looking women with a topknot and skin the color of red mahogany told me. "Got a cache."

"Get them. Get everything you have. Shoot any mage you see but me."

"Wait!" the young man said, as I turned him loose. "What—what's going on?" he looked past me, to where a couple dozen men in black leather coats had washed up against the shield. "Who are they?"

"Dark mages, here to kill you and your *bardric*. And anybody else they can find. Unless you kill them first!"

"What? No, that can't be right—" he began, only to be drowned out by a dozen Weres Changing all at once and howling at the gibbous moon, while the old lady reemerged from inside with an armload of shotguns, which she started handing out to everybody else.

"Kill them first!" she yelled, a refrain which was quickly taken up by the part of the crowd who hadn't been spelled out of their minds.

I heard it echoing down the corridor, along with slamming doors and more wolf howls, but it quickly cut off. The acoustics in here were deliberately terrible, like the non-existent lines of sight. This place had been designed as a killing field.

Let's hope it lives up to his reputation, I thought, and then the mages were through the gate and flooding this way, along with a host of their friends.

They were met with shotgun shells and a mountain of living fur, but they had individual shields up, like the type riot police use that allow them to fire around the sides. Those were common in battle, where you bled energy and needed to reserve every drop, but it was a bad choice here. With shields deployed, only six attackers could advance at a time in the narrow hall, leaving the rest bunched up behind them.

And it didn't take the Weres long to realize their advantage. They surged ahead, like a wave breaking onto a beach, only this wave also washed over top of the mages. I saw a Were go down from a spell and several more get strafed by gunfire, but it didn't stop the rest from leaping over the shields and dropping into the middle of the phalanx, shredding anything they found inside.

Red splattered the mages' transparent protection, soaked the walls beside them, and slicked the floor below. It was rocky here and slippery, and more than one man went down by having his boots slide out from under him. And once on his back, that was usually it.

With Were speed it took all of a second to disembowel someone, and while one or two of the fallen mages was good enough to get off a spell, including something that slammed a Were into the air and backwards over my head, most weren't.

Most died horribly, with a gray wolf I vaguely recognized as the surprised young man of a moment ago, turning toward me with a maw filled with somebody's dripping intestines. He said something, but I was too busy sending a spell to knock back a group of reinforcements to hear. It hit them like a car sized bowling ball, ruining their tight configuration, and that was all the Weres needed.

They jumped them, sending gore flying, but we were too near the arena. The sounds of battle were going to carry, and there'd be more soon—a lot more. Because no way had they attacked Wolf's Head with anything less than an army.

And then the gray wolf spat out entrails and rounded on me. "Where is the goddamned *bardric*?"

I didn't answer, because I didn't have to. The next second, a tawny bullet shot overhead, leaping past us before we could blink, and using the mages' remaining shields as stepping stones to vaunt over top of them. And then—

"Shit!" I said, as Ulmer bolted after the boss.

"What are they *doing*?" the young Were asked.

He had a bad habit of that, like I was supposed to narrate the battle for him when I was busy forcing my way through the remaining mages and out the other side. And across the blown off gate and into the arena. Where I saw—

"Shit!" I said again, as he came up behind me.

I grabbed the mane of fur around the great head. "Get Sebastian. Get him out—"

"He has a right to fight!"

"Not in the arena! Back in the passages we have a chance. We're going to get slaughtered out here!"

That should have gone without saying, since there were more dark mages than I'd ever seen at one time crowding the great space, what must have been five and six hundred of them. And they weren't alone. A group of regular people, probably some of those sent to guard the gates, had been taken to the far, left hand side of the space and were being held there—as bait.

And it was working.

I saw the father and son who Sebastian had charmed in the office among them, the former looking terrified as he clutched his little boy. And then I didn't see anything but Sebastian closing in on them, with Ulmer's great black and gray hulk right behind him. A dozen more wolves blew past us as well, in a wedge of sleek fur that was in no way going to be enough.

"Sebastian!" I screamed, and the gray wolf tore away from me and pelted after his chieftain. Like that was going to help!

The only reason they were still alive was that they were moving too fast for the mages to hit them. Spells detonated on all sides, throwing up sand in great geysers, along with the harder packed, redder dirt below. One hex hit a corpse that exploded in a fleshy firework almost in my face, coating the shield I'd managed to raise with a sludge of gelatinous blood and yellow fat. And the same thing was going to happen to Sebastian's group as soon as they slowed down, and I couldn't do a damned thing but watch!

But someone else could.

"What is *that*?" A woman with a shotgun asked as I stood there, staring across the arena like an idiot.

Because my old truck, which I'd have bet couldn't even fit through the corridors outside, had just burst into view. The roof was missing and the remaining supports were smoking, as if it had been sheared off by a spell. And a bunch of insane teens were screaming and Caleb was driving and the whole thing was headed straight for a large clump of mages near the center of the great space.

"No!" I started yelling. "No, go back!"

They did not go back. They plowed straight into the startled group, and then partially over them, with the mages who were trapped underneath the truck forming a small hill as they pushed their shields upward to avoid getting crushed. And then I was running, even knowing that I would be too late, that they were about to get hit with every spell on the planet any second now.

But they didn't. They were targeted by a barrage, but it mostly failed to reach them because it was coming from the peripheries of the space. The mages that they were literally in the middle of weren't doing shit, other than looking around in confusion. Even the shields they were using started popping, causing half a dozen to get crushed under the weight of the truck when their protection cut out.

Mine did, too, despite me throwing all I had into it. And thereby fueling someone else, I realized, as I gazed up at Sophie, who was standing on top of the seat backs, straddling the front and back and deliberately making herself a target. And glowing like a star.

"Hit the dirt!" Someone was yelling. "Hit the damned—"

It might have been Caleb. I wasn't sure, because could barely hear myself think over the sounds of battle. But I dove for the sand on cue, this not being my first rodeo.

And the next second, all hell broke loose in the air above me. Or to be more accurate, all the spells that had just been flung at Sophie. Her power had absorbed them like a sponge, and then abruptly shot them back out in a hurricane of magical force that just skimmed over my head—and took off a lot of others.

Mages were falling on all sides, people were screaming, wolves were howling and so much sand was being thrown around that I couldn't see a damned thing. I also couldn't hear with shotguns firing, someone turning loose with a machine gun, and spells bursting everywhere. Because we suddenly had a battle, ladies and gentlemen, we had a goddamned—

Somebody grabbed me.

I looked up, a spell boiling in my fist, and then had to swallow it back down because it was Caleb. He was yelling something I couldn't hear, but I didn't really need to when he began hauling my ass off, without even letting me get back to my feet. I fought him to a standstill by the side of the truck, yelling as loudly as I could.

And then a silence spell clicked shut around us, which I was surprised worked, only I didn't see Sophie anymore. Suddenly, I didn't see anybody. And I found myself panicking for the tenth time in the last two minutes.

"—fighting me!" Caleb snarled, shaking me. "Get your butt on board—"

"Where are the kids?" I grabbed him by the front of his coat. "Why the hell did you bring them here?"

"I couldn't have gotten inside without them, and they're not kids, they're *tanks*—"

"They're *kids* and what the *fuck* were you thinking?"

"I was thinking about getting you out, and there are six of them and one of me—"

"You're a goddamned *war mage*—"

"And you haven't seen what they are! They were coming for you one way or the other! I'm just the driver. Now get on the fucking truck!"

And he threw me inside.

I hit the back seat, on top of Kimmie who was somehow still asleep, despite Armageddon going on all around us. I tried desperately to locate anyone I knew—the kids, Sebastian, even Caleb, who had disappeared. Because, instead of launching himself into the driver's seat as I'd expected, he was throwing down with two dark mages a little way off.

I sent a javelin spell at one of them, knocking him off his feet, and my partner promptly turned his buddy into a fiery torch. Caleb's mage fled, screaming and burning, and mine decided on the better part of valor and followed him, clutching his stomach and streaming blood. But that wasn't going to be enough, not even for us to get the kids out of here, because the moment of surprise was gone and we were seriously outnumbered.

Or . . . maybe not.

I'd just sent a lasso spell to bind two mages who'd been targeting us, slamming them together and causing them to hit the dirt, when I felt the ground shake. It was hard enough to rock the truck slightly and wasn't merely the one jolt, as if a major spell had detonated nearby. It was many minor ones, and they just kept coming.

Because the whole arena was shivering. Enough sand was rippling across the great space or sliding off of mountains of the dead that the hiss of it cut through the sounds of battle, leaving more people than me staring around in confusion. And then in worry, because it looked like the beginning of an earthquake, only I didn't think so.

The fortress was as steady as ever, as solid as the rock that had formed it thousands of years ago. No little pebbles were cascading off anything, and no cracks were forming in the massive walls. Just the floor was shaking, and then shuddering, and then something thrust upward out of a nearby pile of sand, something that looked a lot like—

"Zombies!" Somebody yelled, in a magically enhanced voice that echoed around the huge space.

And I finally spotted Jen, the mousy young woman who wouldn't say boo to a goose, but would say "come forth" to a bunch of really fucked up reinforcements. She was across the arena, high on one of the upper tiers of seats, with her arms outstretched and her eyes glowing neon green as she summoned her troops.

And she was summoning a lot.

Bloody arms reached up from the sand and grabbed mages by the ankles, before jerking them down. Headless bodies got up and started stalking others, driving them back even when the mages got over their shock and launched fire bombs at them, which helped not at all. Because if there's anything worse than being chased by a headless monster, it's being chased by a fiery, headless monster. Along with ripped up Were corpses, with trailing guts and blood-soaked fur, who had remembered that they still had teeth and claws and hundreds of pounds of weight to throw around.

And then Jen raised her arms upward in a sudden, savage motion, and the whole arena exploded with the reanimated dead.

I gazed about, not understanding anything. A necromancer might be able to manage two or three zombie servants at once, although at great cost. But this? Who the hell could do this? It would take dozens of necros, all working together . . .

Or one with an extra battery pack, I realized, finally noticing that Jen wasn't alone. Our resident crabapple was behind her, with his hand on her shoulder and his blond hair an electric afro around his head. Jen was providing the talent, but Chris was fueling it.

I stared at them.

Had *anything* been in those goddamned reports?

And then Caleb ran back over, with his coat smoking. "We got a problem."

Chapter Twenty-Six

I spread out my arms, indicating the chaos all around us. "Which one?"

"That one!" Caleb pointed across the battlefield, to where a group of mages had kept their eyes on the prize.

Sebastian and his people were still alive, thanks to a wavering shield wall twelve feet high and what looked to be several feet thick that somebody had thrown up in front of them, and which was absorbing spell fire like nothing I'd ever seen. And still didn't see unless a spell hit it, exploding like fireworks under water, because the barrier was almost transparent. I also didn't see who was casting it, but where a certain person was concerned, that was becoming fairly normal.

Caleb took the wheel and burnt rubber, grinding down the hill of mangled bodies and then tear-assing across the sand, while I searched for a certain elusive student of mine. A spell hit us broadside, rocking the vehicle hard enough to push it onto two wheels for a second, while another tore overhead, just missing setting my hair on fire. But we also broadsided two mages on the way over, and sent a bunch more running and—

"Dimas!" I yelled, pointing.

"What?" Caleb glanced at me. "Where?"

"To the far right of the shield. Hurry—it's starting to fail!"

Caleb swerved that way, spewing sand behind us, and a watery looking, still half invisible Dimas fell to his knees as we skidded alongside.

"Can't hold," he gasped, after letting me through the faltering protection. His olive skin was pale and sweat was running in rivulets down his cheeks. "It's . . . going down."

I tried to respond, but I couldn't hear myself think. Not with Caleb going HAM on the other side of the barrier, throwing what looked like his entire arsenal into the fight. And since he usually clanked when he walked, that was saying something.

He was being helped by Sophie, who had popped up out of nowhere, her red mane a crackling nimbus around her face. And between the two of them, and the maybe fifty mages they had decided to take on all by themselves, the outside of the shield looked like someone had set loose an entire Fourth of July's display all at once. And then Aki was yelling in my ear.

I hadn't even noticed him, but his bright blue hair was suddenly bobbing around in front of my face. "He won't leave!" he screamed. "I told him I'm a teleporter; I can get him out. But he won't—"

"I'm not going anywhere!" Sebastian roared. And then grabbed a mage who had foolishly launched himself over top of the shield and ripped him apart.

Aki stumbled back in horror as blood and guts rained down, and I grabbed Sebastian by the fur. "You have to survive! The war depends—"

"Stop telling me to leave my people!" It was loud enough to almost rupture my eardrums, or what was left of them.

I hung on anyway. "There may be a way to save everyone, including you."

"Talk," Ulmer snarled from nearby, because Sebastian was too busy fighting to listen.

"The Black Circle wants Sebastian. They know if they get rid of him, it'll bring down the alliance—"

"I didn't ask for a summary of the war. What's your *point*?"

"—so they'll follow him. Including into the killing fields," I said, gesturing at the warren of tunnels leading off of the arena.

"Let Wolf's Head do its business," Ulmer said. His maw was dripping blood, but his eyes were calm. I was suddenly glad to have him on our side.

"Yes, the main corridor is big enough for the truck—"

"But can you get him back there?"

That was the question, I thought, as Sebastian tore away from me and I had to use a magical tether to pull him back.

The huge body tried to break it, to leap over the failing shield, to rend and tear and destroy, but I held on. And not only with magic. The strength I shouldn't have had, which had allowed me to crack a rock over Ulmer's head earlier, let me wrestle him down. And get into the huge face, because someone had to make him see sense.

"They want you!" I screamed. "Not them! If you leave—"

"They'll tear everyone to shreds! I won't risk—"

He broke off because the enemy was coming over top of the now barely shoulder high wall. But some of their protection wasn't in much better shape than ours, having had to withstand constant assault by Jen's creatures. Allowing Sebastian to shove his snout through a hole in the nearest mage's shield and—

Goddamn, I thought, and exchanged a look with Ulmer, while his usually urbane boss ate a man's face.

Sebastian wasn't listening and he wasn't going to. Nothing enraged a clan leader more than seeing his people being butchered in front of him. It was primal, the need to protect; it was like a drug, and he was high as hell.

I was wasting my time.

"How far can you take him?" I asked Aki, who just shook his head. Not far enough to keep the stubborn bastard from coming right back.

"What's the plan?" Ulmer said as I narrowed my eyes, and looped the tether several more times around my fist.

"The plan is that he gets in the goddamned truck."

* * *

The goddamned truck had seen better days. But even when new, it had not been designed as a fancy toy to show off at somebody's high school or to brag about to the guys at the bar. This thing was a workhorse, built for hard scrabble labor on a farm or in a quarry, which was probably what it had been doing before I'd bought its rusted green ass to help with my move to Vegas.

Which was a long way of saying that it was somehow still running, despite the blows it had taken, the raw, red flesh in the tire grooves, and the huge wolf that I was forcibly dragging on board.

Sebastian was fighting me, and he was fighting hard, causing me to expend magic I couldn't spare in order to throw a half dozen additional tethers over the massive body. Fortunately, Dimas had flung the remains of his shield outward in a narrow band, knocking the attacking horde off their feet and buying us a few seconds. But seconds weren't going to be enough if I didn't manage to leash Sebastian, and if we didn't move faster than a crawling baby!

I gave a final heave, and the furry bastard slammed down into the front seat.

"Go!" I yelled at Caleb, while wrestling with a good eight hundred pounds of furious wolf.

"I'm trying! Something is dragging on us!"

I looked around and discovered that he was right. The lasso spell I'd thrown earlier had attached itself to the back of the truck and been towing the two mages all over the arena. They were looking fairly battered, but they'd managed to get back to their feet and they were *pissed.*

Until a massive, bloody Were suddenly bounded over from the fray. I didn't think he was one of ours, since he was missing half of his side and most of his entrails and had the odor of someone who had been dead for a while. But he'd nonetheless decided that he was hungry.

He fell on the mages, blood and flesh went flying and the tether snapped, but we were still barely moving.

"We're still barely moving!" I yelled at Caleb.

"Yeah! 'Cause his highness here weighs a ton!"

"Change back!" I told Sebastian as we took off.

The giant face stopped trying to gnaw through a tether long enough to snarl something at me, despite the fact that we hadn't abandoned everyone else. Sophie had stayed behind, forming a rear guard alongside Ulmer and his wolves and some of Jen's creatures. And just as I'd thought, the mages were redirecting their attention anyway, now that their main target had left the area.

Sebastian's people were doing better than we were, but he didn't seem to realize it. And I didn't have time to point it out. Because our few seconds of a head start had most definitely evaporated.

I attached Sebastian's tethers to the truck and left them to fend for self, while redirecting my magic into a shield. I was barely in time. A barrage of spells slammed into us a second later, landing like body blows, like a furious beating hitting all at once. Because shields feel like an extension of a mage's skin, and mine had just been pummeled.

I dropped to one knee, breathing hard and barely conscious for a second, before I snarled and shook it off.

But I wasn't going to last much longer if I had to protect all of us.

And then it got worse.

"What the fuck?" Caleb screamed, and Caleb is not a man who screams. But I was not about to rib him about it assuming that either of us lived through this.

Because if I'd ever seen a What the Fuck, that was it.

He swerved the truck in a large circle, since standing on the brakes was not an option with half a hundred mages on our tail. Although they were suddenly breaking off, were backing up, were falling over themselves in an effort to get away. But not because of anything we were doing.

No, that would be due to the new guys on the field, and while I had never seen anything like them, I had heard of them.

When I was a baby mage, my trainer had despaired of teaching me anything that my father hadn't already drilled into my skull since childhood, and had set me some extra study. Or maybe he'd just wanted to get rid of me; I didn't know. But the upshot was that I'd been allowed to shadow a bunch of mages with different specialties while the rest of the class was learning how to shield and cast basic offensive spells.

One of those, an expert on dark magic, had told me a story that I'd barely listened to at the time, because I'd thought he was just trying to scare me. If so, he'd failed. The reality, on the other hand . . .

"What the hell is that?" Caleb yelled, as our new problems crawled out of a pile of corpses—literally. They were separating dim, shadowy limbs from mangled flesh in jerky, stop-motion actions, like lizards shedding their skin. Or like spirits shedding the bodies they no longer needed, because that's what they were.

"Shades," I whispered.

"What?"

"Shades of the dead! We're not the only ones with a necro on the field!"

And, in fact, there were at least five more. I spotted them the next second, because they were the only ones not fleeing the area. They were huddled together in a dark wad, muttering something and staring at their misshapen servants. Because that was what the creatures I was looking at were: disembodied spirits who had recently died, but had not yet faded from this realm.

They weren't ghosts, not yet, because ghosts fed off the energy shed by the living, and they hadn't had a chance to do that yet. They were souls betwixt and between, as my old instructor had put it. Subsisting off what was left of their own energy for a few hours or days, until it was depleted and they had to choose.

Stay here and scrouge up whatever crumbs of power they could, while being preyed upon by any supernatural being who ate energy and could catch them. Or move on into whatever came next. It would seem like an easy choice, but fear of the unknown could be powerful, especially when combined with resentment from unfinished business in this life.

Ghosts were nonetheless still rare, and quickly learned their way around the supernatural world. They would fight any necro who tried to control them, which was why few made the attempt. But shades were more naïve, confused, and plentiful, especially on a battleground. And powerful necros, or ones working as a group, could often bind them as slaves, forcing them to do their bidding until their energy ran out.

Or so the story went.

And it looked like the old mage had known what he was talking about. Because the mass of souls was getting bigger all the time, as more and more joined the first ones, drawn from all over the battlefield. Their power was boiling darkly over the sands as they streamed this way, like a black sun that casts no shade.

I swallowed and gripped the seat in front of me.

"Why can we see them?" Caleb asked, sounding strangled. Because the only good thing about freed souls was that they were usually invisible.

"You're not seeing them; you're seeing the spell that binds them," I said, trying to think of something that might work on these things. And then several of the latest arrivals happened across a half dead mage and—

"Oh, my God," someone choked out.

It might have been me.

Because the mage didn't just die. He was cannibalized, his soul sucked out of a dozen wounds that had rent his corporeal form and left him vulnerable. And what remained when the now-ghosts finished their initial feed was . . . not recognizable.

I had a brief moment to see his withered face and gray, desiccated skin, with the dried-out eyes sunken and staring. And to wonder if that was what we were going to look like in a moment, because I didn't think that shields would stop these things. Not hopped up on necro power and spoiling for a fight.

And then they were coming, the whole wretched, raging, screaming mass, like a furious cloud studded with ghostly body parts.

And neither Caleb nor I had any idea what to do about it.

But once again, someone else did. Because another hazy, blackened mass tore across the sands like an oversized tumbleweed, carving a swath through the battle and crashing into the first one, right before it crashed into us. And, suddenly, the fight was on.

Take a bokor *with you*, I remembered my old instructor saying, *if you have to deal with one of those filthy bastards. Make sure you have another by your side.*

And so I had, I just hadn't remembered it.

I was still thinking of the kids as kids, but I was starting to believe that Caleb had been right about the whole tank thing. Because Jen was *pissed*, the rational, reasonable, slightly mousy young woman now red faced and screaming her defiance at the knot of necros, while Chris struggled to hold her back. They looked like a supernatural Ken and Barbie, only Ken was looking pretty wigged out, like maybe he'd never seen what Barbie could actually do before. While she . . .

Did not like being challenged.

Her fury had the shadowbinders clutching their bone necklaces and muttering at each other, while the two writhing, clawing masses of horror went careening around the truck, screaming and fighting and finally coming to rest a dozen yards off. It wasn't nearly far enough. It gave us a front row seat as they cannibalized each other, immediately expending any power they received in the fight instead of storing it up, and spilling their life force like blood onto the unforgiving sands.

They wouldn't last long at this rate, neither in the fight nor in this realm, but then, their masters could just raise more, couldn't they?

Or maybe not, I thought, as Caleb suddenly adjusted course again, shifting gears with a savage motion, and taking us straight at the knot of necros.

They tried to redirect some of their latest servants at us, setting up a ghostly barricade. But shades take a few minutes to figure out how this new existence works, and we didn't grant them that. We tore through the middle of them, while I searched around in Caleb's coat for something that might help and not put more strain on my magic. Of course, the big leather number shocked the crap out of me for daring to lay a hand on its master, but for once, I didn't mind.

It felt almost good, the jolt to the system, the buzz in my bones, even the pain. It reminded me that I was still alive, even as the cold, clammy feel of that otherworldly barricade tried to cling to my skin. It gave the impression of bony hands sliding over my body, and was absolutely the worst thing I'd encountered all day.

But then we were through and I was throwing the nasty little device I'd found in an inner pocket through one of the holes in my now tattered shield.

And I wasn't a softball champion for nothing.

It hit them dead center and the Circle's dislocators don't play around. One of the mages got away—the only one who was properly shielded. But the others had been redirecting too much of their magic into the spell trying to counter Jen, and had let their own protection slide.

And the result was just really gratifying. They looked kind of like their creation now, I thought, staring behind me as we swerved away. A jumbled-up wad of heads and limbs and random flesh, with only one torso anymore since everything else had fused together.

I usually hated dislocators and rarely used them, but this time . . .

"Fuck, yeah!" Caleb yelled, pummeling the dashboard like a prize fighter going for the title.

I nodded, feeling almost dizzy from relief.

That was very definitely a fuck, yeah.

And then I realized that someone was screaming.

Chapter Twenty-Seven

The sound wasn't coming from Caleb, who was back to his usual stoic self, and already redirecting us toward our original destination. And it wasn't Sebastian, who was staring at the monstrosity that had been a bunch of men just seconds ago. But he'd leaned forward slightly in his fascination, allowing me to see somebody squashed between him and the door.

Or make that two somebodies, I thought, spotting the Were father, wild eyed and half crazed, with his son clamped face first against his chest.

"What are you doing here?" I asked blankly.

He stared at me for a moment, and then his mouth remembered how to form words. "You said to get on the truck!"

"I didn't mean you—"

"Well, how the hell was I supposed to know that?" he said shrilly. The guy was clearly losing it, having probably never seen combat before, and this was a hell of an introduction. But there was no way to go back, and nowhere safe to drop them off.

And then I was shuddering all over from a renewed barrage, which should have popped my already pathetic shields and fried us all. But, somehow, my protection held, although I had to look down to see that I wasn't shot full of burning holes. And even so, I was left feeling really unwell as we wove through the battle toward the corridor.

Which we were never going to reach if I didn't get some damned help!

I grabbed the father's shoulder. "Can you drive?"

"What?"

"I need Caleb to help me shield. Can you *drive*?"

"No! I have a baby! I can't drive!"

"Sebastian!" But he was no help, either. He'd broken out of his shock and started scrabbling against the limited protection I'd managed to keep up, trying to rejoin the fight.

Which meant that my shield was getting pummeled on both sides now, as what looked like half the mages in the arena converged on our ridiculously slow-moving ride. The fastest were already surging up the sides, blocking the light and threatening to stop us just by their added weight alone. And that was assuming my shields didn't pop, which—

Yeah, that's what I'd thought.

My protection gave up the ghost and they swamped us—which was good, since the ones behind them would have torn us apart with spells otherwise. Of course, these were about to do the same with lead, only they didn't have time. Because Caleb somehow got a shield up in place of mine.

It clamped shut like a vise, cutting off our attackers—literally. Half a dozen torsos tumbled inside the truck as the rest of their bodies fell away outside of the new shield. It also left several very much living dark mages trapped inside along with us, including the one who was staring me in the face.

Sebastian grabbed the other in those great jaws of his, before slamming him repeatedly against the inside of the shield bubble, causing Caleb to curse and the truck to swerve wildly. And the father to yell and cover his boy with his body, hunkering down between his *bardric* and the door. For my part, I barely reacted, because something had just come over me.

But this time, it wasn't nausea.

A shiver tore through me, carrying a sound along with it. It wasn't a scream or a howl; I wasn't sure what it was, except that it was terrible and skin ruffling and deafeningly loud. The dark mage reared back in shock, the spell in his fist dissipating as he lost concentration, not that it would have mattered.

Because my hand shot out at the same time and—

"Oh, my God!" the father screamed, which was rich considering what he'd just seen his *bardric* do. But Weres were used to violence from their leaders, even found it comforting at times. They weren't accustomed to seeing a war mage rip a man's beating heart out of his chest and sit there, seriously considering eating it.

Put it down, I told myself harshly, and received only a snarl in return. *Put it down now*!

And then I realized that Caleb was yelling at me. But not about the heart. But about—

"Fuck!" I said, shoving the mage out of the way and vaulting over the seat. Because Caleb was having trouble walking and chewing gum at the same time.

"You try it!" he snarled, which was fair.

Maintaining a regular shield was usually no problem even in battle, as we practiced it for hours every day in training until it became as automatic as breathing. But expanding it to cover an entire vehicle was something very different, as I'd just had the chance to find out. And splitting your attention while doing so to also drive?

Well, that was why we were about to hit a wall.

I grabbed the wheel with blood slick hands, and Caleb punched a piece of his already tatty looking armor outward, throwing several mages into the dirt. Then crawled around on the outside of the truck, because the front seat was too packed to give him a pathway. The vehicle swerved, he almost fell under the wheels, and we missed crashing into the wall by inches.

And then sped around in a wide circle, spewing sand, because eight hundred pounds of Were had been just subtracted from our load. Sebastian had finally Changed! He was sprawled naked in the front seat, looking dazed for some reason, which might not be great for his dignity but was awesome for our chances.

"Get onboard!" I yelled at my partner, who was clinging to the outside of the truck and somehow continuing to shield even while mages attempted to shoot him through the holes.

"What the hell do you think I'm trying to do?"

Caleb kicked a mage into the dirt, shot another in the face, and rolled over the side and into the back seat. He ended up alongside the still unconscious Kimmie and a very alarmed looking Aki, who had just appeared out of nowhere. And I finally got this ship righted and floored it.

We barreled toward the darkened hallway ahead with what must have been a couple hundred mages on our tail. And although we were outrunning them, it wasn't going to be that easy. Because there were enemies ahead of us, too, having had plenty of time to figure out our destination.

But so had someone else.

And thank God for indomitable grannies, I thought fervently, as the wizened old top knot from earlier reappeared behind the cordon of mages and grinned at me.

Right before her group blew the bastards away, because they hadn't bothered to shield from the back.

And a second later, we bumped across their corpses and into the blessed darkness of the corridor.

* * *

The change was immediate and stark, with us going from brilliant torch light to almost complete darkness as soon as we passed over the threshold. The corridor was at the back of the stadium, like the one with the groundskeeper's office only on the other side. But it was somewhat larger, forming part of the main highway for the complex, allowing vehicles to make deliveries.

It was usually well lit, but all the torches here had been extinguished. I could still smell the burnt bones that were used for the shafts, and the acrid smoke. But there was no glimmer of light remaining.

Leaving us looking at a long, dark tunnel into nothingness.

That was unsettling, but less so than the lack of sound. Because that had cut off, too, the walls muffling the chaos outside as thoroughly as if someone had thrown a heavy blanket over our heads. The effect was heightened as we trundled forward, with it becoming quiet enough that I could hear everyone's too-rapid breathing, along with the soft sounds coming from the father who was trying to reassure his son.

I could see that he'd half hidden the boy in his jacket, even though I hadn't switched on any headlights. They would have made us even more of a target, and anyway, I didn't need them. Because, thanks to my owl tat, my eyes had already adjusted.

Or maybe it wasn't just the tat.

I stared at the left-hand wall, where the old woman's gang was scampering away while still in human form, since the hidden tunnels inside the rock were too small for anything else. And that was exactly where they were—inside the rock. Yet their bodies were as bright as flame, and as clear as if the wall between us was made out of glass.

Infrared, I thought, gazing about in shock. That potion I'd ingested was . . . something else. And then I spotted other defenders ahead, their bodies also glowing redly in the night.

Some were leaning out of rock-cut windows or doorways, while others were peering down from the stony overhang above us, waiting for a chance to strike. The rest—the old, infirm or very young—were huddled in groups in the rooms that studded the passageways, with huge guardians blocking the doors and ready to savage anyone who came near. Wolf's Head was preparing to do what it had been designed for and devour its enemies.

At least, I fervently hoped so. It had been established originally as a fortress during the Were Civil War, when clan had fought clan and a place had been needed for families in the area to take refuge. And now it was serving that function once again, assuming that our pursuers had followed us inside.

Only I couldn't tell, because it was freaking silent in here!

I looked back the way we'd come, but we'd twisted and turned enough that all I saw was rock. I guessed even infrared vision had its limits. And all I heard was my own rapid heartbeat, pounding out a staccato rhythm in my ears.

And then something else, something just at the edge of my hearing that I couldn't quite place. It wouldn't have bothered me so much except that it was immediately followed by a sensation like tiny bugs crawling all over my skin. It wasn't a spell; more a force of nature, like the sensation right before a storm hits, when your body knows it's coming even though you haven't seen the lightning.

I glanced up but saw nothing except for some scraps of tattered cloth flapping in a breeze, the outline of rocks long since scoured smooth by sand-laced wind, and a few scattered stars. But not many of the latter. The light leaking in from the arena had been cut off by bends in the corridor, leaving the open air above us merely a dark ribbon running between darker cliffs.

The battle seemed far away now, with no echoing shouts or called commands, no explosions or gunfire. No signs of danger anywhere except for that skin ruffling feeling that could be excess adrenaline and a sound I couldn't quite place. So why was my breathing getting louder?

"By the pricking of my thumbs, something wicked this way comes," Caleb said softly, leaning forward. Because I wasn't the only one getting chills.

"What are you thinking?" I whispered back. "More shades?"

"One of those necro bastards did get away."

And we didn't have Jen with us, this time. Maybe coming in here hadn't been such a great idea, after all. My eyes started darting after every shadow, seeing strangely distorted faces in the dips and whirls of the stone that weren't actually there, except in my overactive imagination.

Until something cast a real shadow on the ground ahead of us, rippling over the rock.

"There!" the father said, his voice high. "Did you see that?"

"Yeah." Caleb shot him a glance. "Relax. Our shields are holding."

"Relax?" The man stared at him, maybe because we were sitting in a truck full of blood and body parts. "*Relax?*"

"It looked like a bird," Sebastian said, his voice unruffled but his eyes glowing slightly.

"Birds don't get that big," Caleb argued.

And no, they didn't, I thought, searching the river of sky above us. Nothing got that big. Unless a jet liner had decided to wonder off its flight plan and joyride over the desert.

And then to drop down in a sudden plummet, falling on us without warning, and throwing the corridor into utter darkness—

I screamed; the father screamed; and then something else did. Loud enough to slice through the muffling effects of the acoustics and send my flesh trying to vibrate off my bones. It wasn't an animal cry; it wasn't human; I didn't know what it was.

But it wasn't bearable.

I found myself abandoning the steering wheel to clamp my hands over my ears, afraid that my head was literally going to explode. The sound was a knife to the brain, a thousand knives, whiting out my vision and making it impossible to think. And it went on and on until I tried stuffing pieces of my shield in my ears, and then layering more on top, desperate to stop that hideous noise.

Which abruptly cut out.

I came back to myself, heart pounding, vision blurring, and us sliding along a wall, throwing sparks off the stones and causing what should have been ear-splitting metallic shrieks. But I could barely hear them. Even when I shook off the makeshift earplugs, I still couldn't, my head ringing like cathedral bells.

"Up top," Caleb whispered, only he looked like he was shouting. And maybe he was; I couldn't tell. But when I followed his pointing finger, I saw—

"Damn it!" I wrenched the truck to the side, which didn't help much because the corridor wasn't that wide.

But I managed to miss a falling mage, who was screaming and throwing everything, absolutely everything in his arsenal, on the way down. Spells and bullets ricocheted off the walls before the man hit the ground with a thump. But he'd managed only glancing blows on our protection, because he hadn't been aiming at us.

"What the hell is going on?" Caleb yelled, just as my ears popped.

"Those bastards didn't follow us in," I said, staring upward. "They're flanking us from above."

But it looked like something had also flanked them, although I could be reading it wrong. I couldn't see much, and didn't have time for more than glances as I was increasing our speed to try to outrun the problem. Caleb, meanwhile, had started checking out his arsenal, or what was left of it, pawing around in his coat for the little surprises that war mages secreted away for emergencies.

"What's going on?" the father demanded, grabbing my arm. "What's happening?"

"We thought we were trapping them—the dark mages," I said. "But they used magical tethers to scale up the outside walls. And now they're running along the top of the rocks, picking off our defenders—"

"And shooting at us while we're trapped in here?" he started looking around, his face panicked.

"That's . . . probably the plan."

Or it had been, before something up there went wrong.

I had no idea what was happening now and my new super vision wasn't helping. All I could see were the red outlines of moving bodies in between the rocks, where a hell of a fight seemed to be going on. I could anticipate where people were going to fall, allowing me to swerve back and forth across the corridor, avoiding them. Could even tell the difference between Were and human by their shapes.

But whatever they were fighting, I couldn't see at all.

And then the darkness was gone, and the stars were blooming overhead again as something moved on—toward the arena.

"We have to go back!" Sebastian grabbed my shoulder, his eyes wild. "Turn around! We have to help—"

"Help how?" Caleb demanded.

"There's a new weapon in the field! My people can't handle that, not on top of everything else—"

"And we can? The noise that thing gave off almost popped my shield—"

"I don't give a damn about your shield!"

"—leaving us with zero protection if we turn around—"

"Auggghhhhh!" the father screeched from the floorboard, where he'd retreated and wrapped himself around his son. "Look! They're coming!"

I twisted my neck around, staring back in the direction he was pointing, and saw that he was right. Not about some supernatural foe, or whatever that had been, but about a much more mundane threat. And one just as deadly.

The mages who had been up top were scaling down the walls now, and it seemed that I wasn't the only one fighting off panic. Because their tethers were breaking as their concentration wobbled, sending some of them plunging to their deaths; while others took the run down the perpendicular cliffs way too fast for safety, even with magical harnesses. It was more of a retreat from whatever they'd been fighting than an attack, but the result was the same for us.

We were suddenly swamped.

I again tried to speed up, but the infrared eyesight that worked a treat on bodies was useless against cold stone. I couldn't see the path ahead and couldn't risk barreling into a wall and snapping Caleb's paper-thin shield. And then it gave up the fight anyway, after absorbing another half dozen spells, leaving us seconds away from death if I didn't do something completely crazy, right freaking now.

So, I did.

Chapter Twenty-Eight

What the hell?" Caleb yelled, grabbing my shoulder from behind and ensuring that I skidded us into a wall.

Sparks flew, highlighting our location, and I suddenly didn't need to complain about a lack of light. Spells flashed everywhere, from behind us, from above—where it looked like a few of the mages had remained behind—and ricocheted off the walls ahead to come speeding back this way. But instead of us going up in flames, it was something else.

Make that a lot of somethings.

Because I'd just done a blanket levitation spell on the corridor, causing everything in sight to forget about gravity and float up into space, giving us a buffer zone in the form of anything that wasn't nailed down.

So, instead of being the only target in town, we were suddenly surrounded by an asteroid field made up of slowly rotating sacks of garbage; half a forest's worth of wooden pallets; rocks of various sizes, including some that counted as boulders; a number of woven baskets; a line of laundry, all of which was now drifting aimlessly on its clips; and a bicycle, the latter of which was immediately turned into metallic confetti when impacted by a spell.

The remains of somebody's ride sparkled and spun overhead as I righted the steering wheel and took off, not knowing how long our protection was going to last. Or if I could navigate while not running us into something, because infrared vision is not a help when everything is on fire! And then my own eyesight returned, but it didn't help much.

The burning debris cast ominous shadows onto the ground, making it look like we were driving through hell's hallway. It also highlighted the terrified faces of the father and son, who I smiled at as reassuringly as I could manage. "It's okay. We got this!"

But neither of them looked very convinced, maybe because—

"You've got this?" the father yelled, as our front tires started to leave the road. "What, exactly, do you have?"

A problem, I thought, cursing inwardly. Levitation spells were notoriously unreliable if not bound to an item, and the damned thing hadn't excluded us even though I had told it to. I knew I had!

"Change back!" I yelled at Sebastian.

"What?"

"Go furry! We're sailing right into their line of sight!"

But I guessed he didn't hear me over the gunfire now strafing the corridor. And pinging off rock and metal alike as our already panicked enemies tried to shoot the spell that had caught them by surprise. And we weren't much better off, with our last few tires breaking contact with the earth, leaving us completely airborne.

And sitting ducks.

As soon as we floated above the fiery garbage, we were dead. But I couldn't stop us without reversing the spell, which I couldn't do because it wasn't bound to anything! And even if I could have cancelled it, we'd be right back in the same mess as before.

Caleb had started raining fire on the mages behind us, using a magical tether like a whip to grab flaming junk and sending it flying at their heads, which appeared to be making some of them regret following us down here. But the fact that he was resorting to that meant his ammo was getting low. And instead of listening to me and helping out, Sebastian was working on slipping the last tether I'd put on him, since the others had lost their grip when he Changed.

But I'd forgotten—the stubborn bardric wasn't the only wolf in residence. And a moment later, the front seat was crowded once more, courtesy of a now fluffy father and son, the latter of whom must have been wolf born since he'd changed, too. Even combined, they weren't as heavy as Sebastian, but an extra six hundred pounds did help.

That wouldn't have been true in real zero gravity, but levitation charms only give you actual weightlessness if properly bound to an item. Splashed around like this there were pockets of zero grav, and pockets where it was merely lowered, as if we were on the moon. We hit one of those and sank back down again, staying in the gloom, staying hidden. But we still weren't moving, unless you counted an occasional bounce, because wheels don't work too well when they almost never encounter the road. Leaving us vulnerable to any mage with a tat like mine who could see in the dark.

Like that one, I thought, as bullets suddenly strafed the car from above.

Everybody ducked except for Caleb, who one-shotted the sniper off the rocky roof. The body fell into the corridor and then just stayed there, floating about and adding to the confusion, because it couldn't fall. But there'd be a replacement soon enough, and he might have better aim.

We had to get out of here.

"How far does this damned spell extend?" Caleb demanded, reading my mind.

"I don't know. I was just trying to—wait, grab her!" I said, as Kimmie's limp form started to drift away.

"Don't you have a plan?" the father demanded, as Caleb buckled her in.

"Yes, I have a plan!" I really wished people would stop asking me that.

"You do?" Caleb sounded doubtful.

"That depends. Do you have any *fulminare*?"

He stared at me for a moment, and then he started cursing.

The Were father grabbed me. "Does this plan involve us floating out of here like a balloon?"

"No—"

"Then why have we started back up again?"

And, yes, we had. But before I could decide what to do about it, the sound of pounding boots came echoing down the passageway. A lot of boots.

"What's that?" Aki asked, looking around wildly.

"You have to be kidding me," Caleb said, pushing the boy's head down and opening fire on a mass of pursuing mages.

"Where are they coming from?" the father shrieked.

"The arena." I guessed they'd decided to chance it, after all.

And they were coming full bore, with a barrage that would have pulverized us except that we weren't where they were aiming anymore. We had wafted about a story above that, and were heading into a lazy backwards somersault until I threw myself on the dashboard to balance us out. And a moment later, I heard the very unhappy sounds of a bunch of mages who had just run headlong into the same problem that we were having.

I also learned a new thing: spells don't function properly in zero grav. Bullets seemed to work just fine, and there were plenty of them zipping around. But the hexes that had accompanied them were drifting randomly in the air, as seemingly confused as the rest of us.

That might explain why the previous group of mages had been having such trouble hitting us, as their spells drifted off course and immolated somebody's garbage. And it meant that the new arrivals were having to desperately flap about, trying to avoid their own battle hexes. It would have been funny if we weren't rising toward their comrades again, who now had a bunch of suspended spell light to see by.

But suddenly, that was no longer a problem.

"Auggghhhh!" I shrieked, which would have been embarrassing, except that everyone else was doing it, too. And if you've never heard a transformed Were scream in terror, you're missing absolutely nothing, because it's horrible.

But not as much as plummeting from a height with no warning.

We hit down hard enough to blow out all four tires. Leaving us bouncing along on the rims over rocks and hard packed earth, because my spell had just given out. And being pelted by fiery debris as everything else fell down, too, including the dead body.

Which I drove over while trying to control our wildly careening ride.

Caleb was yelling something, but I couldn't hear him over the formerly suspended spells hitting the ground, sending geysers of dirt skyward, and a bunch of howling wolves. Because the Were father's desperate cry had been taken up by hundreds of voices. And, yeah, that *had* kind of sounded like a signal, hadn't it?

The mages, who had just crashed down like everything else, didn't even get a chance to draw a breath before they were hit again. But not by gravity this time, or bullets, or even spells. Instead, a hail of cast-iron pots and pans, large rocks, and nets were thrown from the shadows on all sides.

The nets looked pretty moth eaten, because they were presumably from the last war. But they worked to keep the enemy flailing around on the ground as a wave of Weres jumped them. And all hell broke loose.

Which was probably why Caleb was yelling a steady chorus of *"Go! Go! Go!"* into my ear. And I was trying. Hell, I'd *been* trying, but the truck was not handling well; something was definitely wrong under the hood.

And people were howling and yelling and screeching, and bullets were ricocheting and spells were raining down from the bastards up top. Including one that took out our windshield and sprayed glass in my face. And would have eaten through the dashboard if I hadn't shielded my hand and thrown it off.

And then Sebastian was leaping out of the truck and running back into the fray.

"Son of a bitch!" Caleb said and started after him, but I grabbed his coat because that wasn't going to work. We'd never find him in the churning ocean of fur and blood that the corridor had become, but there was an alternative.

"There's an alternative!" I yelled.

"Like what?"

I stared back at Sebastian, whose tawny fur all but glowed in the spell light. "Give 'em another target."

* * *

A moment later, we had found refuge around a corner, which was going to last exactly no time at all. But then, we didn't need for it to. "Get out," I told the father.

"Here?" he stared at me. And if a wolf could look taken aback, he managed it.

"There's a door right there," I nodded toward a dark opening in the wall, just ahead. It was almost invisible to the naked eye, but there was a warren of slender passageways climbing through the rock behind it. He'd be okay.

Only he wasn't convinced of that.

"*And*? They'll kill us! My boy—"

"Aki will take your son and Kimmie out of here. You can handle two, right?" I asked Aki, who was biting his lip.

"If one is small, yeah. But Sophie sent me here to rescue you. She said—"

"And who are you more afraid of? Sophie, or me?" Considering that I was covered in blood and had just ripped a guys' heart out, I thought that was an easy question.

But apparently not.

So, I growled at him and he blanched. Then grabbed the cub and Kim and vanished into thin air. Leaving me staring at nothing, which even with a lifetime of magic behind me, was damned impressive.

"What the—what just happened? Where is my son?" the father said, looking around frantically.

"It's okay. Aki's a teleporter." This did not appear to reassure him much, judging by his increasingly frantic pawing. "He's taken them outside," I added. "Well away from this. They'll be okay."

"And what about me?"

"Hunker down and stay out of sight."

"And what the hell are you going to do?"

"Save Sebastian's hide," I said, and shoved him out.

He went, looking strangely conflicted, which wasn't my problem. Caleb was. Who had started cursing from the truck bed.

There appeared to be an issue, not with our new propulsion system, which was in place and ready to go, but with the reason we needed it.

"Hurry up!" I encouraged.

"You hurry up!"

"I'm ready to go," I said, and I was. Whether this would work was a completely different thing, but I didn't think that now was the time to bring that up.

Not that it was going to matter if Caleb couldn't support his end.

"What do you think?" he sat back, looking at the monstrosity he'd conjured up. It mostly filled the truck bed, being approximately the same size as Sebastian when Changed. But that was all I could say for it.

"Seriously?" I demanded.

"It's dark!"

"It's not that dark." There wasn't enough gloom in the world to make that thing look remotely like Sebastian. Or a wolf. Or anything besides an oversized orange blob. "It's not even the right color."

"Just go!"

"I'm not going to go! That wouldn't fool a nearsighted toddler!"

"Well, it's going to have to. I used up most of my arsenal and magic keeping us alive back there. I'm running on empty—"

"I'll help you."

"You're no better at illusions than I am, and how are you not out of juice? Plus, you're not even armed."

"Am now," I said, and grabbed the shotgun that I kept under the seat.

"Yeah, because that's going to do fuck all when—"

"Would you two shut the hell up?"

I thrust the shotgun into the startled face of the Were father. Who batted it aside after a second, because he apparently did have some gumption, after all. And maybe more than I'd thought, because the next moment, he was back on board.

"What are you doing?" I demanded.

"Saving my *bardric*." He tried to fasten the seatbelt, which was in no way suited to his transformed body. So, he sunk a massive set of claws through my dashboard instead. But I didn't complain, and not only because I was currently driving a hunk of scrap. But because he was big and tawny and—

"He's too small," Caleb said, while sitting beside his abomination.

The wolf and I both turned and looked at him.

"I'm just saying."

"Get rid of that," I said, waving at his pathetic attempt at magic. And then looked at the father. "You sure? This is going to be a wild ride."

"Not if we never get started. Now shut up and drive!"

Well, okay, then.

I backed up, gears grinding all the way, but managed to get us visible from the battle. Caleb, who was better at whistling than he was at illusions, sent a magically-assisted shriek down the corridor, cutting through the din and turning heads. A lot of them.

"Well, shit," I said.

And then we were moving, with the truck floating up off the ground—because I'd bound a levitation spell to it for a change—and rocketing ahead, with the *fulminare* charm that Caleb had scrounged out of his depleted stock hurtling us forward while lightning scrawled up the walls behind us.

Fulminare were weapons, not engines, designed to electrocute a large field of enemies all in one go. But we were down to bare bones here and couldn't afford to be choosy, and it did do the trick. Its propulsion system wouldn't last long, as the charge was designed merely to carry the weapon through the middle of a group of enemies. But that was just as well, since the initial thrust was in the *oh-shit-oh-shit-oh-SHIT* category, which would have been terrifying enough on an open road. Here it was tantamount to—

"Suicide!" the father screamed, as we barreled right for a very solid looking wall.

But I'd done more than levy the anti-grav spell. I'd also bound it to the steering column, so that, technically, when I moved the wheel it should move us, too. That technique worked for ley line racers, who used the principle to speed through the metaphysical rivers of power that cut around and through the Earth. But they had apparently refined it more than someone in the midst of a battle spellbinding on the fly.

Because, when I wrenched the steering wheel to the side, it did exactly nothing.

Fortunately, Caleb had scrounged up some magic from somewhere, and threw a pillow charm at the wall ahead of us, causing us to bounce off when we tried to faceplant. Which would have been great, since we were about to be meat otherwise. Only there was the small matter of the *fulminare*.

Which did not have brakes.

And, as a result, neither did we.

We ricocheted off Caleb's hastily erected pillow, course corrected, and went barreling right down the corridor again. Since it was in no way straight, that involved a lot of scraping and sparks flying and more ricocheting, this time off the hundred tiny crashes we suffered whenever any rock got in our way. Which was constantly.

That was especially difficult for me, because the formerly courageous Were father was rethinking his life, and doing his best to wrap himself around my body while howling like a banshee. And pieces were sheering off of the sides of my truck, leaving us with little more than a naked chassis after a few seconds. And I was discovering that it *was* possible to navigate, but that this thing no longer had anything remotely resembling power steering.

If I wanted to avoid being vertical roadkill, I had to really lean in on the course corrections. Luckily, with my new found strength, that was feasible. Unluckily, it was made hard by my terrified blanket, and by a crazed mage jumping down from somewhere above us and trying to curse me into oblivion on the way to the ground.

I guess he'd assumed that I'd put the antigrav spell on the whole corridor again. Too bad, I thought, as he dropped like a stone and then got run over in mid-air. Another bastard tried it a moment later, only he was smarter. He aimed for the truck itself, trying to kamikaze the backseat.

Only to land in the bed instead, and have a furious Caleb kick him off into the waiting arms of the *fulminare*, which electrocuted the shit out of him.

And then Caleb was grabbing my shoulder and pointed at something behind us.

Chapter Twenty-Nine

Caleb had been yelling at me, but over the Were's screeches, what might have been a few of my own, and the crackling hell of riding a lightning storm, I hadn't heard him. I still didn't, but I could see. And what I could see—

"Ha!" I said, because as bad as we were doing, the dark mage squad was faring even worse.

They'd taken off after us, with the prime target obviously being Sebastian, as I'd assumed all along. But there was no doubt about it now, with a couple hundred mages abandoning the fight to thunder down the hall in our wake. And using magically enhanced speed, which ate through power like nobody's business, to help them keep up with our crazy pace.

Or maybe that wasn't the only reason.

Because behind the dark bastards, I kept getting glimpses of Weres—a lot of Weres. Whenever we hit a stretch of more or less straight wall, I got a look at the wolves who had attacked the hit squad, and who were obviously not done yet. The unfortunate mages in the back of the group were getting taken down as the Were pack ate at their heels—literally. Which caused the ones in front to pick up the pace even more, to the point that they almost caught us, although they were suddenly less focused on that than on what was chasing them.

And the rest of the squad weren't doing any better.

The people behind concealed doorways and windows sprawling halfway up the cliffs had realized what was happening, and had started throwing everything they could find at their attackers. We're not talking modern weapons or even war surplus here, but toasters, irons, more cooking equipment, paint cans, and somebody's old washing machine. Even a toilet got into the act.

And while you wouldn't think that those kinds of things would matter to shielded mages, the problem was that the battle had been going on for a while now. Most magical battles don't do that. Most magical battles *can't* do that as the mages would run out of magic.

These had managed to hold on for this long because there were so many of them. Some could shield themselves as well as their buddies on either side, and then switch off later to conserve energy. But not in here.

In here, everybody had to use enhanced speed, all the time, or get eaten alive. Everybody had to shield, all the time, even if their neighbors were helping out, because they were being attacked on multiple sides. That included friendly fire from above, which had taken down more than a handful, and those were just the ones I'd seen.

So, yeah, you could share the load, but you still bore the load for part of that protection. And on top of that, you were also trying to attack the bastards gunning for you. And on top of *that*, you had somebody hurling their fifty-pound dumbbells at your head with Were strength behind them.

Sure, they might not get through your shields, although that depended on how thin they were getting at this point. But even if they didn't, impacts drained them—and you. So, the next time the big bad wolf came at you, with shining teeth and jaws that bit down with more force than an alligator, good luck with that.

You expended too much capitol fending off exercise equipment.

Even worse, it wasn't merely the inanimate objects that the mages needed to worry about. I saw a man dodge a flower pot, only to have a huge wolf's head stick out of a shadow and snatch him up. He disappeared without a trace, his scream lost in the darkness of some tunnel or other, as if he'd never been there at all. But other attacks were less subtle—like Granny Top-Knot and her group shot-gunning heads from hidden perches as we flew by.

"Gimme the shotgun!" Caleb said, wanting to get in on the act.

I passed it over, before barely avoiding decapitation from a rock ledge. They protruded out in patches all along the wall in this section, like clumps of weird mushrooms, and should have been knocked out ages ago as a safety measure. But they'd been left intact instead, to catch anybody who didn't know this place well.

Which, unfortunately, included us.

As Caleb demonstrated when he got bonked on the head a second later, making him curse and spurt blood from an ugly wound. And miss his intended target, not that it mattered. The mages were hedged so tightly that the shell hit another guy, right behind the first.

"You okay?" I yelled back, and had Caleb flash me a bloody smile.

"Better than him!"

This was true. The mage had dropped with a yell, holding his leg. And enhanced speed meant that he was left in the dust by his associates as soon as he fell, with nobody going back for him.

Of course, a second later, there was nothing to go back for.

But the wolves were having their own problems. I saw several drop from spells flung at them from above, including a brown Were who was all but incinerated on the spot. More were felled by gunshots and lacerated by exploding rock shelves, which in this section were taking the brunt of the overhead barrage. While another moved just fast enough to avoid a disruptor, the dislocator's nasty cousin.

Ensuring that it hit the mage to the right of him, instead.

If the unfortunate man had been properly shielded, he might have gotten off lightly. A direct hit would have almost certainly ripped apart his shields, as the charge on those things was no joke. Yet, if he was lucky, he might have gotten them back up before anyone noticed.

But he wasn't properly shielded.

He'd taken one too many dumbbells to the head, which was why I was suddenly looking at a statue-like figure, dull red and gloopy, as if a child had made him out of runny clay. The features were no longer recognizable, having melted into the amorphous mass of the head. But the mouth was still there and still screaming.

For a moment, until the rock absorbed it, too, filling it up as if he was gargling lava.

Disruptors didn't send body parts flying off to attach to anything in the nearby area, like dislocators. They did something worse. They sent DNA, swapping it for whatever or whoever's was handy.

The choice was arbitrary, and the spell, unsurprisingly considering where we were, had glommed onto a nearby piece of rock. Leaving the wolves surging around the new, living statue as carelessly as if he'd been just another piece of stone. While, on a nearby piece of rock, a smear of color bloomed.

I looked away, swallowing hard.

The Corps didn't use the awful things. Dislocators were permitted because they simply killed—most of the time, anyway. And were useful for taking on many opponents at once, or scaring a large group away once they realized what you had.

Disruptors were different. They were designed to leave you alive, only as a terrible, twisted version of yourself that would intimidate the hell out of anyone who saw you. The dark had developed them some time ago, but while the Corps studied them, we didn't use them.

But we could still be affected by them.

And, for the first time today, I felt true terror creeping over me.

"Didn't think those worked on non-living things," Caleb said shakily, as if feeling the same way.

"Well, now you know." I gripped the steering wheel hard enough to bruise.

I wanted out of here.

I wanted out now.

But that was a little hard to imagine, after half a dozen mages threw tethers onto the back of the truck, trying to bring us down. We whipped around a corner and they whipped with us, determined to get their prize. Or maybe, seeing their desperate faces, they were just trying to hitch a ride out of here.

I wasn't sure which, but I wasn't having it.

They'd put levitation spells on something under their boots, allowing them to surf along in our wake. But that didn't really help, since the hall was just wide enough to allow me to sling them back and forth across the width of it. They went crashing into walls, smashing into ridges, and in one case, dragging face first over the stony ground, when whatever he was using as a platform shot out from under him. He was smart enough to let go before the rest of his flesh was scraped off, but the others weren't. They doggedly held on, even when they started to get dangerously close to the *fulminare's* electric field.

Allowing Caleb to get a tether of his own around their ropy spells, pull them together, and *jerk*.

That ended that, I thought, as the electrified mages fell away, smoking, onto the corridor floor. But they had accomplished one very important thing in the process. They'd slowed us down.

Not by a lot, but by enough that a spell from above hit the engine hard enough to flip us. That didn't make much of a difference to our momentum, since the engine wasn't propelling us anyway. But it left us hanging upside down and clinging to our seats and whatever else we could find for dear life. Meanwhile, the truck started careening back the way we'd come.

Right over the heads of a lot of enraged mages.

Well, some were enraged. Others ducked the lightning storm, then seemed relieved to have a way out of the trap they'd found themselves in. They made a break for the open corridor ahead as soon as we were out of the way, thus splitting the ranks, with half continuing to pelt down the hallway and the rest bunching up to lob spells at the guy they still believed to be Sebastian.

Who used his considerable bulk to abruptly flip the truck right-side up again, before a dozen spells hit the undercarriage hotly enough to melt parts of it.

That saved our lives, but also unbalanced the truck, which started slinging around the small space in a circle, shedding sparks and electricity onto the crowd below.

I fought with the sluggish steering to get us evened out, while acid from a potion bomb ate away at the floorboards under my feet, turning them to metal lace. I also tried to keep an eye on the battle, although that was difficult through the potion fumes seeping up from below and smoke billowing out of the merrily burning fire that had been my engine. And which finally decided to fall out, prompting a new barrage from those below.

Several more spells tore at us from overhead, and they were better aimed, because they weren't having to deal with dripping potion's residue, smoke and a renewed attack from the pack of Weres, who had just caught up to their prey. The bolts barely missed the madly circling truck, and that was only because they'd been fired at an angle and on the run. The mages who had been pelting along the rocks above had taken a moment to reorient themselves and were now headed back this way.

With a vengeance.

I managed to slam a hex into one, knocking him into the melee below. But it hurt me almost as much as it did him, with the sprained-muscle feeling of bottomed-out magic echoing through my body like a struck funny bone. I wasn't going to be throwing too many more of those.

Which was a problem, since another blast took that moment to hit the wall beside us, bombarding the truck with a hurricane of shards that mimicked the sound of a machine gun. And felt like one, too, when shrapnel peppered my thigh through the missing door of the truck, and a jagged piece bit into my side, leaving me feeling like I'd been shanked.

But I'd managed to get us straightened out again and we rocketed ahead. We were moving in the wrong direction, but right now, I'd take it. Right now, I'd take anything that wasn't here.

Because the mages up top had almost caught up, as indicated by a succession of explosions, creating craters in the walls and floor all around us. Rock flew, spells rained, people screamed. And it was so fast and frantic that I couldn't stop trying to dodge long enough even to attempt to fire back.

Caleb, on the other hand, had acquired a new gun. How I didn't know, but I guessed that he'd used his tether like a whip to snatch it off a mage. He was firing back, and he dropped at least one of the bastards.

But that left plenty more, and we weren't likely to get any help from below.

The fight on the corridor floor had turned desperate, with the mages deploying their entire arsenal to lay down a blanket of deadly fire from a swarm of animated weaponry. They were outnumbered now, but the Weres were outgunned. And everywhere I looked I saw terrified faces of both species, lit up by red and orange phosphorescent spells.

Then a blast hit the truck a glancing blow, but it was hard enough to throw us at the wall, and almost cause me to bite my tongue in two. The main force of it took out someone below and it sounded like a human someone, but the mages didn't seem to care. They were tired of trying to hit a moving target that they could barely see and had decided on a new tactic.

Which was to rain fire until we were dead, and hang the collateral damage.

And it was probably going to work, since our *fulminare* took that moment to cut out.

I heard Caleb curse, probably because someone had managed to get another tether spell on us from below. Someone else had done the opposite, using his tether as a rope to slide down to us from the rocks above. Only to be met by a savage blow to the head from the butt of the empty shotgun when he arrived.

I was the one wielding the gun, because Caleb was busy picking off the tether-holders beneath us. But there were too many of them and he quickly ran out of ammo. I felt us being jerked ever lower, while my beast clawed at my insides, screaming to be let out, and the cluster of mages overhead took aim, planning to finish us off.

But they didn't. Because they'd just been thrown aside, as something else took their place. Something huge.

I craned my neck, because whatever it was, was on our side of the hall. But all I could see was a dark outline against the stars. It didn't look like the bird thing I'd glimpsed earlier; it didn't look like anything except a shadow, one with a Were's snout when it turned its head slightly.

But it wasn't a Were. It was far bigger and strangely misshapen. And was suddenly dropping down on top of us, a jump of maybe fifty feet as if it was nothing.

It didn't hit us, but landed just alongside, crushing several mages in the process. It was tall enough that it could look me in the eyes, despite the fact that I was maybe fifteen feet off the ground. And now that I could see it clearly, splashed with fire and spell light, I felt a cold hand grip my heart and squeeze like a bastard, because it *wasn't* a Were.

It was worse.

"Relic!" I yelled hoarsely, why I didn't know. Most people here wouldn't know what that meant, and weren't likely to have the time to learn. Because three more giants had just leapt down into the crowded corridor, to join the first.

And that, friends, was game over. In a confined space, we couldn't take one of these creatures, much less four. I frankly doubted that we could have done it anywhere, because I'd somehow managed to forget exactly how terrible they were.

There was none of the elegance of their Were cousins. This wasn't a predator; it was a monster, and it looked every inch of it.

From the hideously elongated arms and horribly hunched back, to the misshapen maw of huge, uneven teeth and matted, ugly coat, it was mind-alteringly awful, like something from another world that had no business in ours.

It was also absolutely the cause of Windward's demise, as I couldn't get a scent read on the creatures even with them practically in my face. Except for one, the last to arrive, who had landed by the far wall. Yet my nose picked up on something so bizarre in the air around him that it had me wondering if I was losing my mind.

And then I was sure of it, when the four sent up a terrible ululating cry, almost in unison, and fell onto the crowd below.

But not onto us, despite the fact that we were out of both magic and ammo, and my furry blanket had passed the hell out on the seat beside me. And not onto the Weres, who had stopped fighting and were simply staring at the creatures in a cross between shock and horror. No, the monsters went on the attack, alright, but their target . . .

Were our enemies.

In less than a minute, the four relics savaged every mage there. And nothing the dark squad did made a damned bit of difference. Shields or no shields, magic or no magic, guns, potion bombs, snares, and everything else you could imagine was deployed by the mages who lasted long enough, and none of it mattered.

And then, before I quite knew what had happened, it was over.

The Relics bounded up the mostly sheer walls in defiance of gravity, and with no more effort than I would use to walk down the street. They disappeared over the top, leaving behind red splashed walls, a lot of freaked out Weres, and piles of red, oozing meat. And Caleb and I, bobbing slightly in my ruined truck, and staring at each other.

Chapter Thirty

There had been times after a battle when I'd almost wished that I'd been knocked out, as it would have been simpler. This was one of them. But instead, Caleb and I had to clamber down from the ruined truck, which neither of us had the strength to disenchant, after slapping the Were father around enough that he woke up and tried to eat my head.

I didn't hold it against him; it had been one of those days. I also didn't mind that I sprained an ankle when I landed wrong, after using one of the mages' disintegrating tethers as a rope, and had a limp as a result. I didn't even care that I was bleeding like a stuck pig from the wound in my side, and a bunch more smaller ones peppering my jeans.

But being bottomed out on magic *sucked.*

Mages need magic to live as much as we do food, to the point that we can literally die without it. Getting too low was as bad as losing too much blood, although lucky me, I'd managed to do both. Which probably explained why I was staggering, cold, and clammy, and my skin felt like it was trying to escape from my flesh.

Of course, there might have been for another reason for that.

The area we were standing in looked like a bomb had gone off with us at the center, one that had selectively left out the Weres. Wherever they'd stood, the walls behind them were clean; everywhere else was a landscape of blood and meat and gore that climbed up a couple of stories or more. It looked like a crazy art installation, with broken rib cages and body parts slammed so forcefully into the walls that many had stuck there, like ships riding a red wave.

"Careful," Caleb said, grabbing my elbow. Because I was staring around instead of looking where I was going, and slip-sliding on the carnage as a result.

The Weres were surer footed, and far less squeamish. Sebastian had already taken off for the arena while I was trying to get out of the truck, along with those of his people who remained in fighting form. But that left a lot of others, who had started digging through the mountains of the dead looking for loved ones who'd been buried underneath, and slumping to their knees whenever they found one.

And they found a lot, judging by the howls echoing in the strange acoustics, loud and pitiful one second, and softened to whispers the next.

It was haunting.

"Come on," Caleb said roughly. "We can't do anything here."

I followed him through ankle deep viscera, hoping that things would improve after we left the area. But if anything, it got worse. Because less carnage makes you pay more attention to what is there.

Like a piece of steel, possibly from my truck since it had the same rusted green paint job, that was imbedded in a wall just down the corridor. It resembled a knife that had been stabbed into the stone by a giant's hand. But it had probably been hurled by Were instead, as it was holding up an almost bisected mage.

He had died with a look of profound surprise on his face, as if he hadn't realized just how strong his opponents were until it was too late. His guts were dripping down the wall, making a puddle underneath him. And nearby, a Were, possibly the one who had killed him, was splayed on the floor, a spell stuttering and flaming inside his body, lighting him up like a hairy lantern as it ate its way through to the stone.

I looked away, only to encounter several more Weres silhouetted against the sails overhead, the moonlight just enough to limn them with light. I couldn't see their expressions, for which I was truly grateful. Because everybody I passed felt like a personal failure, like their deaths could have been prevented if I'd been smarter, faster, or made better decisions.

There was no time for recriminations in battle, which was why the aftermath was always harder. Even if you won—and I wasn't yet sure that we had—there were always mistakes. And they were often written in blood.

After a few more bends, we came across a lone patch of my initial levitation spell, which had broken off from the rest and somehow survived. It was moving, caught in some current I couldn't feel twenty feet off of the ground, where it had trapped a collection of body parts. And was now whirling them about like a macabre carousel.

Around and around they went, lit up by the light from spluttering battle spells, plenty of which were eating into the rock and chasing each other across the floor. They mingled with the smoking residue of potion bombs, broken furniture and household items, and still-active hexes fritzing over already dead bodies. But the light they threw off was dim, and left large sections of the corridor shrouded in darkness.

Which was why I didn't see what was in front of me until I ran into it.

I staggered back with a curse, found my footing, and looked up—and discovered something looking back at me. But not something human. Not anymore.

It looked like a column of solidified lava, or a stalagmite that had grown up in the middle of the path for some reason. But it had the vague appearance of a man, including a man's eyes staring out at me from folds of rock. And then they blinked, still alive, still aware—

And I almost threw up.

Caleb came up beside me, breathing hard, although whether that was due to his wounds or to what we were looking at, I had no idea. And I didn't turn around to ask, because I couldn't seem to look away. The mage that the disruptor had turned into whatever the hell this was looked mutely back, unable to speak anymore, but he didn't need to.

We both knew what he wanted.

"Not a chance," Caleb wheezed, catching my hand as I started to lift it.

"Can't leave him." I did look back then and met liquid dark eyes. "Can you?"

"If I had a spell left in me? No. But I don't—and neither do you. I saw your face when you threw that last one."

"Doesn't matter—"

"It *does*. We'll send someone back."

"Yeah, only they can't get in."

And the Weres wouldn't allow them to interfere, even if they could. Most clans took trophies from their enemies to display in their chieftain's hall, both as a point of pride and as a warning to others. And whatever part of the mage had ended up smeared onto the wall wouldn't be enough to satisfy them, not after this.

I glanced at it, but it was already shriveled and brown, like dead moss. It hadn't been able to get a foothold in the stone—thank God. But the rest . . .

I turned my gaze back to the living statue in front of me. That would make a hell of a trophy, for however long he lasted. Trapped in stone, already buried but not yet dead, and internally screaming because his mouth no longer existed . . .

Which was why I couldn't leave him here. I killed in battle; that was part of the job. But this . . .

I couldn't do this.

I looked around, and halfway up the wall, found what I was searching for.

"Too high," Caleb said, eyeing the half exhausted yellow curse eating its way into the rock.

I picked up a stone and tried knocking it loose, but it was too far in. And no way could I climb that high. Not with my hands threatening to shake just standing here.

"I'll do it."

I looked around to see that the Were father had come up behind us. He'd been padding along in wolf form, so silently that I'd almost forgotten that he was there. But other than for being traumatized, he was unhurt, and probably in the best shape out of the three of us.

He looked up at the spell, his face bathed in yellow light, and the next time I blinked, he was beside it. The leap took him up almost two stories, with his weight hitting the wall hard enough to make me cringe in sympathy. But it popped out the baseball-sized spell, which fell to the ground, sizzling in a little in a pool of blood.

I looked back at the trapped mage.

He had brown eyes. They looked strangely normal, like they could have belonged to anyone. Somebody cashing me out in a shop or passing me on the street. Just anyone.

He didn't look evil.

It made me wonder how he got there. And what choices had led to him dying like this, in a desert fortress surrounded by his enemies. Yet destroyed by one of his friends.

I licked my lips. "Ready?"

He blinked.

I hesitated, then started toward the hissing spell. But before I could reach it, the Were father pulled me aside and Caleb kicked it instead. He moved hard and fast, so that his boot didn't touch it for more than a split second, like a soccer player going for a goal.

And sheered the statue's head clean off.

It hit the wall, exploding in a shattering of dust, and the spell finally extinguished, flaming out against the floor. Leaving us in darkness again, which suited me just fine. I didn't want to see what was left.

I didn't want to see any of this!

And I guessed the Were father felt the same. Because he Changed back into human form a moment later and started sobbing. The strange acoustics threw the sounds back to us, over and over, bouncing off the walls from all angles and sounding strangely like hysterical laughter.

I took his hand and pulled him out of that hellish echo chamber, to a place down the hall where the rock was configured differently.

"I don't know what's wrong with me," he gasped. "He was an enemy. I know that. He tried to kill me—and my son! But to die like that—"

"There's nothing wrong with you," I told him harshly. "You're a good man. And you shouldn't have had to see that."

"My father saw worse. He made us listen to constant stories about the old days, when we were growing up. About the war." He looked back at the headless statue, now just a column of rock in the gloom, and his face crumpled. "None of them were ever like this."

Caleb and I exchanged a look, but there was nothing else to say.

We walked on.

It was a shorter trek than I'd expected, because the corridor had doubled back onto itself more than once, while we sped through a maze that had had us crossing and crisscrossing our previous route without realizing it. Yet, surprisingly, there were still stretches with little signs of combat, where you could almost believe that nothing had happened. Although at others, usually bends in the corridor, the bodies were washed up in heaps like flotsam on a beach. The latter presented a problem, because the mages' enchanted weapons were still circulating overhead, protecting their fallen masters.

"No resupply here," Caleb said, voicing my thoughts, as I eyed loaded potion's belts and sidearms still in their holsters, but had no way to get to them.

We edged around, hugging the opposite wall, while the circling weapons obscured what light there was, casting bat-like shadows onto our bodies. It was so dark that the shapes they threw were black on black, visible only in occasional rays of moonlight that caught their edges. It made the place even eerier, sending shivers up my spine and causing my jaw to clench.

And then the torches flickered back to life, all at once.

The father screamed and Caleb and I reached for weapons we didn't have. And then stood there, looking sightlessly for the next threat, because that much light was blinding. But even when my eyes adjusted, I didn't see anything.

Unless you counted the stampede of frightened people from down the hall, which caused us to have to hug the walls again to avoid being swept away with them. Well, the Were dad and I did. Caleb was still trying to play war mage.

"Stay away from the bodies!" he yelled, waving his arms. "Their weapons are still active! Stay away—"

Several huge, panicked Weres all but ran him down, and I jerked him over by the wall.

"It's okay. There are too many targets!" I said, raising my voice to be heard over the crowd. And pointing at the weapons, which were buzzing around agitatedly, but couldn't figure out who to pursue with no masters left alive to direct them anymore.

And then the Were father yelled excitedly at us from Caleb's other side.

"There's a switch that activates the spell! For the torches, I mean. That's a good sign, right? That somebody's turned the lights back on?"

"Sure," Caleb said, and sank down onto his haunches, letting his head sag between his knees. "Heart attack," he added, and it said something that I wasn't sure whether he was joking or not.

I gave him a moment, not least because I could use one myself, and watched the Were father motioning everybody over to the safer side of the hall.

The initial charge hadn't lasted long, but it had gotten the crowd moving. They kept streaming past us in clumps, with many prowling along on all fours or dragging wounded limbs behind them, having stayed in wolf form for the added strength it gave. Others were back in human skin, clothed only in rippling torchlight, and splattered with blood and wounds and sweat and tears.

They should have looked pitiful, but they didn't.

They didn't.

Some were carrying the dead or wounded along with them. One old woman had a gangly young man draped over her shoulders, who was so tall that his legs dragged the ground as she walked. Even untransformed, Weres are powerful, but she was old and hunched and I wasn't surprised when another Were, a large man, tried to take him from her.

And received a snarl so savage in return, that he jerked his hand away and cowered back.

"My grandson," she said. "He fought like a demon! Like a demon, you hear? He died a hero!"

"He died a hero," a nearby woman said. "But he fought like a Were."

She walked alongside the grieving older woman, but did not try to take her burden.

No one did.

I felt something in my chest as I watched them, something primal and fierce and angry, but also very, very proud. They'd done amazingly well for people who weren't even trained as fighters. They were shop keepers and cooks, electric linemen and beauticians, bartenders and nurses. They were regular people who should never have had to face this, but they had, and they'd done better than anybody could have expected.

But next time? Or the one after that? Where could they go that the war couldn't find them?

When even Wolf's Head was vulnerable, what was left?

The answer was that we were left; Sebastian, the Clan Council, and the Corps. We were supposed to be their bulwark when everything else failed, the wall that protected them and their children. And yes, the Corps wasn't technically supposed to intervene in Were business, but now that the war had spilled over into their world?

That made it our responsibility, didn't it?

"Don't," Caleb said, without lifting his head.

"Don't what?"

"What you always do. We did our best, Lia. It's enough."

"And if it isn't?"

"Then it damned well isn't!" he said, looking up with the same pain on his face that I was feeling.

We were supposed to be the protectors, but right now, we were probably among the weakest here. Even a wounded Were was dangerous—maybe especially a wounded Were. But we were currently no better than garden variety humans.

And bleeding, damaged, bruised up humans at that.

I got an arm around his waist. "C'mon old man. We're nearly there."

A hand with a surprisingly strong grip caught my wrist. "I meant it."

"Meant what?"

Dark eyes met mine and they were deadly serious. "Don't do anything stupid. Promise me."

I looked at him in confusion. "What do you think I'm going to do? I can barely stand up."

"Don't know. But we're done, you understand? Getting yourself killed does nobody any good. Remember your training: walk away and save an asset. We can't afford to lose anybody else—"

"I'm not going to do anything," I said, wondering what the hell was wrong with him.

"Even if some of the kids didn't make it?" he asked, his voice harsh. "Even if you see one of those dark bastards standing over their bodies?" The hand around my wrist tightened, just sort of bruisingly hard. "*Promise me.*"

I stared at him, caught off guard. Because, until then, that thought somehow hadn't occurred to me. And then I tore away, limping down the path as fast as I could.

"Lia!"

I ignored the call, and the cursing that followed it, until somebody grabbed me from behind. "Let it go!" Caleb said, and thereby saving himself from an elbow to the liver.

"Let *me* go, damn it!" I twisted in his arms before he had a chance to respond, because I knew he was going to ignore that.

But he'd known me a long time, and we used to spar together; still did, whenever either of us was in good enough shape. As a result, my leg was blocked on its way to do a sweep of his, and I found myself in a tussle with a larger and stronger opponent. I should have been dominating this fight, based on the strength I'd been demonstrating all day, but that was not happening.

"Why . . . are you . . . this strong?" I panted, as he backed me into a wall and got an arm at my throat.

"I'm not. You're just that weak. You've mostly bled out, of blood and magic both. I'm taking you back to the Corps—"

"Like hell!"

"You need to see a healer, Lia!"

"So do you!"

"I'm fine." It was implacable.

"You have a head wound! You're in more danger than I am, but the little woman has to be coddled, right?" I broke his hold, because he wasn't in much better shape than me no matter what he said. "I thought we were past that horseshit—"

"We aren't past it; we never started it! This isn't about your sex or your abilities. I'm your partner, and you're not throwing your goddamned life away on a bunch of—"

"A bunch of what?"

I looked up to see Sophie standing there, hands on her hips, glaring at Caleb. Dimas was with her, and fully visible, probably because he was getting low on power, too. And Kimmie was with Aki, so presumably they were all right, but—

"There's a problem with Jen," Dimas said breathlessly, before I could ask. "You need to come. You need to come now."

We went, all of us, pounding down the corridor as fast as we could go, with my damned ankle slowing me down when I wanted to race ahead. The Were father did that instead, transforming and using four legs to outpace us all. And then coming back just before we reached the tunnel's end, his face telling me how bad it was even before he spoke.

"Clan Council. They're blaming her."
I forgot about my ankle and ran.

Chapter Thirty-One

The arena was so bright, with the blaze of what seemed like a thousand torches, that I was blinded for a moment. But Caleb had two vision tats to my one, and his eyes adjusted faster. And he didn't like what he saw.

"Get away from them!" he yelled. "Get away!"

He took off running and I started after him, tripping and falling because the sands of the arena were littered with debris that I was glad I couldn't see. But my eyes cleared up halfway across, allowing me a glimpse of what had Caleb so furious: Jen and Chris, still high on their perch atop the rock cut benches, and surrounded by a dwindling number of zombies that were being savaged by a group of Weres.

A large group.

A hand clenched my heart so hard that I thought it might explode. And not just because of the danger. But because Jen didn't look like a powerful necromancer anymore.

She looked like a frightened kid.

Maybe because she was running on empty after saving all our asses, with her hair in her face and her eyes huge. Chris didn't appear any better off, with the crackling nimbus of power that had surrounded him gone, leaving just a young man staring death in the face and looking fairly green at the prospect. He nonetheless had Jen slightly behind him in a protective pose, but that was going to do exactly fuck all once their final defenders fell.

I stopped running and grabbed Sophie.

"Can you get out of here?"

The redhead rounded on me, her furious face matching her hair. "I'm not leaving you! Or her!"

"I'm not asking you to. Aki is outside. Find him—"

"I don't have to find him! He was supposed to take you to the parking lot—"

"—and see if he can get Jen and Chris out."

"There's no time!" She looked from me to the rapidly dwindling circle of protection around Jen. "She's almost out of power. They'll be on her before—"

"They won't."

"How the hell do you know?"

"Because I'm going to stop them."

She stared at me for a moment, and I braced myself for more arguments that I didn't have time for. But she surprised me. She turned and ran off toward the entrance without another word.

I didn't know how she planned to get out of here, but I was confident enough in her by now to know that she'd manage. I'd barely had the thought when Sophie's body suddenly disappeared, leaving only footprints in the sand as she ran. Two sets of footprints.

So, she and Dimas were accounted for, as were Kimmie and Aki.

Good, I thought, and ran after Caleb.

He'd reached the bottom of the stone benches, but was being ignored. Sebastian was halfway up and doing better, but that was mainly because he and some of his people were throwing the attacking Weres out of the way, not because he was being listened to. And I was pretty sure I knew why.

The small group of people at the bottom of the sweep of seats were familiar to me, as they were to the whole of the Were world. The heads of some of the larger clans, they helped to form the Clan Council which Sebastian was supposed to lead. But many of them had been bucking him at every turn, some in opposition to the alliance with the humans, others not wanting any oversight into their clan's activities or changes to the ways that things had always been done. It had been an uphill struggle ever since his election.

And now it looked like they had decided to take him down.

Because it was their wolves attacking, with their scents coming to me as clearly as if I was standing beside them. Some of my new powers were fading, but that one was as strong as ever, and it allowed me to link the wolves to their masters with no trouble at all. Especially since most were tied directly to the towering hulk visible above the rest of the group, with the discipline and arrogance to remain in human form despite the carnage all around him.

His wolves shared his egotism, and were utterly ignoring Sebastian's repeated roars to stand down. Caleb was shouting even louder, projecting his voice magically, making me surprised that he had enough power to spare. I didn't, and wouldn't have bothered issuing orders that no one was likely to follow in any case.

I targeted the Clan Council instead.

Of course, I didn't reach them. A line of massive wolves stood in between us, and snarled and snapped at me as I approached. But they didn't attack, didn't bite.

They hadn't been given orders—yet.

But it wouldn't be long. Because the man who rounded on me was their master, the same one controlling the attack. And despite not being in wolf form himself, he gave off the same sense of menace, the same towering bulk, and the eyes—

Were wolf eyes, in a human face.

They burned dark gold, brightly enough to cast light shadows onto the beard that flowed down his chest. It was bigger and fuller than Ulmer's, but had none of the other man's grizzled appearance. It was truly magnificent, a black cascade with only one, stark ribbon of white running through it, the same one that continued up his temple and into his hair.

It looked like a divine painter had slapped him with a brush, but it was the only divine thing about him.

"If you have any influence on your clan leader, rogue," he snarled, "tell him to get back before he ends up dead!"

"I thought that was the idea," I said, only it wasn't me. I'd been about to correct him, to point out that Sebastian's title was *bardric*, as he knew very well. But once again, another voice spoke thorough me, and she didn't seem to care if she got us killed. Because she was speaking to Whirlwind of Rand, one of the most powerful clan leaders on Earth, without the slavish deference he was accustomed to.

Or any at all.

I'd had a speech worked out, explaining that Jen and Chris were fighting on our side, and pointing out that threatening the Corps' assets wasn't likely to end well. I didn't actually expect that to work on Whirlwind, particularly if he was using the attack as cover for another hit on his rival. But he wasn't the only council member here.

I didn't see many of Sebastian's supporters, but there were plenty of clan leaders who fell in the middle politically and they were already looking appalled.

Yet I didn't give that speech.

Instead, I was somehow through the line of wolves protecting the council and into the great man's face. He looked surprised to see me move that fast, but not half as much as I was. Rein it in, I thought desperately. We don't have anything left! Fucking rein it in!

I was ignored, maybe because my other half was busy roaring: "Traitor!"

"Be careful what words you throw around, child," Whirlwind hissed back. "Or they may be your last."

He wasn't kidding. Peripheral vision showed me that the wolves who should have been guarding him had finally caught a clue and whirled on me, teeth bared.

But there was one thing that would stop any wolf in his tracks.

"Or yours," I said. "Fight me! Or I'll gut you where you stand!"

Things abruptly got very quiet in the nearby area. I could still hear the sounds of battle from above us, the moans and groans of the wounded scattered around and the whistling wind overhead. But mostly, I heard the pounding of my heart, as the enormity of what I'd just done sank in.

I mentally closed my eyes.

This was it, the last thing I would ever do. My wolf was insane and we were both going to be joining the corpses in the sand, any minute now. I had just challenged a council member and I was beyond fucked.

Whirlwind seemed to think so, too.

"Are you mad?" he asked, seemingly more taken aback than frightened. "Has the battle rattled your mind?"

I opened my mouth to say something, anything, that might diffuse this, but again, someone else spoke instead. And unlike me, she was not frightened or confused at all. She'd said exactly what she meant, and was still focused on that very thing.

And fuck the consequences.

"Fight me!"

Whirlwind gave what could only be called a roar and Changed. It was so rapid that I never even saw it. One moment, a huge, older man with enough muscles for an aging prize fighter was standing there, and the next—

Damn, that's a big wolf, I thought, staring upward.

And it was a long way up, because he was bigger than Sebastian, a hulking, battle scarred, mountain of fur and savagery. His coloring was plain gray, without any interesting markings, but he didn't need them. And he had the same dark gold eyes as before, because some of the most powerful—and feral—wolves didn't Change back all the way.

He was a beast in both forms, but this one was about to tear my throat out.

But before he could, a slender, dark-haired man ran up. He didn't look like he'd make much of a wolf, but if he was who I suspected, he didn't need to. Farkas of Rand, Whirlwind's Second, was known for being a shrewd, calculating type who fought with his mind not his brawn. He was young for a Second, being barely thirty-five, yet from what I'd heard, he rarely put a foot wrong.

I'd only seen him once before, at a clan meeting, and we hadn't spoken. But those watchful, serious eyes were the same, although at the moment, they were pretty panicked. As were the hands that he dared to put on his master.

"Get out of the way," Whirlwind growled, but his Second stood firm.

"Don't you see what's she's doing?" he asked quickly, and to give the man credit, his voice was steady, at least. "They planned this! They're trying to bait you—"

"Get out of the way!" And Whirlwind knocked him to the side, in a blow that might have killed a human.

But Farkas wasn't one, and he was back in an instant and grabbing onto his leader's massive mane of fur. "Listen to me! She's a *mage*—"

"Gutted more than a few of those in my day."

"That's what Graywind thought," I heard myself say. "Right before his blood stained these sands. As yours soon will."

The bellow that followed that comment echoed around the arena, turning heads, but not enough of them. And not the right ones.

His wolves remained on the attack, and had almost finished shredding Jen's last defenders.

I was out of time.

"Call them off or die!" I said, and in that moment, I meant every word.

I suddenly didn't care that this was beyond foolish, and would have been even under normal circumstances. As it was, with stubbornness and fear the only things keeping me on my feet, it was suicide. I would die, and Jen and Chris shortly thereafter, and none of this would do a damned thing!

My mind knew that, but surging through my veins was something far more primal, something from before higher mental faculties emerged from the primordial ooze, something from the lizard brain that said protect, protect the children at all costs, protect them with blood, with life, if need be, and I couldn't turn away. Didn't even want to. The wolf brain took over and I felt the Change spill through me, not physically, but in every other way. I was suddenly a mother wolf whose cubs were being threatened.

Making me the most vicious animal alive.

The others felt it, too. A shiver went through the surrounding wolves; Farkas yelped and tried desperately to drag his master back; even Whirlwind hesitated. But only for a second, because his honor was on the line. He'd been challenged twice, and before the council.

He couldn't back down.

This was happening, it was happening now, and nothing on Earth could stop it.

Only someone else didn't seem to know that.

"On what grounds?" A woman said, and pushed between us.

That was a good trick, because we'd been all but an inch apart, breathing in each other's faces. But I clearly wasn't the only one who could move fast when she wanted. Although the Lupa of the Red Mountain Clan was looking a little different than the last time I saw her.

The attractive, elegant woman with the silver bracelets and the smooth dark braid now had no jewelry, wild dark hair and a face full of drying blood. She was also wearing an incongruously cheerful, flower embroidered caftan that she'd sourced from somewhere, making it clear that she had Changed during the battle. And the arm she'd reached out to me with was covered in acid burns from a potion bomb that had come a little too close.

But she still had the arm, meaning that it hadn't been that close.

Many of the others behind her weren't so lucky. I finally noticed that I'd stumbled into the middle of a triage area, where people like Laura Brightfeather, Sienna's cousin, were trying to help the wounded. There were a lot of them, and were about to be more if the Lupa didn't get out of my way!

But she didn't. Instead, she put a hand on both our shoulders, with a grip painful enough that it helped me surface slightly from the wolf mind. But not all the way.

"Move," I told her, my voice as guttural as I'd ever heard it.

She didn't try to reason with me; she could see that I was past that. Instead, she asked the only question that might have gotten a response. "Why? On what grounds do you make this challenge."

"My cubs," I snarled. "*Mine*."

"What cubs?"

"There!" I gestured wildly at the two atop the rows of seats. "The ones being attacked—by his wolves! He stands them down or I rip out his heart!"

Considering that I'd already done that once today, it wasn't an idle threat. And Sienna seemed to get that. "The necromancer?" She frowned. "She's with you?"

"She saved you, fought for you! And now his wolves want to tear her apart. Call them off or die!" I snarled at Whirlwind, who snarled back.

"Her creatures threatened a council member," he said harshly. "She used the bodies of our dead, in our sacred grounds—"

"Call them off!"

"—to attack us! That's a death sentence—"

"Call them off, goddamn you!"

Dark gold eyes gleamed at me through strands of gray fur, and then the beast grinned. His back was to the others; they couldn't see him. But I could, like I could see the contempt in his eyes. "No."

And that was it. I couldn't Change, but that hadn't stopped my wolf before, and it didn't this time. It leapt, in a movement so fast that I didn't even know it was happening—

But someone else was faster.

The next moment, I was knocked on my ass and a massive wolf stood over me, but it wasn't Whirlwind.

That was a surprise because it was huge, too, as big as Sebastian only with a pure white coat. And a bloody maw, one that snarled and snapped in Whirlwind's direction until he backed off, too. And then the enormous creature stood between the two of us, tail thrashing.

"Stop it, both of you!" It was Sienna's voice coming from the wolf, and she was looking at Whirlwind. "Call them off. We'll hear what Lia has to say, then pass judgement."

His lip curled, and it was almost a human expression. He didn't even bother to answer, as if I wasn't enough of a threat for that, something that made my beast thrash and howl. She wanted his blood and she wanted it now.

Sienna looked down at me, as if she felt some of my inner turmoil, but her undamaged paw came to rest on my chest. As if to say, let me handle this. My human brain was all about that, but my beast—

I didn't know if I could control her anymore.

And then I knew I couldn't, when I heard Jen's terrified shriek. *"Lia!"*

I looked up to see what I'd expected, which was that the creatures Jen had raised to defend her lay shredded on the stairs, turning them into a waterfall of blood and gore. A few body parts still twitched here or there, but the only creatures still active were in a single line right around the two terrified children. A line which collapsed as I watched.

"No!"

The horrified cry rang out over the arena, not human, not wolf, not anything like either of them. And it didn't need magical amplification to be heard. It surged over the sands, echoed off the walls, and bounced back, over and over again. But unlike most echoes it didn't fade in intensity but seemed to get stronger and louder with every pass, until people were holding their ears and wolves were howling in pain.

And then, suddenly, there were no wolves.

I'd barely had time to register that the sound had come from me, before every wolf in the arena shivered all over, all at once. And I saw a sight that I'd never seen before, that no one had ever seen before, except for some who still remembered the war. And the battles in which hundreds of wolves had suddenly Changed together, only this time it was without warning or preparation.

It left naked, bloody people sprawled on the benches, stunned and slip sliding in the blood their human feet couldn't grip through. It had others tumbling downward, as if the benches were stairs, Changing halfway through a lunge and then hitting hard and rolling. Still others were slumping on rock or sand, unable to move with the dazed feeling that follows a forced Change catching them off guard.

And that included Whirlwind, who hit the ground and stayed there, stunned and cursing, his power deserting him along with his wolf.

Leaving an arena full of people staring at each other in confusion, and then slowly, almost as one, turning to stare at me instead.

Chapter Thirty-Two

I finally got my wish and passed the hell out. At least, I guessed so, since I woke up back in HQ. I could tell by the feel of the wards wrapping around me, even before I opened my eyes. Familiar and powerful, they were like a security blanket I hadn't known I needed.

I wanted to grab them and pull them closer, but couldn't. That sort of thing would set off a couple dozen alarms, even if I had the stamina to attempt it right now, which I didn't. My body felt like a limp noodle, except for the headache pounding behind my eyes.

Or maybe that was something else.

Pound, pound, pound. It was a rhythm, but not like a machine with a perfect, measured tempo. More organic, as if a very determined toddler was whacking the hell out of something with a toy.

It was just on the edge of my hearing, distant but persistent, and very annoying. So much so that I finally groaned and sat up. And opened my eyes expecting to find myself in the infirmary with Sedgewick standing over me.

But he wasn't there.

Nobody was.

And yet, I wasn't alone.

I stopped dead, my body halfway through a slide off of the exam table that I'd woken up on, with the hospital gown I was wearing riding up a thigh. It was an awkward pose that didn't do my back any good, which felt like somebody had been going at it with a baseball bat. Or my side, which had been bandaged up but hurt like a bitch. And all of those small crashes in the car might have given me whiplash, because turning my neck was also really painful.

But right now, my physical state was the least of my problems.

The room in front of me wasn't the expected infirmary, although it was large, tile floored, and bright. But it was also crammed with display cases full of . . . things. Things I couldn't name. Things that my eyes didn't want to focus on, despite my telling them to.

And then my blurry vision cleared up, and I really wished it hadn't.

I finished the slide, the shock of cold tile on my bare feet a distant sensation, because I was too focused on the nearest case. It was suspended from the ceiling on cables as many of them were, as if it was a frame containing a piece of modern art. But instead, it boasted a severed forearm with a hand attached, but not a human one.

It also wasn't Were or vampire or anything else I'd ever encountered. I didn't know what it was, just that it was muscular, to an almost absurd degree, like something off a comic book hero. And scaley, with interlocking gray green plates that flooded down to the wrist, where they became smaller and finer before cascading onto the elongated, webbed hand.

I took another few steps, fascination warring with disgust, and the whole overridden with a sense of unreality. I'd just been in the arena, surrounded by every conceivable kind of gore, but this was worse. I didn't know why, but it turned my stomach into knots even while pulling me closer, although all I wanted was to get the hell out of here.

I ended up nose to glass instead, staring at the hand, which was something else. It had talons that curved like exotic daggers and were absurdly large. They started off black as sin near the nail bed, but shaded into an ombre of gray as they progressed, and finally into white, with an almost translucent color at the tips.

From start to end, they were almost as long as the forearm, which was itself ridiculously oversized. Making me wonder how big the creature had been that it was taken from. And then to decide that I didn't want to know.

Like, really, really didn't.

I also didn't want to see the face on the head a few cases over, which was turned away from me, but which boasted massive, curled horns. I didn't want to look for the body that went with it, or the huge, barbed tail nearby, which was coiled like a rope but was as thick around as a man's leg. And I definitely didn't want to examine the plants in another case stretching up to the ceiling, which had green faces protruding from the stalks with thorn-like fangs.

I stared at them for a moment, because they should have looked absurd, like something out of an old science fiction movie. A prop rejected for being too crazy for any audience to believe and relegated to a corner of a warehouse somewhere. But maybe because of the day I'd had, which would stretch even a war mage's imagination, they completely freaked me out, not least because the fangs had gnawed through parts of their stalks, like a person chewing on their lips out of anguish.

Or someone desperately trying to commit suicide.

Juice from the wounds had seeped down the stems like blood, thick and viscous, along with hanging pieces of "flesh." And it had all been preserved by whatever stasis field was at work behind the glass. Leaving the strange massacre frozen in time, unlike my rising panic.

I moved in the direction of the only door I could see, limping a little from my bad ankle, but limping fast. The door was on the other side of the room, which left me floundering through the trophy section, knocking my head on the very hard edges of suspended cases and setting them swinging. Or barking my shins on the floor mounted kind, which were almost transparent except for their gruesome contents, making them hard to see with vision that kept graying out.

I wasn't sure how much of that was panic and how much was drugs, but I was pretty sure that the latter were in the mix somewhere. Because clumsy I was not, and yet I was quickly turning black and blue after bouncing around like a ping pong ball. And that was before a swinging case that I must have bumped on my way past swung back and almost knocked me off my feet.

And into something else.

I hit a case, palms out and face mushed against the side of the glass. And stayed there for a moment, panting hard. And not just because of the blow.

The case was the floor kind, but taller than me, and held something that would have probably stopped me even without any help. The contents were in the shape of a man, but larger, with areas of stretched out skin as if the musculature of a larger person had been shoved into a too small body. The skin was also discolored, partly by a tat on one arm, the bright colors of which had been smeared out of all recognition as the muscles bulged, and partly by patches of bumpy looking, grayish-black that had eaten up the chest and face. While the lower body . . .

What was left of my brain iced over. Because the creature's entire bottom half was just . . . missing. Replaced by a mass of gray/black coils, slick and shining under the light, like a spill of oversized intestines. Or like what they were, I realized: a snarl of huge, snaky tentacles, with suckers on the bottom halves, several of which were splayed against the glass like open mouths.

And I finally realized what I found so disturbing about the little shop of horrors somebody was running: it was deliberate. The disruptor had done its thing, but it had been random, like the violence in the arena, like all battles. You were in the wrong pace at the wrong time and you got hit, simple as that.

But this was different. Somebody had deliberately done something to this man, had experimented on him, because that tattoo had not come off some otherworldly monster! This was—this was—

My thoughts cut out, because one of the suckers was moving: slowly, awkwardly, leaving a trail of something slimy behind it. The sucker contracted and relaxed, contracted and relaxed, like a tongue tasting the glass. And then the entire huge tentacle suddenly slammed against it, hard enough to crack the surface and to set an alarm blaring.

I stumbled back as the tentacle tried again, and this time managed to burst through the glass to wrap around my arm. It felt like a python, just a single slab of rippling muscle, unbelievably strong. Which was why, when I tried to jerk away, I went nowhere.

Until fire broke out in the case. Jets of it came from all corners filling the interior with flames, thickly enough to come bursting out of the shattered hole almost as far as me. I could feel the heat on my skin, while inside—

"No," I whispered in horror, as the body went up like it had been doused with gasoline, thrashing and burning and—

And trying to pull me inside, to take me with it.

I leaned back, putting everything I had into it, which wasn't much. And then grabbed a jagged piece of glass from the smashed case and stabbed and stabbed and kept on stabbing. Even when the tentacle went limp and the body it was attached to turned to a statue made out of carbon, a blackened, tortured memory of a living being, smoking like a demon out of hell.

My once living bond fell away, and I lurched toward the door. And while I wasn't any more coordinated than before, I was *motivated.* I collected a bunch more bruises, but I didn't care. Didn't care if I broke something as long as I got the hell out, now, now, right freaking now!

And I did, stumbling out of the remaining maze and into an open area of tile in front of the exit.

Where I noticed a man standing by the doorway, watching me.

A very small man.

And then my tongue curled up on itself and I hit the floor, my body jerking and the cold tile grabbing my naked ass through the back of the hospital gown.

Colors danced across my vision as the hex went on and on, until I was pretty sure that my hair was fried and my insides were medium rare. Then abruptly cut out, as fast as it had come, leaving my tortured body arching upward in a spasm of agony. Until slowly, slowly, I relaxed back against the floor.

I didn't try to move again, since I wasn't even sure that I could.

"Get her back on the table," someone said, and I felt myself being picked up and carried across the room.

I hit the exam table once again, the spell still rattling my bones, and for a moment, all I could see above me was white ceiling tiles. And then a face came into view. One that I didn't believe, even though I'd seen it just a moment ago.

"Jenkins?" My numb lips somehow managed to form the word.

"You expected someone else?" He pushed his glasses up.

"I . . . didn't expect any of this," I rasped, too frazzled to lie.

"Yes, they never do," he said placidly, while someone else strapped me down. I tried to turn my head to see who, but my body ignored the command. But a moment later, a burly guy came into view, wearing the same crisp white tunic and trousers that the Corps' medics used, although I didn't know him.

"Where are we?" I demanded hoarsely.

"Research facility," Jenkins said absently, accepting a data pad from the medic. "The Corps has several of them, scattered about the desert, working on different things—"

"The Corps didn't do this!" I said, with more anger in my voice than I should have showed. But I couldn't seem to keep it out.

"No," he agreed. "I tried to help them, but every time I suggested anything, I got those looks—you know the ones I mean." He scrolled upward.

"I gave her the right dose," the man began defensively. "I know I did—"

"Well, clearly not," Jenkins said, and made a note with a stylus.

"What looks?" I said, trying to keep the conversation going while my brain sorted itself out. Which would have been easier without the sound of sizzling flesh and the smell of burnt meat from behind me.

"The same kind you get whenever you do anything less than human. Or more than, really." He shot me an appreciative glance. "Weres are fascinating creatures."

"It's the same dose I give everyone," the medic said.

"Yes, but she's not everyone. This one is special."

"Then . . . should I hit her again?"

"Not unless you want to kill her," Jenkins said testily. "We'll control her manually until time for the next dose, then up it by 10%."

"But . . . she's a war mage," the orderly said, looking less than thrilled with this plan.

"Yes, a beat up one whose magic is bottomed out and who is drugged off her ass," Jenkins said, pushing the pad into the man's solar plexus and starting to walk away.

"Why special?" I asked, my voice a little high.

I didn't know what the hell was happening here, but I knew that if Jenkins walked out of that door, I never would. You don't leave your victim alive, and that was definitely what I was about to be. Another in this macabre collection, or else I wouldn't be here, I wouldn't be seeing this.

Jenkins paused for a moment, the need for discretion warring with the man's love of his own voice. The voice won and he turned around with a little smile on his face. "Gather intel, stall for time, apply a distraction . . ." he said, reciting part of the mantra we drill into recruits' heads. "You know, I forget the fourth one. But you're a trainer. You should know it."

"Overpower the enemy and escape."

"Yes, that's it. Good advice, but I imagine it's a little different in practice, isn't it?"

"No shit."

He chuckled. "I like that about you. You're blunt to a fault. No attempts at subterfuge, no double speak, no lies. It's refreshing."

"Then answer the question."

He debated it.

Then he shrugged and ambled back over, before pulling up a stool and climbing on top. It left him slightly taller than me, even with the height of the table, since I was lying down. He seemed to like that.

I guessed it was a novelty.

"Why not? We both know you're never getting out of here," he said, equally bluntly.

"And here is?"

"I already told you. One of the Corps' own research facilities. I just . . . remodeled . . . the lower level. Turned it into my own little lab."

"Why?" I couldn't keep the horror completely out of my voice, and he frowned.

"You know that, too. We're at *war*. I wanted to help, and my specialty was well designed for it. I could have given us so many advantages, so many new abilities harvested from ancient strains—"

"Like these?" I rasped. I couldn't see much from where I was, but I didn't need to. The leftovers of Jenkin's "experiments" were burned into my mind.

"And more," he agreed. "We have schools full of people who have somehow managed to hold onto talents that we've tried to breed out of us, but which could be damned useful now. I requested the right to do some experiments with them, to see if their power could be enhanced, possibly even brought back to full strength—"

"You wanted to experiment—on *children*?"

It popped out before I could stop it, and it was a mistake. He bristled. "Do you know how many mages we're losing in the field every day?" he hissed, leaning in. "We need more men, they say it all the time, but my point was, we need *better* men. Enhanced ones. Ones with skills the opposition doesn't have or know how to handle—"

"We *have* them—"

"You mean those "students" of yours?" he rolled his eyes and sat back. "Yes, and I'm sure we can trust them, after the life they've led."

"So, you want to make it worse by experimenting on them?"

"I want to make it *better*, for them and for all of us! Do you think the other side isn't trying the same thing? That they don't have people working just as feverishly as I have been? This is an arms race, mage, and we were going to be left behind!

"But the Corps said no; that bastard Hargroves even threatened to demote me if I so much as dared to bring it up again. But when we lose this war, when these so-called gods we're fighting come back and scorch our world to cinders, do you think your precious students will be better off? They will die, right alongside the rest of us!

"But they don't have to. Those kids are repositories of skills that could save us all, but I wasn't allowed to touch them—"

"But you've been experimenting anyway," I said, interrupting the diatribe. "How?"

He smirked. "Because I realized that there was another great untapped repository for ancient abilities, one that nobody else seemed to have thought of. The clans."

"What?"

He nodded proudly, mistaking my shock for admiration. "Yes, I couldn't believe I didn't see it earlier. But think about it—Weres don't trust the Circle, so most of their problem children never show up in our facilities. They get *vargulfed* instead—" his head tilted. "Is that a word?"

I just stared at him.

"Well, no matter." He waved it away. "In any case, I realized that I could use the cast offs from your people to mine the old strains. To suss out talents and abilities that were lost to time, except in rare individuals—"

"Weres don't do magic," I said harshly, my head spinning.

"Yes, but many Weres have intermarried with members of the magical community through the centuries, haven't they? Especially in the lower ranked clans, where a mage in the family might be useful for protection or advancement. And as a result, they carry all sorts of interesting abilities, only the Were strain overrides them, represses them. They don't know they have them!"

"So, when the Corps said no to using the students, you started abducting street kids instead, people no one would miss," I said, struggling to keep my voice even.

He didn't bother to deny it. "What choice did I have? I was trying to save the world, mage, and I've done it."

He took a small vial out of his pocket and held it up to the light. It was a pale green, and cast a sickly pallor over his face, but he regarded it with wonder. "See this? Such a little thing, but it's going to win us the war."

"And that is?"

He blinked at me behind his glasses. "Well, you ought to know. It's been circulating in your veins for the last two days."

Chapter Thirty-Three

The vial was clear glass, allowing me to see that the contents had little bits of what looked like herbs in it, suspended in a syrupy liquid. It looked innocuous, just another potion in a world filled with them, like a salve or balm. But if that was what I'd been given at the grow farm, it definitely wasn't.

"It's distilled from fey wine," Jenkins said, turning the vial this way and that, to catch the light. "Like punch, only better. Punch wasn't designed to bring out latent abilities; that was just a byproduct. So, it was hit or miss, not to mention that it often made people too high to think straight. That wouldn't work for soldiers—"

"And this will?" I croaked.

"You've seen the result; you tell me."

The potion threw shifting green shadows over his face and should have given him a sinister air, even with the Mr. Magoo glasses. Only his expression didn't allow it. His eyes were bright and his face animated, almost awed. He looked like a child delighted with a new toy; one he couldn't believe that he'd managed to create.

"Forget crypto zoology," he said, his voice hushed. "Pouring for hours over old bones, wondering what this or that creature might have been like. This is paleo genetics! And not just bringing back a talent or two, but an *entire ancient being*. One capable of feats that modern man—including modern Weres—can only dream of. Until now.

"My brew can take any old Were and turn him into—well, what you saw. And even untrained, they're ferocious. It took the combined power of your entire lineage in the Corps to take down one, newly turned and untrained example. Can you imagine what an army of them could do?"

I didn't have to imagine. I remembered the way that four of them had carved through a phalanx of dark mages as if they weren't even there. It had taken seconds, and what they'd left behind hadn't even looked human.

Gooseflesh suddenly broke out, all over my arms.

"I intend to use it to create a force of my own," Jenkins was saying. "To deal with this war and the people in our organization who refused to act, even when I put a sword in their hands! But one problem persisted: how to control my new army? How to keep them in line when they are so much more powerful than anything else around them?"

"How do you do that?" I asked hoarsely.

"Well, up until now, I've relied on a charismatic leader to keep them in check, using the Were tendency to unify around an alpha. But that has had its own set of—"

"What alpha?" I asked, but Jenkins was on a roll and ignored me.

"—problems, like that damned clan he found for me, to grow the herbs I need. It was too dangerous dealing with smugglers all the time, not to mention the quality you get is often suspect. So, I thought, why not grow the stuff myself? But those bloody bastards started selling some on the side, didn't they?"

"So, you killed them."

"Ordered it done," he agreed, as if admitting to mass murder was no big deal. And then he saw my expression, which must not have been as blank as I'd thought. "Don't look at me like that! They did the same thing, you know, exiling and then attacking a bunch of their own people who didn't want to be involved with illicit drugs. Killed dozens of them, from what I understand. So, they weren't lily white."

"And the alpha?" I said as casually as I could manage. "Did you kill him, too?"

He looked surprised. "Of course not. I might need him again. I will require Weres for my new army, and they don't trust humans easily, if at all. I had to find someone they'd follow—but even he got fooled. They played him, didn't they?

"Or perhaps he played me." Jenkins scowled. "You can't trust anyone anymore. But I couldn't risk brewing my creation here. I was almost caught smuggling in a body a few months back—practically had a heart attack when one of the guards wanted to check my trunk! *My* trunk—can you imagine?"

"I can't think why they wouldn't trust you," I managed to say without irony.

He nodded vigorously, and then had to push his glasses back up "Exactly; I've been here for decades; they all know me. But war! It changes everything. I managed to talk my way out of that one, but what about the next time? I couldn't risk it. So, I'd go out whenever the clan harvested a new crop and brew up a batch on site, where they were also supposed to store it for me. But I suppose they thought I wouldn't miss a little here or there, and started their own damned business! And I couldn't have my potion going to junkies on the street!"

"Junkies like Colin," I said steadily.

"Yes," he sighed. "It was inevitable that they'd sell to a Were eventually, despite being informed that it was poisonous to your kind. I told them that to keep them from using it themselves, but I guess they didn't care about anyone else. Or else they sold it to someone who sold it on to him. And, of course, it brought my new creation to the Corps' attention."

"How terrible for you."

"Yes, it was," he said, too self-involved to notice the anger in my voice that I could no longer fully control. "Luckily, they turned his body over to me, as it was my area of specialty. And they didn't have the manpower to put a whole team on the investigation, just you—"

"So, you ordered me taken out, too."

Jenkins blinked, as if suddenly realizing that talking about cleaning up the mess to part of said mess wasn't polite. Of course, if he'd killed as many people as I thought, that shouldn't have mattered. But it seemed to, as if the man he'd been before his obsession warped his brain was battling with the monster he'd become—one far worse than his creation.

"It wasn't personal," he said, and actually sounded sincere. "It's simply that the Corps doesn't have anyone else who knows Weres like you do. Eliminate your expertise, and it might be months, years, before any progress was made—"

"But I didn't die."

"No. I told the clan to take care of it, after you stumbled across their operation—that was before I figured out what they were up to. But they didn't follow directions! They could have just buried you in the desert and forgotten about it, but no. They didn't know who you might have told where you were going, and killing a member of Clan Arnou terrified them."

"So, they gave me a dose and dumped me in Vegas?" I asked, in disbelief.

"They wanted you as far away from them as possible, somewhere you'd be seen before the poison killed you. But they weren't sure how it would affect a rogue, so they gave you an extra large dose—"

"And bit me to make sure I counted as Were enough for it to kill me."

"Did they? That's smarter than I'd have expected from them."

"And you had them killed at Wolf's Head because?" I asked, trying to make sense of all this.

He frowned. "What?"

"Wolf's Head! The clan meeting place, out in the desert."

"Oh, is that what that thing was?" He thought about it. "Yes, I suppose it does look rather wolfy. I'd never heard of it before I got your call."

"Never—are you saying you didn't order them to be killed there?"

He blinked at me. "Why would I do that? I just wanted them dead, and told the alpha to arrange it. I didn't care where—"

"Then you aren't working with Whirlwind? You aren't trying to kill Sebastian?"

"What are you going on about?"

"Your . . . the dark mages you sent—"

"Dark mages?" He looked at me as if I was the crazy one. "Why would I be working with them? I told you; I'm trying to save us *from* them! Haven't you been listening?"

I just stared at him some more, trying to figure out where I went wrong. But I hadn't misread the situation. Those mages had been laser focused on Sebastian.

But if our Dr. Frankenstein hadn't sent them, who had?

“And now I’ve found a way to do that,” Jenkins said, pushing bothersome Were politics aside. “You are the last piece in the puzzle, the one I’ve been searching for.”

“Me? I can’t even Change.”

“Well, no, which puzzled me—until I did a blood test on you while you were out. I understand now why you didn’t want to allow that. Neuri,” he mused. “I must say, you played it off well. I really believed you just wanted to follow in your father’s footsteps.”

He pushed up his glasses, and waited, as if expecting a comment. But hearing the hateful word on someone else’s lips had done more to freeze me in place than any spell. I didn’t say anything.

“Anyway, I arrived at that place—Wolf Head—just in time to see what you did,” he said. “You roared at them and they . . . fell out. Just fell out. Stunned, back in human form, and greatly chastened. Some of them couldn’t even move! It’s exactly the kind of control I’ve been looking for. It turned out to be fortuitous in the extreme that my incompetent associates didn’t kill you.”

He beamed at me.

“But . . . I don’t know how I did that—”

“Of course, you do—I just told you. A latent ability brought out by the potion you consumed. It seems that Neuri can’t block everything. Or maybe the magnitude of the dose opened up a crack in its protection and something slipped through.” He reached over to pat my shoulder and his glasses fell down. “Don’t worry. We’ll figured it out,” he assured me distractedly, reaching to push them back up. “And then we’ll—”

I cursed him into oblivion.

Jenkins collapsed on top of me, a literal dead weight, while I gasped at the ceiling like a fish. I’d used what magic my body had produced while I was out for the spell, but it hadn’t been enough, not even close. But I’d forced it, anyway, taking some of the magic I needed to live.

And now, I wasn’t sure that I’d left myself enough for any of this to matter.

I hurt, but it was worse than that, way worse. It felt like opening a vein, like bleeding out, like I’d cracked a bone and fed the damned spell my marrow, and I wasn’t sure that I hadn’t. I could feel my heart stuttering in my chest and my veins shriveling up, and would have curled into a tortured ball but the restraints wouldn’t let me.

Breathe through it, I told myself savagely, biting back the screams that battered against my teeth.

Fucking breathe!

And, after a moment, I did. In little gulps, like someone who has been underwater for too long, doesn't remember what to do with oxygen. But the Corps teaches techniques in pain control, and slowly, the breaths got longer and deeper, and my starved brain cells started to be able to think again.

Everything still hurt, and probably would for days, as this sort of thing was extremely ill-advised. But it was better than the alternative. Only the alternative was still a good possibility if I didn't figure a way out of here!

And that wasn't looking likely when I was strapped down and exhausted. I couldn't even manage to throw Jenkins' body off me, leaving me stuck under his weight until Igor decided to come back and check on the boss. Which probably wouldn't be long because there were cameras all over this place.

But try as I might, I couldn't dislodge him. Or free myself, no matter how much I struggled. Which I continued to do until worn completely out, to the point that my muscles refused to obey commands and my heart started doing that stuttering thing again.

I lay there as the room swirled around me, panting and desperate and staring at Jenkin's balding head. It was getting familiar with my stomach, with what felt like drool leaking out onto the thin material of the hospital gown. Like his hand, which had landed near my breast, but couldn't be said to be groping me because he was dead.

And because there was something in it.

I stared at the tiny thing I could just see peeking out from between his limp fingers, and swallowed. There might be a way out of here, after all, but it would require taking a risk. A big one.

And I wasn't going to get any help from my magic. Even a tiny spell would leave me dead before it left my lips. No power, no weapons, and drugged half out of my mind . . .

Did I have a choice?

No. Yet I hesitated, remembering how bad that particular solution had been last time. But that had been an overdose meant to kill me; maybe this would be better?

Yeah, sure. Because that was how my day had been going. But I nonetheless twisted with my body and pulled with my fingers on the lab coat that Jenkins was wearing, and finally got his arm to drop away.

Leaving a small test tube behind, full of faintly green liquid.

There was strength in that vial, but also a whole lot of crazy. And that was assuming I could even get it to my mouth. It was on my chest, having rolled into the valley between my breasts, with unnatural cold seeping from it that felt uncomfortable even through my gown.

But there was no other option, so I didn't debate it for long. I managed to get my chin down and my body up, bucking as hard as I could against the restraints, letting gravity help me. And it did, with the little thing rolling up my chest to land against my chin—

Before wedging itself halfway between it and my neck.

God damn it!

I strained my ears, trying to hear if anyone was coming, but all I heard back was an echoing void. The last dose had completely worn off, it seemed, and my super senses were super gone. I needed another hit.

And if I didn't get it, I was dead.

But that was looking less and less likely. The test tube Jenkins had used was short and squat, maybe half the size of a regular one. And the cork at the end didn't look to be shoved in very well, meaning that I might spill it if I wasn't careful.

But I didn't have time for careful!

I followed that thought up with a bunch of contortions that did nothing but waste time, and wedge the damned thing further under my neck. Where it was doing a pretty good job of burning my skin. I didn't know why there wasn't ice on this thing, it was that cold. Or why the contents hadn't frozen instead of sloshing sluggishly against the sides as I struggled.

I finally stopped for a break, panting and desperate, and accepted that this was never going to work. I was never going to get it into me that way, which was why I let the tube fall onto the cot and maneuvered my body down to it. I couldn't go very far within the restraints, but that wasn't the problem.

The problem was that the test tube was almost flush with the mattress and my mouth couldn't reach it. Even when I almost broke my sore neck twisting it to the side, and stretched my lips as far as they'd go, like a horse. And breaking the restraints with my strength gone wasn't happening.

But I tried it anyway, half sobbing from effort and fear, an emotion that war mages weren't supposed to feel, which were bullshit! You felt it, you were just trained to manage it, to think past it—so think, damn it! Now, while you still can!

And now was all I had, because the door had just slammed open on the other side of the room, and somebody cursed.

Chapter Thirty-Four

The thing about being a trainer is, you never have a chance to forget your own training. Other Corpsmen die occasionally for stupid shit, the kind of thing they were warned against by somebody like me, screaming in their faces, pounding the correct behavior into their heads, and forcing them to practice it day after day until it became muscle memory. But that was when they were cadets, and thirty, forty, or fifty years later, things sometimes got sloppy.

But not for me. I did this stuff every day. I *taught* this stuff, hammering into young minds until they finally started to listen.

Which was why I heard my own voice in my head, reciting the type of thing I'd said to dozens of students while they struggled with some seemingly impossible task. "Slow your breathing; this is no time to panic. Concentrate on the task at hand, and nothing else. The only thing in front of you, soldier, is the job you have to do.

"Not the pain, not the fear, not the pressure. Time *doesn't matter*! Distractions *don't matter*! They are for the other guy, to throw him off. You are focused on what you are doing. You have seconds, and every one is precious, every one can save your life. You don't waste them, but you don't hurry and flub it, either. You are a war mage.

"Act like it."

So, I did.

I used my shoulder to make a make a wrinkle in the mattress. It wasn't much, just a small hill poking up in the plastic underneath the vial, barely an inch high. And I couldn't push it anymore or risk the little thing rolling off into the floor.

I stared at it, as intently as if my gaze could fix it in place while I maneuvered into position, stretching the bonds as far as they'd go, and twisting my neck to the breaking point.

Meanwhile, somebody was coming this way, barking his shins on the maze of cases as I had, and firing a gun that he didn't know how to use. The gunshots sounded as loud as cannon fire, with nothing to muffle them in a room with tile floors and almost empty walls. They ricocheted off various metal cabinets, breaking glass and making me want to flinch. But I didn't; all those years of training, of running obstacle courses in full gear, a hundred-pound pack on my back and live fire rounds exploding all around me, had to be good for something.

And they were.

I moved, hardly at all yet just enough, and the vial rolled against my face, burning a line of cold down my cheek. I ignored that, too, and caught it between my lips, before working the stopper out with my tongue. And then—

Gah!

Gag-inducing bitterness hit my mouth, along with mind-numbing cold. It froze my lips and made my throat want to close in shock, to the point that I had to almost force the solution down. But I barely noticed because this stuff kicked like a *mule.*

I immediately felt it spreading through my body, a wave of shocking cold followed by intense heat, allowing me to easily trace how far it had reached. Although I would have been able to do that anyway by the feeling of life surging back into my veins. I gasped, my pupils blown wide, and every capillary I had suddenly roaring with blood like a raging river. I still had no magic—that takes time to build up—but I had everything else.

Including the power to pop the heavy restraints like they were made out of paper, to roll off the table onto the floor, and to miss the hail of bullets that peppered the cot a second later.

Igor, I thought, as he came bursting out of the maze. And looked surprised when I sprang at him like a wild animal and brought him down, not with a curse or a weapon, but with my teeth in his throat. His blood spurted everywhere, speckling my face, soaking my gown, and this time, it tasted good—hot and bright and like victory in my mouth.

I felt when he died underneath me, thrashing and panicked one second, and limp and lifeless the next. And then got onto my haunches in a deep crouch, waiting for the wave of backup that should have been behind him. I licked my lips without thinking, my heart hammering in my chest, but nobody came.

It finally dawned on me that the idiot had come alone!

But there was a red light over the door now, and a new siren blaring through the building, so they wouldn't be long.

A quick search of Igor's limp form came up with a card key that might help, and a gun that probably wouldn't, since he'd emptied the clip. I threw it aside with a curse and started for the maze, only to find that my left leg didn't work. It was still fighting off the effects of the hex Jenkins had hit me with and was dragging behind, threatening to throw me off balance.

It didn't help that I was barefoot and the glass from shattered cases littered the floor. Or that the room was wobbling at the edges, although the full-blown psychosis I'd experienced last time had yet to show up. Maybe that took a while to kick in; I didn't know. I just knew that I had to move, now, leg be damned.

And in a strange twist of fate, the gruesome collection saved me, the cases providing useful hand holds as I pulled myself along. Even better, the key worked on the door and there was a gurney just down the hall. I threw my battered body on top of it and started pushing with my good leg, hoping that it was too late or too early for a full complement of guards.

Or any, considering that a raw recruit could probably take me out right now.

Fortunately, I didn't encounter any.

I did, however, encounter somebody else.

I'd been looking in the windows of the rooms as I passed, hoping for someone—or something—that I could let out to provide a diversion. But the creatures I found inside were just as gruesome as the supposedly dead ones in the lab, and were looking at me like lunch had come early. I couldn't risk it.

But there was one exception.

"Jack?" I stared through the small, rectangular window in a door half way down the hall, and met a single brown eye looking back at me. Sienna's son blinked in surprise, his pupil blown wide. And the constant pounding I'd been hearing all this time suddenly cut out.

"Let me out," he said, although I could barely hear him over the alarm and the warded, four-inch-thick door, even with heightened senses. I mostly lip read, which was tough since I could only see part of his lips. The window was really narrow, I guessed to keep people from putting a fist through it.

I used Igor's key instead, and the door swung inward.

And then I just stayed there for a second, because the room was trashed. There were huge slashes that had ripped off most of the drywall, all the way down to the reinforced concrete behind it. Some of that was gone, too, with missing chunks and pieces of bent rebar that stuck out in places, twisted almost out of recognition.

"I wanted out," he told me awkwardly, and tried to pull his hospital gown closer around him.

I didn't answer. I was staring at the pattern of slash marks on the nearest wall, which did not look like they'd been made by wolf claws. I was about to ask when boots started hitting stairs somewhere above us, and I decided I didn't care.

"They're coming," Jack said, his voice suddenly high. "They're coming, and they'll spell me again, like that weird guy did outside of Wolf's Head! I was hurt in the battle and he found me and brought me here—"

"No one's going to spell you," I said. "We're getting out."

"How?"

"That depends. How fast can you push me?"

The answer was pretty damned fast. We took off down the corridor like a bat out of hell, racing the sound of the boots to a set of metal stairs at the end of the hall. We hit it first and took refuge in the shadows underneath, while what looked like a whole platoon clanged their way downward, right over our heads.

Jack's eyes were huge but he didn't say anything, and they didn't immediately see us. We'd parked the gurney just beside the stairs and were huddled behind it, with the sheet pulled down to help hide us. But that little trick wasn't going to work for long.

The Corps has procedures for searches, as with most other things. And while the majority of the mages had run for the lab, the supposed source of the disturbance, half of the rest were fanning out to check the doors along the hall. While the remainder stayed by the stairs, blocking the way out.

Somebody was listening in training, I thought grimly.

And then I thought, what's that?

On the wall beside the stairs was a pad. It was blinking, I guessed because some of the war mages had opened a few of the empty rooms to check if anyone was hiding inside. The little device didn't like that, and was blinking a message: SHUT ALL DOORS?

I stared at it, and then got a hand between the metal side of the stairs and the concrete block wall, because I knew that pad. There was one like it at HQ on the lower levels of the prison wing. It acted as a way for guards to shut the place down in an instant in case of a break out, because wards were great and all, but a steel door was still a steel door. And redundancy was a wonderful thing.

But the rescue squad hadn't used it, because the doors were already secured.

But what closes things down also opens them up, right?

I decided to test a theory.

Of course, a mage took that moment to step in front of it, half obscuring the screen. His coat was inches from my outstretched fingers, but he wasn't looking at me. He was staring down the hall toward the lab and there was nothing in this direction to redirect his gaze—as long as I didn't screw this up.

And I didn't. I *stretched*, calmly, quickly, and silently, and passed the key card through the scanner attached to the monitor. I held my breath and waited for the screen to change and give me some options.

The screen did not change.

I gave it a second, then tried again, thinking that maybe I'd wobbled a little and it hadn't gotten a good read. But the result was the same. It seemed that Igor didn't have high enough clearance to do me any good, and that was bad.

That was very bad, because people were starting to come back this way, having not found anything in the lab but a couple of fresh bodies. Something that was likely to make them trigger happy, and with this many mages crowded into a small space, they'd spot us in seconds. Not to mention that talking my way out of a problem had never been my strong suit, especially with somebody's blood still dripping down my chin—

I felt a tug on my sleeve and looked back to see Jack mouthing: "Let me try."

I didn't know what the hell he thought he could do, but I was out of ideas. We switched places, slowly so as not to attract attention, and he reached out. But not all the way because he didn't need to. A tiny filament of electricity arced from his fingertip to the pad, reminding me of the lightning storm that had briefly broken over Wolf Head, lighting up the night—

And then things suddenly got a lot more interesting.

The pad burnt out in a suddenly flame, doors clanged open simultaneously all along the hall; someone screamed a warning, and blue, green and lavender shields bloomed everywhere, so closely packed together in the limited space that I didn't see how anything could get in between them.

Anything managed.

To be more precise, the things in the cells managed, with the corridor suddenly awash in fur and fangs and scales and claws. Not to mention spells slamming everywhere, one of which melted a section of the stair railing right over our heads. I jerked Jack back from the dripping metal, as screeches, roars and the sibilant sound of a massive snake broke out in the formerly quiet space.

And then the sound of bodies being thrown everywhere, as all the things rushed for the stairs.

But we were there first. I climbed onto Jack's back and he went running upward, right through the middle of two mages who hardly reacted, because they were too bust reacting to whatever was headed their way. I had half a second to see wide eyes and hastily reinforced shields, and then we were past, and we were moving.

"Should've gone out for track," I said, although it sounded more like sh-sh-sh-should've, because that's how fast he was taking the stairs.

Jack laughed, and while it was a little high pitched and a little manic, I'd take it. He wasn't the kind of kid who broke down in a crisis. Which was good, because we still had one.

"Hold it!" I told him, and we paused to use the key card on another door. And then to hide behind it as more mages thundered down to join the search.

I got a better look at them this time, through another tiny window, and they weren't dark. They were Corpsmen, as familiar to me as the wards down here, with their shiny service pins winking on the front of their coats like badges of honor. But that was just it—I didn't know who was honorable, and just happened to be assigned to the upper levels of Frankenstein's lab, and who might be another Igor.

And in the shape that I was in, if I guessed wrong, it was game over.

So, as soon as they'd passed, we ran out behind them and kept climbing—and climbing, and climbing. The little room I'd woken up in turned out to have been a grand total of twelve stories below ground. Which was why Jack was panting and cursing under his breath by the time we finally reached a floor with no more stairs going up.

"Careful," I mouthed at him. He didn't answer. He probably couldn't, as he was mostly concentrating on sucking in air. But his expression lightened when I unlocked the door on the last landing and carefully cracked it open . . .

Onto a desert vista with the sun just beginning to peek over the horizon.

I felt the wind in my hair and the pinkish rays of a new morning on my face as we stepped out onto the top of a small, two-story building. It was plain concrete block and looked to be part of an abandoned mine, with several corrugated tin outbuildings and some rusted mining equipment scattered around. That probably meant that we weren't all that close to Vegas, which was a problem if I couldn't find a vehicle to hotwire.

Or maybe not.

"Climb on," Jack told me, only it wasn't Jack anymore. It was—

"Sienna *Thunderbird*," I said, staring at him, and finally understanding.

"Yeah, only it missed mom. I'm the first in the family since grandpa," he said, crouching down and shaking a mass of iridescent feathers at me.

They spread out in great wings the size of a small jet's, shading the whole roof and then some. I didn't know what color they actually were, because they seemed to take on the surrounding hues of nature. Which right now meant that the rising sun was painting them a glorious, fiery red-gold.

"Hurry!" he added, as the sound of boots came from below, this time heading up.

Probably had cameras in the stairs, too, I thought, and clambered onto the great back.

I didn't bother locking the door, since presumably everyone had keys, and of course, I couldn't do a spell. I just grabbed hold of a handful of feathered skin and hoped that I wasn't going to regret this. And then *really* hoped that, as the great bird stood back up and started running for the roofline in great, leaping strides.

The power thrumming underneath me was unreal, with little electric sparks glittering in the air all around us. I couldn't tell if that was the drug kicking in or just the way this whole thing worked, and didn't have time to figure it out. Not before—

"Oh, my God!" I yelled, as we dipped downward, almost touching the ground, close enough that I could have reached out and touched it if I hadn't been holding on for dear life. And then swooped upward, so fast and so hard that I'd have gone tumbling off the back if not for the potion lending me extra strength.

I almost did anyway, when I heard the door slam open behind me and felt a stun spell zip through the air beside me. And miss because we weren't merely flying. Feels like a jet, too, I thought, laughing in disbelief, with the roar of the wind tearing the sound away almost before it left my lips.

I looked back to see a bunch of war mages pouring onto the roof, but no more spells came our way, because we were already out of range, souring high into the fiery ball of the sun, the great wings bearing us aloft.

And then we were gone.

Chapter Thirty-Five

"Are you *insane*?" Caleb asked, his voice sounding hushed over the phone, probably because he was within earshot of someone. "Seriously, I'm asking. Have you lost your goddamned mind?"

"Possibly," I agreed, watching Vegas traffic stream by the tinted window of the limo I was riding in. "But if you don't go in now, whoever else Jenkins was working with might wipe the camera footage or destroy the evidence, and we need that."

"I want you to listen to yourself," Caleb said, slowly and carefully, so that I got every word. "You killed two Corpsmen, committed acts which led to the injury of seven more, and trashed a Corps facility—"

"I didn't trash it. It may have ended up that way, but—"

"—and not surprisingly, there's a warrant out for your arrest!" His voice had risen on that last word, and then abruptly cut out when he remembered where he was, which was in HQ's infirmary.

He was finally getting his injuries checked out after spending half the night being debriefed, and most of the day holed up in his office writing his report. And I knew without asking that it had been thorough, because my scruples didn't apply to my partner. He was willing to overlook certain things, but a major battle wasn't one of them.

I didn't blame him, but I did need him, and he seemed fixated on the warrant. Which . . . wasn't ideal. But on the list of things that I had to worry about right now it was sitting pretty low.

"I hear you," I began, which only seemed to infuriate him further.

"People only say that when they do not, *emphatically do not* in your case, hear a goddamned thing! I don't need you to hear me. I need you to come in—"

"I can't do that—"

"You have to! Lia, anybody who comes across you will shoot on sight! You killed two people and turned a dangerous predator loose on the city—"

"Which one?" I asked, suddenly worried.

"Which—the one you flew away on!"

Oh.

"He's a fifteen-year-old boy, Caleb, and he's currently wrapped in his favorite blanket, eating cereal and watching anime—"

"He's a *dangerous predator* and he's loose thanks to you!"

"Yeah, well there's a lot of that going around. And there's going to be more if I don't deal with it."

There was a good chance that it was already too late for at least part of that, as I'd been out of things for most of the day, swimming in a sea of colors and lights courtesy of Jenkins' brew. It hadn't been like the first time, or at least not quite as psychedelic, but I'd felt floaty and very strange and so exhausted that I could barely lift my head. I didn't even remember most of the flight back to Wolf's Head, where I'd woken up around five in the surprisingly comfortable home that Sienna had managed to make for herself and her boy.

I'd almost immediately started trying to contact Caleb, but that had been a challenge since he hadn't been answering his phone and I couldn't risk identifying myself. Corpsmen had already been by Sienna's, asking for me, so I knew about the warrant before he spilled the beans. And if they were checking with everyone at Wolf's Head, taking time out of the investigation that Sebastian had surprisingly allowed to go door to door, they meant business.

But so did I, and I didn't have time to debate this.

"You can't handle the Were side of things," I said. "Nobody in the Corps can. While I can't get near that facility again without getting taken down like a dog. But you can check it out and let me know—"

He hung up. That was not particularly surprising, as that was how about half of our conversations ended. I sighed and gave the phone back to Sienna, who was sitting beside her cousin on the other side of the limo and looking concerned.

"He'll deal with it," I assured her.

"I'm glad you're so certain," she said grimly. "But that still leaves your old clan—"

"What about her clan?" Laura asked, fussing with her gown.

Sienna's somewhat fluffy cousin was wearing a gorgeous gold evening gown covered all over in curling silver feather designs. They were huge and in-your-face, like her bosom, which was strapped high and shown off by a plunging neckline. But it matched the piled high dark hair and silver feathers in her ears, and the teetering silver heels just peeking out of the hemline.

The whole look was over the top, but people dressed up for the opening of a new Great Council, which was usually the centerpiece of the Were social calendar. The business part of things didn't start for a couple days, but the showing off was well underway. And it was considered that leaders were embarrassing their clans if they weren't sufficiently blinged out.

It was one reason I was wearing a plush outfit that I'd borrowed from Sienna, who had agreed to let me join her entourage. The chiffon looked like a desert sunset, with orange, red and purple hues mixed into the delicate layers around the hem. The rest was a plain column of sand-colored silk running all the way up to a loose-fitting drape over the head.

It wasn't quite a hood, but if the wind was blowing right, it could be used to obscure the face—and the fact that I wasn't Sienna's Second, a formidable old battle axe who had been happy to stay behind with her feet up allowing me to take her place.

Not that I figured prominently enough in Were high society to be easily recognized. My name was known, but my face shouldn't be to many people. But I wasn't taking chances.

"Lobizon has declared her *vargulf* and put a price on her head," Sienna informed her cousin shortly. "I know what you're trying to do, Lia, but I really think—"

"What? But they're not even your clan anymore!" Laura said, looking outraged. "If they have a problem with you, they can take it up with Arnou! How dare they—"

"They claim that she was never eligible to join Arnou," Sienna said, meeting my eyes. "And therefore, remains under their jurisdiction."

"Not eligible? That's preposterous! What are they talking about?"

Sienna didn't answer, leaving it up to me. It was my secret, only it wasn't a secret any longer. After I passed out in the arena, Farkas, Whirlwind's eagle-eyed Second, had noticed something. The famous rogue, Lia de Croissets, who had refused the bite for years despite the status and wealth it would have conferred on her, *had* one—on her leg.

The wound I'd taken at the grow farm had been revealed by my shrapnel-shredded jeans, along with the fact that it wasn't fresh. He could tell that it was at least a day old, and while that wouldn't always be time for a Change to take place, under that kind of stress, with blood all around and my very life on the line . . . well. It had made him curious.

Before Jenkins had shown up to claim his new guinea pig, then, Farkas had taken a blood sample. Nothing scientific, just a smear on a handkerchief, but it was enough. The test had come back positive for Neuri and now Clan Rand was trumpeting it to all concerned as a way to further blacken Sebastian's name.

And it would. The charges against him were adding up: allowing an entire clan to be butchered, allowing Wolf's Head to be attacked, and having no idea where these Were-like monsters were who were terrorizing the community came from. The fact that the butchered clan had been butchers themselves—of other Weres—as well as a bunch of drug sellers was irrelevant. Like the fact that he'd fought for his people at Wolf's Head, and that no one else had any more ideas about the Relic threat than he did. All that mattered was that it had happened on his watch.

And now the Were community learned that he had also adopted a rogue into his clan, knowing that she had Neuri. Or that he'd been too careless to have her tested first to find out. Things were looking grim for Sebastian's chances of remaining *bardric* for much longer, or of me remaining anything.

Because Lobizon was on the prowl, hunting me to remove the stain from their house, and to avenge those who had died trying to turn someone who knew that she never could. The Corps might shoot me on sight, but Lobizon would do far worse. And they were sure to be there today.

"If anyone accuses you, I put you under a compulsion," I told Sienna, as we joined a long line of cars inching toward our destination. "I forced you to help me."

"That sort of thing doesn't work on our kind," she said levelly.

Sienna was taking a risk helping me, and she knew it. It was in the darkness in her eyes, and the faint line on her forehead. She wanted to do the right thing, but she also had her clan to think about.

And she was all they had.

"Doesn't usually work," I said. "But I'm a rogue *vargulf* mage with Neuri Syndrome—"

Laura gasped, and covered her mouth with her hand.

"—so who knows what I can do?"

Sienna nodded, looking as if she was revising her speech for if we got caught, while Laura abruptly leaned forward and grasped my hands. Her reaction surprised me, both because of the concern on her face and because carriers of Neuri were treated worse by the Were community than lepers. Nobody wanted to touch us; nobody wanted to get close.

But her fingers closed hard around mine nonetheless.

"You have to go back!" she told me breathlessly. "Now! We'll . . . we'll call you a cab. You can hop out and run across to another hotel to wait for it. Nobody has to see you—"

"I'm not going back, Laura."

"But they'll kill you! And that's assuming Whirlwind doesn't get you first! You have an open challenge—"

"Not anymore," Sienna said, her jaw tight. "That's why that bastard Farkas was so quick to spill his guts. A *vargulf* can't challenge."

"Lobizon will hunt me to the ends of the Earth regardless," I told Laura softly, because she was looking seriously distressed.

I'd saved her favorite nephew, and to Weres, that kind of thing creates an obligation, and a bond. She felt responsible for me, although she should have been running as fast as she could in the other direction. I gently removed her fingers.

"But today, most of those people in there still don't know what I look like. It's the best chance I'm going to get."

"To do what?" she said angrily. "I don't understand—

"There's someone I have to see."

She would have grilled me some more, it was all over her face, but we'd just pulled up. Only not to a Were owned facility, since the only one large enough in the area was Wolf's Head, which was still a crime scene and would be so for days. And even for Weres, holding court among a field of bodies was a bit much.

So, they were holding it here, in Vegas's only supernaturally owned hotel and casino, the gaudy, overly themed, Halloween-all-year-long monstrosity known as Dante's. It was where most of the out of towners had been staying anyway, so it was convenient, and the meeting of a bunch of Weres didn't even raise an eyebrow in these parts. Weird occurrences were so much the norm on the property that the Corps had almost stopped responding to calls.

Not that that seemed to concern the vamps who ran the place overmuch. They just brushed any problems under the rug and added the cost to the culprits' bills. And hid the fallout from the regular folk who came here to party and gamble by adding even more spooky kitsch to the crap ton they already had.

Thankfully, we weren't going in the front, which was part medieval castle, part hellmouth, and all wince inducing. The lobby was currently undergoing refurbishment, so the long line of shiny cars had been routed around to the back. Where the local glitterati were exiting onto a literal red carpet.

I thought that was a bit much considering that the back was mostly a large parking garage where the buses arrived, but maybe that was why they'd needed the carpet—to cover up the oil leaks on the cracked concrete. Like I assumed that the planters of evergreens along either side of the plush were supposed to mask the scent of urine in the corners. It didn't help with a bunch of Were noses, but everyone was politely pretending not to notice.

The torches spaced regularly inside the evergreens were a nice touch, though, and sent rippling shadows over the faces of the beautiful people heading inside. It helped that Dante's looked better at night, where the fake rock on the façade more easily resembling an old European castle, and where the weeds in the landscaping weren't as noticeable. With the clan banners arrayed in a long line over the façade and fluttering in a mild breeze, it was actually pretty impressive.

Especially when you considered that they'd had less than a day to pull it off.

The limo Sienna had rented, because her clan might be small but damned if she'd arrive in a taxi, glided to a halt and she and her cousin got out. Laura still looked trapped between anger, worry and sadness, but I doubt that anybody else noticed. Because Mamma Thunderbird knew how to put on a show, and today she'd gone all out in an attempt to keep eyes on her and off of me.

It worked spectacularly.

I slipped out of the limo behind the two ladies, head down and partly turned into my neck, allowing the drape of the material to largely obscure my face. But it was a needless precaution. And almost caused me to step on the hem of the gown, if it could be called that, that my hostess was wearing.

It was constructed of a sweep of long, blue green feathers that had an iridescent quality to them, shifting their hues depending on what she passed. They were mostly gold and green at the moment, with crimson around the hemline where they reflected the carpet. Although the whole flowed with color as she moved, like ocean waves or swiftly moving clouds.

The feathers also glittered with gold at the tips, as did the low-cut bodice, which was all gold, to match the diadem in her long, dark hair. And as if that wasn't enough, she had iridescent blue and green tones feathering out from her eyes like wings, and demarcating her high cheekbones. In short, she looked like a goddamned supermodel and nobody so much as glanced at anyone else as she swept inside.

I followed them at a short distance, then broke off when we were through the main doors because several members of Lobizon were headed this way. Even worse, it was Wulfgar and Simeon, both of whom had been there that night that dad and I fought to keep them from giving me the bite, and thereby to retain my secret. We'd been essentially fighting for my life, and we had acted like it, which was why Wulfgar was missing an eye and Simeon had a face of pockmarked skin from the potion bomb I'd thrown into it.

I didn't know why they were here instead of prowling for me in the city. But here they were, sniffing the air, testing for my scent. And I wasn't wearing perfume since I'd woken up at a Were's house that didn't have any.

Shit.

I quickly hung a right into a hallway I was familiar with from one of the aforementioned weird occurrences, which led to the banqueting kitchens. And made it halfway down before they caught me. The kitchen would have confused my scent with the smells of whatever was on the menu tonight, as well as the skin ruffling odor of the workers, who weren't exactly human.

But I didn't make it that far.

I felt them Change behind me, without a word or a shout of warning. They weren't interested in talking; they were interested in killing, and they knew from past experience who they were dealing with. At least, they thought they did.

But I'd changed a bit since then, and while I didn't have my magic, or even the stored variety I usually never went without—potion bombs, magical snares and lariats, and spelled guns, knives and hand grenades, a war mage's typical arsenal—I did have something else.

Which was why I let them get almost on top of me, and then jumped up and over, somersaulting backwards above their heads. And landing, not behind them, but on top of them, hitting down on the broad, hairy backs, which had been shoved together by the confines of the hallway. And before they could react, while they were still turning in surprise, I grabbed the massive heads and slammed them together with every ounce of strength I had.

And right then, I had a lot.

They went out like sleeping babes and I jumped down onto the crazy carpeting behind them, slightly dazed but mostly all right. I hadn't even managed to tear my dress. But I had been distracted for half a second, and that was all it took.

Someone grabbed me my shoulder with a grip like steel, and I swiftly found myself slammed into a wall.

Chapter Thirty-Six

It's not a great idea to jump a war mage, especially one as keyed up as I was. Which was why I had a fist halfway to a face before I stopped and stared. And then did some slamming of my own, after dragging my captive over the fur mountains and around a corner.

"What the hell?" I asked Sophie, whose only reply was a snarl worthy of a wolf. But it sounded more like a giant cat, and looked it, too, when I focused on the shadow behind her.

"My offensive form," she told me, while Jen peered back into the other hall, I guess to see if we'd been spotted. And why we hadn't been was beyond me, but not because of my wanted-in-seven-states ass. But because—

"What the fuck is *that*?" I shrieked, staring at Jen, before Sophie clasped a hand over my mouth.

Jen turned toward us, relief on her face. "I don't think anyone saw."

"Don't think. Know," Sophie snapped, and Jen dutifully let loose one of the three creatures she was holding onto by black, smoking tethers.

The hideous thing took off like a shadow itself, albeit one with hideously elongated arms and a face that looked like the guy in *The Scream* painting, only worse. But it blended into the horrible wallpaper that was plastered onto everything around here until you got past the public areas. I watched it go, then switched my attention to the two snarling and snapping creatures that she still held by their smokey ropes, like maddened dogs.

Only they weren't dogs.

Jen tightened her fist and jerked them back slightly, bringing them to the hem of her purple mini dress. "Stop it," she said, and they settled down.

I looked at her. "What the hell?"

But I guess my expression was more gob-smacked than accusatory, because she beamed and swirled her hem at me, making the purple and silver beads draped on strings all over the scrap of satin shimmy and dance.

"It's Versace," she told me proudly. "Sebastian said we had to fit in, so he gave us his credit card and told us to get whatever we wanted—"

"Jen—"

"Whatever," she repeated, sounding a little awed. "And Ulmer said to go high end, because Arnou's rep was on the line, so—"

"Not the dress," I said, sounding strangled. "Them."

"What?"

"Them! Those things!" I pointed.

She looked down. "My shoes?"

She twisted her legs so that I could see that the soles on her four-inch stilettos were a bright these-cost-the-earth-and-then-some red.

"She means your pets," Sophie said, crossing her arms.

"Oh," Jen said, combing blond hair out of her eyes with her fingers. "They're the necros from last night. I found them after everything."

"But what are they doing *here*?" I asked.

She shrugged. "Seemed a shame to waste them."

"What arc *you* doing here?" Sophie said, before I could figure out a reply to that. "And what the hell was that out there?"

"Self-defense, and I could ask the same of you!" I said, turning on her.

She had gone more subtle than Jen in the bling department, but was still chic in a smart little black dress that probably also bore a designer label, but I wasn't well-versed enough in such things to know which. It was a cute, off the shoulder cocktail dress with two rows of sparkly buttons down the front that she'd paired with thigh high black boots that had to have had a five-inch heel. The ensemble shouldn't have worked, but it did, giving her a slightly pirate-y vibe, which went well with the stubborn look on her face and the still crossed arms.

I wondered if we were going to have a problem, and my face must have reflected that, because the tilt of her chin got a bit more pronounced.

"You're not supposed to be here," I reiterated. "And what do you mean, your offensive form? What the hell was that last night?"

"Self-defense," she said, throwing my own term back at me. "It takes less energy, since it just turns an enemy's own spells . . . on . . . them . . ."

She trailed off, her bravado faltering in what was probably a withering stare, but I was in no mood to soften it. "You're a Were?" I said harshly. Because that was just great. Nothing the clans liked better than being spied on by other shapeshifters.

"Nagual, but I can only shift at night, into a jaguar—"

"I know the legend!"

"—and why are you so freaked out?" she said, rallying. "It was in the folder—"

"It was not in the goddamned folder!"

"—or haven't you gotten around to reading that yet?"

I glared at her. She glared back. Her shadow on the wall paused to lick a paw, apparently unphased. I liked boring old human students, I decided; they were easier to intimidate. And then I had to pause to stomp at one of the shadow things, which had gotten a little too close.

Damn it all to hell—literally!

"You can just do a repulse spell," Jen said helpfully. "They don't have much power left—"

"Neither do I!"

"Could have fooled me," Sophie muttered.

"Your magic hasn't built back up?" Jen said, looking surprised. "I thought war mages were supercharged or something."

"I used what little I had this morning—"

"Wait. You really don't have magic?" Sophie interjected. "And you came here? Do you know what they're saying about you? Cyrus almost had a fit when he got back—"

"And you didn't call him," Jen said, disapprovingly.

"I haven't had time," I said angrily. Because I was feeling guilty about that myself.

"It takes, what, ten seconds to send a text?" She reached into a sparkly purple bag, because the girls had apparently soaked Sebastian for all he was worth, and pulled out a phone. "Here, I can do it for you—"

I caught her wrist—for about a second. Before one of her "dogs" grabbed mine in a grip like ice, and the other snapped at me. "God damn it!"

I let her go.

"What is it?" Sophie snorted. "Afraid he'd forbid you to come?"

"Cyrus and I aren't in the habit of forbidding each other to do things—"

"But?"

"—but he might try to come with me, and he'd be killed on sight!"

"And you won't be?"

"Can we talk about you?" I said bitingly. "This isn't Wolf's Head, but the idea is the same. You can't be here—either of you!"

She spread her hands. "It's a hotel. Plenty of people are here—"

"Not in this section!"

"—and besides, Ulmer brought us as part of Sebastian's retinue. He has us guarding the *bardric*—"

"Or the guy they have pretending to be the *bardric*," Jen added. "We helped to smuggle him in, all wrapped up in this gorgeous caftan. I think it was Dolce and Gabbana—"

"—as back up for some of the guys they lost—"

"Wait. What?" I said, because the girls were talking over each other, almost too fast for me to keep up.

"It's a whole thing," Sophie said impatiently. "You'd know if you hadn't gone AWOL all day."

"It's been so exciting!" Jen said. "We spent all day in one of the upper floors here—Sebastian took over a whole one, just for his staff—"

"What kind of thing?" I asked Sophie.

"—and he has his own private plane, did you know?" Jen continued, unabated. "And it's not one of those little things, either. It's a converted Airbus—"

"Stop perving on the old guy," Sophie told her.

"He's not old. He's forty—"

"That's old."

"Not for a Were. And he's hot. And a widower—"

"Who has a daughter your age!"

"Who isn't me," Jen tossed her hair and turned to me. "Anyway, he used it to get here, the plane I mean, so his wolves are flying commercial. They'll be here soon, but we're covering in the meantime—"

"We were told to check around for anything weird," Sophie added. "All of us, the guys, too. Ulmer said to look for something a wolf wouldn't notice. He said his gut is grumbly, which I think means he's worried—"

"I don't give a damn what he is," I said furiously. "He can't just throw you into the middle of—"

"Tell him that."

"I will! And what is this thing you're talking about? And why the hell didn't you go back to the house with Caleb last night?"

She sighed. "Yeah, you missed the fun, didn't you?"

"It was not fun," Jen said, suddenly serious. "It was not fun at all."

"What happened?" I demanded.

"Oh, nothing," Sophie said. "Except that you almost missed the start of another Were civil war. People were pissed—"

"Mostly at you," Jen interjected.

"—at what you did, and Whirlwind wanted to have a go at you, once he'd recovered. I think he was planning to finish the job while you were out cold, the bastard. But Caleb hexed the fuck out of him, and then he fell over onto his face—"

"Whirlwind?" I said, my confusion growing.

"No, Caleb. Or rather, both of them—"

"He was out of magic. He shouldn't have tried it," Jen said, while my head spun.

"And then Whirlwind's people started for both of you," Sophie continued, "but the townspeople got in their way. And it was looking bad for a second, because that Whirlwind guy brought, like, a private army with him, and the townspeople were not in the mood, you know? I mean, you'd fought alongside them, bled for them, and where had the council been? It was intense—"

"What happened?" I asked, because Sienna had glossed over a lot of this, maybe because, to a Were, the news about Neuri was a far bigger deal. And I hadn't questioned her too closely, being focused on getting here.

Because Ulmer's gut wasn't wrong; Jenkins hadn't been the only problem.

I just didn't know for certain who the other one was.

"Sebastian intervened," Sophie said. "He got out in front of the townspeople, facing off with Whirlwind, who had started to come around. But he was hurt pretty bad—"

"Defending me," Jen said fervently. "Sebastian was—I would have died without him. I would have *died*."

It looked like the teenage crush she was having was built on more than just Airbuses and sparkly dresses, I thought.

"—but I think he and Whirlwind would have gotten into it anyway," Sophie continued. "But then that weird mage showed up with a dozen others and the council put a stop to it. I don't think they wanted trouble with the Corps on top of everything else—"

"A dozen?" I repeated. "He was supposed to come alone."

"Well, he didn't," she said, and then sighed, as the updo she was wearing to complement the dress came cascading down. She pulled the froth of red curls back into a ponytail. "There were at least that, maybe more. And the mage in charge—"

"Jenkins."

"Yeah, him. He was on the phone with the Corps the whole time, loudly reciting the names of the council members and bigshots that were there. So, I guess the Corps would know who to come after if they didn't turn you over—"

"So, they did," Jen said. "Sebastian didn't object; I think he was grateful for someone to get you out of there. Only, in the confusion, we didn't realize that they'd forgotten Caleb until they'd already left—"

She and Sophie kept talking, but I was no longer listening. Because it seemed like Jenkins might not be the only true believer among the Corps. That sort of treachery wasn't supposed to be possible; there were tests, one in particular known as the Trials, designed to weed out potential traitors. But that was just the thing: Jenkins hadn't thought he was a traitor. He'd thought he was saving the world—what if others agreed?

Damn it! I hadn't even been here fifteen minutes, and things were already falling apart. "Do you have a phone?" I asked.

"Are you listening to me?" Sophie demanded. "You left, and then it was like you fell off the Earth or something. Cyrus has been going crazy. He called HQ, but they said you weren't there. You didn't seem to be anywhere—"

"Phone?" I asked Jen, because I knew she had one.

"—and then the news broke about Neuri. Is that true? You have to be batshit to come here if so—"

Jen handed over her phone and I punched in a number, while holding up a finger to stop the torrent of conversation from the girls.

To my surprise, it worked, and then a familiar voice came on the line.

"Don't hang up," I said.

"Oh, God. Not you again." Caleb sounded almost tragic.

"Are you on the way?"

"Yes! Yes, I am on the way! And I'm fine, incidentally, not that you asked. Just a mild concussion—"

"And they let you out of the infirmary?"

"I didn't ask for permission!"

He seemed stressed, so I cut the pleasantries. "How many are with you?"

"Two, Jacobs and Singh, why?"

"You're going to need more. Twelve war mages picked me up last night—"

Caleb started cursing.

"—and I don't know how many more might be compromised. You can't go in there with three—"

"If I ask for more, I'm going to need authorization—"

"So, get it."

"—from the old man! Who is already on the warpath after hearing what you did. And by now he's had time to read my report. It's why I scarpered before the bastard could find me—"

"Scarper back. Tell him what I said—"

"And he's going to believe you?"

"Maybe not. But he's old school—he'll have to check it out. And he won't let you go in there with your ass hanging out."

"And when he asks where you are? What the fuck am I—"

"Tell him the truth. That you don't know," I said, and hung up.

"You guys have an interesting relationship," Sophie said.

I was about to respond, but Jen's third slave had just returned, and was whispering something sibilant and awful into her ear. I didn't understand a word, but she apparently did. She looked up, biting her lip.

"It's starting."

"What is?' I asked, wondering if I wanted to know.

"The thing."

The girls took off, clambering over the hairy mountains of Lobizon's finest, who were making noises but hadn't yet come around. We didn't stop to help out, or to assist a couple of room service types on the other side, who were looking unconcerned except for the fact that they couldn't get their cart past. I followed the two well-dressed troublemakers back to the main hall, and discovered that something was happening in the big ballroom.

Or one of them, anyway.

There was a row of large rooms with unusually bland décor running down one side of this wing of the hotel. They'd been recently redecorated, part of the major refurbishment currently going on, because instead of eye searing patterns and colors, they were a tasteful beige and white. And the only bling in sight were glittering chandeliers and sconces.

It looked like the Council had taken over all of them, probably for security reasons, but also to accommodate the mass of people here for the first day of the session. That was also probably why the separators had been removed from the individual rooms, each of which could accommodate hundreds of guests. Leaving one massive rectangle that was teeming with a crowd of thousands.

But things were going down in this one.

What things, I couldn't see, because of the crowd attempting to get in through the huge, double doors. I could have forced my way inside, but that would have made too much of a spectacle. But being polite wasn't doing me any good, because we'd basically stopped moving while still being in the hall.

The room was already packed out, it seemed, and nobody was interested in giving up their place. So, I had no clue what was going on, except for the fact that somebody was yelling. A very familiar somebody.

"Fuck," I said with feeling, and began being more aggressive in my attempts to worm through the crowd.

“Wait. Come this way,” Sophie said, and started pulling me in a different direction. It worked because she currently smelled like cat, something extremely unusual in this setting, which had people unconsciously drawing away from us and a few sniffing the air in disgust. And because we weren’t headed inside any more.

“Wait. Where are we going?”

“Where Jen and I were before you showed up. It’s a great vantage point.”

I hoped so, because where we were at the moment was a narrow set of stairs, obviously meant for the help. There was almost no light in here and I could touch the sides without spreading my arms. But it was short, only half a dozen flights, so maybe three stories up. And when we burst out of the top, it wasn’t onto another floor, but onto a rooftop.

A rooftop made almost entirely out of glass.

There was a narrow walkway around the sides, I supposed for repairmen, but the whole of the center were glass panes in a vaguely golden hue, or maybe that was the light coming from the room below. And it had a triangular top, extending up another story or so for dramatic effect. Part of the remodel, I supposed, as this room had had a normal ceiling the last time I checked.

But this one was better, and not just because it looked more impressive. But because it allowed me to see the trainwreck happening below perfectly. And to hear it, too, thanks to the drug coursing through my veins. Not that either of those things was helping, only I didn’t know what would.

Because Cyrus was standing in the middle of a circle of wolves, half of them in human form and half with their fine clothes shredded around them, about to get ripped apart.

Chapter Thirty-Seven

But it seemed that there was some kind of plan, because Cyrus raised a hand holding a large golden medallion on a red, black and yellow ribbon. I couldn't see the face of it, but I didn't need to. It was the badge of office, the symbol of the *bardric*, and made like a necklace so that he could wear it in either form.

"You see it?" Cyrus asked, turning in a half circle to show it off to the thousands of onlookers. And there were thousands, and not just in the large circle around him. People with cell phones had done like me and tried to get higher, including standing on chairs or climbing onto other people's shoulders, uncaring about the elegant venue or their fine clothes.

And at least one of those was running a feed to another room, because I could hear Cyrus's voice echoed at a distance, just after he spoke.

It wasn't surprising that there would be interest, as a *vargulf* at a Great Council meeting was unprecedented. No one knew what it meant, but they smelled blood in the air, they just weren't sure whose. And neither was I.

But Whirlwind and a dozen bodyguards had just shoved their way through the crowd and into the open area at the center, so it wasn't looking good.

"Your entire family has a death wish, it seems," Whirlwind snapped at Cyrus. The great mane of black hair, with its ornamental white streak blazing down the side and into his beard, was shaking in anger.

That seemed an odd emotion. Annoyance I could understand, maybe even disgust, as a *vargulf's* presence could be considered insulting to the council. But anger? Yet it appeared genuine, with his face flushed and those strange eyes snapping.

It made for a powerful picture, despite the fact that he was still in human form, his bulk encased in a flowing black, watered silk caftan. I couldn't see where the tearaway seams were, as they'd been cleverly concealed, but I knew they were there. It was the sort of thing people wore when they suspected a swift Change might be necessary.

Whirlwind had come prepared to fight, but the only person it would make sense for him to challenge was Sebastian, who was nowhere in sight. I scanned the crowd, but although I recognized a lot of the people there, Sebastian wasn't among them. I didn't understand that—until I remembered what Sophie had said.

"How badly was Sebastian hurt?" I whispered to her.

"Bad enough that he couldn't get out of his chair."

So, bad-bad. Because a Were would fight with both legs broken and one arm ripped off if need be. Sebastian wasn't injured, then; he was half dead, or he would be here. But that still didn't explain what Cyrus was doing.

Or why the hell he was laughing!

"A death wish, indeed. Yes, you could say I have a death wish," he agreed, grinning.

It seemed to be making Whirlwind nervous, as he cut his eyes to the side, to meet those of that bastard Farkas. Who, for once, didn't seem to know what was going on, either. Or maybe they just couldn't figure out what Cyrus was doing here dressed like a prince.

It was a sight to behold, and one I had never seen before. I'd met him after he and Sebastian pulled their little scam, in order to get someone competent in charge of the Were community. And by then, he had dressed like what he was: a regular guy.

But not tonight.

The ever-present western shirts and blue jeans had been replaced, not by the elegant suits that Sebastian favored, but by a flowing caftan in gold silk. It had black and gold embroidery scrawling all over it, and a neckline low enough to show off the hard lines of his chest and to almost reach his navel. Even more telling, he was barefoot, which on its own could be considered aggressive in this setting.

The whole outfit said he had come to fight, not to talk, although he did some of the latter, in a booming voice that he didn't need, because you could have heard a pin drop in there.

"I do have a death wish," he said. "Yours—in payment for what you have done to my brother."

"I've done nothing to him," Whirlwind spat. "And the only one who will die tonight is you, for daring to show your face—"

"Yes, I dare!" the smile was suddenly gone from Cyrus's expression and voice. "And I have your *bardric's* permission. As indicated by this." He held up the badge of office again, in case anyone had missed it. "You tried to have my brother assassinated, repeatedly tried to remove him in the most cowardly way possible, so that you could steal his office—"

"Lies! And from a traitor's mouth!"

"—and when that didn't work, you took advantage of his injuries to come here, prepared to challenge a badly wounded man, who you thought you might be able to beat. It was another cowardly act, but you knew he'd have to fight, that he wouldn't have a choice. A challenge for the *bardric's* position must be answered by him or a close relation, and I was gone—"

"And for good reason! Remove this bastard," Whirlwind told his guards. "He defiles the Council by his presence!"

"Yet he has the badge," someone said, and I saw Sienna come forward. She managed to stand out in a room where everyone was putting on a show, but not just because of the outfit. But because of the air of quiet authority she wore like a cloak.

She was a council member, I realized, tiny clan or no, and tonight, she looked like it.

"He must be allowed to speak," she added.

"And who are you to say must?" Whirlwind sneered. "Your tiny clan—"

"Fought off an army yesterday, one which yours . . . was not quick enough to face."

There was nothing in her words that directly accused him of anything, but she somehow conveyed the impression that he'd been late on purpose. And the insult landed. The wolf eyes, already so disturbing in a human face, flashed and narrowed, and his lip curled.

But Sienna didn't back down, or even act as if she'd noticed, and the room was trending her way. "Let him speak," echoed from every corner—although less, I was pretty sure, in support of a *vargulf* or even a minor council member, and more about the drama. Cyrus had piqued their curiosity, and for the moment, it was enough.

"I was gone," Cyrus repeated. "Exiled and disgraced, and you cleverly removed Lia by having her proclaimed *vargulf,* too, by lying to the entire Were community—"

"There was no lie!" Whirlwind snarled. "Your whore has Neuri, and now everyone knows it—"

"For that, I'm going to kill you slowly," Cyrus promised, with a strange smile on his face.

"She has it!" Whirlwind looked around at the crowd. "Bring the bitch here and we'll have her tested, in front of everyone!"

Some people seemed to like that idea, sending a cold chill up my spine. But Cyrus had the floor and he wasn't ceding it. Nor did he look worried.

"Your delaying tactics won't work, old man. You thought to discredit the Lady Accalia, Laurentia of Lobizon's only daughter, and the adopted daughter of Sebastian of Arnou! Thought to besmirch her name and send the craven dogs of her old family chasing her, to make sure you did not have to face her again. You feared her—"

"I fear nothing!"

"She beat you—"

"She used magic—a trick—"

"She was out of magic, to the point of death. She used no trick. That was the gift of the *Ulfheðnar*, once the captains of our people. Long thought lost, but now reborn from a line known for it."

At that, a murmur went around the room, because some people had clearly understood what he was talking about. Which was more than I did. But he ignored them, moving on.

"You thought that removing her would clear a path to victory. But you forgot—Sebastian has a brother. And now a champion!" Cyrus threw the badge of office onto the ground in front of Whirlwind, where it lay, gleaming under the lights. "You want it, old man? Then pick it up. But only after you've won it—the old-fashioned way. The Blood Path."

A bigger murmur reacted to this, because the Blood Path was not merely a challenge. A regular challenge could end at any time, if either combatant chose to concede. Or if one was too badly injured for that, a family member could do it for him. It might come as a surprise to outsiders, but most Were challenges did not end in death.

Except for one.

The Blood Path was ancient, from a time far crueler than the present, and it was bound by different rules. Or to be more accurate, it was bound by none, save one: it only ended in death. Of one combatant, of both, it didn't matter, but the fighting didn't stop until someone had paid the ultimate price.

Whirlwind snarled, an echoing sound that reverberated around the room. But he didn't bend down. He didn't take it.

"You're *vargulf,*" he scoffed. "You can't challenge anyone, much less a member of council!"

"I am *vargulf,* it is true," Cyrus said, looking around the room. "And I deserved it, if ever anyone has, for thinking that I could rule better than my brother. For casting family aside and challenging him for a position that I had no right to. Unbridled ambition made me determined to rule our clan, and possibly even all of you!

"I was wrong.

"I did not realize how much until afterward, at the sight of my family turning their backs on me. Then I felt true remorse, knew burning shame for what I had done. But there was no recourse. I accepted my fate, I left the family, and came out here to make my way however I could, thinking to trouble Sebastian no more." His eyes slid back to Whirlwind. "But when I heard what had happened, when I understood that you had tried to fight him when he was half dead from *protecting our people*—"

"He was hurt protecting a *thing*, a filthy necromancer—"

"Dick," I heard Jen whisper.

"—not one of ours—"

"That 'filthy necromancer' fought for us, as did a number of other powerful individuals—including my 'whore', as you called her. Where were you?"

"On my way," Whirlwind snapped. "And had I been there, with the might of the great Clan Rand behind me, far fewer would have died! Your brother lost how many—"

"But you weren't there," Cyrus said, cutting him off with that simple truth. "You didn't fight. They did—my brother, my mate, a handful of children, and a group of townspeople with only shotguns to help them against an army of well supplied mages. Yet they held out; they won. And you came in, conveniently late, to accuse them?"

Cyrus's voice had been loud before, but now it had reached a crescendo that shook the rafters. Or, in this case, rattled the glass. For a second, I was afraid he'd break it, like an opera star going for a high note.

But then it went in the other direction, from a shout to a whisper, but one that carried. One that crawled up the spine and back down again, bringing shivers with it. Because he meant every word.

"My brother made it clear: the only way back is the way I left: through challenge. Your blood is the price of my redemption, and I *want* my redemption. Fight me."

Whirlwind gazed about at the circle of faces, all of whom were silent, waiting. They weren't tilting one way or the other, not yet, but they easily could. Challenge had been given, and while this wasn't the usual place, with none of the ritual that went along with it, that didn't matter.

At its heart, Were society hadn't changed much in hundreds of years, maybe not in thousands. A challenge was sacred, and could take place anywhere, including a dusty street with no pomp or circumstance, no anything but blood and courage. It didn't matter when or where; it was just as sacred, just as important.

And yes, it was barbaric and cruel, and sometimes let the wrong person win.

But I couldn't deny that my blood flowed a little faster through my veins, just at the sound of those two simple words: Fight Me.

But Whirlwind clearly didn't feel the same way. It was the proof of a leader, that he or she was willing to put their life on the line for their people. And since he'd missed that opportunity last night, he couldn't very well turn away from this one. Not if he wanted to become *bardric;* not if he wanted to retain control of his own clan.

But he had a problem. Cyrus was young and hard bodied, and that was in his human guise. As a wolf, he was every bit as big as Sebastian, and a trained fighter. Arnou would have allowed nothing less.

Of course, Whirlwind had been trained well, too, and had decades of experience on the younger man. But he didn't know that he could beat him. He must have thought he had it in the bag tonight. As Cyrus had said, fighting for the position of *bardric* required that the chieftain fight himself or that a close family member did so in his name. But Cyrus was out of the picture and I was declared an outcast, leaving no one else close enough by blood or adoption except for Daniela, Sebastian's teenaged daughter.

There was no way that Sebastian would risk her, so he would either have to do it himself or forfeit.

But now Cyrus was back, and Whirlwind was worried. It was all over his face, and in his words, which should have been a resounding growl and an immediate Change. But instead, he tried to wiggle out of it.

"You may have been offered redemption, but you don't have it yet! You are outcast, and cannot challenge—"

"I'm not challenging. Sebastian is. I am merely his champion."

Cyrus took off his beautiful robe and handed it to a nearby wolf, who hurried to take it, while I hid a smile. Cyrus was *vargulf*; the wolf should have done nothing but look at him in disdain, if not attack him for the insult. But Weres admired nothing so much as courage—unless it was loyalty to family.

And Cyrus was currently showing both.

Whirlwind noticed, and whatever else he might be, the old man could read a room. "You are *vargulf*!" he snapped. "You cannot be a champion, either!"

"And yet, there's nothing in the rules about that," Cyrus said, removing the silky trousers he had on underneath the caftan. Leaving him clad only in a loin cloth that itself would fall away as soon as he Changed.

Someone drew in a shocked breath and I shot my eyes over at Sophie, who was almost as red as her hair. After a second, she noticed. "He's, uh, he's very fit," she said, swallowing.

"Stop perving on the old guy," Jen muttered, and I decided to ignore both of them.

But Sophie wasn't wrong. If ever anyone had looked like a Were prince, Cyrus did. I didn't know if he'd oiled himself up before coming or if it was just the effect of the lights, but he shone like a bodybuilder going for the gold. The heavy musculature of a Were in his prime was a beautiful thing, and spoke its own challenge, without another word.

But again, Cyrus drove the point home. "There's no rule that prohibits a *vargulf* from being a champion—"

"Because no one in their right mind would appoint one!"
"—giving you no excuse. Fight me!"
"I can't." A murmur started to go through the assembled crowd. "I can't!" Whirlwind insisted, his eyes darting from them to Cyrus. "I already have a challenge on me, from your woman. I have to finish that one first—"
"A fact that did not stop you from challenging Sebastian."
"And she is *vargulf*," someone else said. I recognized Laura, Sienna's cousin, pushing her way through the crowd. Her voice was breathy from exertion, but it carried. "Or so you've been telling everyone. And you said it yourself, *vargulfs* can't challenge."
Whirlwind looked at Farkas, the Second with all the big ideas, and received panicked eyes back.
"She . . . she wasn't *vargulf* when she challenged," Farkas said, but as an excuse it was weak as hell and no one cared.
"Fight me," Cyrus said, not giving the old man time to come up with anything else. "Or name yourself coward in front of all here assembled. But let me be clear, old man. I am not going to be kind. There will be no easy death for you. You who were too cowardly to challenge until Sebastian was injured and exhausted. You who tried to have him assassinated repeatedly before this meeting could even take place. You who hate the alliance with the humans, but don't offer anything else in its place. Just the same old tired traditions that haven't been updated in hundreds of years—which is the last time they may have actually worked!
"No, no quick death for you. I will take you slow, piece by piece, and I will enjoy it."
It was a verbal slap in the face, and a taunt no Were leader could possibly ignore. And to his credit, Whirlwind didn't try. The dark gold wolf eyes suddenly seemed much more appropriate in the face of a very different creature.
"Shit, that's a big wolf," Jen whispered, awed.
"Are you sure Cyrus can take him?" Sophie asked, sounding slightly panicked.
I opened my mouth to reassure her, only to find that my throat had closed up.
Because Whirlwind was huge. And even though Cyrus matched him in size when he suddenly Changed, causing the crowd to quickly

back the hell up, he wasn't any bigger. Not that size was everything, but this fight was to the death, and Cyrus was out of practice and I—

I needed to trust him, I thought, mentally slapping myself. I couldn't do his job for him, but I could do mine, especially now that he'd given me the final piece I needed. Which was why I wasn't watching as the two huge beasts clashed together, hard enough to rattle the windows in front of me.

I was looking at Jen. "Can you open the pics on your phone?"

She blinked. "My pictures?"

I nodded. And then took the lavender case she passed me—no need to guess what her favorite color was—and quickly scrolled back to the bar-b-que. It didn't take long, as the only stuff in front of it was her and Sophie trying on literally everything in the Caesar's Palace shops.

"Here," I held up the phone, showing her the picture of a man. "Can you find him for me? I can't easily move around here, but you and your . . . friends . . . can."

"This guy?" Sophie took the phone and looked at it, frowning. "Are you sure he's here?"

"No, but I suspect it. But don't engage. Just find him, and let me know where he is."

"So that you can . . . compliment his cooking?" she asked carefully.

"Something like that." My voice was steady as I watched my lover get thrown against a wall.

"Ooookay. Time to go to work," she told Jen, and a moment later, I was alone.

Chapter Thirty-Eight

The girls' departure left me on my own for the first time in hours, which was not a plus. The wind wasn't bad up here, as the main bulk of the hotel blocked it, but the myriad scents borne on the breeze confused my nose, making me almost scent blind. And the sounds from the Strip made it hard to hear small noises.

Like the scrape of a shoe over concrete.

"Tell me, did you send them away for their sake, or for yours?" Someone asked, coming out of the night.

I couldn't see him very well; the light shining from the room below was bright. And he was standing in the shadow of the hotel on the other side of the pyramid. For a moment, I couldn't even tell which form he was in, as the panes shivered in sympathy with the crashes from below, making him seem to morph and blur.

"How would it help me not to have back up?" I asked, fighting an urge to stand up as it might spook him.

The figure shrugged, a tiny movement, but I felt it in my body like a struck piano wire. "If you're not planning to fight, you don't need back up," he said, walking closer. "And we don't have to fight."

"Don't we?"

He didn't answer, but kept moving around the mountain of glass. "You know, I have to give you credit. When I heard that you'd been taken by that bastard Jenkins, I didn't give much for your chances."

"Didn't you used to work for that bastard?"

He laughed, and it was a rich, full sound, almost catching. "The operative phrase being 'used to.' I plan to kill him, once this is done, unless . . ."

"Took care of that for you."

"Ah. Thought you might have, although I was looking forward to it."

"You can go back and desecrate the body, if it makes you feel any better."

He shook his head. "That was his thing, not mine."

"And what is yours?"

The wobbly, indistinct body paused, and the head came up at that. "Really?" he said. "You don't know that yet?"

"I have an idea."

"Oh? Tell me. Let's see how close you came."

"I know it has something to do with the council. Jenkins didn't choose to kill the Windward clan at Wolf's Head; he didn't know anything about it. Just wanted them dead for stealing from him and imperiling his great plan. But someone chose that venue, and then turned a dark mage army loose on us all—"

"Not on you," he corrected. "You weren't supposed to be there."

"No. I was a last-minute addition, after Sebastian called me to consult. I never thought the attack had anything to do with me; I'm simply not worth that kind of risk. But once I had time to think about it, I realized that nobody there was, including Sebastian himself.

"Killing one man, even one who has proven difficult to assassinate, hardly requires an army, although they *were* after him. So, I started to think: what is Sebastian? Not just a man, but the head of something—"

"Very good."

"—something that showed up shortly after the battle was over, and should have been walking into a massacre—their own. And they always travel with an army of bodyguards and retainers. They *would* take a large force to overcome, particularly when you couldn't be sure how many they'd bring. So, you wanted the council dead, but you missed them at Wolf's Head. I thought maybe you'd try again tonight."

He clapped, the sound echoing dully off the fake stone behind us. "Excellent, except that I didn't miss them. The damned mages saw Sebastian's back up squad arriving from Vegas, and assumed it was the council. They jumped the gun."

"And attacked too early."

He nodded. "And once it was on, it was on, with no way for me to stop it. The mages had been given orders to take out the council for me—as my payment for setting everything up—but their masters were mainly after Sebastian. They honed in on him and I thought he was a goner. But then you decided to ride to the rescue."

"Wasn't much of a rescue," I pointed out. "I failed. They were about to gut us all when you saved us . . . Danny."

He laughed, and again it sounded genuine. His head popped out from behind the pyramid. "Boo."

Looking at him, it was almost impossible to believe that we were having this conversation. He looked the same as he had at the bar-b-que, when he'd been grilling us some next-level ribs: greasy dark hair falling into his eyes, scarred up cheek, and stained wife beater/dirty jeans combo. He could have been any homeless person checking the slots for spare change.

But he wasn't; he was something very different. Yet, I still couldn't see it. Even when he walked closer and smiled at me, although he still kept some distance between us.

"Why so cautious?" I asked.

His head tilted. "I'm still not sure about you."

"Yet you saved me."

"Did I?"

"You know you did. Caleb and I would both have died in that corridor if not for you."

"Then I guess you owe me a life debt, huh?" I didn't say anything, and after a moment, he chuckled. "Worth a try." He paused to light up a cigarette. "The truth is, the boys didn't give me much choice."

"Lee, Noah and Jason."

He nodded. "They were very upset to learn that Cyrus's mate was involved in all this, and the idea of letting you die when you'd fought for them . . ." he shook his head and blew out smoke. "Weres."

"Thank you anyway," I said.

He shrugged and looked around for stars, which he didn't find. "I hate it here, in the city," he said. "It feels like my clothes are too tight all the time."

Cyrus had said the same thing to me, more than once, but Danny looked like it, too: antsy, hyperaware, and keyed up. But also oddly animated, almost as if he was high on something, and maybe he was. But the cigarette didn't shake as he paced back almost to the edge of the pyramid, before suddenly returning.

"How'd you guess?" he asked abruptly.

"That you were Jenkins' Alpha?" I shrugged and kept my hands where he could see them, because he kept looking that way. "A bunch of little things. Like the boys being too willing to take on the Corps, almost eager for it, when no sane wolf—much less an outcaste with little back up—would even think of such a thing. But someone who could Change into a Relic . . . they wouldn't have the same reaction to perceived danger to their Lupa, would they?"

"Touché."

"And their concern when Noah mentioned Lyall, the name you use in Tartarus when preaching rebellion to young outcastes. It freaked them out, not because he was telling on some street preacher, but because said preacher was right outside. Who had already given me part of the spiel, one too practiced to be the first time you'd delivered it."

He grinned. "This is fun. But those seem pretty thin reasons to suspect me?"

"I didn't suspect you; I just noticed things that seemed out of place. Like at the funeral, when I had a vision about the massacre at Wolf's Head. I didn't realize what it was at the time, just thought I was remembering the grow farm assault. But later I began to wonder. The only other visions I'd seen had been of Jace, one of Cyrus's boys.

"Maybe the same thing had happened again."

"And I asked you how you were, just afterward." He pursed his lips. "Bad timing."

"It made me think of you," I agreed. "I have a link to Cyrus; maybe it gave me a link to all of you, as well. Enough to get a flash of something when your emotions were running high, as Jace's had been, because you know what was about to go down. But the real kicker was your cologne—"

"My cologne?" He laughed. "Come on!"

"It's true. When I first met you, you had on enough Axe Body Spray for five teenaged boys, even though Weres don't usually wear scent. But you didn't have a choice. You'd just massacred an entire clan at Wolf's Head as bait. And while you'd bathed afterward, you didn't dare go around people with sensitive noses without insurance. Insurance that was still clinging to you when you rescued me later that day."

"Ah. I had wondered why you looked so strange, when I jumped down there."

"You're also older than the rest, when it's unusual to survive on the streets for so long without someone to protect you. Like I suppose Jenkins was doing?"

"Part of the deal," he said, and then his head tilted again, and after a brief pause, he came over and sat down beside me.

The cigarette was almost overwhelming this close, and a distraction—like the no holds barred fight going on below. I could hear it perfectly, as if I was ringside: every body blow, every grunt and gasp, every scream from the crowd as the combatants rolled into them. I desperately wanted to sit forward, to see what was happening, but that would have left me vulnerable, so I didn't.

"But you didn't arrest me," Danny said. "Didn't come after me. Not even today."

"I knew you were helping Jenkins. What I didn't know was if you were the mastermind or just another follower. Whirlwind also wanted Sebastian dead, and no offense, but he seemed more the type. And he had the entire resources of Clan Rand behind him."

"And you didn't want to tip him off." He looked thoughtful. "But you figured it out. That was my picture you showed the girls. What finally gave me away?"

I shrugged. "Nothing you did. I knew when Whirlwind tried everything he could to avoid the challenge just now. If he was coordinating this, and you were just an employee, he'd have the potion, too."

"And if he had the potion, he'd have accepted."

I nodded. "As challenger, he can choose any form of combat he wants. Most choose their Were form, as it's stronger, but he doesn't have to. And even when unchanged, the potion gives strength, heightened senses, speed. He'd have won easily, yet he didn't want to fight.

"Therefore, you were the one behind all this."

"Smart." He leaned back against the pyramid, smoking for a moment. "You're not wrong about Whirlwind. My associates were actually kind of pissed at him. He kept sending people to kill

Sebastian, and they kept getting in the way of the people *they* were sending. It was entirely too many assassins, and made the clan appoint Ulmer—"

"So, that's why there were so many attempts."

He nodded. "And Ulmer is paranoid, so security got increased tenfold, making it impossible to get at him. Which is when I offered them the deal."

"And you knew the Dark Circle how?"

"They're all over Tartarus, recruiting. We were competitors, you might say. I'd planned to bring onboard enough people to take out the council on my own. After I realized what Jenkins was working on, and what it could do, it seemed feasible. But I'd only managed to find three I could trust, and I didn't know if that would be enough.

"In peacetime, maybe, but everyone is getting antsy since the war, and I kind of wanted to survive the attempt. I thought, why not let the mages die for me? The alliance between the Corps and the Council has really been harshing their buzz, so they were happy to accept." He laughed suddenly. "Probably less happy now."

"There is still one thing I don't know," I said, and saw him quirk an eyebrow. "Why? Why do you want the council dead so badly?"

Once again, he looked surprised. "You get the hard stuff from some bad cologne and a little youthful bravado, but the easy part you can't fathom?" He leaned back against the glass, giving me plenty of time to attack him if I was going to.

But it was too easy. He was making it too easy, almost as if testing me. And the jitteriness—could that be an extra dose? Did more of the potion make him stronger?

I didn't know, and in my uncertainty, I didn't move.

He smiled suddenly.

"You know, I couldn't figure you out, back at the house. Here you are, Laurentia of Lobizon's daughter, a noble of one of the oldest houses out there, yet you're slumming in Vegas with a *vargulf* and a crew of street rats. When I first heard about you, I assumed you were one of those women who go gaga over a guy and trash their lives running after him. But when we met . . . you didn't fit the bill."

"Thanks."

He inclined his head. "You looked like the poster child for a Were noble, yet you opened your house to a bunch of outcastes. You chatted with us, ate with us, sympathized with us—and with that stray cat from the magical community and her crazy pack of friends. And it wasn't the usual do-gooder dynamic, not that *vargulfs* see a lot of that. Mages don't like us 'cause we're Weres and bad ones to boot; wolves don't like us, well, because we're inconvenient. Losers who get in the way of the nice world they've built for themselves.

"Yet there you were, taking us in. Didn't make sense—until today. When the news broke about your unfortunate affliction. Then a lightbulb went on, and I got it."

He sat up and leaned closer. "You like us because you *are* us, and even worse as far as the posh types down there are concerned. They'll exile and revile us, but if we stay out of their way, they'll let us live. But not you—"

"Does this have a point?" I asked, and hated that my voice was hoarse with emotion when I said it.

But it only made him smile more. "Yes. The point you were asking about, in fact. I realized that you understood what it's like to be outcast, rejected, persecuted. You'd done nothing wrong to deserve your fate—neither had I. Neither have a lot of us."

He paused to take a drag on his cigarette. "You know, being made *vargulf* used to be a rare thing, reserved only for the most heinous deeds. There weren't a handful made every year, if any. But now? There are hundreds turned out of their clans every year; thousands every decade. Thousands of people left friendless and alone, cut off from others of our kind, abused, taken advantage of, even killed—and no one cares."

"And you do?" I asked. "You were turning boys over to that bastard Jenkins. You must have known what he was doing with them!"

He didn't answer for a moment, looking up again at the field of non-existent stars. It suddenly felt oppressive, that unnaturally darkened bowl. I began to understand what he'd meant.

"Yes, I knew," he finally said. "But say I hadn't helped them. Say I'd taken them in instead, begun a fake clan like Cyrus. How many could I have saved? A dozen, maybe a couple hundred over my lifetime? I'm playing for more than that.

"We don't need charity, Lia, we need change. Real, lasting, meaningful.

"Lia," he said again, rolling my name around on his tongue. "You don't use Accalia, the name of a Were noblewoman, because you aren't one. You couldn't be; you were outcaste from birth. Instead, it's Lia, a human sounding name. Because that's all you are, all they'll let you be.

"Like this is all they let me be. They turned me into this—whatever I am anymore."

He had been facing me, leaning forward, as if trying to recruit me as he had all those boys. And I could see why they'd gone with him, trusted him. He had charisma, dirty jeans and all.

But now he half turned his face away. "I know how it is to lose a name. I lost mine; I lost everything. That story I told you in your backyard? It was true, every word of it. But I didn't tell you the rest."

"And what is the rest?" I found myself asking.

"The reason this has to change, has to burn down, right to the ground—all of it. Every last goddamned piece of the tradition they use like a lash to beat us with."

"Like they beat your father?" I guessed.

He turned back to me then. "No, I wouldn't be here for that, for a mere beating. But he did go to see them, after we lost everything—after it was stolen from us. He went to beg the council at a session just like this one. They allow that, you know, on the last day? They allow the little people to present grievances . . . only most never do, knowing the wrath they'll face from their clans if they dare to make them look bad.

"But we didn't have a clan anymore. My parents raged at the leaders after I was outcast, and thus became outcasts themselves. But that didn't stop my father. He went to Wolf's Head, a *vargulf* daring to enter those great jaws, and not only that, but to petition the council. It was a small group that day, just a rump they call it, but enough to make a ruling. Enough to hear him, or so he thought.

"But they didn't hear. They killed him instead. He had no badge of office to protect him, no noble blood in his veins, no friends or money or anything they respected. Just a simple man asking for justice, and they spilled his blood on those sands instead."

"That's why you did it there," I said, understanding.

He nodded savagely. "They should have died there, all of them! And not just for my father, but for the rest of us. There will never be lasting change until they're gone, Lia. You talk about Sebastian, but he won't do anything. Oh, he'll try," he said, when I opened my mouth to protest. "Perhaps even sincerely. But he'll fail.

"They'll throw everything in his path—procedure, tradition, and worst of all, procrastination. Yes, they'll say, and you're right, and of course . . . yet nothing will be done. Or it will be some surface change that doesn't do shit, because it doesn't apply to them. And if it doesn't apply to them, it doesn't count.

"So, we make it apply to them."

"Make it . . . how?" I asked, starting to get a very bad feeling.

He smiled. "I think you already know. I knew, as soon as I realized what Jenkins was doing, what he wanted with all those boys. I'm the one who persuaded the clan to start brewing up some punch for me to sell on the streets. Very hush hush kind of thing, just to humans, why should the mage make all the profit when you're doing all the hard work?

"It was easy."

"But you didn't sell it," I said.

"Oh, I sold some. I had to, to keep them flush and happy. But some of each batch I saved. Gave a little to my boys, the strongest ones, the ones who *got it.* They didn't go to Jenkins."

"But they did go to Cyrus," I said. "So you did, too."

"Some of their friends were already there. They said he was different." He shrugged. "Maybe they're even right. But soon, he won't have to be."

He turned on me suddenly, and quick as a blink, was in my face. But not to hurt me. His eyes were feverish, almost fanatical; he wanted me to understand.

"You remember that trip to the desert, where Colin used some of the stuff he'd swiped from one of my boys and you had to put him down?"

I stared at him. "Of course."

"Well, a question was asked that night. Allow me to answer it. Colin wanted to know where Weres came from. If he'd lived, I'd have eventually told him: we were made by the gods to be an elite fighting force, the best army of the ancient world. No, it's true," he insisted, seeing my face. "Jenkins told me himself. He saw the info in a secret Circle memo, with very restricted access, over a year ago.

"The Circle leadership found out from some vamp operative and had it confirmed by the fey. The gods were always fighting, and needed help to tilt their wars one way or the other. They experimented on humans, turning some into vamps, others in Weres, and still more into things that haven't always survived.

"That's where Jenkins got the idea for his private army. He was already playing god; it was the logical next step. But it told me something else, something more. We were special then, all of us. There were no *vargulfs*, just soldiers. Everyone was valued, everyone mattered, everyone was *important.*

"But now, it's all politics, designed to favor the higher clans to the exclusion of everyone else. They keep the lower ones in line with threats of making them outcastes, so nothing ever changes. And nothing ever will, until *they* do—the bastards who did this to us, to me, to the boys, to you."

"Change . . . into what?" I asked carefully.

"Into what they already are—monsters. Let them look on the outside the way they do on the inside, the way they did on the day they condemned an old man to death for seeking a little help. And after I turn them into creatures out of a nightmare, and watch them savage each other in a bloodbath for the ages, I'll get to watch the other clans turn their backs on them. Just like they did to us. Just like they did to him. Then we'll have a return to the real tradition, to the old ways, when we're all the same.

"Then we'll finally have justice."

I stared at him, caught completely flatfooted in spite of myself. "No, you won't. You won't get what you want, not like this."

"Lia," he said, shaking his head. "Beautiful, courageous, smart—who nonetheless doesn't get it. I already have."

Chapter Thirty-Nine

I didn't have to ask what he meant. The screams from below, which had been rising and falling as the fight progressed, abruptly reached a crescendo. That could be a result of somebody winning, but I doubted it.

Because Danny was laughing like a fiend, and then grabbing me in order to clap a hand over my mouth. I didn't understand why for a second, and then I got it: he didn't want me using my gift to stop this. The one that Cyrus had talked about, and that the potion had apparently brought out in me.

He wanted to keep me silent.

I had been letting him talk in order to get the full story while I looked for a chance to take him out. But he had been stalling for this, to make sure that I wouldn't be able to interfere when his plan went down. And I'd let him play me!

I started struggling, and I wasn't holding back.

But despite that, and despite the Corps' training, which was not kind and gentle, I went nowhere. He was stronger than any opponent I'd ever fought, and while he wasn't as well trained as I was in hand to hand, he wasn't a slouch, either. I guessed living on the streets taught you something.

But he wasn't trying to hurt me. He still wanted me to see what he'd done, what he'd managed to accomplish. He kept trying to drag me closer to the pyramid, to let me look, and I kept fighting to break away.

And then stopped abruptly, and falling limp, as if the choke hold he'd had me in had done its work. He loosened his grip to check on me, a rookie mistake. And as soon as he did so, I broke away, whirled around, and slugged him with every ounce of strength I had, all while screaming my fucking head off.

It was the same scream I'd used at Wolf's Head, but it had a very different result. Namely none. Maybe because the people below hadn't Changed yet, although a number of them were writhing on the floor, decorum forgotten.

Or maybe because the glass between us was too thick, and had muffled the sound.

I started to use my elbow to break it, but got punched in the gut before I could, with a blow that should have ended things, right freaking there. Because Danny was no longer playing. Whatever had been happening before, whether it was respect for someone who'd helped others like him, or just a desire for an audience, was gone.

I was suddenly in a fight for my life.

He hit me again, but not before I'd gotten a guard up—which did exactly no good at all. He punched right through it, and almost punched through me, but I'd jerked back at the last second and lessened the blow. It still left my ears ringing, like my stomach felt like it might have collapsed in on itself from his previous strike, and I didn't seem to be able to breathe properly.

Not that I was complaining. I should have been dead, but I seemed more resilient than I should have been. A lot more, although not nearly as much as him.

I landed punches and kicks, half a dozen in quick succession, because I had to find one that worked. But unlike the two Lobizon members, who'd been knocked out with a single hit, the blows hardly seemed to register. And then he shoved me into the glass, his hand found the back of my neck, and he repeatedly slammed my face into the heavy panes, until one shattered and my field of vision turned into a sea of blood.

I'm getting my ass kicked, I thought, and tried to channel my inner trainer, but Danny wasn't giving me time to think. He wasn't giving me time to do anything, include breathe, which took shouting off the table. Or living, if I didn't come up with something soon.

But nothing I did worked, and while I finally did manage to draw in a breath, it was shallow and quickly knocked right out of me again. My vision, what I had left past all the blood, started to go dark, and only a wash of pure fury kept me conscious. I wasn't going out like this. Not like this, goddamn you!

Except that he wasn't giving me a choice. He hadn't even Changed, so why couldn't I beat him? We'd had the same drug. Think, Lia!

But I wasn't thinking. The choke hold was back, and this time, I couldn't break it. I scrabbled against it, tried every trick in the book, my hands wet with blood that I was pretty sure was all mine.

But things were getting darker and I was out of time.

I felt myself sag in his grip, and this time, it wasn't fake. The scene in front of me grayed out, and all I could hear was my heartbeat. And I wasn't close enough to the ground to grab a shard of glass as I had in the lab, and try to free myself that way, if I could even have found one because I couldn't see it.

I couldn't see anything.

Except for a pair of demon red eyes, glowing in the haze in front of me. Huge and terrible in color, but not narrowed in anger. They were oddly kind, and in that moment, I felt a completely incongruous wave of peace flow over me, as if someone was saying, this will be all right.

Although how it was, I didn't know, because I couldn't see and I couldn't breathe, and now my mind was failing, too. At least I assumed that was why it felt like my body was melting in his arms, twisting and shifting, the muscles and bones and everything suddenly out of place. Like plastic that gets too near a flame, it didn't feel like I was holding shape.

Or maybe, like I was suddenly holding another.

He abruptly released me and stepped back, and I hit the ground, but not on two feet.

I landed on four, and not the normal kind. They were huge, with massive paws, and were covered in fur that was as black as night. And which flowed up into heavily muscled limbs covered in that same fur, and a body that—

That I'd never seen before, except in a dream.

I couldn't see any more of myself, but I didn't need to. And a series of memories, flashing across my vision, provided all of the context I needed: Farkas being surprised that I had a bite but hadn't turned at Wolf's Head, because serious danger to a Were almost always prompts a Change; my wolf straining against her bonds when meeting Cyrus's beast for the first time, awake and aware and wanting OUT; and Jenkins, goddamn him, bending over me, pleased that his brew had worked to bring out a single, lost gift. "It seems that Neuri can't block everything, doesn't it?" he'd said cheerfully. "Or maybe the magnitude of the dose opened up a crack in its protection and something slipped through."

Yeah, I thought, crouching low to the ground. Maybe it had. And maybe the second dose had shattered Neuri's hold altogether, and let my true self out into the world for the first time.

Let's find out, I decided, and leapt, going straight for the throat of my opponent, huge teeth bared and tearing into him.

Blood spurted, he screamed, and the body I bore to the ground turned and twisted. I felt him Change underneath me, even as I kept my hold on his jugular. But unlike the last wolf I'd tried that with, this one didn't care. He wrenched away from me, an arc of his own blood shining in the light, his neck gushing with it.

And then healing over a second later as he lunged for me, the hideous Relic form greatly overshadowing mine in size and ferocity, even in this guise.

But he never touched me. Because three more fell creatures caught him halfway through the attack, and those he didn't counter so easily. Those, he didn't counter at all.

I scrambled back, a little unsure on my new legs, and watched a sight that mortals are rarely gifted to see. Jen's starving, captured shades tearing into the thing that had been Danny, looking for the life energy that they believed to be in there somewhere. But I guessed in their frenzy they had forgotten a simple fact: Weres aren't made like humans.

Our souls do not make ghosts, for they are bound to our bodies, and do not leave it until the body has completely disintegrated. It was why we were cremated at death, to speed up that process. And why the starving shades found no sustenance to sustain them.

They screamed, a terrible sound, ripping and tearing at him in their frustration. Only to find a tiny, tiny thread of spiritual energy floating free, due to the amount of damage they were inflicting. One of them spotted it, consumed it, and shrieked the information to the others.

Who immediately realized what it meant. They had to literally rip him to shreds to feed. And they had to do it fast enough that he couldn't heal through it.

So, they did.

"I thought you said they were weak!" Sophie yelled, crouching down with her hands over her head as blood and meat and viscera started flying.

"Even starving animals find strength when confronted by a meal," Jen said, and remained standing, her voice completely neutral as she watched her creatures at work.

"You know, you're fucking scary sometimes!" Sophie raged, staring up at her.

"Thank you."

The four combatants staggered back a moment later, and fell off the side of the building, with the shades, or ghosts as they were slowly becoming, clinging to the disintegrating body like remoras to the sides of a whale.

I didn't hear them hit down; I didn't know that there was enough left to hit down.

But I heard something else.

"We have another problem," Sophie said, not even commenting on my new form in her panic. "It's why we came up here to get you."

"I know."

A look through the ruined window showed that things in the banquet hall were falling apart. I didn't know where Danny had put the potion he'd been saving up, but it had reached a lot of people. Maybe the wine—it didn't matter.

What did matter was that people were Changing all over the expansive ballroom, and not into Weres.

New Relics were being born everywhere, bursting out of their finery to tower over the crowd, screaming their birth pangs at the skies. And then immediately attacking everyone in the vicinity, who were Changing, too, as the extent of the danger became clear. But it didn't matter; a regular Were couldn't stand against these things, as I'd just found out.

Which was why I felt a scream building in my throat when Whirlwind Changed, his already altered form bulging and twisting as something even more ferocious was born—

And immediately leapt straight at the hunched body of Cyrus.

I heard the girls' scream beside me, felt my body go cold, saw my paw slam against the glass, seeing shards cascade down into the ballroom like falling jewels—

And then I let it out, putting everything I had into it, giving off all my terror, all my desperation, all my hopes in one, long, earsplitting howl.

It was loud enough to have the girls covering their ears in pain, to have more glass shiver out of its panes and fall to the floor, to have me feeling like I'd coughed up part of my soul as it echoed and echoed and echoed . . .

And did nothing else. Except to cause a lot of the assembled Weres to fall back into human form, dazed and in some cases stunned, while their attackers remained untouched. My gift hadn't worked before because it didn't work on Relics, I realized, and then Cyrus went flying at the wall.

He hit hard enough to break every bone in his body, and to leave me choking on the end of my cry. But his bones didn't break. I knew that because, at the same second, he Changed.

And what came off of the wall wasn't Cyrus.

Instead, the biggest, most terrible Relic of them all hit the floor and caught the creature that had been Whirlwind halfway through a leap. And bit down—but only once. Because once was all it took.

Whirlwind's altered form fell to the ground in two pieces and Cyrus, or what had been Cyrus, stood up to his full, towering height and roared at the room. And if I'd thought my puny shout was anything, I was now learning how wrong that had been. His call was loud enough to shatter glasses like miniature fireworks popping all over the room, to send cracks running up the newly painted walls, and to break the remaining panes in the pyramid and send them pelting down like golden rain.

It also caught the attention of every Relic in the room, all of whom paused their own fights to look at him, expressions of surprise and then of something else on their features.

One by one they moved away from their victims and toward the summons. Because that was what it had been, I realized, as each took a knee in front of him. The mass of Relics had found their captain and were awaiting instructions.

That would have been wonderful, only this wasn't Cyrus anymore. I didn't know who this was, and in all likelihood, neither did he. Because Jenkins had said that his potion should allow a person to think through it, at least in a basic way, but I hadn't had too much success with that.

Neither had Colin.

And now the alpha of alphas had manifested, and was about to send his troops to rip everyone else apart.

And there was only one thing left to do about it.

"Wait! What are you *doing*?" Sophie yelled, because she knew what my suddenly bunched muscles meant.

I didn't have time to reply. I jumped through the now open roof, fell three stories, and landed right at Cyrus's feet. And looked up, searching desperately for some sign that my lover was still in there, just in another guise.

I didn't find one.

The room had gone silent, except for the heavy breathing of the Relics. Nobody spoke; nobody moved. Including Cyrus, who was completely unrecognizable, and yet who hadn't immediately gone for my throat.

That could have been surprise, at someone being foolish enough to deliberately put themselves in harm's way. Or it could be something else, some sliver of memory, or maybe only a sliver of scent, because he had never seen me in this form. But I knew how powerful scent was to Weres.

So, I took a chance. And instead of backing up or attempting to talk, or doing anything human, I did what my wolf had done when first meeting his. She'd been coy and cute, and played around for a while, but then she'd gotten down to business, winding her body around his, letting her scent fill his nose, letting him feel her warmth and strength and softness as she brushed against him.

I did the same, first looking into those horrible, yellowish eyes, and then not looking into them. Because I didn't need to keep an eye on him. I wasn't an enemy; I was his *mate*. And he would remember that, he would smell me, feel me, *know me,* if he would ever know anyone at all.

For a long moment, nothing happened. I didn't know if that was good or not; if he was just struck dumb by someone being insane enough to try this in the middle of a massacre. But I kept on doing it, and added little flourishes as I went along: a tickle of a bushy tail here, as my mother had sometimes done to me, a slow slide against that horrible hide there; and then a short walk away, to sit cleaning a paw with my back to him, because I wasn't worried.

I was Lupa, and he needed to remember that. To woo me, to placate me, to greet me properly, as he still had not done. Come on, I thought, not turning around. Even when I felt a presence come up behind me, even when I tasted that terrible breath on my neck. I just sat there, unable to do anymore, because I couldn't take him in battle.

And not just because I physically wasn't strong enough. But because he was Cyrus and I loved him. I couldn't hurt him; I could never hurt him. We who had been through so much together, who shared a bond that the accepted, the loved, the approved members of society could never know . . . no, I couldn't hurt him.

So, he would know me or he wouldn't.

There was nothing else.

Other than for a weird snuffling behind my head, a great snout poking into my face, and a paw—massive and horrible and with claws like daggers, softly patting at me, trying to get my attention.

I felt dizzy with relief, but also felt another emotion. Because my wolf . . . was not pleased. She turned an annoyed shoulder to him, because he'd taken too long to acknowledge her, and that was unacceptable.

He pawed a bit more, and then whined, low in his throat, because she was being mean, she wasn't giving in. She left him like that for a long moment, letting him worry, letting him stew. Unbothered by any chance that it might make him mad, because it was her anger he had to worry about, her pique that must be satisfied.

And then it was, and she turned and playfully leapt around him, bouncy and happy once more with her mate at her side. And then he was doing it, too, carnage forgotten, because it was play time. And time to introduce her to the rest of the pack he'd found.

They quickly slunk forward, heaving great monsters with heads low in obeisance, to sniff her paw and to make the acquaintance of their new Lupa, their new queen.

And then to follow her, as their captain was doing, up the walls of the ruined room, out onto the roof, and down, leaping onto the concrete. A few stopped to sniff the scraps of flesh littering the ground, all that was left of another of their kind. But he wasn't pack; didn't matter. And Lupa wanted to run!

They ran after her, joyously burning up the concrete and then the pavement and then the sands of the desert as the hateful city fell away, and the open skies beyond beckoned them. The stars burned overhead, a glorious full arc, and the scents of the desert caught their attention, as a whole world opened up to them. Their captain bayed his happiness at the moon, the mate of his choice at his side, and declared the night to be theirs, and theirs alone.

Chapter Forty

I awoke in a cave, somewhere in the Nevada desert. It wasn't a nice cave. There were animal bones in it, some looking disturbingly fresh. There was scat in it, thankfully not fresh, and toward the back. And there was a man in it.

A naked man.

He was considerably nicer than the rest of the cave, with a long, lean, well-muscled body, a light mat of brown hair on his chest, and a thicker, tousled mop on his head. His face looked like he hadn't shaved in three days, but that was simply because he was a Were who had left his razor at home. I kissed him, and he had morning breath, and also possibly dead animal breath, if the bones were of some feast that we'd shared the night before.

I was terribly afraid that they were, and that I had a tiny bit of rabbit fur caught behind a molar.

"I think I ate a bunny," I told him tearfully, when we broke apart.

He laughed, all white teeth in a suntanned face, and kissed me again. And it was so good, so full of so many things: fear, relief, joy and happiness. And most of all the love that had saved the day when violence couldn't, that I didn't even care about the breath.

Much.

And then someone was yelling from outside.

I crawled over Cyrus and poked a head out, since I was as buck ass nude as Eve. And saw a lot of other naked people wandering around, looking dazed and confused, probably about being out in the middle of the desert when they were supposed to be sleeping off the excesses of the night before. Only last night had held a bit more excess than usual.

I looked back at Cyrus, who appeared to be admiring my butt, and shoved him a little with a foot. “You gonna tell them or am I?”

“Tell who what?”

He poked his head out. And then, very quickly, drew it back in again. “Coward,” I said.

“I defeated Whirlwind,” he whined. “Don’t I get some consideration for that?”

“Consideration meaning?”

He batted eyelashes at me that were longer and thicker than any man had a right to. “Could you maybe deal with this? You’re so much better at explaining things than I am.”

I sighed, and pondered logistics. Because I was not going out there naked; I didn’t care how common that was for Weres. But I wasn’t seeing a lot of other choices.

And then I heard one, because somebody was approaching on what sounded like a vehicle gasping its last. Another quick peek, and it turned out to be Caleb and the kids, in the ‘school bus’ he’d stolen from the Corps. They were throwing clothes out of the windows to the poor unfortunate ex-Relics, who seemed glad to get them.

I waved an arm.

And shortly afterward had a clump of cotton tossed to me, because the cave was a little way up a hill.

It turned out to be jeans and a western shirt in Cyrus’s size, and jeans and a loose fitting, cotton V-neck in mine. There was no underwear for either of us, but I didn’t feel like complaining. I emerged first and stood there, blinking in the sunlight, and then picked my way down the hill to where Caleb was waiting for me.

I hugged him, which wasn’t protocol, but screw it, he’d brought me jeans.

“Thank you,” I whispered.

“For what?”

“Not making me have to hitchhike back to Vegas in the nude.”

“Oh. I thought it was for leading a raid—with a concussion, I might add—on a Circle establishment riddled with traitors.”

“That too.”

I kissed his cheek, which seemed to surprise him, and then I swear he blushed. I would have ribbed him for that, but I was feeling too good. And then the moment was lost when half a dozen shiny black jeeps and SUVs came bumping over the rocky ground, I assumed courtesy of the council.

Sophie came up and handed Cyrus, who had emerged after me still pulling on his shirt, a phone. “Sebastian,” she said, and he nodded and walked a little way off.

I sat with Caleb on the side of the hill as water and tea and juices were handed out, along with a variety of sandwiches.

“Thank you,” Caleb said, grinning at a pretty brown girl with ringlets.

Right before he discovered that his sandwich was mostly made out of cucumber.

“What? Just because I’m the human, I get the shit sandwich?” he called after her, and she tossed him a pert look over her shoulder.

I traded him for my ham and Swiss.

The least I could do was eat the rabbit food, since I’d already had the rabbit.

“Am I still wanted?” I asked, after some chewing.

“No. The camera feeds at the base exonerated you. Clear cut case of self-defense if I ever saw one, although the way you took down that medic was a bit . . . extreme.”

I laughed, and then kept on laughing at the look on his face, until I got a piece of watercress stuck in my throat and almost choked.

Extreme.

Yeah.

I was gonna need a new definition for that one.

And then something occurred to me. I sat there, chewing cress and cucumber and cream cheese, and flexed a hand, summoning an apple from a basket a guy was passing around. It was sluggish, because my call had been tentative, but the fruit moved.

And then zoomed into my hand when I tightened my grip, and pulled.

“Still hungry?” Caleb asked, with a raised brow.

“Wait,” I said, and looked at my other hand.

It was dirty and had some disturbing stuff caught under the nails that I decided not to think about. But that didn’t matter. Only one thing did, and I licked my lips, wondering if I wanted to know.

But I had to. I couldn’t live like this anymore, not knowing who or what the hell I was. Not after last night.

I concentrated, and it was easier than I'd expected. As easy as it had looked when mother had sometimes transformed her legs only, to give her extra height to reach something off of a shelf, and then shrank back down as if nothing had happened. Only in my case, it was a paw, with black fur and long, dark nails.

"Son of a bitch!" Caleb said, scrambling back. *"What is wrong with you?"*

"Nothing," I said, as I looked from one hand to the other. "Nothing at all."

"Could have fooled me!"

"It's . . . a long story," I said, looking up at him. "But you need to trust me; this is wonderful. A cure for a terrible disease. Or it might be, if Jenkins left any records intact."

"He left them," Caleb said. "The loyal Corpsmen locked everything down once the situation you created was contained. They were subsequently attacked by the others, but followed procedure and sealed themselves behind the lab's wards until we came to sort everything out. Whatever he had, it's still in there."

"Good. Jenkins did a lot of terrible things for his research. It would be nice if at least something good came out of it."

"Uh huh." Caleb was still looking at my hand. "Does that . . . come off?"

Cyrus came up and deliberately kissed my Were hand, then sat down as I let it melt away. "Thought Weres couldn't do magic," he said, crunching my apple.

"Guess I'm the exception."

"Always were," he said, and kissed me.

It tasted better with apple, I decided, and deepened it.

"Would someone tell me what the hell is going on?" Caleb said.

But no one did.

* * *

Half an hour later, everyone had been rounded up and accounted for, and we were riding back to town in the old van turned school bus. Caleb was driving, but kept shooting me glances, probably wondering how to mention all this in a report and whether or not he should even try. I left that up to him.

I was who I was, and for the first time in as long as I could remember, I was good with that.

"What did Sebastian have to say?" Sophie asked, leaning forward from a middle seat.

"A lot of things," Caleb informed her. "No one else feels like challenging—"

"I bet."

"—and as a result, he's *bardric* for another year and the alliance with the Circle has been confirmed."

"So, basically, everything stays the same?"

"No. No, it does not."

I'd been looking out the window, watching the desert stream by, and enjoying the scent parade. I'd been able to tell where we'd caught the unfortunate rabbit, where we'd scampered around and over a hill, what had to be a dozen times, chasing each other in joyous abandon, and where we'd paused to—

Huh. Well. I guessed our beasts knew each other pretty well now, all things considered.

But at Cyrus's comment, I turned to look at him. "What?"

He had a look on his face that I wasn't sure how to read. Happy but anxious, excited but wary, hopeful but unsure. He saw me noticing and gave me a kiss on the top of my head.

Weres were always touchy feely, but today he couldn't seem to keep his hands off me. I didn't mind, but it showed even more than his expression what he was feeling, and that he needed reassurance. I covered his hand with mine.

"I proposed an idea I had, and Sebastian accepted," he said.

"What kind of idea?"

"You told me what Danny said."

I nodded. We'd caught up, briefly, while everybody loaded into the vehicles, although there were a lot of pieces yet to be filled in. However, I'd given him and Caleb the basics, Caleb for his report and Cyrus . . .

Because Danny had been one of his. Maybe it had all been for show, to keep close to the boys he was cultivating, I didn't know. Or maybe he'd had some feeling for the one man who had actually cared. I thought I'd seen a glimpse of that, a time or two.

But either way, it hadn't been a show for Cyrus, and that made three boys he'd lost in less than a week: Jayden, Colin and Danny.

It was in his voice when he spoke again, the loss, the grief, and the despair that everything he'd tried hadn't been enough. "He was wrong in what he did," he told me. "But not in what he said. We do need change—and now, not whenever the war ends. There will always be another war, another problem, another reason to keep things the way they are. There will never be a perfect time to act.

"So, we don't wait for the perfect time."

"Meaning?" I asked.

"There are a lot of *vargulfs*. Some deserve it, many don't, but either way, their clans don't want them back. But leaving them on their own . . ." he shook his head. "Weres don't do well on their own. They attack someone and the Corps takes them out; they kill themselves out of loneliness or desperation; or they're preyed upon by others. There are a thousand stories but they almost always end the same way.

"But what if they didn't have to?"

"It's the way it's always been," I pointed out.

"But not the way is has to be! I asked Sebastian, what if we could establish clans for the outcastes? Places they could go where they'd be welcomed, where they could belong again. Where they could have a name, have brothers and sisters who cared for them? If they get thrown out again, if they can't learn to live in peace with others, then so be it. They're on their own. But a second chance—it's all some of them need. It's all any of my boys needed, and most of them I think will make it in the end."

I thought back to what Danny had said, about how it was three outcasts who had come after me, who had insisted on saving me, and for what? Because I made them dinner? Because I talked to them like people for once? It didn't seem like much, but it had meant enough for them to spare my life.

"How would it work?" I asked.

"We're still ironing out the details, but there will be a number of second chance clans established, in all quarters of the Were world. There's even going to be one here in Vegas," he said, and then let it trail off, before looking at me hopefully.

"You're not going back to Arnou, are you?" I asked evenly.

He shook his head.

"Are you sure? You bled for it. You risked your life for it—"

"And I love my old clan. I always will. But . . . it doesn't need me. They do."

"And you want me to come with you?"

A dark eyebrow raised. "It wouldn't be a clan without a Lupa."

Three clans in a lifetime, I thought. It wasn't unknown, but it was unusual. Still . . .

"Sounds intriguing," I said, and Cyrus grinned.

"Don't promise too soon," Caleb said. Glancing back at me. "You got a lot on your plate."

"Like what?"

"Like whatever Hargroves is going on about. He received a proposal from Sebastian about making a joint Were/mage force to fill out our numbers, and also to investigate Were crimes. Have you ever heard of such a thing?"

Yeah, I thought. From Sienna. It looked like she'd been busy.

"It might be nice to have some extra hands on board," I said mildly.

Caleb shot me another look. "It might. Might be kind of wild, too."

That, I thought I could guarantee.

"What about us?" Someone blurted out.

I turned around to notice that all of the kids were looking a little lost, suddenly. Even Sophie had gone quiet, and was staring down at her hands. But not Jen.

The mousy young woman seemed to have found her voice, and she was the one who had spoken, with eyes blazing.

"I don't hear anything about a place for us in all this," she added. "Or are we supposed to do a Chris and just melt away? Go back and be locked up like nothing ever happened?"

"Go back?" I asked, confused.

"Chris already did, this morning," Sophie told me quietly. "He said his chances of survival were better at school."

I remembered his expression at Wolf's Head, when the private army Whirlwind had brought were climbing the stone seats toward him. And I couldn't say he was wrong.

"But you didn't go with him?" I asked. "I wouldn't blame you if you did—"

"We want to be here," Aki said quickly, and Dimas appeared out of nowhere to nod in agreement.

"It's been . . . weird," he said softly. "But I like weird."

Kimmie didn't say anything. But the sandwiches she'd been multiplying, because even the council's heaping baskets hadn't been enough for Were appetites and the kids had missed out, suddenly cascaded down to the floor, threatening to bury the backseat in salmon paste and turkey clubs. She looked up, her dark eyes huge.

"I like weird, too," she whispered.

"We all do, or we'd have gone back with Chris," Jen said impatiently. She glared at me. "The question is, do you?"

I held up a furry hand. "Don't really have a choice."

They didn't seem reassured by this, so I spelled it out. "What? You didn't really think I'd leave you guys behind?"

And then Caleb was yelling and swerving off the road, as the front of the van was mobbed by screaming, crying kids.

* * *

It was a long way back to Vegas. Apparently, Relics can cover some damned ground, and we had. Four hours' worth, to be precise.

Fortunately, Were trackers had been able to find us. Unfortunately, that left us jouncing over dirt roads, when they existed at all, for hours until we finally hit some blacktop. And then we still had miles to go.

I watched us eat up the road and wondered how life could change so much so fast. Someone once said "There are decades where nothing happens; and there are weeks where decades happen." And it felt kind of like that. Or like Alice falling down the rabbit hole, and wondering where it went.

I guessed I was going to find out.

"So, does it help at all?" Cyrus asked me quietly.

The kids were eating sandwiches, and playing some game where you had to guess the pop song in as few notes as possible. Only Aki couldn't carry a tune in a bucket, adding an extra layer of difficulty. People were laughing and throwing things at him when he told them his latest answer, which had sounded nothing like the song it was supposed to be.

I watched them with a small smile, and then looked back at Cyrus. "Does what help?"

“It seems to me that you’ve saved a lot of kids lately. The five of them, from those internment type schools, Jack from imprisonment by that bastard of a mage, and you’re joining me in my mad crusade to save who knows how many from the streets.”

“What’s your point?”

“Does it help? With the one you lost? With Adam?”

I finally realized what he meant. And for a moment, I was back there, standing in the doorway of my laundry room, watching a boy’s blood seep out onto the blindingly white tiles. I felt a shiver rip through me.

“Does all this help you?” I asked. “With Colin and Jayden and Danny?”

He smiled slightly in understanding. “No.”

“Me either.” I thought some more. “But it’s nice.”

He pulled me close, and his warmth immediately banished the chill. “How about we go home and do some laundry?” he whispered, against my hair.

I rested my head on his shoulder. “Yeah.” I said. “That sounds good.”

Also by Karen Chance

The Cassie Palmer Series

Touch the Dark
Claimed by Shadow
Embrace the Night
Curse the Dawn
Hunt the Moon
Tempt the Stars
Reap the Wind
Ride the Storm
Brave the Tempest
Shatter the Earth
Ignite the Fire: Incendiary
Ignite the Fire: Inferno

The Midnight's Daughter Series

Midnight's Daughter
Death's Mistress
Fury's Kiss
Shadow's Bane
Queen's Gambit

Standalones

Masks
Siren's Song

Author's Website

KarenChance.com/Books

Made in the USA
Middletown, DE
17 July 2023